The Exit

Blue Moon Chronicles

A SCIENCE FICTION FANTASY

TODD BODDY

Broken Club Publishing LLC
Mckinney Texas

DEDICATION

To Steve, and all those who fight in the dark.

ACKNOWLEDGMENTS

There are many to thank; my children: Darla, Amber, Dustin, Colton, and Lexi, who were relentless in forcing me to tell them bedtime stories even when I was deliriously tired, the lovely Ms. Loretta who has supported me through all the hair-pulling, Sue who gently moved me to write and rewrite, Shari for wading through multiple manuscripts and loving it, Michelle for connecting me full circle from the past, Mom and Dad loving unconditionally through all life's ups and downs, Mark & Timothy who were the first to read the concept, Dennis for helping me stay on track, Robert giving me much needed breaks on the course, my church family who never thought I was crazy for taking on this project and helped make this possible, John who showed it could be done over soups and salads, Troy for the rock support of a brother, Denise for all the prayers, and friends everywhere who have kept the motivation alive. Of course, lastly, thanks to the One who Sails the Magnificon.

The Exit

BROKEN CLUB PUBLISHING
MADE IN TEXAS

Prelude

++

Blue Moon Chronicles Book III, 12.1

Date: *At appearance of last Juwaan,*
Third generation G-Class star formation,
Fourth generation Angelus,
Beginning of mass exit to Sanctuary
Subject: *That which led to the Exit*

Long ago, before the final transformation of the humans, the sealing of the gates of the Wounded Heir's Kingdom, and the disintegration of the original creation, the golden planet Siyon and its turquoise Blue Moon, roamed as glowing orbs between universes, galaxies, and civilizations, independent of the fabric of space and time. All kinds of intelligence, conscious and unconscious, dappled across the celestial planes owed its origin to these starless planets, which cast their seed by messengers, known as Winds of Light as they burrowed through the hot fermenting cosmos.

Starless indeed, that is not to say that they did not have light; for at the center of Siyon existed a primordial realm called the Magnificon, the headwaters of all creative and life giving power, flowing into and becoming the glorious universe that was. From this place was birthed the compressed pinpoint of light-love energy from which all worlds blasted into being from seemingly nothing to form a canvas across the heavens. In response, this new creation yearned for relationship with an awaited breath of life.

Yet, some witnesses to this event did not yearn for relationship, but rather envisioned a world of their own. Hence a darkened light appeared, first as an infection among the Winds of Light who began to desert their legions during the third generation of star formation. It tried to compete with the light from Siyon just as the earliest strands of proteins were being sown among the habitable solar systems. This eventually resulted with the infection mutating and crossing into a select species on the planet Earth; the humans, who had been set aside for a future return to the Magnificon in their next stage of development.

The Heir, saddened by the desertion and spreading infection into his select species, departed Siyon without the protection of his legions of Winds, left quartered on the Blue Moon. However during his sojourn, the worst happened. He became wounded by former members of his legions and took on the contagion himself. Back on Siyon the ruling council called for the annihilation of the Earth, but the Heir would have nothing to do with this, instead opting for a declaration of amnesty to all species infected if they would declare their contagion as self-initiated. There were a few takers of this offer among the humans but none among the more ancient darkened Winds, whose hope remained focused on a mythical new realm of their own called, "The Sanctuary," immune from the reach of Siyon.

I have recorded this story as a memorial to a fallen hero among the Winds of Light, misunderstood and slighted by friends, who made attempts to counter this dark insurgency, and also to give support for those clinging to faith, that subspace channel of knowledge and inner power, if this darkened light should prevail. "The light shines in the darkness, but the darkness has not understood it."

God help us all if we can no longer recognize the true light.

Shem, from the Blue Moon, the caverns of Sharu

+++

Prologue

"And from the days of John the Baptist until now the kingdom of heaven suffereth violence, and the violent take it by force." – Matthew 11:12

Westminster, London

"Come on Pam, we can't run this bloody story as the lead. Push it down in the teleprompter, and tell the editors to cut the base story in half. This isn't news anymore. This is pure hype for the biggest snake oil rip off in history after the virgin birth."

"Rulanda, I'd kill to have your paycheck, which is not bad for a reader in a tight dress, and FYI the BBC has been commercial for two years. Guess who now owns fifty-one percent?"

"The Sanctuary Corporation... I read, remember? Aren't we glad we're kissin' their arses as news whores?"

"At least their pockets are getting deeper."

"Pam, they're going to own a third of the world markets whether this works or not. This puke your guys have for me to regurgitate is meant to escalate the run on these Hub tickets. The real story here is this whole sham is going to backfire. Look at the thread of the feeds we are featuring today: mega-preachers, self-help gurus, Hollywood, UN, climatologists. Why aren't we featuring the naysayers?"

"The kooks? It's been tested. It works. How can you argue with the Archbishop of Canterbury?"

"Funny, no journalists with independent spines have been asked."

"I tell you what. You're on in fifteen minutes. I'll give you the opening paragraph to put in your spin, after that you read the script and run with the clips as edited. Deal?"

"Thanks, Pam."

———

Cusco State, Peru

"Look at him, Lucas. The rainforest is his playground; no fear of spiders or snakes. He'd just as soon swing on a vine or run barefoot than ride home with us. Call him down and remind him of his curfew – he hears better when dad says it."

"Daniel! Come down here for a second; we need to talk."

"Why does he have to choose the highest trees?"

"Because they're there, why else? He's all boy. Love the perpetual scab on the knee."

Victoria, still not satisfied, poked his shoulder with her left index finger and added, "And your father encourages more risks, taking him exploring deep into those old Inca mine shafts and playing with those antique Conquistador swords."

Lucas caressed her finger and kissed it saying, "Vic, we can't over protect knowing what's at stake."

Daniel bounded down to his parents, immediately appealing for more time, "Let me stay a little longer," Daniel used the puppy-eye look on his best target, "Please, mom?"

Vic let the sneaky, puppy-eye attack roll over her and stuck to her guns. "Sun sets in two hours. You know the rules."

"Climb with me to the top dad!" Daniel tried to persuade his other parent. "This Ceiba tree is the oldest out here, it's massive. It'll be fun. Whadda ya think?"

"Daniel, please listen to your mother; you need to be on time tonight. The clock is running while you stand here arguing."

Remembering the occasion, Daniel focused like a laser. "Mom, baked Alaska for my cake? You promised."

"Out here? Absolutely, I'll see what I can do, but no party and no dessert if you're late for dinner, Mr. Tanner. No make-ups for tenth birthdays. Sure you don't want to get in with us?"

"I have a shortcut. Don't worry."

The Land Rover began to inch forward, slowly navigating the water-filled potholes of the old logging road. Lucas looked back in his side mirror as his gangly son with his dark mop of hair, shirtless, shorts, and barefoot, waved good-bye, then darted back for the thicket.

"Honey, when you get to the first switchback, pull over," Victoria said as they went up the hill. "I want to test the broadband reception for my web visor."

Pulling over to a rotted log guarding the edge of the three thousand-foot ravine, they found a clear line of sight to the tower in the valley. Among the peaks' shadows twelve miles to the southwest, Lucas could barely make out Machu Picchu.

"It's getting much worse, Lucas; put yours on too. I want you to see this. Go to preset five."

"This is Around The World with BBC correspondent, Rulanda Lakee. The DOW dropped another five percent today on news of more people leaving behind homes, jobs, and family for the Sanctuary Corporation's new transport hubs. Located in over one hundred cities around the world, they are being touted as the gateways to the new Shangri-La. Many Fortune 500 employers are complaining of lack of job applicants because people are making plans to leave."

"Lucas?"

... ... *"...and the stoppage of basic city services like fire and police where civil servants are walking off their jobs, unannounced for good... ... ..."*

Lucas cupped his hands around his temples to block the periphery sunlight obscuring the micro-projection being broadcast from his web visor to his retina, "I see it."

"Don't you think it's incredible, all the masses of people camped around these hubs. Even in places like Boston, people are panicking, being fooled that they're gonna miss the greatest boat of all time. What's the nearest hub to us? Lima?"

"They've auctioned off over half a million tickets so far in Lima. In LA, over 700,000; in sub-equatorial Africa, they're trying to double the hubs."

"Hold on Vic, listen."

"With the world on the brink of global economic collapse from the dismissal of the Euro currency five years ago, the unification of anti-western

Mediterranean rim Caliphate, harsh Asian outbreaks of both H5N1 and military strains of smallpox, and major shifts in weather patterns and crop yields in North America, you can easily see why the world's self-proclaimed ninety-nine percent are throwing in the towel. Rallies are being held in sports stadiums around the world with the fervor of old style evangelistic crusades."

"Watch this clip from well-known televangelist and prosperity minister, Hugh McKenzie of Dallas, Texas 'You've been told all your life you had to suffer to find God's will. I am telling you that this is a lie from the devil. God has given you the keys to take ownership of the biggest land grab in history. God's not interested in improving this world. Some things need to be thrown away, like old shoes. You ask, what is required to experience a new world and a new life? It is very simple. You have to have faith to leave everything that is broken behind you. No eye has seen nor ear has heard what God has in store for those who love him. There is none who has forsaken mother, brother, father, wife, or child who won't receive, a hundredfold over, mothers, brothers, fathers, wives, children, and with this, eternal life.'"

"Here's another clip from Jinnah Sports Stadium in Islamabad Pakistan, from Al Jazeera network. The Imam Jafar Hammam speaks highly of the Sanctuary..."

"Take 'em off, Vic. We don't need to see any more of this. We knew this day would come. Watching won't make it go away."

"Lucas, your eyes! It's happening."

He opened the driver's side makeup mirror. "Usually takes more than bad news to get this reaction."

"We should have made Daniel get in."

"Honey, stay calm. This is his backyard. Nothing bad is going to happen. He'll meet us with his grandma and grandpa to celebrate his birthday. Good luck to anyone who thinks they can catch that kid in the rainforest."

As they pulled off the main logging road and made their way across several acres of clear-cut fields before diving into the jungle again, they drove through a swarm of black beetles that peppered the driver's side of the vehicle and windshield like small hail.

"Yellow guts on a black paint job. Why do I bother?"

"I don't like this, Lucas."

"Not to worry. If it were them, they would have stayed with us. They're gone. Everything is fine. No more bugs. Let me stop and clean the windshield so I don't hit a tree."

Lucas got out of the vehicle, released the back hatch, and opened the hidden tool compartment under the carpet. Beneath the squeegee and glass cleaner was a bath towel wrapped around a scabbard. He uncovered the hilt and grasped it with his right hand. To his surprise, the handle was warm; after releasing it, his hand retained a slight shade of blue.

Cleaning the bug guts off the windshield, he didn't notice the stirring wake of debris moving rapidly as it followed the vulture-like shadow towards his vehicle. Victoria saw it and froze. There was no time to warn him.

Rocking the SUV in its vacuum and pelting him with dust and gravel, the shadow roared over them into the thick vegetation from where Daniel would be returning.

Lucas cleared his eyes and ran to the back of his vehicle for the sword and the small velvet sack underneath.

"Take the Rover to the shelter. Lock it down. Get everyone packed. I'm going to find our son. It's happening."

Chapter 1

Follow your desires and new doors will open. Some doors should remain closed.

(Ten Years Earlier)

Ambling into Starbucks had, for better or for worse, become Dr. Lucas Tanner and Dr. Victoria Pruett's anchor to the world outside their lab. Once again, the caffeine zombies ordered their usual afternoon dosage and found a table for two among the sales people, soccer moms, and other fellow coffee addicts.

Life so far was following the familiar droning script: pay the price of tenure, publish new findings, establish patent rights, sit on a few boards, and then reap the academic and financial benefits for a good long life. As they relished their latest progress in the quantum mechanics playground, Lucas sipped his watered down espresso while Victoria caressed her caramel macchiato latté. For a few minutes, they enjoyed their semi-private solace, until Lucas fired up his laptop to hold off the daily onslaught of bellyaching undergrad emails and search for funding.

Victoria's gaze narrowed. "Lucas, tell me you didn't just raise a toast to the vogue tramp in the corner, the one peeking over her Mac?"

"What are you talking about, Victoria? You mean, like this?" He lifted his Americano again and flashed a grin at the lone diva.

"Vic, why are you always looking out for me? What, jealous or something, are you?" Lucas teased. "Don't the baristas here all remember your name?"

"That's what happens when you tip."

"Well, compared to your texting relationships in our lab, where's the crime in passing on a warm smile to a fellow professional who came here to work and sip a mocha? She's tricked out for somebody. Could be me; who knows?"

Victoria rolled her eyes back. "How do you know she's drinking a mocha?"

Lucas sighed and shook his head. *How long can Vic keep up this "big sister" act?*

"Admit it, Vic, you purposefully use your white lab coat, PhD badge, and thick black frames to keep anyone on your level at bay. What are you going to add next? A burqa? It's not you."

Dr. Victoria Pruett leaned over the table and pushed her thick, black-framed glasses back over the bridge of her nose. She kept her flame of red hair short and muted to a more conservative auburn; collateral damage, a result from a date who said her natural perm reminded him of Bozo the Clown.

"She's not your type, and you're not hers. Trust me on this one, Mega Mind, I believe her only missing accessory is a live beating heart. With this one, you'll have regrets, I promise."

Victoria had the qualifications to be an expert on regrets. She blamed her father's exit at a young age for her insecurities. Before the lab coat, there was the "promiscuous, desperate undergrad" era, as she referred to it. Away from her mother and the small-town church, the mutual exploitation of hookups made a mockery of her abstinence vows, picking up something of a reputation in the process – and nothing else to show for her efforts. That's when academics became her friend. They loved back, provided insulation, and paid her well to find answers.

"Why do you guys go for such sleazes?" she muttered to herself in frustration as she stood up to go order a second round. She couldn't resist taking a closer look to check out her rival as she strode with her own runway walk. *How COULD Lucas be so stupid as to not see what was right in front of him, every day – and what do I have to do to wake him up to see me as a woman? It's ridiculous to keep watching him play these idiotic man games, like this one;* scanning the bimbo as she approached. On the surface, she saw nothing to contradict her initial gut check*: White to olive skin, skank model wannabe, yeah, 5'10", dark short sassy hair, poker face, sunken cheeks, black pearls, white sleeveless blouse, tight black leather pants, long thin heels, physique that's spent too long at the gym, vein visible in her left bicep, and white MacBook. It all speaks to more to fashion sense than common sense.* And yet there was something she couldn't quite put her finger on. *Let's see ... if I keep staring at her...*

The woman's gaze met Victoria's for a fraction of a second, and she immediately reached for her iPhone. There was an "I told you so" smirk on Victoria's face when she came back to the table. "Oh, how you said she might be here for you? I think you might be right. Let me see your laptop."

"Huh?" Lucas said, confused by both the comment and the instruction.

"Let me see your laptop. Act as though there's something on it you want me to see."

"Okay," Lucas sighed, "but I'm still checking my email..."

The laptop changed sides, and a few keystrokes later, Victoria confirmed her suspicions. "Keep smiling, Dr. Tanner."

"Lighten up, Victoria, this is a public place. You're going to draw attention from other men. You wouldn't want that."

"Maybe I do, Mr. Heartbreak. She's not your type, Dr. Tanner: mysterious, sexy, no character. And if I didn't like my feet, I'd wear those heels too. I give her kudos, though, for the Mac and matching phone."

"Hey, can I have my computer back now? I'm doing work on it; honest!"

"Gotcha. Just what I thought. You've been hacked. This connection is going to end right now. None of our research is on here, is it, Lucas?"

"You know I'd never risk that."

"All regulars in here, except for your new friend in the corner. What do you make of that? Lucas, keep smiling for her."

Lucas tilted his head as he faked a smile at the intriguing woman, "Victoria, you don't really think...her...? Alright, I just raised my cup to her again; now she's leaving."

Victoria's face remained focused on the computer screen, "Just got an IP. A proxy server; definitely covering tracks."

"She's getting up, she's headed for the door...damn."

Lucas sputtered again, "Victoria, you don't really think...her...?"

"Yes I do. There she goes, on her little white crotch rocket. How fitting. What if I wasn't around?"

"Nice Ducati. Goes with the MacBook too. You know, I'd protect myself. Vic, guys'd be all over you if you got a ride like that...and... aw, look...you have the prettiest blush when you get angry."

"Glad you noticed. Coffee break's over, Dr. Tanner; time to get back to research."

Backpacks slung over their shoulders, they walked cautiously back to Lucas's Land Rover and climbed in.

"If you're right, who do you think she's working for?" Lucas asked as he turned the key.

"Someone with deep pockets or tied to industrial espionage. Word's out on the street that the dynamic duo of Tanner and Pruett is being shorted by their funding partners who keep throwing dollars at hogs like the Large Hadron Collider and their search for the Higgs Boson or 'god particle.' In all probability they will find it. But what next?

When they do, I want to deliver more than a particle. Expectations are high to put central University of Texas systems back on the Nobel map and do it on the cheap. Our University President is snowing us to believe he's been protecting us from budget cuts the last two years when we need more cash. Some investors think we ought to take our research private. So, Dr. Tanner, with so much riding on this, please don't give it all away because you're a sucker for a pretty face and you need to prove you've got a lethal flow of testosterone."

"Eyes wide open. I agree, Vic, but I'm not the only one who attracts coffee shop and other groupies. I have to admit, I'm not immune to your particular seductive powers as an 'Ugly Betty.' As much as you try to play yourself down, it doesn't work with me. You have your own admirers closer than you think. However, in the interest of fair play... I have to bring this up: what about your last date?"

"That was two months ago. I've forgotten him. You haven't."

"How could I? 'Mr. I'll-Stalk-You-Until-You-Go-Out-With-Me,' the ex-marine undergrad student with the six-pack abs who showed up at my gym? He thought I was his competition."

Victoria laughed. "Are you still jealous of his bench press?"

"How can I be jealous of someone who challenges me to a bench press competition for you?"

"Ouch. So you weren't up to the challenge of my 'Ugly Betty' seduction powers?

"You were using this undergrad to get me to prove myself? That's why the moment I get an exotic admirer in my corner your claws come out and try to ruin my fantasy?

"Think what you want, but wouldn't you rather have the real thing? I'll surprise you one day with the leathers and high heels under my lab coat."

"And I'll surprise you with a tattoo of Leonardo da Vinci under mine."

To his surprise Victoria reached over and touched the back of Lucas' neck and said, "Agreed."

"Hey, ah, before I drive off the road, what about our agreement? You know I want you to find the right guy and succeed in our research. We've been friends eight years, and during the last couple I've had to become your Dr. Phil over these guys trying to gigolo their way through your intro to physics class. Why would you even give them a chance?"

"Lucas, I am so glad you brought that up. That only happened once, a one-time mistake, because I couldn't find any men with real class. What about you, Dr. Tanner? I'm still make-believe friends with all your little graduate assistants who think you're the hottest thing since the sun, and think they can get into your pants through me. You know what it's like being asked what your relationship status is? I tell 'em they can just look it up on facebook/BradPittsCousin."

"My little what?"

"Those dreamy-eyed emos trying to get to you through me. They all sound the same: 'Ah, now, ah, Dr. Pru-ett, could you tell me if Dr. Tan-ner is married or has a serious, like, girl-friend? Does he need a lab assistant or intern or something?' Did you ever think of that? I don't tell them anything."

"What's to tell?"

"What you really like in a woman, for one."

"Like what I just saw fly out of the Starbucks? Okay, Vic, I'm just kidding. Don't throw your lab coat at me while I'm driving; I'm not used to seeing you without it. Hey, nice calves; you got a waistline, too?"

"Wouldn't you like to know? Shut up and drive. And by the way, I'll take that last remark as a compliment. Maybe we should renegotiate our agreement."

Feeling they had called each other's bluff, Dr.'s Pruett and Tanner went silent for two blocks not knowing what to say next. Lucas stopped at the red light, and turned to Victoria to find her already staring at him and asked her, "You mean that?"

She nodded her head up and down, "Yes...and I want to say something else."

"Sure."

She met his eyes and held them with her own. "You have a green light. That means go."

Chapter 2

Hindsight is hell. Hindsight with faith is revelatory.

She had stopped her work to watch him fumble through the scrap notes on his desk. It was the little things that attracted Vic to him, like the way he ran his hand through his streaked blond hair when he was stressed, or that he wasn't yet conscious of how handsome he was in his special nerd-coming-of-age way. If she was mad at him, his innocent smirk with the dimples made her forget why. *The man is tall and lean, six feet, one hundred and ninety pounds of bridled brawn. Now, all he needs is a good men's store.*

He called her, "Vic, come over here and take a break for a minute. I've got something to bounce off of you."

Back to reality. She removed her glasses as far as the safety cord around her neck, struck a mock pose with a ballerina-like hand in the air, pursed her lips and gently sucked in her cheeks. "The mystery diva, right? She contacted you again?"

"I wish! No joking on this. Look, we're going to need a human guinea pig. Our test dummies are taking us about as far as we can go. Intuition is telling me 'move faster.' This is huge, and it goes without saying we're in a bind. Do you trust me?"

"Slow down, Mr. Ambitious. We're not desperate yet. For starters, this isn't like hiring a test pilot for the next stealth fighter; it's too dangerous."

"Alright, Vic, maybe we can contact the guy who dives with the red devil squid down in Baja?"

"Better idea: the sexy magician's assistant who survives being sawed in half every night? Seriously, I agree on cashing in for the right partner, but we can't go public or let the department know about this yet. Last year we were rock stars with our publications, and this year we're in danger of budget cutbacks."

Lucas braced his hand down on her shoulder, lifted his brow, and continued. "How long do we keep saying 'no' to funding and rearrange the lab for every military aide who drops by to schmooze? Prestige and publicity are only as good as today. We've moved mundane objects and a few small animals through three feet of concrete and steel-reinforced walls. The military wants this real bad for Special Ops applications. If we don't make a deal soon, this could be ripped from our hands for national security interests."

"Dr. Tanner, do you want to be owned and told that everything you are working on has to be kept hush-hush so the military can find more ways to bloat their budget? If we have to make a choice, I'd rather be on a shareholder's leash. This has to stay off the books. We'll keep documenting everything in secret and tell them this work was on our dime when it comes up."

"The energy we use is a dead giveaway. We both know that's not on our dime."

"Lucas, we'll pay it all back eventually, no problem."

"We don't have to do it like this. I have a confession, Vic."

"What are you referring to?"

"Ever heard of the world's worst secret? It's going to be us. Where do you think our test subjects are going?

Floating somewhere as space junk? We need money right now to do this justice and work on the up-and-up."

"And?"

"And I've been in contact with a private investor. Remember when I flew to the UN for our honorary award nomination last year? Everybody and his neighbor wanted a piece of this, especially a few small countries who've been bidding for acceptance into the European Union. They want to quit being treated as second class."

"Lucas, you're getting in over your head. Did you make any promises?"

"I took a courtesy deposit out of goodwill. The only promise I made was to give updates on any new developments. They also get the first crack at the opening bid for private investment."

"Oh my God. How much?"

"Ten million is sitting in a Swiss account, wired from Prague. I have the code, but haven't moved on it. I swear this is the truth. You have to admit, this is a good problem to have."

"You don't get it. The woman at the coffee shop? And now this? There's a connection."

"Victoria, the nature of what we are working on is the problem. Money is how the world works. This is freedom."

Chapter 3

Obviously, there are slips and gaps in the system
where it appears a door was left open on purpose.

Across the chasm of time and space, he would be the first
of another kind to greet them. Secretly creating micro-
singularities off the books, Dr. Tanner and Pruett
assumed they were discreet on their side of the universe.
The attention they gained on the other side, however,
was a different story. They could have just as easily come
across another life form with far more sinister plans as
they graduated from sending garden statues through
concrete walls to punching them into what they fondly
called 'statue heaven.' Hunting for clues to their stoic
passengers' final destination, they filmed the quantum
jumps with high-speed video.

As Victoria and Lucas were combing over the data from
the last portal launch, they had a hunch that Galileo II,
like the other conscripted volunteers, didn't take the long
way home. Rather, the concrete statue had slipped
through the fabric of the cosmos. When the energy
vibrations stirred the quantum marrow of its atomic
structure, the statue itself ceased to be constrained by
the scaffolding of space and time. Poof, gone, a torn
bundle of smoking electrical conduits, the only telltale
signs of a directed free fall.

Of course this was exciting, but there was still something
very important missing; proof of a real destination, and
better a round trip ticket.

"Dr. Pruett, if you think there is a heaven, then maybe we
should send Jesus or the Buddha next? Our friends may
need a mediator since we can't find them. So far, the
jump looks like a one-way trip."

Vic thought about it. "So you want to save the Thinker, David, the Galileo brothers, Leonardo, and St. Francis? I feel bad for them, being all alone out there."

"I wouldn't say 'save,' but we need to know where they went."

"Lucas, I know you don't like to talk religion, but what do you think of the 'Anthropic Principle?'"

"What, that intelligent design crap where the entire universe is fine-tuned to support us alone, homo sapiens sapiens, the prima donnas of the cosmos?"

Victoria sighed, "Yes, that crap where the entire universe is at least fine-tuned to support shower scum and nail fungus. Feel better?"

"I'm with you, Vic, but you have to choose your words carefully. They'll end up defining you. You mention I.D. and our potential list of benefactors and emergency funds could dry up overnight. They want practical uses of this technology and profits. Cosmological and metaphysical speculation ought to be left up to priests, science fiction writers, philosophers and theoretical physicists, in that order."

"Alright, Dr. Tanner, in your estimation, which has more intelligence behind it? Political correctness or intelligent design? Or are you trying to play neutral?"

"I tend to think they need each other. When people are searching for what they don't know, they start first by defining what they don't believe. Vic, with our research, that may all become a moot point. We are talking about the chance to visit extra-solar planets with this technology: secure world peace. I'm not looking for heaven. There are too many other places to visit first."

"You know what bothers me most about your semantic cage, Lucas?"

"That it's true?"

"It's that we have to prematurely excuse ourselves from the possibility all this may have been started by a force beyond our capacity to know. If it makes you feel more secure, we can call it the 'evolutionary conscience.'"

Man, she's still on an esoteric roll. Why can't she let it go? Should I tell her about my dreams? Lucas said to himself. "Obviously there are slips and gaps in the fabric of space where it appears a door was left open on purpose. But now we know we can force open the door."

"Don't you think some people have already been holding the door open more than we give them credit for? People have been experiencing other realms in ecstatic moments of prayer and meditation for centuries."

"Come on, Vic, let's leave the 'déjà vu all over again' stuff alone. They didn't do it this way, without all the mumbo jumbo."

"Seriously, Jedi Luke, artists, musicians, and Zen masters try to move through these branes of spatial dimensions in space-time all the time. I think some of them succeed long enough for a short glimpse. But what if it was possible to travel through the barrier of human existence, take a good long look at the other side, and return to tell about it?"

"Then maybe your creative friends will be there waiting for us. If we can cut down on the light years of travel needed even to get to Vega, I'd be happy. There are enough vacation destinations here in our own back yard."

"Lucas, you made the confession a few weeks ago about the money. I didn't ask who or where? But--"

Interrupting her, "Vic, you know it's better that way. It was someone from one of the Balkan countries, Swiss bank account, leave it at that in case something happens."

"No, I have a confession too."

"What, you took a down payment as well? Now we have a problem!"

"Let me finish, Einstein. No! It's different than that. I don't have a good way to say it." Exasperated she took a big breath and blew out her cheeks, "I had a dream. No, really I've had dreams."

"Healthy, Vic, good for you."

"Seriously Lucas, not this one. It's been the same dream for several months, over and over; the only reason I give it credence. And it always involves you."

Lucas stroked his chin, "I'm flattered but maybe this isn't the time. How about this weekend we go out? Keep emotions out of the office just in case."

"In case? Listen, this trained, reasoned brain has had this dream, over and over again! It goes like this; you jump from a cliff into a deep canyon where I run to the edge and watch you fall for miles until you disappear. I look for your body and never find it. I keep hoping you are alive, but no one will help me find you." Wiping the sweat from her forehead, temples and neck with her hand, she waited for a response. "Are you going to say anything, Dr. Tanner?"

"You're not setting me up for embarrassment?"

"You know me better than that."

"Alright, I've had dreams too. I've tried not to take it too seriously. As a kid I had a reoccurring dream of a warrior angel with immense wings, but nothing ever came of it. Probably from stories my mother seeded. Kid's stuff."

"How interesting."

"For the last few months I keep seeing a golden gas giant like Jupiter with a large moon the size of the Earth. The closer I fly towards it, I am embraced by a golden warmth emanating from the core of the planet. The moon doesn't glow like ours. It's the most beautiful shade of aqua blue. And I also see what looked like meteorites, flying streaks coming and going from both spheres. And I hear beautiful music beyond description. When I wake up, I feel like I've been there."

"Dr. Tanner, your secret is safe with me. That is beautiful. Do you still feel like a scientist?"

"Enough, that's between you and me only. Doesn't mean anything."

"Maybe our dreams correspond?" Victoria paused, waiting for an answer then asked, "Not ready for that leap of faith yet?"

Chapter 4

How hard we try to avoid the attraction to the sins of the father.

Ru knew that Cuzak, like herself, rarely slept. That was one of the few things they had in common, another quirky mix of their shared genome traits she inherited from him. For all his talk of bringing her into his network of underground power and deal making, so far she was left in the dark as he relegated her to gathering intelligence and acting as an enforcer. The closest thing to love he demonstrated is when he took pride in showing her off as a tool of intimidation.

How ironic. The oneness she had hoped for of a real father-daughter relationship hadn't happened yet. Of course that would be impossible. The two of us will never have a normal relationship. We aren't normal. Ouriano says, "That doesn't matter. You aren't the first one to be split in your loyalties between your blood ties and your conscience. Your father has the same choice."

Cuzak's private quarters were buried deep below the reactor's spent fuel pool, past three sets of security personnel. She had examined the security logs and knew he never hosted any visitors there except her. *Who would make this their retreat? Who wants to don radioactive gear to socialize? No one human, for sure.*

At the last check point, the guard asked, "Is he expecting you?"

Ru condescended, "So he is in, you imbecile! Yes, we are going over new security protocols," then bullied her way by to the industrial stairwell. *If his private apartment is locked down and I feel the pulse, he'll be in there, re-*

energizing, plotting, communicating, analyzing, maybe worshiping? Which will it be?

Away from the sight of security, she opened her wings and stealthily glided down the five floors of the metal stairwell, avoiding the clank of the steps and rails. Her heart began to heave as she felt the pulse. Her night vision picked up the purple vapors seeping under the bottom of the thick steel door. Carefully, she placed her hands over the exterior casing of the two deadbolts. Twisting her palms, she felt the bolts turn and release the door. Holding most of the weight of the door, she slipped in without a sound.

There across the room, in front of five thick white candles with his back to her, Cuzak sat in a lotus-like position on a small carpet. He was covered by a dark blue robe and looked to be in a trance. Purple smoke circled around his head and twirled up around the maze of pipes and valves. *What is in the purple vapors? Whatever it is, it's wonderful, in a different way.*

He's talking to someone! Who is it? "Don't you think those aspirations are too high, my lord? Why not be content with the Sanctuary and leave it at that?"

The conversation stopped abruptly. Without looking up, Cuzak asked, "Why, my daughter, have you come unannounced? Do you really want to know the sins of your father?"

"If you're asking, 'do I want to know what my father does in his strange man-cave and where his loyalties lie?' Yes, but actually I would settle for just getting to know him."

Cuzak blew out the candles and stood up as the fluorescent lights flickered on and the purple vapor evaporated. He put his hands in the pockets of his robe and smiled. "Ru, I am glad you are here. Listen carefully to these words, 'mutual respect.' Do I inquire about all your whereabouts and contacts? Do you have the freedom to leave now if you like? So, let's go over our agreement again: you don't ask too much, and I won't tell you what to do with your life. After all, I would imagine you have other good advisers to turn to?"

"I only have one father."

"I thought you found love among the Russian oligarchy? What do you need with a father?"

"You are the one who introduced yourself out of nowhere at my husband's funeral, helping me put the missing pieces together."

"Yes, and you were left a fortune as a young bride, weren't you?"

"I resigned it all back to his estate to disappear and work for you. Isn't that what you wanted?"

"What I implied is, 'You are like me. This world can never be your home if you are going to fully develop into who you are. In that case, we must stick together. I don't know exactly what you expect me to say. Is there anything else?"

Dejected, Ru started backing out the door. "No, that's all."

"Ru, knock next time. You may not like what you find."

Chapter 5

Are not all angels ministering spirits sent to serve those who will inherit salvation?... Well, almost.

Victoria put her glasses back on. "I've let our conversation about the dreams ride all week. If you're not going to respond about our sixth sense encounters, then let's review this latest scientific contribution we've made to the universe of the unknown."

They began to playback the high-speed digital recorders that documented the shift of objects and animals through their created gateways of space-time, without any extraordinary results at first. Then they switched to infrared light spectrum filters and experimented with the depth focus.

"Stop right there! Back up!" Lucas shouted. "You didn't record over old footage, did you?"

"No. Oh my God, he looks like a hologram." Victoria's nervous system began to feel the bleach of panic rush through her synapses as she tried to process the unmistakable human figure who looked to be investigating them.

"Look at it! This guy is half pro wrestler, half Greek god!" Lucas quipped.

A full thick mane of unkempt hair like a '70s rock star followed the intruder's head as he turned and winked with his left eye at the camera.

Lucas rubbed his forehead. "This isn't a joke, is it? I've seen this image before. You imposed this didn't you? Not funny."

"Are you crazy? I wish. How would you fake this? You know what, I don't feel so good." Her panic rose as her brain tried to process the reality of this obvious contact, her autonomic nervous system going into overdrive and pumping adrenaline and blood to her heart and lungs away from her brain, causing dizziness and freezing her muscles.

"Vic, are you going catatonic on me? If this is real we may have leapfrogged over your anthropic principle. Some like Sir Dawkins hold that aliens may have seeded asteroids."

"Find my purse, Luke – the Xanax."

Lucas dredged through the bottom of her purse for the prescription, then handed her two pills with the advice, "You don't need those."

"Bad relationship, old prescription, special occasion," explained Victoria.

The alien image was frozen on the monitor. She sat stunned for a few minutes as her anxiety meds seeped into her bloodstream.

"Does he look menacing to you? The form looks humanoid enough. Vic, are you with me yet? Judging by this...entity's boldness to communicate, we must not appear to be a threat. Why didn't he show up for the SETI people?"

Victoria guzzled down the last half of her water bottle with her head cocked back, then put her hands on her knees. Her brain kicked in as the meds took effect. "Let's see if we can repeat. We need another test statue."

"I'll go talk to security in the lobby and tell him we need to borrow the three-foot bronze of Leonardo da Vinci for a photo shoot in our lab."

As Leonardo's dimensional shift neared the threshold, they decelerated the last twenty percent of the power increase. With cameras recording, to the human eye, the sculpture disappeared instantaneously; to the digitized replay, he faded away, leaving a longer window to observe.

Lucas slapped himself when the friendly green eyes under the guitar hero hair stared at them and motioned this time with his hand to follow.

"My God, tell me this isn't happening," Victoria, said, still returning from her stress seizure. "Here he comes again, head and torso, then the entire body, taking a look around the lab. He's an eight foot holograph of a romance novel model."

"You still read those? Tell me Vic, what's this superman made of? Look at the muscle striations under his clothes. They look more iridescent than pigmented."

"I've read my share; ever pick one up? Our virtual friend appears to be self-aware."

"How do we look to him?" Lucas asked, mesmerized. "And why would I ever read a romance novel?"

"Beats loneliness."

"Guess what? We're not alone."

The mane of long hair flung to the side as the figure faced the primary camera with a grin of confidence and amusement. He wore a long scar along the right base of his neck, running down the inside of an overdeveloped trapezius muscle that disappeared under the neckline of his simple toga. A wide belt supported a long sheath bearing a glimmering hilt of a sword. He then retreated back through the quantum aperture in the space of a millisecond.

Black spots appeared in front of her eyes and her head swam. Victoria pulled down an emergency kit from the wall. "Break open the ammonia for me, now!"

Fumbling the green container on the floor and spilling the contents, Lucas kicked and chased several capsules until he secured one and snapped it under her nose. Her head jerked back as she seared her sinuses.

Lucas reached for his own bottled water, squeezed and sucked down the entire contents, tossing the empty bottle on the floor. "We did it," Lucas said, chin trembling as he mustered the words. "We successfully opened a temporary gateway, twice – and entertained a guest!"

"It's no longer theoretical," Victoria added in a subdued voice. "The multi-verse has travelers." Surprised she saw Lucas slump down on a stool with his lab coat touching the floor behind him, fully inhale an ammonia capsule for himself, then close his eyes.

"I have to ask you though," she said, "is this the angel of your childhood dreams?

Without opening his eyes or saying a word he raised his right hand as if about to speak, then lowered it.

"I am going to take that as a yes, unless I hear something else from you," added Victoria.

When he finally moved, Lucas checked the internal infrared GPS unit avoiding her question, "Our Leonardo emitted a location signal from this spot for five seconds after disappearing! There was no linear movement. Next time, he'll have a stronger isotope packed up his orifice."

"That's your specialty. In the meantime, I'll run an analysis of anything exchanged between realms and run a light spectrograph to see what this Fabio is made of. Congratulations, Dr. Tanner, looks like your dream's come true."

Chapter 6

"He fashions winds as messengers, flames of fire his servants." – Psalm 104:4

"Uhh." Victoria scratched the back of her head, continuing the closed loop nervous tic. *Why us?* she thought as her nails dug in searching for relief. *Is this Pandora's box? The discovery of the second atomic bomb?*

"Dr. Tanner, are you ready for the report?"

"Shock me."

"Pure wide-spectrum light entered the opening when Leonardo was absorbed. Light waves, neutrinos, possibly some antimatter radiation, detected. No gases, no loss of air pressure, nothing unusual. Lucas, is there any credible documentation of non-carbon-based life forms? I may need to double my prescription."

Lucas ran his hand through his hair, "Documentation is the problem. Some speculation on silicon and arsenic. Nothing close to this."

"What do we call the... uhhh... entity? Do you like the name Fabio?"

"How about Methuselah? You remember Methuselah, the oldest man in the Bible, lived like nine hundred years?"

"But he didn't look that old."

"Our Methuselah is old in a different way."

"What way?"

"Methuselah is an intelligence composed of light, with no classic elements from our universe essential for life. No carbon, hydrogen, nitrogen, oxygen, phosphorus, or sulfur composing his essence to deteriorate."

Victoria clamped her hands together behind her head, "So you're thinking he's a being of light? You think Methuselah was sent to us in response to our poking around? Each wormhole makes a discernible disturbance in time and space fabric because of the focused energy involved."

Lucas walked up to the idea board and began drawing a familiar shape. "Kind of like a bug hitting a spider's web. As a little kid, did you ever pull the legs off a grasshopper and throw it into a spider's web to see what happens next?"

"I don't follow."

"The vibrations of the poor tangled grasshopper signal the weaver that lunch is served."

"Lucas, that's sadistic."

He gave a smirk, ghoulishly enjoying her typical girly reaction. "Well on Earth, our insect world has no mercy. The spider will come down, sink her fangs into the tangled bug, spin a cocoon coffin of soft silk, and wait for the victim's guts to liquefy for a tasty shake."

"Can you change the analogy? How about a gatekeeper or sentinel for anything that crosses over? I don't want a giant spider coming through a hole we made in time and space."

"Well it was just a quick illustration. In reality, that's not what I'm saying. The truth is, we put several objects through the fabric of time and space, and somebody noticed."

"Once again, who noticed? Who sent Methuselah? I know that's a religious or at best metaphysical question, but be honest: you want to know if that thing is a sentient being, an angel, a demon, some kind of a Bodhisattva, a spirit guide, a hallucination, or what?"

"A Man In Black or a Matrix's Mr. Smith? Vic, can we answer the question without embracing a worldview or religion? It could be a higher-level species or ..."

"You can, but then you would be a liar, Lucas."

"We can't perform a verifiable experiment on something we have to have a religious belief in. I can see that in a journal now: 'Scientists Discover Angels and Demonic Entities in Lab.' The only publication we'd be in is the National Enquirer."

"Skip the lecture. It's you and me here, Lucas. We've accomplished something which is taking us beyond science. Not everything in life is verifiable, especially when you play with the curve of time and space. We don't even have to go there yet, but who can verify a dream? Or falling in love? Or why we don't say what we feel towards someone?"

Victoria paused to judge his reaction, which looked confused. "Let's face it: the progress we've made with these quantum leaps has come from an intuition – you said it first – which is beyond our explanation. There is an order here that begs to be discovered."

"Vic, let's stick to Occam's razor for the most obvious explanation first."

"You're forgetting, Lucas, there's an Occam's razor for coincidence; it's called *your dream*."

Chapter 7

"I heard the Father say, (You have to go!) You're going to the Land of Zion!"

It was late afternoon. Lucas scooted down to the end of the hardwood pew to leave the old church sanctuary but was met by someone who stood in the back. He guessed the well-dressed suit was none other than the Senior Pastor, the Rev. E. S. Gardner whose name hung on the aging metal sign over the sidewalk by the church office door. He judged the pastor to be at least seventy-five-years-old, distinguished by his gray goatee-mustache, short black hair, and chocolate skin. The reverend, wearing his gray-silver suit, crisp white shirt, shiny cufflinks, partially shaded glasses, red tie and handkerchief, greeted him. "I didn't hear your prayers," he said, "But I know someone who did. If your heart is troubled, this is the right place to start."

"I needed a safe place to be for a few minutes and gather my thoughts. I've driven by here numerous times. This looked like a church that helps people. Thank you for lending it, but I'm alright now, really."

"Prayer's more than a one-time event," he said, offering his hand in friendship. "Emanuel Gardner, officially Pastor, caretaker, subordinate to God's flock, unofficially 'all dressed up and no place to go.'"

"How long have you been a Pastor here? What size congregation?"

"Twenty years. We've become a mission more than a traditional church. We help people who are passing through, many for whom the bottom fell out of their life but they can't afford to move."

"Sorry. I'm Lucas Tanner. I work at the university down the road, research. I have to go – you know, deadlines – but can I ask you something?"

"You are always welcome back, but I have a few minutes now."

"I have a friend who lives in fear that he may have made a big mistake because he turned his back on God a long time ago. Now he's having weird dreams, second-guessing himself – even though he's experiencing what others tell him is success."

"And your question?"

"Pastor Gardner, how does he find God and make up for it?"

"Your friend, he presumes God has lost track of him, like he went off the map?"

"Yes, I suppose something like that. I guess you're going to tell me that God doesn't lose people?"

"How lost can he be, since he has a friend praying for him? That would be a beacon to God. What did you tell your friend?"

"I told him he was an idiot for presuming he knew so much."

"You are tough on your prodigal, aren't you? I bet he knows the way home but he's not sure of the welcome. Do you think he is open to being un-lost?"

"I think he's open to it, but doesn't want anyone to know."

"I see; spiritual but not religious. And what does he think God wants him to do to make up for his past?"

Lucas wrestled with the question for a few seconds. "Risk, maybe?"

A female voice from the front of the church surprised both of them. "Reverend Gardner, we're ready to rehearse the song you requested for Sunday." Twelve choir members trickled into the choir loft while they were talking as the pianist-director warmed up.

"Pardon me, Lucas, we have to prepare for Sunday's worship," the pastor said before walking up to the choir loft. Glancing back over his shoulder to speak over the choir and musical warm-ups, the pastor's voice carried clearly to Lucas, "I believe we all cross paths for a reason. You are an interesting young man. Someone has a hand on your shoulder. Let's meet again."

Lucas almost left, but he decided to stay in the back of the sanctuary a few more minutes. It had been ages since he had heard a live church choir. He watched the pastor take his own microphone and stand next to the piano opposite the choir.

The choir began humming and swaying to the vibrancy of the rich piano chords. The pastor hummed his own antiphonal sounds, and then they all started in, the choir singing first. On the second line of the first verse, some internal premonition switch flipped on inside Lucas. How can so much sound come from such a small group? His hand started tapping the back of the last pew.

"Taaaake my haan-annnd! I'm going to meet the man from Zion!
Taaaake my haan-annnd! I'm going to meet the man from Zion!
'Cause He, 'cause He, He won't leave meee!

Early in the mornin', I'm going to meet the man from Zion!
Early in the mornin', I'm going to meet the man from Zion!
'Cause He, 'cause He, He won't leave meee!"

The joy of the singing found an empty lake inside of
Lucas, void of this kind of pleasure. The pastor readied
his mic to begin singing with the choir like a seasoned
blues artist. For the next few moments, Lucas stood
outside himself.

"Taaaake my haan-annnd! (He's got to go!)
I'm going to meet the man from Zion!
Taaaake my haan-annnd! (She's got to go!)
I'm going to meet the man from Zion!
'Cause He, 'cause He, (Cause He-He-He)
He won't leave meeeeee!

One fine mornin', (He's got to go!)
I'm going to meet the man from Zion!
One fine mornin', (She's got to go!)
I'm going to meet the man from Zion!
'Cause He, 'cause He, (Cause He-He-He)
He won't leave meeeeee!

He's comin' from the ea-east, (Sista, you've got to go!)
He's going to the land of Zion!
He's comin' from the ea-east, (Brotha, you've got to go!)
He's going to the Land of Zion!
'Cause He, 'cause He, He won't leave meeeeee!

I heard the Father say-ay, (You have to go!)
You're going to the Land of Zion!
I heard the Father say-ay, (Jesus, You have to go!)
You're going to the Land of Zion!
'Cause He, 'cause He, He won't leave meeeee!
('Cause He, 'cause He, He won't leave meeeee!)
(Jesus, You have to go!)"

"And Jesus said, 'I will never leave you nor forsake you, I will be with you always, even to the end of the age,'" the pastor finished. At this cue, Lucas left the church for his car filled with a joy that he didn't have a place to file. He never heard Pastor Gardner tell him at the end of the song, "Godspeed Dr. Tanner, Godspeed. You will need it."

Pastor Gardner then turned around to face the choir and musicians to thank them. When he dropped the microphone to his side and bowed toward them, they all bowed likewise and began to fade into nothingness. As they dissipated, he knelt down and prayed. A few moments later, the old sanctuary and choir loft sat eerily empty.

Chapter 8

There is a lonely road which leads to my lover.

Lucas had no problem making live-or-die decisions. On the back wall of his office, under his framed and matted MIT PhD, hung a poster board sign on a string that said, "Deliberating fate is counterproductive."

"Victoria, I have a core philosophy. It's what I tell my students all the time: 'The big decisions in life are better off left to short warning. Split-second decisions leave no wasted time for obsession. They reduce you to your base personality and force the gut decision born of real passion. Buy the winning lotto ticket and you can experience a miracle. Buy a loser and you won't bother to tell anyone.'"

"Dr. Tanner, do you really believe that your passions should be your true motivation? Because I have a secret sign hanging on the back of my desk where no one can see it."

"What is it? 'Welcome to my conspiracy?'"

"It has a little more weight than that, thank you, and tends to agree with your prescription for passion. Mine reads: 'There is a lonely road which leads to my lover.'"

"Deep. I like it." They looked at one another with a new awareness. The wordless communication within the silence of that one look broke down the pseudo-barriers and hastily built, presumed self-saving obstructions, and both knew they had found that solid connection and base – that it had been there all along, just waiting to be pulled from the shadows. The truth and peace of it settled in their hearts, and souls. They had found each other, and it was right, and good. And knowing that, they also knew they had to keep on with their work.

"Hey Vic, my cell phone is going off. Can you reach it for me?"

"So is mine. It's a text from the University President's mobile: 'Drs Tan and Pru, !IMMED secure all data drives, logs, lab to be shut down tomorrow pm, plan B, NSA HS, requesting orig dat in 48 hrs. Bring to my office tomorrow 8am!"

"Same text here. No on the plan B, Vic. We're going into our plan C phase!"

"I know plan B includes uploading our most important data to a secret offshore server. What's plan C?"

"We are going to destroy the latest data regarding the quantum jumps. Except one exceptional overseas server only we know, and then..."

Interrupting him, "Are you crazy? We can't destroy the official records of our best work! We'll be fired from the university. They obviously want us to leave everything intact for National Security Agency and Homeland Security to evaluate, then sit down with us." Victoria paused, frowned, "Oh, here's where your little overseas slush fund comes in. That won't bode well. You're suggesting they'll keep us on a homeland vacation while they farm out our work on some military installation? Gotcha. I suppose they won't let us leave the country to work for your investor either?"

"That's my guess. Besides, our latest work is off the record. They had to be monitoring the energy fluxes we caused on the local grid. The Prez and I had an agreement if something like this happened, at least give us twenty four hours."

"That was some heads up. What was the 'and then,' earlier?"

"After we destroy our server drives, you are going to send me through to the other side."

"What? Excuse me? I had a premonition one of our government agencies would be monitoring in case they wanted to nationalize. They had to know you were on the verge of private investors outside the US. But you, punching through to the other side? That's not worth risking your life! What's the urgency? This is *our* work."

"The urgency is *your* dreams, *my* dreams, Methuselah, the whole thing. I don't want to see it all cut off. Who knows? I am afraid they might want this project boxed up, mothballed, when they learn things can travel both directions. Victoria, grab the other half of the suit. It's now or never."

"I want to agree with you, but this is not like you. You are really putting on the suit?"

"It is me, but I had myself boxed up. My hunch is the being we saw from the other side will help. That's my gut feeling. Like you said, it's not scientific. I didn't want to admit it, but my recurring dream, and yours, and *yes*, the confirmation of *the angel*, has changed my outlook. I would think you would be happy?"

"I, I am. Happy you are more open to life. But I want to make sure you are rational too."

"Ha ha ha. A week ago, I felt so conflicted that I pulled into an old downtown church off 10th street on the way home from the lab and sat alone on a pew, trying to figure out the dream until the Senior Pastor there hounded me. Felt like he was reading my mind, but then he had to leave to practice with his choir. I watched and listened from the back; a mind-blowing experience."

"What?"As Lucas told her the story he continued to put the lower half of his pressure suit on.

"Well, there's more. I stopped back two days later to finish our conversation. A different church secretary told me there was no Reverend Gardner or active choir at that church. And the sign with his name was gone. In fact she said, 'Our parish is getting ready to close and sell off the building. My job ends next Friday.' I told her, 'That can't be! I shook his hand and heard him sing with his choir.'

She asked, 'What did they sing?' I said, 'Something about *Brother, Sister, You've got to go, to the land of Zion, cause he won't leave me.*' The secretary told me, 'I've been here fifteen years, and we haven't had a choir in the last two. And I used to be the director of music. I don't even know that song.'"

Chapter 9

*I'll do all I can to contact you from the other side and I
know you'll do the same.*

Victoria's mind was running in two directions; one
preoccupied with the checklist for the quantum jump
and records destruction, the other bemoaning life after
Lucas was gone. *What will life be like if I never see him
again? Why does my dream have to come true now
when we've had this awakening between us?*

"Hey Vic, do you think we'll meet the dead line? I'm
sorry, are you crying? Stop, stop a minute. Talk to me."

"We can't stop. This is meant to be. You know Lucas,
better our relationship never got too serious, otherwise
I'd feel like a widow the rest of my life."

Victoria continued, preoccupied with the task at hand,
"Holes drilled, bombs away hard drives into the acid vat.
Does this feel like treason to you? Only four hours until *I
meet* with the University President? Of course, you have
other flight plans."

Pointing to his temple Lucas said, "It's OK Vic, we've got
the important details up here; that's leverage. Me and the
man upstairs haven't been on speaking terms since I left
home, but the recurring dream has become more
detailed. Two nights ago I saw others like our
Methuselah singing in unison where the melodic sound
of their voices streamed out from their lips in a rainbow
of colors."

"You're determined, Lucas. All the equipment is powered
up. Put your arms in." Blue *NASA* was emblazoned on
the left edge of the thick white forearm sleeve.

"Remember when you were back in high school and you cranked up your favorite song on the car stereo?"

"What? 'Alone Again, Naturally' or 'Can't Touch This?'"

"Come on, Vic, the fantastic feeling you got singing at the top of your lungs? That's how it was. I didn't want it to end. I could actually see their music."

Victoria helped him continue to suit up. "Arms in the jacket...life support harness. Like old people making smoke rings?"

"It sounds crazy even trying to explain it. Help me pull this down. I really have to go. They might cut power or interrupt us."

"Lucas, I believe, you, but we shouldn't be rushing this."

"We have one chance. I'll do all I can to contact you from the other side and I know you'll do the same. I mean, we don't know if there *is* 'another side.' Maybe I'll still be here; who knows? That's the point. Our work is so much more than us; no one has the right to hijack it."

What about us? "Okay, that's the last seal on your suit. You secure the helmet."

"Plug me in. Ready the cameras, upload the info then destroy the local data after the event. Oh yes, Victoria, I have to say this."

There was a pause between them as they both wondered if they should officially cross over the line about their true feelings. Lucas crossed first.

"I love you."

Without missing a beat, Victoria planted a quick kiss on his lips. "Lucas, promise you won't leave me forever. Remember my dream too, where you disappear for a while. This is crazy, Lucas, but I believe something good will come of this. Remember me and all the questions I'll have to answer when no one can find you."

"Victoria, I'm ready."

"No you're not. Here are your gloves. And you forgot the GPS unit and the isotopes. Find some way to signal me."

Victoria followed through on the wiring harness and the checklist. After reopening the extra power circuits required, the hum of the quantum vibrations began. She pushed the control throttle into the red threshold, where Lucas would either slip through the fabric of space or light up like a bonfire.

Lucas began to fade. "Are you feeling any pain?"

"No, just... cold. Numb."

"Testing transmission, one, two, three. Someone's banging on the door, Lucas..."

"Don't let them in."

That was Lucas' last transmission. The raiding party now stood outside the old hardened oak lab door. "Open up now! We have a warrant from the Justice Department to cease and desist from your experiments!"

They didn't wait for a response. The custom steel, two-man battering ram slammed against the door three times before the surrounding frame finally parted from the wall. A flash-bang grenade trailing smoke skipped across the black and white tile floor. Hearing the cartridge hiss, Victoria dropped behind a lab table, to no avail: the shockwave forced her into fetal position with her hands on her ears and her retinas temporarily scorched. As soon as she realized she was still alive, she cracked open her eyes and peeled her hands off her ears, all in time to be embraced by a military swat team, guns pointed. They zip-tied her hands behind her back as a man in a business suit stepped through the dissipating smoke.

Victoria lay sideways on the floor looking at his dress shoes, still dazed from the concussion but growing angry from the over the top intrusion, blurted, "Surely, we weren't this dangerous!"

"We're from the National Security Agency and we have a federal cease-and-desist order in conjunction with Homeland Security. You are hereby relieved of your offices and will be taken into temporary custody for questioning. All files and data regarding your work here will become temporary property of the United States government. Where is your partner?"

"He's gone."

"Where?"

"I don't know, but I need my pills."

"Your what?"

"Nothing, to hell with em. Medication can't help this," she mumbled as she made a futile attempt to roll on the floor.

The dress shoes squatted down next to her, "Hold still! What are you saying? What were you doing just before we entered?"

"Toasting marshmallows."

"Sir," one of the uniformed interrupted, "a huge power flux was just directed to this building."

"How long ago?"

"Two minutes."

"*Stand down!*" the suit suddenly barked. He stared hard at Victoria. "He made the jump, didn't he? Tell me...did Dr. Tanner allow himself to be shifted into another dimension?"

His voice was rather calm considering his entrance. "Answer me."

"I don't know who you think you are or what you are doing in my lab, but get the hell out! And get your hands off me!"

"No, Dr. Pruett, you're the one who will be leaving. Take her. Gather all the cameras, the computers, the storage devices, and seal the doors and windows. You've just lost your partner forever and I hope for your sake that's all that's happened here."

"I don't know what you're talking about!"

"Really? You strike me as so much brighter than you let on. You might not fully understand now, but you'll talk."

Chapter 10

"For is it not to angels he subjected the future world,
about which we speak."--Hebrews 2:5

As Lucas was sucked into the vortex of the beyond, Victoria forced a smile as she raised the energy level to the mean threshold for the jump. Peering through his airtight visor, he saw her head whip around at something behind her. Victoria disappeared as the darkness engulfed his view. This was a knee-jerk decision mixed with apprehension for leaving her behind and hope for answers on the other side.

So this is what the netherworld of the cosmos is like? Lucas thoughts were magnified by the sensory deprivation. Stillness, complete darkness, no weight or reference for my equilibrium. What if this was the wrong juncture, or my gut instinct just led me into absolute nothing?

At age twelve, Lucas began thinking about absolute nothing in his cerebral attempt to find God. It always ended the same way: he'd lie in his bed pondering until his imagination reached the terminal edge of creation, and then go to sleep. He wondered now if this was the proverbial hell, or perhaps nirvana.

All right, quit the esoteric philosophy, turn on the camera and voice recorder. Be calm, relax, breathe regular, deep. Hold the breath in, purse the lips, slowly let it out. Switch on my helmet lamp. Good, the body parts are still with me: gloved hands, fingers moving, legs, boots. Still nothing beyond my immediate view. How's Vic doing? She probably won't receive anything but a slap on the wrist. What she knows is too valuable.

Reviewing his heads-up display, "All systems are functioning properly. Blood pressure high, 145/92, understandable given the circumstances. Definitely feeling some gravitational acceleration, like the initial first drop of the roller coaster. Need to get turned around. I hate going backwards on thrill rides, makes me nauseated. There, a distant light and growing larger, a ring of fire at the end of this portal." Lucas' commentary paused as he rushed toward his destiny.

"Woo! Woo-hoo! I've come through the void! Ahh, Victoria, I am still conscious. The view is stupendous. The star formations and nebulae, absolutely beautiful. Oh, let me catch my breath and figure out my bearings. I am obviously in another section of the universe. Off to my right, intersecting pin wheel galaxies with a black hole center. The violence, the power, unprecedented view. There, below my feet ... the planet and moon of my dreams?"

He floated a few more moments in silent wonder where his imagination and experience united, then resumed his report, "But, where is the star for this system? I can't find it. They shouldn't exist as spheres, or spin without the gravity of a nearby star, not by themselves? Ahhhh, a new worry Vic, looks like they are moving toward me. The dream--just like in my dream, except I didn't get bowled over by a pair of flying rogue planets, drifting alone through space. This is strange. The golden planet is glowing without any reflective light. Where is the source? Its radiant light is penetrating my suit. Feels warm, feels wonderful! Today will be a good day to die even if I don't figure something out quick. Hope you get all this."

"That can't be, apparently this euphoria is giving me a flash back to my upstairs bedroom back in Cleveland. There I am, the little guy falling asleep. I must be two years old. My parents must be in their early twenties, young and strong. Mom is so lovely. She is putting my stuffed bear, Boo, next to my pillow and they both are giving me a kiss, tucking me in to my baseball print sheets. They don't notice me behind them, 'mom, dad, it's me'--they're praying,--now leaving the room--fading, 'don't go!'"

After a few deep breaths Lucas resumed, "We are alone now, me and this vision of my younger self. I am walking over to the bed and putting my hand on this little man's forehead. I can feel him! He is warm. Oh my, his eyes just opened, they are searching the room. I am freaking out here Vic. I can look through his eyes. He sees me! He's frightened, screaming! I jerk back my hand, close my eyes ... wait ... he's gone ... what was that ... what happened to me? I think I need oxygen or something... let me breathe a minute..."

"Sorry, I'm back drifting in an apparent alternate universe again. This is wild. The planet and moon are still advancing toward me. The space around me continues to spark with other wormhole entries. That's my best guess and yes, for good reason. I see other humanoids moving toward the golden planet. Victoria you won't believe this--they have no protective suits on. One just waved at me, and there, another one above me with no clothes on at all. Some appear calm, others are flailing their limbs in a panic? This must be a known destination, who else has this technology? Maybe I should take off my helmet. If this doesn't kill me, then falling into orbit surely will. Maybe I am expected? Wait, I hear a voice. Can you hear that?"

"Lucas, keep your helmet on! I am moving you before you incinerate."

"Who said that? Where is the voice?"

"Lucas, be calm, steady, I mean you no harm."

"Something has just grabbed my arms? Ahhhhhhhh--
Vic! the Methuselah. What a grip. He is pulling me.
Release me! What do you want? So much for friendly
aliens."

Lucas quit the struggle against him as he realized he was
completely defenseless. He pictured himself as a squirrel
in the talons of a red tail hawk. Powerful hands held his
waist as they dipped and veered to the right. He
wrenched his head around inside the clear helmet dome
managing to view the most magnificent wings trailing
behind his first class seat. This Methuselah kicked in his
galactic afterburners and made a wide arching ellipsis to
put them in orbit between the golden gas giant and the
blue, Earth-like moon. The big splat was avoided.

Neither said anything as they evaluated each other for a
few minutes.

Gathering himself and trying to continue his narration,
Lucas said, "Victoria, this blue moon reminds me of a
primordial earth. The atmosphere has a light turquoise
haze canopy with cloud formations and weather patterns
beneath. Hold on, spoke too soon, something is moving
rapidly below this blue firmament and now breaking
through the canopy."

"Strange, I swear, thousands of Methuselah-like
creatures moving rapidly in a diamond formation. My
chest and visor are vibrating as they pass us. I see where
they are going, a rip in the space fabric, an opening
before them like a wheel of fire. They are transiting
through, gone. The ring has closed behind them with a
dissipating wake of red and yellow glowing energy."

Overwhelmed, Lucas asked his captor, "Who were they?
Angels headed to Earth? Are you one of them?"

He answered, "A legion, yes, but not for your time."

"And you are the Methuselah? You actually saved me, didn't you?"

"I am called Ouriano."

"And this place?"

"Remind you of anything?"

"You gave me those dreams? And those who passed by, more like you?"

"Your visions are unique to your kind. Have you read the prophets?"

Lucas fumbled for an answer. "Hubbard? Nostradamus?"

"No."

"You mean Jewish, like Bible, old school?"

"Exactly," said the angel.

"I own one, somewhere."

Ouriano asked more questions as they drifted on. "You are familiar with the story of the mountain? The Timeless One?"

"This is a God thing?" asked Lucas.

"The Son of the Magnificon?"

"Faintly; you'll have to remind me. Maybe you've got the wrong person."

"You are here to fulfill another's imagination. I have been sent to orient you so that you and your kind may survive and continue your propagation."

"No disrespect, uh, 'Ouriano?' But I'm gonna check my oxygen levels again – alright, saturation perfect. I mean, this all sounds pretty heavy-duty. Just where is *here*? Survive what? You're saying I'm here because of someone's imagination? I mean, pardon me, but who are you? My suit has limited life support. Tell me I'm dreaming!"

"So many questions, so random in your priorities as you accelerate through time and place, all the possibilities. This won't be easy for you, Lucas. There are many questions in both life and death. Your wisdom will grow to recognize what you do not hear or see. Here is the center of everything, the source. Your future survival will require great wisdom. With your lack of the basics, I am surprised you are here. But there can be no mistakes."

"You are asking me why I came here?"

"Yes, you don't strike me as a real Juwaan, for you know nothing of what I speak, do you?"

"Whatever a Juwaan is... Sorry to disappoint Mr. Ouriano, 'Dr. Tanner' will suffice. I came as a scientist with some extra intuition."

"Ah, I must explain. A Juwaan is one who knows that which he does not know and has a mission with no real place to lay his head. For now, we'll accept your self-definition as a starting point, Lucas--Tanner--P-h-D. You discovered an alternate way through as was planned and we can ill afford for you to fail. May the power of the Magnificon send us mercy, for you are known in Siyon and beyond. Hold on again, Son of Stardust!"

Chapter 11

If you give up the power of choice, you have lost.

Ouriano clutched Lucas to the side again as he pulled him at light speed. A horrible depression suddenly displaced Lucas' satiated sense of wonder at this new world. His stomach convulsed as he witnessed a green light emanating out of dark space far below them. Angelic creatures rushed toward this gateway to receive and escort the exotic craft now puncturing through this rift in space. Behind it trailed a wake cloud of light-absorbing darkness. This stealth ship covered with jagged diamond edges came to a full stop, then fell nose-ward toward the surface of the Blue Moon like a long, spiked icicle off a power line in winter.

Weakly Lucas asked, "What was that? I have so many questions, but it is hard to focus..."

"You feel the infection, don't you? Through your own raw wound. That is a construct you may not believe in, but which must be respected all the same. If ever approached here or in your world, resist at all costs and pray. Don't allow fear or depression to gridlock your choices. If you give up the power of choice, you have lost." Ouriano continued, "There is a scheduled trip by an ambassador of the dark winds, a representative of Beltshzan. They may only come by approved request. We know they spy while here. But then we also have uninvited guests who slip through the grid by dubious means."

"Did you know I was coming?"

"Of course, or you would be dead. This Beltshzan I knew, before the infection took them away. Like your primal vision of your parents bestowing on you nocturnal affection, all the winds of light and darkness share familial memories. In the early years of Yare'ach Kachol – the Blue Moon, in your tongue – Beltshzan stood above every order of the angelic species. Once known as Lucifer, he was loved by all, a noble wind of light, filled with joy and co-creative powers. At that time, he was the beautiful one of Siyon, the golden planet."

Absorbing the information, Lucas queried, "And now?"

"And now, is the time to prepare you."

"For what?"

"Dr. Lucas, you have a meeting with the one who holds the destiny of all that has been, is now, and shall be. The timing seems odd because you are one who is yet to be born. Cherish these experiences."

Ouriano took hold again and continued their orbit around the golden planet. The invigorating vibes from the light defeated the internal melancholy set off by the dark ship. Accelerating, they passed an endless supply of developing wormholes, like flak explosions chasing a World War II bomber.

People arrived through the wormholes from every continent, race, and tribe of the earth. Some arrived with their clothes on: military, athletic and work uniforms, street clothes, pajamas, suits, tatters, hospital gowns -- and others with none; the full gamut of humanity. None looked to be more than thirty years old.

Upon further inspection, there were other species of mammals, reptiles, and sea creatures also entering this orbital zone. Most came by way of earth, but there were others from epochs foreign to Lucas, grotesque and unrecognizable as a species. These new émigrés were insignificant dust particles compared to the sheer size of the golden planet, which was unique in many ways, but most of all, it had the power to pull life from other dimensions.

When Lucas looked back, he noticed the edge of a thin orbiting disc, which collected these non-angelic life forms as they burst through space to begin their slow descent to Siyon. Likewise he asked, "Why are we not going down with them?"

"Because this is their appointed time and not yours. You will have your day, at the ordained time, when you too are called. But for now we need to confirm that you are indeed a Juwaan and prepare you before returning to Earth. Most of these you observe descending will remain or go on."

Continuing around the back side of Siyon opposite the Blue Moon, a faint shadow was visible from a smaller debris field funneling away from the atmosphere. The twirling thinning hubris disappeared as if vacuumed by something unseen.

"A black hole?" asked Lucas.

"That place is unknowable. The winds, including myself, have never been sent there for support. Those who survive in that cavity of space must do so independent. Yet your kind have spoken that the Son of the Magnificon has ventured to that far region alone. That place is void of a name. The descendants of Stardust who go there have given up their right as heirs, for they preferred their infection just as those who follow Beltshzan."

"Enough questions for now, Lucas. If you indeed are a chosen one, then you have the capacity to see more than one like me. We will now go down to the Blue Moon to prepare you for your encounter. We must hurry before your suit and your body expire."

Lucas scanned his sagging life support gauges. The oxygen level had dropped to critical. "Victoria, this trip is beyond belief. Out."

Chapter 12

Everyone has a breaking point. Ask Judas.

Lucas' coffee shop fantasy woman woke Victoria up with an annoying knuckle wrap on the forehead. What's worse, she was dreaming of Methuselah who was about to share something important when her waking nightmare was reaffirmed. Perspiration drenched the back of her neck. Her stomach craved a shot of Maalox. This predicament opened a junior high school memory where her eighth grade class was forced to document the feeding of a rat to a boa constrictor. Victoria had left the lid off the corner of the terrarium. The rat saw the opening, but made it only as far as the top of the glass.

The shoes and voice confirmed the ringleader. "Dr. Pruett, we have examined the tapes and data."

"I don't have time to answer your questions. Dr. Tanner needs me to get back to the lab."

"You don't have a lab. Not until you cooperate."

"Then start by telling me who you are and what you are looking for."

"I am a case lead for the National Security Agency of the United States of America. My name is Colonel John Smith and we have been monitoring breaks in space-time and energy drains on the electrical grid from your lab for the last year. We have reviewed the tapes and data on your work, including Dr. Tanner's disappearance. Where did he go? Start talking."

"Colonel John Smith, huh? Okay, then. I'm Olive Oyl and my partner Popeye stepped out of the lab to go and buy some spinach so he can come back here and crush your head between his fingers. Judging from this conversation so far, he won't have to press hard."

"We don't need to get hostile, Ms. Oyl. You'll get what you want, which is to contact and help Dr. Tanner. We'll speed the process once you've dissected a few bits of information with me."

"I'm not talking. I want to speak to my lawyer."

"You are more delightful in person than your dossier. If you want to pursue that route go ahead, but time is a precious commodity, Dr. Pruett. With national security at stake, Homeland Security has guaranteed a bureaucratic nightmare for you."

"Look, Mr. Smith, you already know more than I do. I don't know where Dr. Tanner is, only where he isn't. I can only guess what happened. For all I know, he's hiding in a closet somewhere waiting to jump out and yell 'boo!' at me when I pass by. Can I go now?"

Dr. Pruett tried getting up but was shoved back down by her adversary, now in a trendy black business suit. She was further immobilized when the femme fatale pulled out a stun gun, let it crackle in demonstration, then held it to Victoria's neck. Colonel Smith waved his hand shooting his assistant a grimace of displeasure causing her to back into the corner. He then ordered her, "Bring me the file."

Turning back to Victoria, Colonel Smith said, "I am on your side, but this country needs your help. Let me show you something."

Sliding the file like a professional card dealer, it glided between Dr. Pruett's hand and the table. It was a sketch of Methuselah. She glanced at it wondering if they figured how to focus the camera through the infrared filters? Why a sketch?

"What is it? A drawing of Hulk Hogan's grandpa?"

"A physicist and a wrestling fan. You are full of surprises. Please, can you identify this person? I think you can."

"Where is this from?"

"We found this in Dr. Tanner's home. Was he into angels and demons, the whole Judeo-Christian 'good-and-evil' philosophy?"

"Not really. His work was his life."

"Here's another picture."

"It looks like the same image."

"Yes, it does: a copy from a 1400-year-old drawing from St. Catherine's in the Sinai Peninsula. An archaeologist with connections in the Greek Orthodox Church identified it. When did Lucas travel to the Sinai?"

"What's the connection? I've never rummaged through his passport. He probably found it on the Internet."

"Really? While searching for what?"

Miss Killjoy stepped forward again, demanding in a grating, high-pitched voice. "Enough games! Where did he find this picture?"

Colonel Smith called her down. "Back off and begin the video."

It looked like restored 16mm film, streaky and grainy. "This video is from a camera mounted on a satellite which was launched in 1975 to monitor solar winds. The camera was for routine inspection of solar panels. In 1978, the satellite ceased to function in a disturbance triggered by a large solar flare."

Victoria watched the grainy video as the satellite camera panned the panel's surface. A green aura appeared at the end of the solar panel. A black hole emerged from where the green light was emanating, pulling the craft towards it. The satellite began shaking, snapping the solar panel in half and rotating into a violent horizontal spin. After ten seconds the spasmodic flight, however, was halted. Then he was there: holding the solar panel and steadying the probe. She instantly recognized Methuselah as the one who kept the satellite from being sucked through the space aperture.

As the video ended, Colonel Smith leaned forward, giving Victoria an unfortunate close-up view: a yellow film build-up in the bottom of his corneas and pockmarked cheeks and neck from past bouts with cystic acne. His nose had taken a few brawl shots over the years, healing at a different angle each time.

He said nothing for at least a minute while he waited for more information from her. First one to speak loses. They both understood the tactic. He then raised his eyes and shoulders with a smug smile and said "I'm sorry it has come to this."

With the remark, Victoria heard the crisp sound of black stilettos and I knew the woman she hated was coming in for the sting. Her whole spine cramped with the surge of 700,000 volts arcing through her muscles and neurons. She passed out.

They drug her back to the discount gray concrete guest room where she woke wet and shivering. Her shoes and socks were gone along with her lab coat. The overhead fan spun like a propeller in this special refrigerated room nicknamed 'the meat locker.' The first thing she noticed when she came to, was the empty water bucket laying on the cold concrete floor next to her; the second was her pounding headache. She rubbed her temples and neck.

In her anguish, despair and pain, she ached for confirmation of Lucas' safety, and his quick mind and steadying strength. "Lucas, where are you? Why are these people interested in Methuselah? *Ohh, my head.*"

There was nowhere in the room to escape the cold as she stood up and walked the walls. Her teeth hurt from the chill. As the light torture tactic did its work, she could no longer distinguish between her involuntary muscle contractions and her fear. In anger she took the one piece of furniture in the cell, a single metal fold-out chair, and flung it into the fan blades overhead. Four of the five blades snapped off, leaving one bent fan blade to rotate lopsidedly.

Homeland Security? NSA? Unlikely, but she knew she would have to make a deal.

Staring at the mess, she heard the little sadist's steps echoing down the hall, then the beeps of the punch pad on the door. She wondered what her story was. Her English sounded too clean; more like a second language.

"Sit in this chair, Dr. Pruett," as she tapped the back of the now bent steel folding chair with her little electric negotiator. "Why are you shaking so much? All you need to do is start answering questions and the thermostat will be raised. Here is a gesture of my friendship: a hot cup of coffee."

Victoria's quivering hands wrapped around the warm ceramic mug. As she sipped, the heat radiated through her teeth, tongue and stomach, the excess dribbling down both sides of her chin. Her interrogator threw a plastic bag on her lap and started to close the door. It was warm, dry set of clothes, including a lab coat.

"I'll be back in fifteen minutes."

"Frapping hench," shot back Victoria as she tossed the bag aside.

Her interrogator poked her head back in the door, smiled, and said, "You just drank a powerful diuretic. You'll die of dehydration in only a few hours. There's an antidote waiting in a nice warm lab with a restroom through the door down the hall. Get dressed and meet me there." The door shut, but no lock imprisoned her.

Immediately Victoria's bladder began to constrict and her mouth became like cotton. She hated herself but went ahead, dressed and headed down the hall. Colonel Smith opened the door wearing his instant smile, placed his arm around her and handed her a small cup.

"Drink. This will help you."

They have me, she almost said out loud. She drank from the proffered cup. The layout of the facility was confusing: no windows, no signs to help orient any sense of direction. There were no numbers on hundreds of identical doors. Colonel Smith led her through a maze of hallways before finding the lab.

Even if had been built for the wrong purposes, she could appreciate the scale of the facility. "Wow, spectacular. So this is what you get when money's no object? The ceiling must be a hundred feet high. State-of-the-art, Colonel Smith, a larger version of our lab back at the university. You've been duplicating our work, but you can't duplicate us?"

"How do you like this, Dr. Pruett? You should see your apartment next door. I'm sorry you had to temporarily stay in the unfurnished quarters."

"My apartment? How long do you plan on keeping me?"

"Shh,"--with one finger over his lips and the other hand up in the air. "We're helping each other. No harm. You have little time and I have little time, so we don't have to negotiate for months. I have an offshore account with $2,000,000 waiting for you and you alone right now, along with a new beachfront retirement condo for your mother. See her on the screen."

On the monitor was a live shot of her mother sitting in a oak rocking chair, accented by a scarlet bougainvillea wrapped around a white porch column. To her side Victoria saw the turquoise water of the *Caribbean*? They had moved her from her home she always hoped Victoria might come back to.

"You have me hogtied, Colonel Smith."

"My office, Dr. Pruett, is right above your new one over there. Now, my technicians need your cooperation. Let's get started."

Chapter 13

*Most people operate out of fear, including their
motivation to do good.*

Victoria barely expressed any emotion except for the
telltale slight tremor of her right index finger she held to
her lips. Her thoughts were a different matter. Cursing
the Colonel in silence, she vowed, *You control-freak-
sleazy-coward, hiding behind your anonymous name.
I'm going to find out who you really are.*

Leaning forward and pressing both hands on the table in
front of her, Colonel Smith began, "Dr. Pruett, these are
the films and energy readings of your quantum jump
experiments, including Dr. Tanner's disappearance. You
will help us to interpret them."

"It's all in your focus. Slow down the frames by 98% and
run light filters. Play with the zoom settings and you will
find your person of interest."

Within a few minutes they had a picture of Methuselah.
The faces of Smith's team showed disgust, but no
surprise at the discovery. Victoria overheard one of them
mumble, "It's the parasite, Ouriano. This breach may be
left unguarded. Let's move. We have a confirmation,
Colonel Smith."

Smith answered, "Then what on earth are you waiting
for? Bring him out."

Victoria was ill prepared to comprehend what transpired
next. She watched as a muscular, medium height, dark-
haired young man in an international orange prison
uniform was brought out, hunched over, in heavy chains.
Her friend, the Taser-master followed behind him. They
walked him up the ramp to the round, elevated launch

area. This was a larger version of their university lab where they transferred energy into a hyper-vibration phase, enabling test objects to slip through dimensional boundaries. A warning horn sounded, and a heavy blast door with a red flashing light above slowly opened on the side wall of the main lab. The pungent odor of a decayed animal grew as the door raised. Victoria felt like she might vomit.

When the horn and door stopped, an oriental man in a white lab coat pulled out a flatbed cart that carried a leather-bound, medicine ball-like object, two feet in diameter. The cart stopped at the base of the jump platform where the bound leather began to expand like a vacuum-dried sponge doused with water.

The roadkill creature slowly unfolded to a wingspan twelve feet wide and shoulders seven feet high. Instead of hands were large talons. The eyes were bulging, glossy, black with fluid stains seeping from the corners. The head was a cross between the head of a bald man and a well-weathered vulture. It cried out a deafening screech, daring anyone to stare into its eyes while it scanned the room. All looked away in fear, except for the woman who delivered the shock treatment to Victoria. She stood behind it with arms crossed, unimpressed, ushering the creature to move onto the platform.

This demon seed walked up to the terrified convict, then placed its talons around his torso like an iron maiden, so that the man began to scream, "What are you? I didn't volunteer for this!"

The man's strength was no match as he flailed and kicked. Opening its mouth, like a viper the jaws of this beast unhinged, and enveloped the convict's head – muffling his screams. Victoria bent over and vomited, but when she looked up, the beast had disappeared and the young man was left standing alone where he straightened his shoulders, raised his head and stretched a grin across his face. With a perky Londoner's accent he said, "lets saddle up for the ride shall we, I've been away too long."

But his wasn't the only voice. As they brought a life support suit and were dressing the convict, the original personality with a southern redneck drawl spoke up, "What are all y'all doing with me? Is this the state's method of execution? I want to see the chaplain, my lawyer."

When it looked like rigor mortis had set in to the apparently frozen redneck, the Englishman inside spoke again. "It's been a while, but now that we've settled into the cortex, we shouldn't have any more outbursts. Poor chap; someone's been here before and never cleaned up. Most likely Beltshzan's league before the coup. Let's forgo the helmet, shall we?"

Chapter 14

What if the Earth has one last epoch, and we are halfway through?

As they descended toward the Blue Moon, Lucas now had confirmation of at least one comparable exo-planet to Earth, a sister blue marble, with the immediate, obvious similarities of being mainly covered with water and dappled with spinning, white cotton clouds. He wondered how many rogue planets like this lay beyond the scope of any current deep space observation, and how would he get back?

Lucas' quest for information was again interrupted, this time by another vision. It was a hot summer day as he helped his father groom the yard. The abused four-stroke Briggs and Straton engine belched out oil-burning exhaust in exchange for mown clumps of fresh chlorophyll scented bermuda. In the corner of the lawn, marked by a couple of standing shovels, stood the leftover sandy loam they vowed to level by the end of the summer. The yard had to be the best on the block. When finished, his father handed Lucas a glass of ice water, condensation dripping down the sides. Lucas drank it all at once then pressed the cold, wet glass against his forehead.

Next they set a little Hibachi grill under the big red oak. His mother brought out the steaks when the coals were cherry red then left the cooking to her boys. In between flipping the steaks, they slumped in their lawn chairs, basking in the burnt orange sunset.

Lucas admired his version of a Norman Rockwell painting, then shook his head, awareness returning back his presence inside his life support suit. Red warning lights blinked. Green gage for oxygen was down. Dehydration was setting in, emotions were depleted.

"When we reach tree level of Yare'ach Kachol, remove your helmet," said Ouriano.

Passing through the blue-tinted fog of the canopy, Lucas' clear head dome collected the fine mist, channeling them into streaks of running droplets. He fumbled to remove it, tucking the helmet under his arm, and filling his lungs with precious oxygen. The ruffle of friction from the atmosphere buffeted his suit, swept through his sweat-slicked hair and cooled his face. Ouriano's wings and feathers made small adjustments, leaving vapor trails at the tips where his wings cut through thin blue fog.

The doctor's eyes were treated to the blue, turquoise, and silver hues from the surface of the moon's oceans. In his euphoria of a now freshly oxygenated brain and the stunning visual feast, the colors and hues mixed to become a pearl reflection of rainbow colors. Continuing their flight path to the surface, they passed mountains born out of the battering sea and foam, many snowcapped and guarding plush jungles and yellow flowered valleys below. The most outstanding feature of the Blue Moon was the continent-sized dark hole in the surface toward which they soared.

The Earth had a distinct way in which it absorbed light from the sun, especially on a cloudless day that left many shadows; but here on Yare'ach Kachol there were few shadows on the surface. Everything was lit by two sources: the iridescence of the vast oceans and the warm glow from the mother planet Siyon. These tropical seas generated enough light to cast shadows of the clouds on the upper atmospheric canopy when viewed from the backside of the moon.

Visiting the Blue Moon invites speculation. As their flight path continued toward the ominous mega canyon, Lucas interrogated Ouriano with several more questions, to which he received no answers. "What event hollowed out a galactic body of this immense size? Where is the star which holds Siyon and this planetoid in orbit? How does the Blue Moon spin on its axis as it circumnavigates Siyon?"

Lucas couldn't help but think this planet operated on radically different physics, and the limited crust or islands must be only part of its habitable area. *"How can the planet be hollowed out without collapse? Or exist without a magma core?"*

Continuing their descent, the two glided in a corkscrew pattern like a C-130 and then flew parallel to the rim of the great hole. To Lucas, this was Niagara Falls times 15,000 miles long by 300 miles deep. He tried to imagine a hole in the middle of the Pacific where the oceans tumbled into the center of the Earth. Already there were more questions than answers.

He observed the rim was packed with island-sized reserves of forested mountains, jungles, volcanoes, canyons cut by snaking rivers, white water, and clouds of low-lying white fog. There were land-blotting formations of fowl-filled beaches. Pods of whales shot bursts of powered mist. Square miles of fish schools broke the surface of the sea with glimmers of yellow and silver at each change of direction, chased by great sea creatures.

Finally they dove over the edge of the great chasm, passing below the surface of the moon's tropical crust and following the great waterfalls down. Descending, the light of the giant canyon made everything look like a technicolor dusk on Earth after a thunderstorm in late afternoon. The falling drizzle of water was emitting its own light – though far less than the surface oceans.

Heat-generated lightning exchanged between thunderheads floated down inside this voluminous depression. Lucas took deep relaxing breaths. The smell reminded him of the approaching rain of an overdue summer front.

Water also burst out in torrents from concurrent canyons, ravines, and underground rivers, adding more mist to the air and waves of blue-tiered rainbows. Giant trees and thousand-foot hanging vines were anchored into the crevices by bulky, twisted roots like they had been buried in concrete.

Mile after mile, they passed rock-hewn sculptured masterpieces on the canyon wall. There were uncountable tunnels, caves, and cliff dwellings which reminded Lucas of the ancient city of Petra and Indian dwellings of Mesa Verde.

Ouriano became more luminous the deeper they traveled, as did the others they crossed paths with. As the surface ocean's cascaded mile after mile, they dissipated into a fine translucent mist. Some fifty miles down, the humid and warm air turned to a chill, nipping at Lucas' ears and cheeks. "Surreal" would have been an understatement of what transpired before him as they traveled through this geological strata scored with pictogram remnants of an alien epoch.

Chapter 15

Who is going to believe my quantum trip if I do make it back?

Ancient etchings on the canyon walls encompassed more area than Lucas could see. One art form catching his attention as they continued to descend were two skyscraper-sized angelic beings with outstretched wings touching tip-to-tip. Radiant beams were engraved all around them. They stood watch over an ornate rectangular opening in the great wall at about their knee level. The opening itself had four smaller hieroglyph creatures with three sets of wings hovering at the four corners.

Above the opening and between the two large angels stood the etching of a bearded and barefoot man dressed in an ankle-length, flowing robe. One hand held a bowl at his waist while the fingers of the other dipped into it. Each foot and wrist was scarred with stigmata Lucas recognized from old iconic church art.

How ironic that he would be forced to grapple with the myths of another world when he had given up understanding those of his birth planet. The deeper they flew, his perception of how well he knew himself shrank to the size of a grain of sand. Only last year he had made the confident announcement in an NPR interview, "If I have to choose, please put me down as a conscientious objector to all manmade myths. There is enough mystery in the cosmos to fuel my intellectual passion without need of God!"

You fool, reflected Lucas as he loathed himself in the mist, *Tanner, your truth has never been more than convenient massaged reason. You wouldn't recognize truth if it bit you in the ass, and it just did.*

And then it happened a third time, another vision, but less pleasant. Lucas found himself in the darkness inhaling the rotted air of a damp basement of spawning mold spores. He lit a match and walked forward until he found sitting in a high-backed, wooden rocking chair the figure of a brooding old man, with cross-stitched facial wrinkles and bruised, sunken eyes. The old man flared open a pair of stretched leather wings, which had been wrapped around an object in his lap, revealing a pair of talons holding Victoria. She wore a scar across her neck like Ouriano, and lay in a deep trance.

The dark angel set her on the ground, then took the same talons and wrapped them around Lucas' chest and began to suffocate him, with an ever-increasing compression, while lifting him in the air. The creature tilted its head back and forth as it examined him, nasal cavities and eyes inches from Lucas' face, then said, "You, you are no Juwaan," then threw him backward in disgust.

In shock, Lucas heard Ouriano's voice calling him back, "Lucas, Son of Stardust, are you listening to me?"

"I just had another vision."

"What did you see, Lucas?"

"I don't know exactly. Something dark and oppressive, holding my friend. It said, 'You are no Juwaan!'"

"Don't listen to that voice. It is not the voice of confirmation. How quickly they are already organizing against you, but somehow you still have an impotent comprehension of the insurgency. So much misinformation from the dark winds. The Morning Star's Spirit will guide, if you trust."

"Who are you talking about now? The same person as this Son of the Magnificon?"

"Let's start over. Dr. Tanner, what does your keen intelligence tell you about me?"

"You're not carbon-based. You converse verbally and telepathically. And you're made of some kind of energy which can restructure itself into solid form and can therefore withstand the radiation and harsh conditions of space. You're also trans-dimensional or multiverse-capable and appear to be subordinate to another being or organization."

Ouriano asked slowly trying to keep a straight face, "Subordinate to another being?"

"And you appear to mean me no harm, good natured."

Ouriano laughed, "Good natured? How scientific! Haven't you heard, 'there is no one good, but God alone?' We are here."

Lucas turned to his head to the left for a second, then back. In that instant, Ouriano disappeared.

Chapter 16

If you can't explain it to your mother, then you're in trouble.

The Colonel began with his fluff as normal, "Oh Dr. Pruett, you've helped us so much all ready. If you hadn't advised us to abort yesterday, we would have wasted our test pilot."

"The unwilling possessed convict?"

"Nomenclature, all for the betterment of human kind. Now that we've made the adjustment, I want you to have a front row seat. 'To infinity and beyond,' someone once said. But first, more good news. We are going to let you talk to your mother right now. There will be a four second delay, in case you get cute. Go ahead, you are now on conference call. Keep it short."

"Mom?"

She answered with the time delay, "Is that you, Victoria?"

"Yes, how is the new place?"

Ms. Pruett, who always made an effort to be positive with her daughter, replied, "Absolutely wonderful, but how did you afford all of this? Everyone here is treating me so well, like I was some kind of celebrity. I have my own hot tub and bridge group on Wednesdays."

"So you like it?"

"Oh, honey, at first I couldn't understand the rush, the movers, the money. A nice man in a tan suit from the university visited me saying that you and your friend Dr.

Tanner had made some great discoveries and had been rewarded handsomely for your scientific breakthroughs. Speaking of, how is that handsome young man? You couldn't do much better than Lucas. Is there anything happening between the two of you? The university man said you were still locked in research and for security reasons unavailable, but that you needed me moved before media caught wind of your breakthroughs, thus ending my peaceful life. Is this true, honey?"

As Victoria began to answer her, she noticed the black widow was keeping one hand on her electric negotiator. "I am sorry mom, but I had to meet deadlines and yes, I did not want people hounding you or worse, hitting you up for money. Our work here has some national defense ramifications and I just wanted you to be safe. So you like it?"

"Victoria, you already asked that question. The answer is yes, it's a dream. If you hadn't moved so fast or had given me time to think, I would've never moved out of the old house. Remember your pink bedroom? Never changed it from the day you left to begin your career. Thought you might come back one day. But this place, blue oceans, sunshine, new friends – is growing on me, and they let me bring Blitz. They even have a dog park here lined with purple, pink and orange bougainvilleas, can you imagine?"

"No mom, I can't imagine. Glad you and Blitz like it in paradise. Sounds better than the brochures and what they promised. Now *you can't imagine* how much work I still need to complete here, so I'll come and visit you as soon as I can. Got to go."

"Wait, let me hold Blitz up so you can say goodbye to him too."

"Bye Blitz, bye mom."

Blitz responded with a quick, high-pitched, "Ruff, ruff."

The dog's bark eked out a little smile from Victoria as Smith hung up the line. He began talking to her but she wasn't listening, as she held the picture of her mom's happy face in her mind. At first her focus was idly drawn to his pockmarks along his cheeks, nose, and neck, and then to the thick black hairs which needed trimming on his upper ears.

His voice faded in as she let go of her mom, "And you will see her again if you continue to help us. She is healthy, secure and comfortable. Better than she was before. She also is out of US jurisdiction and could easily disappear without a trace. Now, if you will turn around to view the lab floor with an open mind, you, Doctor, are about to help make history."

Looking through the safety glass of her office, she saw that the young man in the orange jump suit was fully harnessed up with the jump clock on the back wall counting down from 00:45. To her horror, he had no space suit on to protect him from the vacuum of space.

"Stop, stop this right now! You are going to kill him."

The Colonel answered calmly, "It's too late. Believe me, in the long run it makes no difference. There's no one waiting for him."

She watched in helpless dread as the jump clock counted down, '00:03, 00:02, 00:01,' and felt the low rumble of the power current increase exponentially until the fabric of space itself ripped. The man and his vile internalized parasite faded away in a few seconds as Lucas had.

Colonel Smith put his arm around Dr. Pruett and said, "You don't know what you've made possible do you? This is a breakthrough of epic proportions."

Chapter 17

This creature was disfigured eons ago in the great war.
Your God made him that way.

Colonel Smith led Dr. Pruett out to the post-jump platform. He considered offering her a permanent way out, but based on centuries of experiences with her kind, he also knew how unpredictable these image bearers could be. It was difficult to determine how they were marked. Nevertheless, the jump technology was far from ready for its true purpose. He needed her and Dr. Tanner back in his lab. They were so close to developing full-blown travel for the insurgency.

"You know, Dr. Pruett, the human soul has a natural GPS device of its own."

"I don't understand."

"At death, souls have the ability to slip through space and time. You've given them a new choice, even your own soul."

At this moment she tasted the horror and shock of what she may have become party to. Her eyes did not blink for a minute as she walked among the smoldering cables, "I am concerned about the man you just sent. He didn't have a protective suit on? How will he survive? ... ... That wasn't the point was it? That hideous thing was inside him like a maggot, using him as a host? What for? Did you send him after Dr. Tanner?"

"We did him no harm. He was well on his way to the same destiny through lethal injection--a death row inmate convicted of murder. What happens to him over there is something he should have taken responsibility for already. Naïve doctor, you didn't believe your Sunday School?"

"I quit when I went to college but I still believe there is some hidden truth to the stories. I remember a story about a man Jesus confronted who lived naked among the tombs. A wild man no one could chain."

"And why did the myth say he lived naked in a graveyard?"

"Because he was host to a legion of demons."

"And what precisely were the demons hoping for by invading this sad case of a pathetic image-bearing human?"

She responded, hitting his target. "They were hoping to make a jump?"

The Colonel's hand caressed Victoria's neck as he inspected her buttoned shirt. Two had come loose, reminding him she was more than just a brain geared for intellectual exercise. "Please hear me, Dr. Pruett. People may know the truth but rarely do they act on it. They love their passions more." While he talked, he took the liberty to push the buttons back through their holes and organize her collar.

She froze, her skin crawling with revulsion, not knowing where this was going or what she could do to defend herself against any unseemly advances in her precarious position. By his mere touch, he could feel her pulse and the tenseness in her muscles. What she did not know was how much she aroused him with her combination of intellectual pride and fawn innocence. Her neck flushed in an autonomic response, but Smith understood now was not the time to pursue her in this manner.

Nevertheless, Colonel Smith knew that he had her full attention now, though her recall of childish theology surprised him. "Yes, Doctor, these abandoned spirits only wanted to do what comes natural to humans. Jesus knew jumpers hovered at death hoping for a chance to ride the deceased's spirit back to their original domain, and so he maneuvered to cast them out. They are desperate in their suffering for home."

The Colonel was already anticipating what her next question would be and said, "You would like to say 'you seem too acquainted with this story? You have too much personal knowledge?' Is this what you wanted to ask?"

"No, I wanted to ask if this is why Jesus is reported to have cast Legion into a herd of cliff-jumping swine? Could it be he didn't want to see your kind in his kingdom. So you are claiming you were present?"

"Very clever to remember such detail, so now you are putting hope in those stories? Your bio and emails left little to suggest you had this type of interest. I thought you were a practitioner of science and empirical observation?"

"I am all of that, but you have brought my childhood to the forefront."

He wondered if she could be turned, after all, from the conspiracy of the loyalists? A woman of her acuity would be very valuable. "The myths are partially correct. Has it not been two thousand years? Do you see a kingdom, or any of the promises materialized? No, none whatsoever, just protracted suffering of the peoples of the earth while your fallen hero works his plan. Don't you see, Dr. Pruett, the glory of your technology? You have enabled us to jump at will. No longer will these defanged creatures depend on sub-occupation at the time of death for the chance to jump. You've turned the tide for the good of all people, races, and species. You may not understand now. The creature you saw up here did not always have such a hideous appearance. He was disfigured eons ago in the great war. Your God made him that way."

Chapter 18

*And now what? I've helped this cultic used car salesman
hijack the kingdom?*

Victoria was escorted back by the diva of security to a
secured internal apartment with no windows or means of
outside communication. She wanted to know, *What was
her story in all of this? How did she come to work for
the Colonel? Did she dress in anything but black?*

When she pulled opened the apartment door Victoria
noticed the green and purple mixed tweed carpet in
contrast to the drab grey tile of the outside hall way. Her
escort gave her the nod to follow her inside.

"Looks like you do your decorating from a big box
Scandinavian furniture store. We've got the tan corner
sofa and a rose print living room chair with the bonus
long fluorescent light fixtures above, mounted on a white
latex rolled concrete ceiling." Victoria clapped her hands
together in mock glee. "The prison dorm room I always
dreamed of."

She continued to squeeze out her anger, "In kitchenette
number one we have the yellow pine square table and
four matching chairs with small cheap five bulb
chandelier suspended by a link chain with three feet of
excess banded together, in case we later shorten the
table. For food preparation we have all industrial steel
decor for the sink, stove, and fridge chased with— look
here, a free case of bottled water!"

Everything else was sanitized white; a single bathroom
with shower, sink, cabinet and toilet. In the sole back
bedroom was a queen size mattress on box springs with
overhead fan and white dresser. A few fresh changes of
clothes were folded neatly on top.

Her tour guide started to leave and secure the front apartment door when Victoria spoke to her. "Wait. Was that a demon I saw today?"

The mystery woman stopped. To Victoria she appeared vulnerable for the first time. "There are worse things than what you saw today," she assured her. Victoria heard two mechanisms lock as the ice queen swung the heavy metal door shut from the outside.

She plopped down into the living room chair and pinched her cheek to insure she was indeed alive. Closing her eyes, Victoria felt apart from herself, the scientist in her almost separately witnessing her brain trying to process the bizarre unfolding drama: the images of the unraveling black leather flesh, claws, the smell, the voice; her mother's kidnapping; the helplessness of the convict. None of this made sense.

She thought the pseudo-Colonel was right about one thing, I didn't believe Sunday School much anymore. But then, did he assume I'd quickly buy into his twisted version? My repertoire of the Bible was limited, but did he think I'd dare take the liberty to reinterpret the basic figure of Jesus? Why bother to twist an irrelevant story to say something different? No hard feelings for whomever these little therapeutic stories helped, like my mom. After all, I was as spiritual as anybody but not over-the-top religious. Colonel Smith did have a point. If Christ was so powerful, why then was he so slow in converting the gross suffering and pain of the world to goodness?

Speaking aloud to collect her thoughts, "Ah, metaphysical introspection, not going there! I can't allow myself to get sucked into this. Hey self! I just witnessed the intentional sacrifice of another human being, for a jump? I need a sign to make sure I haven't broken with reality. Methuselah is the key. He didn't look anything near as awful as the giant Alice Cooper bat I witnessed swallow that poor man."

She scratched the back of her head attempting to pull out answers, "Think, think, Victoria, what do you remember about the Bible?--the kingdom, Jesus preached about the kingdom of God coming soon. And now what? I've helped this cultic used car salesman begin to hijack the kingdom?"

Victoria threw her shoes against the metal front door and screamed the beginning of her dialogue *to somebody, anybody,* "This is a like a new Grimm's fairy tale, except I'm in it! God, don't you see what is going on? When your Jesus walked the earth (I can't believe I am going down this road of conspiracy), did he show up to stop a mass jump by demons?" For the first time in a long time she wished she had a Bible, even though she liked her old presumption better, when the world could become whatever she desired. "Maybe we're all a pay grade short." With that quip, she walked over to the fridge and pulled out a water bottle and placed the cold plastic on her temple and fell back on the couch. *What a mess. Blackmailed with my mother, held prisoner until they execute me with my own invention, and likely never to see Lucas again.*

Victoria reached internally for something she had not exercised in a long time, a prayer. *I know it's been a long time. I need you. I should have listened better, but please deliver me from this evil. We need to get reacquainted real fast. God, don't let that bastard touch me again. Where do I start?*

Chapter 19

The mythology line was angels serve the just and demons the dregs of evil.

"Do you ever get used to this view?" In awe Lucas stood gazing off a cliff balcony into the great chasm of neon blue iridescence. Sentinels sliced through the ocean air like speeding barracuda. The traffic was continuous. His inner ears felt the pressure change as they rushed by. He turned back to Ouriano, waiting for an answer, but he was gone.

The air was fresh, cool. A faint fragrance of antique roses caught his attention. As he turned around, his olfactory sense lured him toward a tunnel running some four hundred meters through the canyon wall. Fragments of white light columns flickered at the other end.

"Why did Ouriano ask me to stay put until he returned?"

Against what he considered a suggestion more than anything, Lucas pulled off the pressure suit, retaining his gun, flash light, and data recorder. Led by his flashlight, he began traversing the rocks and rubble of the decaying tunnel. Along the way, he passed multiple corridors, vertical, horizontal, diagonal shafts. Lucas, like a boy crossing a forbidden train trestle, was eager to discover the unknown. Climbing his way around the edge of one intersecting vertical shaft, the near-miss vacuum of a high-speed transient nearly sucked him down.

Resuming uninhibited, he followed his rabbit trail to the end to an empty lava dome where the original alluring scent hit a crescendo. Peeking over the edge, the paralyzing panic he had experienced earlier returned. Some five hundred feet below, he saw a flat rock square pad, fifty yards across, surrounded by blue lights.

Gazing upward, he viewed an ancient hollowed out magma shaft heading toward the surface at a fifteen-degree angle. Pasted along the walls of the old melted rock were masses of velvet red flowers interspersed with green ferns, the source of the aromatic temptation. Before Lucas could enjoy them, he began to feel queasy on and off. From above came sweeping bright lights and the source of his former bad feeling floated down past his hiding place, emitting a growing hum and low vibrating pulse.

It was a craft similar to the one he and Methuselah had passed coming out of the worm hole. The dark icicle-shaped craft's de-acceleration cushioned its horizontal landing, kicking up a small dust storm and swaying the vegetation on the walls. The stealthy, jagged triangular transport landed.

A door opened on the side of the ship and a man in a western-style suit exited last escorted by five shadowy creatures. One seemed to unfurl dark leathery wings for a second, but Lucas couldn't be sure. Emerging out of a lower tunnel, a small contingent of twenty or so sentinel beings like Methuselah surrounded them. The suit pointed up towards Lucas, disclosing his surveillance.

In terror he hastily retreated, tripping into a vertical shaft. Fortunately his hands and elbows snagged on a narrow outcropping six feet down, stopping his plummet. With his legs dangling over the dark hole, he looked over his shoulder to witness the twirling beam of his flashlight in a free fall and the clanking of his gun fade away in an abyss. Next, a heavy buzzing vibration pealed over his head like a giant hornet draining off the last of his fight-or-flight adrenaline rush.

No doubt, he assumed, *if they were to seek harm, resistance would be futile.* His mother had homeschooled him on the lore of the Egyptian and Assyrian death angels who eliminated the firstborn and slaughtered armies. He reminded himself that the mythology line was supposed to be, "Angels serve the just and demons the dregs of evil."

Lucas asked himself, "What's wrong with this picture?" as he strained to climb out of the shaft, heart pounding in his ears. Pointless resistance or not, he wasn't one to stand there and be overtaken. Regaining his bearings, he turned and ran, but in his second stride he collided with a pillar, the stout-as-stone form of his sentinel, Ouriano.

Chapter 20

I could show you black holes which consume more mass than your entire galaxy every single day. They have no regard for your technological singularities.

Ouriano focused on Lucas' heat signature at the other end of the tunnel, then darted towards him as he recalled the words of his mentor: "Faith, though almost an impossible concept for angels to practice, is only a perceived difficulty for the latent image bearers. Their entire life is a wakeup call. Little do they understand how much they need to exercise their wisdom of the will for what lies ahead."

He then prayed, "Far be it from me, Lord, to teach Lucas."

Landing directly in his escape path he sensed Lucas was shaken, so he asked the most ancient question to him, "What did you do? You've seen something."

"I thought you encouraged me to observe - so I was observing."

"Yes, Lucas. Be careful; your heightened metabolism makes you vulnerable prey. Creatures of emotion are a dead giveaway."

"I saw a craft resembling the one we had to avoid earlier, and I thought you..."

"You've been brought in at an interesting time. Something has reawakened which I have not dealt with in eons, now breaking out in your world and spilling into this realm. We were not sure where they had gone. Somehow you are connected, but it is not under my auspices to speculate. I have been wrong about your kind before."

"Ouriano, what are you talking about?"

"A few of my genus have the freedom to operate on faith. Most take orders and follow them precisely. The questions you ask about good and evil, beginnings and endings, the purpose of this place? I repeat, you are at the center of it all. Your place here is much more important than mine. This phase of your life has been waiting for you. My mission is to prepare and protect. You are of high esteem in the eyes of the Morning Star who rises beyond Siyon."

"Okay, you know I just saw something at the other end of this tunnel which isn't right, the black craft of the dark winds, landing, mixing it up with your kind?"

"Your life is but one more generation born into this long era of struggle on earth. Juwaan, I am so surprised at your suppression of this. Willful ignorance will not make your enemies rest. For ages, rogue elements have tried to upset the balance with the blind hope of igniting universal sabotage. You have a saying, 'the enemy of my enemy is my friend,' correct?"

"My enemies, rogue elements, universal sabotage, your friend? Something's wrong here. You better explain what I'm up against, Ouriano."

"Angels have strong social bonds going back millennia. In the initial rebellion, Lucifer, who we now call Beltshzan, made us sympathetic to the promise and cause of finding our own universe, where we could develop and propagate with no bounds. My species cannot breed new offspring, and yet he succeeded in creating a subspecies in his likeness before he was judged.

His offspring were genetically engineered with precursors of modern humans and had the ability to replicate. We were happy for him. Yet his offspring bred down into its purest form as a meme, a 'thought virus' of sedition – looking to multiply and oust our original allegiance. This was long before your kind was developed and gifted as the most recent image bearers on earth. There was chaos and mixed emotions as we were instructed to bind Lucifer and the others who adamantly wanted to find another universe to develop as an independent home apart from the one who rules Siyon.

Lucifer's imagination of what could be was boundless. He was warned against his creative expression, yet he persisted. He had no patience for the mysterious limitless wisdom of the Creator to unfold. He wanted to push the limits of his own imagination into creative genius for all to glory in. His plans, while we had never heard of such a thing, were not expressly forbidden. Lucifer 's ideas were unique, different; but then he turned violent, ripping apart those sent to arrest him. He began to use force and intimidation against all who opposed him.

Instead of finding an independent universe, he was transferred to yours until his time is completed. Some of his offspring were so violent and unreasonable they were placed into the abyss of Gammeroon, an alternate universe full of chaos, younger than yours, without hope of cohesive development. Others escaped, never to be heard from again except in whispers and rumors. These offspring, no one really knows how many, were a hybrid of human and angel. They had the ability to travel through space-time and multiply, begetting the genetics of humans, angelic powers, and the image of the one on Siyon. They were at one time referred to as Nephilim. By birth, they also carried the subversive virus of Beltshzan."

"Go on. I am trying to process what you believe to be true."

"Lucas, I marvel at how little you know of these stories about this great tragedy – a temporary setback for the evolution of creation, but not forever. You are here to help change the tide."

"Wait, you're saying that these rebels, Nephilim... or bio-engineered angels... are real? Otherwise, I'd stop you from rambling except I can't explain anything I'm seeing here. What you are telling me seems so hidden from plain observation. So what did I witness?"

"Some of Siyon's judgments are without appeal. You saw emissaries of Beltshzan under guided permission to make, let's say, an unofficial diplomatic visit. The mediator of Siyon is not without mercy. Their cause is fruitless and suspect. They try to persuade the Morning Star through us, knowing we secretly weep over our kin who have been infected.

As of now, they are trying to improve their position by reporting on the rogue elements and Nephilim. We have reports of this renewed insurgency infiltrating into this realm by unauthorized jumps. They are grooming and harnessing the technology you discovered. On their own, they lack the dexterity and creativity of the image bearers. Unless..."

"Ouriano, do you believe all of this smoke and mirrors conspiracy? On Earth we have Moore's law, which we can thank to predict the trend of the exponential growth in technology and knowledge. This is leading to more technological singularities like our discovery. Why are we adding religion to this? Anyway, can't your God stop them? Why would they come here. How long have you lived? Why...?"

"Juwaan, excuse me, Dr. Tanner, did I make a mistake in stopping here? Can you identify what you don't know? Before we ever go to Siyon, you must expand your capacity for faith. Allow your intellect to take a back seat to new experiences as the Spirit works. Integration will take time. Your mind is strong for what you have been, yet weak for what you must become. You have new enemies who do not rest. Worry, for what you cannot control is a fatal flaw as much as dread of your enemies and pride of your strength. You must step past your science and walk the bridge of the incomprehensible. I could show you black holes which consume more mass than your entire galaxy every single day. They have no regard for your technological singularities. But even those black holes must exist within the boundaries of the living universe. And so, no conspiracy of evil can thwart the Self-Sustaining One. In time you will know, and be known."

Chapter 21

*What say you, image bearer? Have you come
to save us?*

As he observed with disbelief from the balcony, the sly fantasy diva from the coffee shop was now fraternizing with Ouriano!

A few minutes earlier Ouriano had encouraged him to, "Please relax quietly up in the corner of the loft. Anyone or thing which attempts to communicate with you, harasses you, telepaths, or asks questions, refer them to me at the bar. Avoid direct eye contact."

Lucas bit his lip. In his assessment, she stood apart from the rest with her high heels and look of an assassin. Her wings were dark and sleek. They involuntarily expanded and contracted to emphasize a point or emotion when she spoke. While holding a drink in one hand, a seven inch tongue pulled the straw to the near side of her cocktail glass. This femme fatale had a powerful and grotesque quality which both repelled and attracted him. She looked up at Lucas with a smile while still sucking her straw. He in return mocked the raising of his Starbucks cup. Ouriano glanced his way with a stern expression, then turned his back as he leaned into his conversation with the complex woman.

Lucas' seat enjoyed a good view of this way-station café and bar deep inside the hollowed rock of the Blue Moon. To his back was a thirty-foot-high, blue-tinted quartz wall dividing the café from the sea. Shadows passed by the fractured window revealing ocean predators on the hunt. Patrons like himself could feel the vibrations of attacks, chomps, and wakes; and hear the muffled bursts of painful screeches and mating calls. For his amusement, he hummed Armstrong's "What a Wonderful World" while he soaked it all in.

Sensing someone standing behind him, Lucas turned to be greeted by two Ouriano-class sentinels. Avoiding their faces, he looked between them at the glossy sea wall. By focusing on the reflections in the crystal panes he could see they had mid-shoulder-length hair, carried swords and engraved symbols on their arms, indicating a military rank. The heavier one looked older and more weathered.

He spoke in a rich baritone voice, "Hard to digest your insignificance, isn't it? Out there you would be less than a snack and an anachronism to your species' existence. Let me buy you a drink."

Lucas wasn't sure if Ouriano's rule was to be broken again, so he smiled but remained silent.

"It is considered an insult to refuse hospitality here. This is a sanctuary to all visitors, friends and foes. What say you, image bearer? Have you come to save us? You may have enemies in this room. Are we expected to fight for you?"

The wings of the younger fanned him with a rush of annoying air when the familiar voice of Ouriano interrupted. "Veezon, this Juwaan has just arrived into my custody. He needs time to take all this in. He has yet to know his left from his right. In time, I will introduce you."

The one called Veezon spoke to him, "Haven't you heard? People of the Earthen realm have no need of another Juwaan or illegal half breeds."

When, the two angels turned toward Ouriano, Lucas spun around to inspect their backs where two magnificent pairs of white wings flared and receded. They both wore a brownish red military knee-length tunic leaving their back shoulders exposed where the wings attached. A short sleeve covered their right shoulder to the upper edge of the developed triceps but no covering for the left shoulder or arm. The three stood close, conversing in a language completely foreign to humans.

Past them Lucas looked to the floor below. The mystery woman was gone, but new creatures came and went replacing her spot at the bar. Some had the heads of lions or water buffalo with torsos and hoofs like horses. Others like Ouriano's friends were armed and varied in age, uniforms, and masculinity. The new Juwaan felt so small, like a lost child standing on the floor of Grand Central Station, an accident waiting to happen.

Chapter 22

My best prayers are embarrassing. They arise out of anxiety, not piety.

Victoria awoke from her emotional wasteland to the water bottle wedged next to her wet thigh and the aroma of fried chicken and fries. She sat up from the soaked spot on the couch and attacked the white plastic sack on the kitchen table. With a chicken leg in one hand and pacing the walls of her apartment cell like a hungry rat, her eyes searched for a way out but found nothing interesting, except that the apartment was wired for 220 voltage, a standard common outside the United States.

Tilting her head back and extending her arms she said, "I don't have a new desperate prayer, the ball is in your court. In the meantime, I need to do what I can control. Alright? Ms. Manners deserves a taste of her own medicine. Can you help me with a little vengeance today?"

Thinking it an answer to her prayer she at that moment had flash memory of a college cafeteria prank of rolling up the edge of the plastic table cloth to transfer sticky lemonade to the victim's lap at the end of the table. In this case the revised plan would be to: split the living room chair seat cover, fill the sponge cushion with salt water, and set up a power supply with the refrigerator's cord. When the target sits down, in an instant she'll wet herself and trigger the circuit of the makeshift electric chair. *It probably won't kill her, but I'll be able to take control of her weapon.*

She finished lining the cushion with the plastic shower curtain to hold the fluid and set the contacts. *Is this a sin, Lord? The bait?* Well, that's me. Victoria heard what she labeled as the "Junior Goose-Stepper" coming down the hall, then the bang on the door.

"Dr. Pruett, get yourself together. You're requested in the lab. Do you hear me? Acknowledge. Acknowledge or it will cost you." The key pad was beeping with the code. The handgun proceeded first. "Let's go, rest time is over. You're needed."

Victoria acted dazed as her security hostess, dressed in her patent black, and donning dark grey sun glasses walked up to her and put the muzzle of the Beretta to her forehead. "Can I eat first?"

"Where's the food I brought earlier?"

"I put it in the fridge."

"Stay seated." She walked to the small fridge and opened it. She grabbed the bag and she threw it in Victoria's lap. "Eat quickly, or the Colonel will get suspicious."

"What are you talking about?"

"Not right now, I'll explain later," Ru said as she started backing toward the booby trapped chair.

Victoria wondered if she had the wrong target? "Hold on, I don't need to eat now! We can go if you'd like."

It was too late to stop. Ru plopped down into the new electric lounge chair. "What!"... ... ... The fluid squished up between her legs as she looked down in astonishment. The circuit completed and the current hit. The lights in the room flickered on and off. In the flashes and sparks, Victoria witnessed the bizarre. Expanding through the strobes was an immense set of dark wings with fine to long feathers in a tight and symmetrical pattern. A spider web of protruding veins ran underneath the wings and were also now visible in her arms and neck. Then the lights went out completely. A buzzer alarm sounded.

"You've ruined our chance to get you out alive," said the electrocuted creature as the lights stuttered back on. The smoke and steam were rising off the chair's cushion, accompanied by the strong stench of burnt and melted foam. Victoria's plan failed. Unscathed and still holding the gun, her nemesis fired hitting her in the inner and upper thigh. Shock set in the moment Victoria looked down at the blood palpitating out, realizing the pain was about to follow. Quickly, the shooter moved towards her, placing two fingers in the wound. The pain never came.

"Act as if you're in pain! I've fixed your femoral artery. You won't bleed to death. You didn't see anything, understand?" All Victoria could answer was "What?" as she tried to comprehend what she just witnessed.

"No time to explain," said the dark angel. As Colonel Smith's henchmen moved into the room, she pistol whipped her cheek, knocking her to the floor and forcing her eyes to tear up. Then she made the sadistic suggestion, "Prepare her for jump fodder. She's become uncooperative. Look at the genius' work. If I hadn't noticed the fridge light was off, she might have toasted me."

The Colonel stopped in the doorway examining the collateral damage. "Take her back to solitary after you examine the wound. Ru, I'll make the calls on the jump fodder. See if you can keep Dr. Pruett in one piece. Right now, she's worth more to us than you are. Don't underestimate her again. Why did you let your guard down in monitoring her? She would have killed a regular guard. This is too important."

The madam put her head down in disgrace. Colonel Smith softened momentarily and said, "I am glad you held back, only shooting her in the leg. What is the extent of your injuries? You appear intact."

"Colonel, I was suspicious but underestimated her cunning, so I put my foot on the cushion, setting off the circuit."

"Then why are your pants wet?"

"Ru," as he called her, turned away from the Colonel and walked up to Dr. Pruett's face while setting her sun glasses above her forehead. She stared at her, dilated her pupils in and out as a sign of intimidation, "We struggled. I shot to disable the good doctor when she shoved me into the seat after the circuit prematurely completed. As she was intent to kill me, the next time I will show no restraint."

Chapter 23

Even the local entity speaks of the need for a new creation – giving up on his own cesspool.

Ru brought out the sentimentality reserved for lonely discarded old men. What Colonel Smith really wanted was her philosophical support over her filial sympathy. Her buy-in had to overcome her resentment for what she saw as coldhearted. He put his arm around her shoulder, "Can we talk for a few? Let's leave the floor and go into my office. Anything to drink?"

She exhaled, rolled the eyes up, "No, fine."

"Have a seat. You have done a splendid job coming on board so late with all of this. I hope you will release your feelings of abandonment long enough to embrace a new future for both of us. Yazad will be so pleased with developments. Ru, please smile! With jump capacity at our will, the players will come out of hiding along with their offspring. The potential havoc they will wreck on these corrupt image bearers and the loyalists is unprecedented. We will bring in a new age."

She kept toying with her smart phone. "Ru, do I have your attention? How is the good doctor's leg?"

"Her thigh is healing nicely. Arteries and bone are intact. On cue with her work, slight limp. Do you doubt me?"

"This is grand. Her anger is seeping from her gray to white matter for a way out. Clean slates, sincere egalitarians, believe nothing and so believe anything. Of course there is truth. It has many angles. Her faint, civil God caused all this pain and suffering through the ages.

"We've risen to right all that has been wasted on these insolent image bearers. We are no longer interested in being part of the experiment for the progressive growth of this local entity. Beltshzan was on the correct path to establish a new home, then he gave up on his own vision and became content as the puppet 'bad boy' provost of this world. Now he is backpedaling to ingratiate himself. Who would believe that ploy?"

Ru answered, annoyed, "I don't know anyone like that. Is class over?"

"Bear with me. No, he is up to something again. It is about buying time and disturbing rival factions who might unseat him and pull the only power he has away from him – his diminutive lost angels and technology. Also, I believe Dr. Pruett still holds faintly to the myth of a sovereign God who sees the beginning from the end and can consistently rearrange the dominos to fall his way."

She was beginning to listen, "I have to be honest with you, can your faction do better?"

"Better? There may have been good and evil, but we've redefined the rule makers. We will persuade Dr. Pruett to join the third way, as have many others. We will show her that the local entity has created a rock too large to be moved. We are the new cosmic brokers!

Beltshzan is weak and will give way to new bold leadership. He'll have no choice when we begin to terrorize Yare'ach Kachol. He'll be on the defensive outs from all the attention and assume the terminal countdown has begun. His methods have gotten to be such old hat – racism, tribalism, classism, Marxism, socialism, religious fundamentalism and fascism, all an attempt to further corrupt and frustrate the image bearers, raising and suffocating all hope, over and over again. Beltshzan has experienced temporary wins in a losing cause and everyone knows it. Even the local entity speaks of the need for a new creation – giving up on his own cesspool."

Like her father, Ru had trouble submitting to anyone. While he talked she sketched on a legal desk pad a picture of a sad small girl walking with one hand holding that of a winged savage, then responded, "Cuzak, I really don't need to know all these details. A zero sum game, until now? I'm on the hit list with no other options, save the details for someone who might give a damn."

Cuzak took the pen from her and drew his own picture of a drooping cross in the little girl's other hand and continued, "What you don't know can kill you, too. The local entity loves these pathetic rats so much he visited and became one of them. When they die they filter toward him between the membranes. No longer! We'll make them slaves in the new world. When Armageddon or the singularity of bloated civilization arrives we'll mass jump all those who want to escape their own funeral."

Ru tried to finish his sentence, "where there'll be no return? *Hakuna Matata!*"

"Be careful what you say my young leopard. Imagine, a mass jump of symbiont surrogates to a new world governed by an entity of their choosing! They will come in droves over their fear of death and the promise of immortality."

"My kind of place, where the buffalos hit the ground beneath the cliff."

Chapter 24

You're talking about the death of God. Wasn't he counted out once before?

Ru stood up and began to pace as she thought about the holes in Cuzak's ideals. "That's impressive; sounds so easy. Do you think the one in Siyon will show up himself if he stands to lose a mass of loyalists? It's one thing for them to die and float back to him, but what will he do if they leave town permanently?"

"Those pitiful corralled sheep mean nothing to him. Once they have been translated to the Sanctuary, there will be no return. Yazad has complete control of this new universe. If his winds come to help, they will be attacked and dismembered. And if their holy one enters our domain, there will be no resurrection for him. With Yazad, we own the fabric, the code, of this new time and space. He'll enter a black hole of no return. His unity will be broken for good, Ru!"

"You're talking about the death of God. Wasn't he counted out once before?"

"You sound like Dr. Pruett!"

"What I really want to know is, what about me?"

"Ru, Ru, early on when we were experimenting with our failed jump technology I spared you from our partners. I kept you hidden and alive all these years, a precious gem growing in beauty."

"Colonel, you know that since I have become part of this I will have to leave too. The one whose name you will not say, you know he will come. And what's with the sparing me crap? Am I not your flesh and blood, even if I am one fourth?"

"Ru, you're my daughter. You weren't born with all the traits of the Nephilim, granted. When I speak of humans, I don't include you. You are more noble than they. You will rule over them. I'll make safe passage for you. You have to trust me. The partners have worked it all out. There are a few more like you."

"Cuzak. If you didn't save my mother, then why should I trust you?"

"Be careful when you use that name, damn it! Your mother was just a human who fell in love with me. Before you were born, she began leaning toward the loyalists. The ties had to be severed. She knew what she was getting into."

"So how did she die?"

"She died in childbirth, holding you. She bled to death. You were born in a secluded place."

"So there would be no record of me? You abandoned me to an orphanage in the Balkans."

"When you were ready, I came for you. You lived through and survived several massacres, did you not? You will survive more, I tell you, all in preparation. Do you think your survival was all of your own doing? Of course you are exceptional, but still you lack experience. Already you suppose to hold back some of your abilities from me?"

"What do you mean Cuzak?"

"There are always exceptions and the possibility of mutations. The way you came out of that skirmish with the doctor, her healing, and my inability to read you lead me to think you are developing advanced traits which could be to your benefit in the Sanctuary. In our new world, the sheep get bred, enslaved, then slaughtered. No different than here. Ru, look in this mirror: you are a queen, an entirely different class."

Chapter 25

"At that time, Michael the great prince who stands guard over your descendents will arise." – Daniel 12:1

"Methuselah, I've got to sleep. I'm not sure if I'm hallucinating or totally out of rhythm on my sleep cycles. Argh, let me ask you, do you sleep? Do angels need to sleep? Can you tell me why humans sleep?"

"No, we don't sleep. But we do something similar. We praise and lose ourselves to Him. We become unaware of our desires so that they match His. Let me show you."

Lucas watched as his eyes dilated and a smile came over his face. His wings expanded and the veins underneath them pulsated with a heart the strength of a Mack truck engine. He began to sing in an unknown language that was both beautiful and striking. As Ouriano's visible praise vented from deep within his enormous chest, luminous colors flowed from his mouth and nose. This rainbow of smoke, even containing some palettes of colors he had never seen, drifted gently up along the rocky ceiling and then slipped toward the entrance of the tunnel.

"Where are they going?" Lucas asked.

"Back to their owner, the same as yours. If you curse, your breath of life returns to that owner. Give to God what is God's. My dear Lucas, your sleep is mysterious to us. When tired, you sleep. When in danger, you sleep. After procreating, you sleep. When depressed, you sleep. All your life, you sleep. I cannot answer this question as well as you would like. Your greatest dreams, thoughts, passions, are set free to fly when you sleep. It's your opportunity to pray and reassess your hopes. All image bearers are on equal footing in sleep and prayer. The one in Siyon has blessed the image bearers with imagination and love. They all culminate in worship. Do you practice a form of worship?"

"No, Methuselah, I am agnostic at best. I am trying, but it is hard to trust myths and ancient stories."

"Ha, Ha—You have a misconception about what is ancient, and you deny your own existence. You are saying 'I am not here.' Say this for me, 'I, Dr. Lucas Tanner, am not here.'"

"That's ridiculous. I won't say such a thing! Am I your specimen?"

"Then verify you are here! Not as one just asleep, nor caught in a vision, or hallucination? Without relationship you have no personality. You don't exist."

As Lucas stood in the tunnel yet another vision came over him. On this occasion he was walking behind himself and Victoria near the campus research facility. He observed them mashing the traffic walk button, trying to hurry past the live annoyance of an itinerant preacher making the campus circuits: 'Sister Susan,' in her long black skirt holding up a large black Bible.

She was ragging on, "Repent, all you brood of vipers! Woe to you who live in gated communities, woe to you who worship beauty and spend more on caffeine and alcohol than your homeless shelter, woe to you who find no time for God, ignore the prophets, but search diligently for aliens and sales. Woe to you who conveniently worship your education yet remain ignorant of the poor--Jesus saves!--flee from your worthless lives, this corrupt and damned virtual, latte, generation. I tell you, God's wrath is real!"

Wedging his apparition between Victoria and himself he saw the two had a smug smirk on their faces, trying not to laugh at Sister Susan's vindictive preaching of epithets all the while despising her judgments. When the crosswalk light turned white, Lucas watched himself look down and away from the preacher. He heard himself think, *What right does this street fanatic have in entering my private world and criticizing me? I am doing something with my life. You go do something constructive.*

"What did you just see, little Juwaan?"

"Nothing, Methuselah, I am so tired. Let me sit down here."

Lucas braced his hands on his knees and then squatted down leaning his exhausted body against the tunnel wall. He closed his eyes and conceded the fight against a much needed sleep. Ouriano lifted him up in his arms and took flight, his mane blowing across Lucas' face.

Chapter 26

Oh my love they will call you Eve, the mother of the living.

Blindfolded, they escorted Victoria for a short walk to a new building for a tour. In transit she could smell the sea and feel the humidity. "We were on a coast line!" she told herself.

Arriving at the next building, they removed her blindfold. Colonel Smith arrived in a new, dark blue suit, with light blue tie and white shirt. His winsomeness reminded Victoria of the used car sales manager glad-handing the mark when his salesmen couldn't close the deal.

"What can we do to let you know how important you are? Never again will so many be indebted to so few."

She looked back at him, transitioning her face from serious to the same fake grin he used on others, then back again.

"Ingenious, Dr. Pruett. Your improvisation is exactly why we chose you. I actually admire your attempt at escape from Ru. Tell me, were you surprised that she was not electrocuted?" His smile continued as Victoria ran through all her possible answers. "You realize she wanted you to attempt an escape so she would have an excuse to kill you?"

"I'm sorry, Colonel Smith. I saw an opportunity and I took it."

"Jealousy, I suppose Doctor, and for good reason. You are a prodigy, underrated, underappreciated, and underpaid. What you have invented is priceless. It will save your people. You are like Moses, except you won't abandon your people to die in the desert, will you?"

"Colonel Smith, who are my people?"

"The avant-garde, those who are tired of shirking future responsibility by holding to a false faith in someone they cannot see or hear. Your people are those who believe in the evolving potential creativity of humans to solve the perennial global pariahs of social injustice and inequality. You have redefined 'equal access beyond your own species!' Let me show you something, but you must promise not to tell anyone--promise?"

"Yeah, uh, sure," as she shrugged her shoulders and dug her hands down in her lab coat pockets. They walked down a long pale blue concrete block corridor with black and white checkered floor tile, then descended down a long flight of stairs, two hundred steps by her count. Victoria heard and felt the unmistakable hum of generators as they entered the control room, which to her resembled those set to monitor nuclear reactors. "How could you...?"

"Impressed? You don't have to be concerned with how this was obtained. We call it a 'lease agreement.' The camaraderie of corporations is much greater than nations. But you, my dear, should be concerned with the miracle this will empower. With your help, you will be called the 'mother of the living.'

A mass gateway will be opened to wherever we please. A power once reserved for gods will be at our fingertips. Look around and see what is happening. You can take your mother to a place where she will be safe and free forever. The end of the world will come with a whimper after being precipitated by a mass exit, not a ruthless takeover. We will leave this world and its god behind forever to let those left sort the remainder out for themselves."

His long rant allowed time for Victoria to question more about how this might play out, "Colonel Smith, are you talking heaven and hell now?"

"If there is a heaven, a hell, a purgatory; this local entity can have it all, but we won't be here to wait any longer. We don't care."

"I must ask, you will outflank God, the rapture, the second coming?"

Cuzak, aka Colonel Smith, paused a second, cleared his throat with a grunt, pulled on his suit-tails, then said, "To keep it simple, if you believe that kind of hysteria, yes. The truth is, the local entity is not that interested anymore in the human race. For now, I want you to build on a much larger scale what you have already designed. We'll arrange for your partner to join you."

"Colonel Smith, what did I just hear you say...? Something about Lucas? You know where he is? How to get him back?"

"You love him don't you?"

"Where is he? Show him to me now? I want proof Colonel Smith!"

"Follow me, then," Smith said. They entered a pristine white conference room except for a large flat monitor serving as one of the wall panels and a board room table made from a single piece of polished white marble, surrounded with eight high back black leather chairs. The wall monitor opposite Victoria's seat lit up. There was a broken stream of video with static lines.

Victoria took a deep breath, "Oh my gosh—it's him--standing up on the cliff looking down. Where was this taken? When? His suit is off. Is he alive?"

"We can retrieve him if he can stay alive long enough for us to reach him."

Mr. Smith, you bring Lucas back and bring my mother here and I'll help build whatever your scamming heart desires. And, by the way, don't you consider it only fair to give us a piece of the patent--the least you could do. Surely you can agree to this? After all you now have control of the only two people in this life who matter to me. Harm them and I'll die before you get what you want."

"Oh my love, they will call you Eve!"

Victoria heard herself described in such a way for a second time; however, she didn't take them as a compliment.

Chapter 27

Your world is but one front of many in the war, soon to be the most active.

Ouriano was seated forty feet from where Lucas lay, next to an ochre-tinted arcing wall which rose to a domed, white ceiling thirty feet high. The smooth dome illumined in dancing mellow hues, patterns, and brightness in sync with Lucas' racing thoughts and emotions.

"Greetings, Dr. Tanner. You must be feeling better, rested. You've been sleeping deeply for two of your days."

Lucas strained to speak through his sticky, cotton-filled mouth, "Methuselah, Methuselah, what is this place?"

"You needed rest. This is my private place of recovery. Over the ages, I have come here to heal. I bear many scars of battle with those suffering the infection of Beltshzan. Your world is but one front of many in the war, soon to be the most active. The war goes deep into the cosmos, separating me for long periods from my home; a test of endurance. You are the first Juwaan to be here. I am privileged to have you."

"So angels have private apartments? Wives, spouses, children?"

"What do you see in my home?"

"It's fairly simple, but elegant. You practice Feng Shui?"

"Juwaan, dreams can be valuable. Dream all you want. Of this, I am envious of you image bearers. Here, drink this, sit up. I will bring you a meal soon."

Lucas tilted the gourd in faith and drank until his stomach felt bloated. In a few seconds the tissues of his mouth and throat rehydrated. He then sat still for a moment reflecting on the odd taste and twinge he was feeling, then asked "What is this? Sweet with a taint of salt? Electrolytes? My arms, the muscles are twitching!-- what have you given me to drink? Look, the skin on my belly is rolling in waves."

"Juwaan, what do you feel?"

"It feels like a deep tissue massage, hurts but in a good way. Spoke too soon. Ahh, not that one, a mule kick in the chest."

"I am so pleased, I was afraid this might kill you."

"What, Ouriano? You risked killing me! Do you understand human anatomy? After all aren't you thousands of years old? Don't angels help humans and save them all the time?"

"We rarely save anyone by our own decision. The winds comply with what they are asked. We can save bodies and tissues or break them down. We don't claim ownership. You are a Juwaan and I have orders to prepare you for a visitation to the owner of the planet above. This hasn't been done in ages and only on the edge of great calamity. My problem is I don't know exactly how to prepare you or when you will be summoned."

The rolling response of Lucas' outer tissue increased. He grimaced with each sharp pain, "Ouriano, ahh, you must have a manual, uhh, or a book on this type of preparation? Are you telling me that, yow! My, my back! Arrrh, that I am the experiment of an angel? Ohhh."

"Your symptoms will subside in a minute."

"Great mother of massage parlors, a great party joke. What's in this?"

"Think of it as an inoculation against your own infection, an enzyme which temporarily suspends your body's cellular and molecular laws which bind you on Earth but are worthless near the golden planet. You've been given a temporary pass. Your neural pathways are now subject to governors, limiting sensory stimulation. Without this your subatomic structure would become so excited that your body could disintegrate from overload--an overdose of too much reality, otherwise you would..."

"Go insane? Thank you, Methuselah, I would hate to have come this far to be vanquished by too much of a good thing."

"Lucas, you would not believe how many do."

"What, is that some type of angel humor?"

Ouriano smiled for the first time, placed his hand on Lucas' forehead and said, "Now relax, look at the dancing colors above you. They reflect the depths and shallows of your mind, spirit, body, and connectivity. We need to explore them all until you can focus the bands as one white light. Then you will truly be a Juwaan. Go ahead and try."

Light shades of yellow, blue, red, browns, zig-zagged frantically across the white, smooth dome above them. "Does this mean I am scatterbrained? What do I do next?"

"Try emptying yourself in prayer."

"Rusty on that one."

"Walk through a memory of an important time in your life."

"Alright," Lucas replayed a vision of a family Christmas when he received his first telescope at age nine. His grandmother was visiting from Detroit. The entire family gathered around the tree with all the home lights off except for the decorations and surrounding white and red glowing candles. His mother played her favorite, Bing Crosby's, 'White Christmas,' as everyone karaoke'd together, '*I'm dreaming of a white Christmas, just like the ones I used to know... ...*' Afterward they watched, 'It's a Wonderful Life.'

"You are making progress," said Ouriano, lifting his hand off Lucas' forehead and motioning up to the lights. "Make them converge. By the way, the wingless second class angel was Clarence."

Lucas chuckled and focused above on the beautiful kaleidoscope of oscillating colors. He tried harder by leaving the Christmas memory to concentrate solely on converging the colors. It had the opposite effect. The patterns dissolved into scattered beams and disjointed patterns.

Ouriano asked, "What happened?"

"I tried to consciously bring the colors together."

"This is where you failed. 'Not by might, not by power, but by my Spirit, says the Lord of Hosts.' The seed of your species makes you restless to know, explore, control. Yet your defect leads you to see without seeing, to hear without understanding, to control for no purpose."

"What else are we to do with our intrigue into the mysteries of the universe? Chalk it all up to religious philosophical speculation? Your path for me doesn't fit. I didn't come here out of a religious pursuit. I came on a scientific quest. Sorry for the disappointment, but right now I am doing the best I can."

"Oh Juwaan, many of your kind hold to the pride of advancement beyond the previous generation--they both hope and fear the closure of a unifying theory. Why is this?"

"I imagine, because it would be the end of the quest."

"The end of the quest? That discovery might merely get them to the 'on ramp.' You will discover here many levels to reality. Can you tell me the difference between your conscious life, dream state, and aspirations? On Siyon they come together as one. You've been brought to the unifying principal which lives and breathes. I pity your struggle to find a way out of birth and death, love and suffering. You image bearers all suspect something more perfect."

"Why do you refer to us as image bearers? Are you referring to my genetic affinity for my mother and father?"

"That's part of it, but you are not going back far enough."

"Ouriano, 'far enough' would take me back to primordial ooze, correct? With the breath of God thrown in?"

"That's not what you want to hear Dr. Tanner; so then, if not an image bearer, what are you?"

Lucas slowly breathed out the words, "I don't know--I, don't, know." As he said this, the ceiling light patterns for the briefest of moments converged as a whitish yellow light.

Ouriano admired the ceiling encouraged, but said, "Oh Juwaan, in this, I do not envy you. You may be severely wounded on this quest or horribly disappointed at the prospect of returning to your world."

Pausing for words, Lucas pressed his two index fingers into the corner of his eye sockets and wiped out two encrusted coagulations then asked, "Methuselah, I thought your species didn't suffer anxiety or speculate about the future? Are those outcomes sealed?"

"May it never be. Life is more complicated than my mission and your philosophers. There are consequences for everything. I accepted the stewardship of your preparation, and you are far from ready for a trip to Siyon. You need a detour to Sharu."

"What's a Sharu? I'm at a loss figuring this place out."

"Sharu is an island on the surface, a place time has forgotten, where you will be tested to expand your powers. Make the effort to experience what it means to be a Juwaan. I wish I could tell you the entire story of the island; better you discover it on your own. Some means of understanding have to unfold."

Chapter 28

"When he lies, he speaks according to his own nature,
for he is a liar and the father of lies." – John 8:44

Delighting in the life vibes Victoria gave off brought back memories of many women from his past. Before he spouted any more of his twisted dialectic, Cuzak's conscience tried to draw a line to rein in his passions, *Humans are such feeble creatures. They multiply like rabbits, soft-shelled and short-lived, easy prey if it weren't for their guardians who haphazardly interrupt on their behalf. I hate to get attached, especially fall in love. The daughters of Eve will sacrifice anything to bring forth new life. I promised myself to never take advantage of this flaw again.*

"Colonel Smith, Colonel Smith? Just what are we aiming for? If this nuclear reactor was designated to power the opening of a wide door to another universe, how will we know where to aim the coordinates?"

"First things first Dr. Pruett, how is your leg wound?"

"I won't be a swimsuit model with the scar, but then I never have been. I'll take a rain check and die another day."

"I am surprised how quickly you have healed. Dr. Pruett, in time you will come to be satisfied about all of these things. Let me ask you a question, can you explain where your original portal opened into? Of course not. Long before there was science and reason there simply was the infinite multiplicity of universes longing to be understood and explored. What if I told you some of them have been and new ones continue to be explored by beings more intelligent and powerful than you or I?"

Victoria responded by placating him, "I don't have a problem with that scenario. Without someone to understand them, they don't exist? I will defer to your experience on this. I mean my scope of training is limited to lab work. You're a man of the world."

Though he judged most of her answers to be insincere, it weighed on Cuzak's mind that he might soon need a breeding partner, *If she shows signs of turning, then maybe I should preserve her? I'd take her now except I need Dr. Tanner back in the lab. Let me build a bridge to her sense of justice.*

"How do you think we arrived here Dr. Pruett? I tell you these explorers of the cosmos are very much alive today, and by no means desire to be at enmity with the local entity. That is entirely of his doing."

"Colonel, I am not sure what you are saying? You speak passionately about things I don't fully understand."

Colonel Smith masked his feelings for Victoria behind even more elaborate academic, haughty explanations, "Abraham's progeny have tried to sew that lie under the umbrella of domesticated monotheism. The truth is this local entity came into this universe only to hijack this evolutionary seedbed called Earth, and plant his own myth and domination. This entity came to earth spinning out a cute myth: Genesis, Moses, Jesus and the whole bit. Some other religions have hitchhiked on the skirts of this grand narrative."

"It's this narrative which bothers you the most though?"

"Because their adherents are the most closed-minded. Thankfully, other explorers saw through this treachery, culminating in his plea for pity with his atoning sacrifice. Since becoming educated, you probably lost most kinship with the whole God of Abraham myth. Guilt is what keeps most adherents on board that sinking ship. So, I want to simply state, there are many universes and many gods. You're not turning your back on anyone."

"Yes, Colonel Smith, but what about part two to the myth you are bringing up?"

That she would try to deliberate upon his remarks intrigued him, "Go ahead, what is on your mind, the part two?"

"My framework on these matters is considerably less than yours, but what about the coming kingdom? That's all my mother talks about, the prophecy, the imminent return?"

"That is pure rubbish from Biblical propaganda. Look at the changes through the Bible stories. Some have seminal truths, but the text does more to document his failures. There is one truth, however: this god, or entity, does have the upper hand of power here. This is why, going forward, we will no longer waste our time on rehabilitation or rebellion on this planet."

The Colonel (Cuzak) Smith was trying too hard and he knew it. His hands became fists, the knuckles turned white. His suit coat was about to rip at the seams. Stepping back he again straightened his jacket and tie then said, "I am sorry if I am over the top. I promise you this, we will relieve pain and suffering."

Victoria stepped up to him and extended her hand out in peace. He gently accepted it with both hands as she said, "You are a very sincere man. I will help all I can. No more games?"

Smith raised up her hand and kissed the back of it, "Thank you. Your blue eyes reveal a remarkable rationality and goodness. The entity you saw transported a few days ago was once a beautiful creature. But in the mayhem it was maimed and designated for destruction."

"Between the gloom it cast and the melodious stench it gave off, who would have known it righteously suffered. Thank you for enlightening me, Colonel. "

"The hideous creature inhabiting the death-row inmate once sailed the solar and galactic winds in search of a new home. When the local cosmic squatter caught on to what was happening, he clipped its wings out of spite and forced it to forage off the earth and humans for survival. Until now, it had no other choice!"

Chapter 29

"If God places no trust in his holy ones, if even the heavens are impure in his eyes, how much less man who is abominable and corrupt, who drinks in evil like water?" – Eliphaz to Job, Job 15:15-16

From where Lucas stood in the ankle-deep surf of the primordial island, his suspicions about what lay beneath the servant-hood of angels like Ouriano surfaced. "Your kind are aloof from the human experience. You don't die per se, so how can you fear death?"

Although Ouriano didn't show it, he felt disappointed, "Lucas, give this time."

"Your code of honor probably includes, 'No crying in heaven allowed.' 'Don't get too emotionally tied.' Right now, what I need most is to get back to Victoria. I know you can return me. What are you, some type of disengaged surgeon of the soul? You force yourself to be coldhearted, don't you, so you won't get hurt?"

"It is for your good that I leave you. Don't forget the consequences here are real. Intellect alone won't keep you alive."

"I don't know what is real anymore. What am I supposed to do?"

"Discover who you are, Juwaan."

"That's it?" Before another word was spoken, Ouriano vanished. Lucas' first thought reminded him that all displaced aliens in action flicks become either the hunted or hunter. If he stayed put, someone or something would find him.

"Oh well, such is fate," he announced to no one but himself, kicking the warm salt water before fixing his vision on the rising Siyon, which filled three quarters of the horizon. "You up there! I really want to know what lies below your warm golden glow!"

His intrigue about Siyon was short lived and displaced by survival instincts. Taking inventory, Lucas found himself on a pristine white beach lined with windswept palm trees with smooth trunks ninety feet high, fronds waving a third of the way down. Behind the palms hung a thick green curtain of vine-woven trees and shrubs decorated by orchids. From within the canopies and ground below them he could hear abundant jungle life by way of grunts, coos, cackles, whistles, the staccato tapping of woodpeckers, the rustling of leaves. Over them, twenty miles away rose twin green volcanic cones, the left one smoldering.

The peaceful shore and warm ocean breeze reminded him of a serene dive vacation to Costa Rica until a hundred pound fruit hit the sand with a dense thud ten yards to his right, leaving a small crater. Frightened by these wrecking balls, he retreated up to the blue foaming surf's edge. Next he watched in shock as the nose of a rhino sized brown boar rustled its snout through the bordering jungle and plucked the giant coconut. The hogzillian swine crushed the hull with two loud pops and chewed the pulp while keeping attention toward Lucas. White slobbery milk dripped down its jaws under the long tusks. Satisfied, it reversed into the dark entangled woods. Lucas decided then, his answers were not in that direction.

From a quantum portal to a continental sink pocked with angelic relics to a Jurassic island beach, Lucas' old life was drifting further away. Judging the beach as secure as any place he sat down in the shallows, and leaned back on his hands hypnotized by the rhythm of the luminescent turquoise water lapping over his out stretched legs.

The retreating foam went around his feet as he talked to himself, "Surf in... ... surf out. Surf in ... surf out. Not the worst place to be stranded, but stranded nonetheless. Victoria how am to contact you? By now you've probably written me off as dead. I should have told you more than just 'I love you' – I should have told how you make me whole; how I really feel, that I can't imagine my life without you in it. All this would mean a million times more if you were with me. If there is a heaven, a paradise, what good is it by yourself?"

With the end his self-pity, he tilted his head back, sunk his elbows in the wet sand of the slight undertow, and finished, "Alright Lucas, you are long overdue for some R & R anyway, and don't forget, you are a Juwaan, which so far hasn't netted any benefits. That must be good for a few free nights in the beach bungalow."

With his pep talk over, something suddenly moved into his peripheral vision. He looked down the long strip of sandy white and saw a black lab mix with a white underbelly and four white paws playing in the surf. Lucas clapped his hands to get the dog's attention, who then paused, turned towards him, and ran full throttle. Standing up he moved backwards to deeper water in case of an attack. The dog continued the sprint until it crashed into the first wave and then paddled closer, still wagging its tail.

"Lucy is that you?" She had the purple collar he had buried her in. His parents called him home his freshman year of college to see her before she died. They had been inseparable before then, fishing, hiking, even a date.

"Come here girl. I never got to say good bye! You passed away before I could get back home. Why are you grabbing my wrist and pulling me toward shore? How did you get here? I am so happy to see you! OK, I am following you, but let's not go into the trees over there."

"Now for our big hug. Stand up Lucy, big hugs!" His arms went out to her but instead of embracing him, the dog took a defensive stance, fangs exposed, hair on the back raised, mucus dripping from under the flaps of her muzzle.

"Whoa girl, take it easy. I didn't mean to scare you. We can be friends again. Lucy, it's me Lucas. Remember how you slept on my bed at home even when I moved away? I still have your blanket on the foot of my bed."

Before he could say another soothing word, something rubbed against his upper left calf, causing him to jump, "Snakes!" Around him fish, sea snakes, horseshoe crabs, mullet, otter like creatures were racing toward shore leaping up on to the beach. Lucas heard the sound of crashing waters and turned to see a front end wake the shape and size of a nuclear class sub bulldozing the water toward him about one hundred yards out. Adrenaline kicking in, he high stepped the waves toward shore competing with the other frantic small sea creatures, screaming, "Lucy!"

Chapter 30

We have a Juwaan among us.

Lucy disappeared in the jungle as Lucas dove in the underbrush behind her, tripping hard and landing face first. As he rose to his knees, a long pain-filled, wild boar squeal cut through the jungle. Lucas peeked through the vegetation down the beach at what looked like a monster croc, with no legs and a thick round snout -- almost matching the width of its sausage shaped body. It was wiggling itself in reverse to the surf with hogzilla lifted up in its jaws rear first. It shook the boar like a rag doll and repositioned it deeper into its throat with every smashing crunch. The poor victim continued to squeal until the panic filled lungs were compacted and ripped by the inner smashing molars of the sea invader.

"So much for the beach as a safe haven," he told Lucy. As this menace of the sea receded, it stopped to bellow out an eardrum breaking screech as a warning to all who challenged its turf. Lucy licked Lucas' face and he in turn gave her a hug in their little hiding place beneath the shrubs. She grabbed his wrist and started pulling him toward a thin trail inland, where upon he stood and followed her at a brisk pace.

After visiting the island's version of SeaWorld, he tended to agree with Lucy's urging, "Perhaps the jungle is more appealing." Thinking of what ifs, he added, "If I had only gone to pharmacy school, none of this would have happened."

The vegetation was lush, a paradise of orchids, flowering vines, clear creeks and canopied ponds with schools of colorful fish, varieties of ferns and tall hardwood trees. Three miles inland, Lucy led him across a patch of matted down undergrowth and broken tree limbs where she paused in the middle as if unsure. Her tail went down and she ducked her head sniffing the buried trail. Lucas soon caught on, to the side of the matted limbs, ten thousand flies were buzzing around a steaming dung pile, shoulder high, enough to fill a dump truck.

"Lucy, or whoever you are, this is not good. Did Ouriano put you up to this?" Lucas began to curse under his breath and added, "God... Methuselah, what have you done bringing me here? A twisted angelic game of Survivor?"

It was clear who was the hunted. Surveying the ground he determined they were standing inside a foot print, next to them another, and another. The broken tree branches ran alongside the path of the prints. Lucy lifted her head up, looked at him, then began trotting down the original trail.

Lucas followed of course, realizing everything around him was a point of no return. He chattered on to the dog while he tried to keep pace, "Such a lush and violent world you live in Lucy. I don't give us twenty-four hours to survive, but at least there are no nights here given the luminosity of Siyon and the waters of this Blue Moon. I'd hate to be hunted in the dark."

They hiked for at least another seven miles, resting briefly at the base of the extinct volcanoes, then continued through more crystal streams, mazes of green ferns, patches of open red sand and rugged black volcanic rock. They walked through soaring groves of giant redwood-sized cedars covered with white and reddish brown peeling bark along walls of wet limestone grottoes. Lucy, content, continued to listen to his self-help talks. The warmth of the ever present Siyon above and the blue iridescence of the surrounding sea gave everything a chromatic tone.

In an overdue break along a small stream, Lucas rubbed her neck and ears. Lucy nuzzled his hand in return. Still expecting the worse, he noticed the jungle had become uncharacteristically quiet, though she didn't raise an ear. All the abundant bird life, monkeys, boars, insects, which had provided background chorus to the adventure, were now oddly taking a nap.

He whispered, "Lucy, something is watching us," as he dropped into a belly crawl beneath the ferns for at least thirty yards, then periscoped his head up praying silently, Please don't be a meat eater.

The humanoid had coarse shoulder length dark hair. The rest of the body was hairy like the back of his uncle Larry, who always took off his shirt when working on his father's 77 Mercury. It carried a spear and rope, with several animal skins hung bundled over its shoulder. Lucas went down to the ground again, contemplating his next move, *It's part of a hunting party. Why didn't Lucy bark? I have to find her.*

Attempting to periscope through the ferns again, he met a foreign resistance which forced him down to his knees. He tried to stand up but slipped as the net began dragging him through the ferns, vines and limestone patches. Lucas yelled, "Hey, stop, stop, stop, this is a mistake, ... Ouriano, Ouriano!" To no avail -- his back and head bounced and skidded through the rocky growth.

From Lucas' perspective, the primates paused to decide the fate and value of the alien prey laying entangled at their feet. In all there were eight biped humanoids of the Neanderthal or Cro-Magnon variety in need of a body wax. His paleontology escaped him. He voted for Neanderthals.

Still enmeshed, Lucy remained faithful, sniffing and licking his hand. But Lucas pulled it back in shock when he saw her transform from a black lab mix to a creature resembling a tiger-sized crustaceous shrimp, with clear exoskeleton scales over the visible internal pumping organs. Long feelers bounced up and down on its head between two high mounted black eyes. One of the Neanderthals fed it the head of a small deer for a reward. Its side-clamping mandibles easily cracked the skull as a siphon extended down to suck out the soft brain tissue.

The humanoids unraveled Lucas from the net then outstretched his arms and legs staking them to the ground. Next a female with bloodshot eyes and a tangle of rough quartz necklaces came forward waiving a five foot long, green celery-like shoot with a three inch brown thorn on the end. She slapped the thorn into his upper right thigh with the force and pop of a whip. It stung like a Japanese hornet.

Lucas tried to communicate through his scream, "I am from the Earth, Ouriano sent me, no more!" Blood spurted out of his trembling leg as pain shot through his sciatic nerve. The welcoming party mumbled to each other as they watched how his body dealt with the shock of the wound.

The female who struck him dropped her weapon and stuffed dried leaves mixed with spit into the wound. Next she pulled back on his scalp and with a sharp stick in the other hand, pried open his mouth. Discovering no fangs she let go of his head, stood up and declared waving her hands over her head, "Juwaan, Juwaan, we have Juwaan among us!" Several of the males shook their heads and knelt down and cut his ties.

Chapter 31

The Nephilim were on the earth in those days (and also after this) when the sons of God were having sexual relations with the daughters of humankind, who gave birth to their children. – Genesis 6:4

"Mom, I need your help. I've had no time off and I'd like you to come stay with me here at the lab facility. I've already arranged for your plane. We're sending you a private jet."

"Victoria, where are you?"

"Mom, ah, due to national security I can't tell you. But some reliable people I work with will bring you."

"Secret Service? Honey, if you need your mom, I'm on my way. I'm not sure what to pack, but I guess I can do some shopping after I arrive? So you're not at the university?"

"I'll answer all your questions when you get here. I haven't had your homemade lasagna in ages."

"I bet you are getting too thin again. I'd love to be needed. Can Blitz come too?"

"Mom, you want to bring Blitz?"

Victoria motioned at her guardian for permission--who nodded in the affirmative.

"Of course. Look, mom I have to get back to work with some important deadlines."

"Victoria, one more question, do you know of a church nearby I can attend?"

"Plenty... OK, bye mom, I love you and can't wait to hug you."

"I'm glad you need me. We'll go to church together like we used to. Look for one where they pray. See you soon." The communication with her mom ended.

"Dr. Pruett, we need to talk," Victoria's seemingly ever-present watchdog shifted into view.

"I am not sure what to call you, 'the femme fatale' with a penchant for goth? You shot me, then you healed me? I don't understand, but then again, so many things around here are not what I would call normal."

"My name is Ruvale Marija Zvonimira. Please call me Ru or Maria. I am the daughter of the one you call Colonel Smith. His real name is Cuzak. But please don't associate me with him. He may be my father, but he never helped raise me. We have very little in common. I came to him because I have a unique set of problems and needed to discover some things about myself."

"Ms. Ruvale, I could almost believe anything now, but I caught a glimpse of something abnormal about you too when the lights flickered. You took an electrical charge which would have stopped the heart of any human. Are you like one of those creatures Colonel Smith, ah Cuzak, is trying to jump? You don't smell like one. If so, how come you haven't tried to possess me?"

Ru stood before her with her arms crossed trying to temper her answer, "There is one reason you are still alive: your technology is not yet perfected to open the full corridor and be replicated. After that, you and your mother are fodder unless you work with me. Are you listening to me? Dr. Pruett?"

Victoria distantly heard Ru while a vision overtook her. Her mother was taking her to meet her father at the Burger King for the weekend exchange. While they waited for him to show, her mother tried to follow Victoria through the yellow, red and blue tubed playground equipment. She asked her mother, "Why do I have to do this every week? My dad said I could live with him if I wanted to. It's not my fault you got the divorce."

"I am sorry Victoria, but that's not the agreement your father and I worked out."

Victoria climbed up to the third level of the tubes and looked over at the parking lot for her father. She spotted him there – scrambling down to run into his bear hug when he came through the door. He lifted her up to his beard-stubbled face, which tickled her cheeks. His arms were the safest place in the world.

He took her for the weekend to a surprise trail ride. On separate horses they meandered through the foothills. The scent of the tall pine trees and the horse-worn mud trails were a relief from the aromas of her generic apartment and its commercial cleansers. Brushing against the low-level pine needles and oak leaves, their cool dewdrops ran down her neck.

Victoria experienced complete happiness for a moment, but as quick as it started the vision began to dissipate. She gripped the horn of the saddle and tried to stay with her dad. To no avail she faded back with Ru, who was holding her wrists.

Unbelievably Ru understood. "You know I've had the same thing happen to me. You've had a vision."

Victoria was dazed. "I was with my father. We were riding horses together."

"Did you recognize where you were?"

"Ru, I don't ever remember riding horses with my father. He promised to take me before he passed away."

"Victoria, close your eyes and get back on the horse -- please trust me and do this. Our time is limited." Ru closed her eyes as she held Victoria's wrists. Closing her eyes also, Victoria immediately found herself drifting down through layers of fog and tree limbs as she descended back into the saddle.

"Dad!" she proclaimed, with an alto voice, as he leaned over from his saddle and hugged her. It felt good to be loved by the father she had missed most of her life. Examining her arms, legs, and body told Victoria she now was an adult, she wondered, this is not the same story, has Ru changed my vision?

Her father touched her shoulder, "Vic, I've got someone here to see you." He pulled his reins to the left and nodded toward a small adjacent field. Approaching out of the fog and trees were three mounted white stallions. Pewter medallions on wide black waist belts held down their long gray robes. Hoods shadowed their faces but she sensed innate goodness the closer they came. Two moved around her father's mount and pulled back their hoods; Lucas and Methuselah beaming with joy. The third kept a distance and was unrecognizable.

For Victoria, this manifestation of Lucas was more handsome than she remembered; his arms and hands were rugged and tan like that of a warrior, not a man limited to cerebral work. As her heart rate increased, he reached over, lifted her hand, and bowed his head over it, allowing his long blond hair to fall across her arm. He then pressed his lips to the back of her hand, delivering a shock. The energy of the kiss almost knocked her out of the saddle. Her pounding heart was embarrassed and melted at the same time. In their years working together, he had never kissed her.

"Victoria, Methuselah brought me here to see you. And I suppose you have met Ru. She must be helping you now. I hope you have lost your jealously. She is courageous and is helping us, despite great danger to herself. I promised to contact you. I don't understand everything, except it wasn't an accident and now we are in the middle of a counterinsurgency if we are to survive."

Lucas speech kept accelerating with excitement, "I love you so much and miss you. Real angels are not sweet little valentine cherubs like we may have thought, and our earthly lives are not the center of this universe. Our forensic knowledge is only the beginning of understanding. Our epistemological deficiencies don't limit the one in whom we live and move and have our being. I've seen the genetic reserves, the seed beds of the Earth -- gazed beyond the multi-verse. I had my doubts, and was asking the wrong questions, while I missed you horribly and thought I never see you again, and they call me a 'Juwaan' ... and ... ...ah ..."

Methuselah intervened holding his arm up over Lucas' chest, smiled and said, "And nothing can ever separate your love for each other. It has created something wonderful. Hold on to this dearly."

There was silence for a moment. Then Lucas spoke, "I pleaded with Methuselah for a way to communicate with you. He circumvented some normal channels through Ru. He tells me the essence of your life is secure and you have been given a front row seat for some nasty galactic fireworks. Yes, you and I helped to speed up this demonic insurgency. Our work has fallen into the wrong hands. Already we have been attacked and held up from returning. I have been holding on to what Ouriano, or what Methuselah, has said, 'the end isn't always the end.'"

Victoria reached out her hand to his again. But they were gone. Her eyes refocused and she found herself looking into her guardian's viper-like eyes. She ripped her wrists out of Ru's grip and demanded, "What did you just do?"

Chapter 32

To your devil, your dysfunctional family,
blood is thicker than water.

Ru put her hands on her hips to defend her matter of fact reply, "You needed confirmation to trust me."

Victoria's hands went to her own hips to mock her, "Was that real?"

Ru lowered the attitude, "Yes and no. You were not physically outside of this room, but by means of Ouriano, I communed with them and you. The winds of light can communicate with each other across distances, times, and dimensions. For those who have become darkened, it is much more difficult."

"How then could you communicate? You strike me as sort of dark."

"I'm not sure. I am a mix breed; a fallen angel, and like you a fallen human. I have the conscience, body, and eternal spirit of a human, the ability to transverse and heal like some of the angelic race. Yet I also carry the infection of Beltshzan but have yet to come under judgment. When the death eater came for me it was Ouriano who struck a deal to allow me to live because I might become an asset for a time like this. He appealed my need for capture and immediate death. I lived with Ouriano on the Blue Moon for mentoring and later returned to my orphaned life in the former Yugoslavia. I don't remember all of it, unfortunately I have to rely on what others tell me. Still trying to sort it out.

Ouriano is greatly feared by the dark angelic stock, *angelorum lapsus*, because he doesn't play by the rules. He is one of the few loyal angels given free range. He receives assignments which require something most angels do not have, faith. This makes him unpredictable to his enemies.

I am a second-generation Nephilim. Most like me only lived for a few hundred years, millennia ago, because of our domination of humans. The unexpected genetic experiment was cut off. And, most like me were killed, or were exiled to a world of their own where they slowly preyed on each other to extinction. A few escaped.

We were part of Beltshzan's plan to disrupt the genetic sequence of humans and build a new world with him when the edict to end the experiment was given. Cuzak is one of those who escaped. His father is Beltshzan, his mother was from the human line of the ancient warrior Lamech, a descendant of the line of Cain. Beltshzan helped him find a secret refuge, but later lost Cuzak's allegiance because he couldn't transform this world or find a new one."

Victoria was trying to follow Ru's story. "Whoa, Goth girl! I saw the wingspan, and now you are telling me that you are not a demon, an angel, nor a human, and your father is the son of the Devil?"

Ru nodded. "Yes, I am afraid so. And like all angels, I too have a natural internal homing for Yare'ach Kachol, the Blue Moon of Siyon. I was given a temporary stay on my infection which allows me to transmigrate between what you would call heaven and earth. Cuzak does not know the extent of my development or training, but he suspects something. For now, please do what he asks."

"Do I have a choice? You have me in a cage."

"You are almost free, Dr. Pruett. Please don't hate me. Ouriano told me, 'Some things must come to pass.'"

"And why would I hate Ms. Zvonimira? Because you might have to prove your allegiance?"

Dr. Pruett almost read her mind. Ru kept looking around the room then answered, "Allegiance?"

"To your devil? Your dysfunctional family? Blood is thicker than water. 'Woe to those through whom evil comes to pass.'"

"Yes, I have heard that, but it is not always true, Dr. Pruett. The future is up to us to shape. I am of the belief that while I acknowledge a barbaric heritage I choose a new fate. Ouriano has taught me about faith."

"Does your father know of your, how do I say, abilities?"

"He may know more than he leads on, but he is proud of me."

"What if he finds out? From what you've told me, I wouldn't put it past him to play us against each other. So the million dollar question is, 'Would you kill me if he asked?'"

"Dr. Pruett, seeing as you have already made an attempt on me, I'll tell you when he asks. Fair enough?"

Chapter 33

Can you find something which cannot be known?

As the blood flowed back into Lucas' hands, a juvenile male Neanderthal ran up, spouting a guttural language and pointing back to the jungle thicket. At the same time, three small wild boars bounded in through the ferns, then transformed themselves into the chameleon species. They huddled with the humanoids who were negotiating the fate of the alien Juwaan.

A mature male and female lifted him to his feet, then handed him over to two younger males. Their clothing consisted of leather loincloths, their necks adorned with rough-hewn jeweled necklaces of red, yellow, blue crystal and turquoise. The skin of their backs were studded by small pieces of similar stones. Aided by short stocky legs, solid torsos, wide feet, and thick ankles and wrists; they carried his six foot, one hundred and ninety pound frame with ease. When he stood unassisted, Lucas' thigh throbbed worse when he put weight on it, but the bleeding had ceased.

The caravan descended single file through a valley of steaming cauldrons of reddish brown mud, which belched bubbles of septic and sulfur gas. Little breeze and high humidity added to the misery. In one such pit, the remains of a reptilian predator resembling a feather covered T-Rex lay with the lower half of its body boiling in the mud. The rotting neck and head rested on firmer ground where Lucas paused to examine the fist-sized eye. Even the hardened hunting party paused to appreciate this flesh eater by laying a hand on the snout and wrenching out trophy incisors.

Leaving the smog and death pits behind they carried their souvenirs up a high barren hill. From this vantage the humanoids celebrated the last leg home. Cupping his hands over his forehead, Lucas focused on a far off beautiful peninsula of rolling, green jungle-covered hills, with outcroppings of red and orange rocks. Having crossed the pits Lucas could see this primal community was naturally guarded on all sides. The desert dunes bordered the backside of the peninsula, fading off into a blur of brown dust. On the left the self-illuminating blue sea greeted the steep cliffs with pounding waves. His guides pointed and proclaimed, "Sharu, Sharu." Two of the party ran ahead.

Excited children and adults poured in behind Lucas' entourage and escorted him beneath a grove of immense cypress trees: root knots the size of cars. The trees formed a solid canopy the size of a soccer field with a round clearance in the center. Here lay a circle of seven six-foot, blocked red-orange sandstones inlaid with lines of white quartz. Along the inner edge of each block was a carved seat. They stopped at one of the stones and motioned for Lucas to sit. As his escorts left the circle, new arrivals with shaved heads, ornate colorful tunics and tan sandals walked in single file before him. One by one they bowed, kissed his right hand, then walked to their respective seats. All held solemn faces except the last. He kissed the back of Lucas' hand, raised his head with a smile and said, "Ah, the last of the Juwaans. My name is Shem. We are glad you are here. This is a great blessing." He turned and continued to his seat.

"Have we met? Are you the leader?" Lucas said to his back as this distinguished elder walked over to the next stone chair and sat down. Shem and all those accompanying him were more human-like, taller, than the original captors. With tranquil expressions and closed eyes, these six turned their faces upward, then raised open palms, waist high.

Lucas wondered, *What are they thinking, I am their lost guru?" for each sat in his own stone chair, positioning themselves to pray. I make the seventh. Who was my predecessor?* As the other six continued to slip deeper into a meditative state, he tried to keep his brow low, but couldn't help from peering around. The Neanderthals stood twenty yards distance from the circle curiously watching as they clung to each other.

Lucas contemplated confronting all of them right then, *Hey, don't you realize where you are? You're on a nonsensical, time forsaken, isolated island floating on a blue moon with a giant hole orbiting a starless planet! I call myself Lucas Tanner, not a Juwaan. I was dropped off by a hapless, semi-retired angel into your Jurassic park. Now please, if you would just show me the way out!*

Chapter 34

I am looking for a new world and a way home.

Lucas burned on the inside to say this, but he kept silent for the small chance that maybe he could learn something after all. Shem opened one eye toward him from his block stone chair. Lucas caught this and quickly darted his eyes another direction. He finally went along with what he called "the show," then closed his eyelids and extended his palms out as the others. His shoulders slowly sagged with pain until he opened his hands, palms up.

To his surprise, his open palms became like solar panels, channeling energy to his soul. A cool micro-climate crept upon him like the aftermath of a summer mountain rain. Each breath now also added new life energy to Lucas' depleted state. Floating in the moment, his analytical mind came to rest. He wasn't sure, ten minutes or two hours may have passed by. Just when he was soaking in the serenity of the moment and the mystical force drawing his palms higher, a voice interrupted the calm, "What are you looking for?"

Lucas opened his eyes to see that everyone in the circle was still motionless, their eyes closed. "Who said that?" he questioned loud enough for all to hear, but none responded.

Again terror pricked his mind as he unmistakably heard the audible words, "What are you looking for?" The voice was a low female tone with slight rasp, unknown to him, and unique. The crowd surrounding him remained silent as if they had heard nothing. A small mid-air arcing of sparks appeared and started to grow progressively brighter. Lucas used his arms to shield his eyes when in a few seconds this spot of energy became unbearable.

Not sure how it had come about, Lucas found himself standing at the foot of the chair. Spinning around he observed his own dark silhouette against the high back of his sandstone chair, the lines of quartz shimmering with energy.

Glancing over at Shem, he was perplexed that there was no bright light cast on him or his chair. Slowly turning back and filtered through the shield of his hands, he saw a brilliant blue white arc of lightening, floating in the air about three feet off the ground and ten feet high.

The voice returned and vibrated every cell in his body like an earthquake, "Lucas, what are you looking for?" and opened a flush of chemical emotional charge--a concoction of fight or flight, love and terror. Lucas mouth became slow and uncoordinated as this light compelled him to answer the question, "What are you looking for?"

Lucas strained to speak, "I don't, I don't know, what I am looking for. Who, what, are you?"

The voice responded as the arc popped in the background, "You have answered correctly, for I am the one you struggle against, the one you pretend to deny. My ways and thoughts are beyond you."

The skeptic in Lucas struggled to dismiss this experience and thought, *Could Ouriano be playing a parlor trick?* but was persuaded to confess aloud to the voice, "I am looking for a new world, and a way home."

Illuminating everything around him like a lightning strike he heard what he was determined to reject, "You have been summoned. I have pronounced that you shall be a Juwaan."

Lucas' independent streak still emboldened him to demand, "Reveal yourself to me. Let me see your face! Why do you hide?" Even so, his body began to cower at the energy before him.

The light intensified again as it spoke, "Am I like you that you should evaluate or critique me?"

For Lucas there was a numbing silence in the circle of stones. Everything was perfectly still, the trees, the elders, the surrounding Neanderthals – awaiting the answer.

"But you shall know me along your path. Answer me, how does this sea glow? Who gave the winds their swift wings? How many worlds do I keep hidden like a fetus in its mother's womb? How many stars have you walked on? How many galaxies have you danced across?"

Falling on his knees out of desperation Lucas, realized no hoax could go this far. "I confess, I do not know. Who, what are you? The unifying principle?"

The voice spoke again with a simple answer he did not want to hear, "You are a Juwaan."

With that pronouncement, the glowing arc disappeared. Time, motion, wind, sound began again. Lucas fell over face first in the red dirt. His stomach undulated with nauseous heaves as everything around him spun.

Tears mixed with sweat burned his eyes. He now lay in the dirt in a semi-catatonic state, suffering embarrassment before his more primitive captors with an alien voice engraved in his heart. At this low point, a wrinkled hand with long sinewy fingers reached down. The chief elder Shem helped him to his feet as all the five others arose, laid hands on him and prayed. Shem ended the prayer, and whispered, "Godspeed, Dr. Tanner, Godspeed."

Chapter 35

Your faith can make time a servant.

"Did you see the lightning? Shem, tell me you heard the voice?"

"Is this voice strange to you, Lucas? We hear it every day."

"No, I am not talking about some ethereal quasi-spiritual voice, I mean a real loud audible experience with lightning and energy -- right here in the center of this circle just a minute ago."

Shem turned away from Lucas, lifting his arms to make an announcement to all gathered at the circle while the other elders still held him, "God has many voices. He has to speak louder to some. That is why this stranger is sick. You of Sharu must help him." Then he turned back toward Lucas, and asked in front of all, "What did the voice say?"

Lucas hesitated with the response as an over humble person would, but finally repeated the voice, "I have pronounced, that you shall be a Juwaan."

With those words, Shem moved quickly back toward Lucas with brisk steps to within six inches of his face. The other five elders now left him standing alone under his own power. The Neanderthals reacted by all waving their weapons in the air, taking a knee and bowing. The elders, less responsive, looked at him like he was an innocent man sentenced to death.

Shem leaned in close to his ear as if he were examining his brain or taking in his scent, then spoke with a volume only the inner circle could hear, "Yes, I suppose you will be tested as a Juwaan. I am both happy and sad for you."

"Why, what is a Juwaan?"

"Ouriano did not tell you?"

"Yes, but it was too much to understand as it still is."

"It is hard to explain, but a Juwaan has something beyond intellect and good luck. When there is no way out, they can find a way. When evil comes, they run toward it. When others' vision narrows out of fear, a Juwaan can see in all directions. The gift and call does not come naturally. It must be developed."

Lucas asked with trepidation, "I must pass through more mud pits?"

"You will pass through more than mud pits." Shem moved his toe in the dirt, then spoke again, "Yare'ach Kachol may be the home of the angels, but it still suffers from the scourge of Beltshzan, as does your remote home."

"My goal is to get back to that home and put this behind me. Victoria is in danger. I don't have time for all this. I've been gone too long already!"

Shem answered, "If you survive this, you will make it back in time for all things. Don't confuse your time and agenda from where you came with those here. Your faith can make time a servant. Time is deceptive in your world. You may think it begins in your birth and ends in your death. That is a misguided platform to judge that which has gone before and will happen in the future. This encounter needs to be digested slowly. What else did you hear the light say?"

"The Light kept asking 'What are you looking for?'"

Shem reflected the question, "What *are* you looking for?"

"What is this, therapy? Isn't it obvious? Can't it be something simple? I was looking for a wormhole to a parallel universe, to probe the unknown. If notoriety among my peers and money followed, great."

Shem replied, "To probe the unknown? Is it possible to find something which cannot be known?"

"Shem, that is a good question."

"When you are a young warrior and energized by the hunt, all things look to be within reach."

"Yet Shem, you admit we have the drive to hunt the unknown? Where did that drive come from? I hunt for the euphoria of discovery. For us lab jocks it is exhilarating to explore the next something. Ouriano thought I was looking for a unified theory."

"Ouriano, he is unpredictable, so unlike the others, a dreamer. One day he may fall by his own pride. Have you ever wondered, 'what if I ran into something which was too big to hunt?' like the Leviathan which roams our seas? I understand from my pet, you became the hunted. Hah!"

"Shem, since leaving Earth, I feel like I'm trying to ignite a star by rubbing two sticks together. On the other hand, what is the story of this place, and what are you doing here among these cave people?"

Shem responded, "I have never understood why Juwaans don't appear here with more understanding. They are babes thrown into the mud pits with but a wicker basket to float them. Go with Peleg, eat, rest. He will be your guard. The echo of dark winds is near."

Chapter 36

We receive no signs from God; no prophets remain and none of us knows how long this will be. – Psalm 74:9

After feeding Lucas, Peleg led him to a compound guarded by four crudely armed Neanderthals. It was hidden by sagging cypress fronds from the soaring trees along the red-orange cliffs. They guided him through a bent, switchback of a gate made of tar-soaked, rope bound logs sunk into piles of boulders. A crude, carved wood double-door wedged between more boulders opened for them into a common area. Illuminated by a spring-fed pool at the center, the twenty-foot square walls and flat ceiling came alive with thousands of hieroglyphs. Many resembled patterns Lucas had viewed on his subterranean trip-- angelic beings, ancient rituals, flying crafts, but with personal story lines, including war, domination, and enslavement by a taller race of humanoids. Catching Lucas' attention in this narrative was a drawing of the sun and crescent moon.

Two of his guards stood either side as he tried to interpret sections of the wall. The epochs portrayed varied panel to panel. After a half hour, his guards walked up to the wall and put their hands and forehead against the engravings and shook their heads 'no.' Lucas' anthropology time here was over.

Next they led him through a crawl space entrance into another room. A small central wood fire burned there and lingering soot rose to a channel cut in the ceiling. The smoke irritated his eyes but the floors caught his attention, teeming with abundant soft animal furs. They motioned for Lucas to sleep. He lay down and soon fell asleep with his hand on his thigh wound as he searched for reality.

When Lucas awoke, he was being attended to by the stocky female from the hunting party who had both injured and mended his thigh. His old clothes were gone. She washed his feet and then rubbed oil on them. She smiled with her filed-down, perfect milk-white teeth.

Lucas said to her, "This makes up for everything. Not exactly Margaritaville here, is it?"

Just when he wasn't sure how much she understood, she spoke, "Ah, beautiful Juwaan you are. I will make you stronger than Shem. New clothes for you. You must look good for the hunt."

She curiously continued to examine him, washing and massaging the rest of his body. She pat dried his refreshed skin with soft hides, then clothed him with a loin cloth, gray tunic, and wrap boots. While dressing, he asked, "So what is your name? Will you be joining the hunt in case I get hurt?"

"Please call me Wayla. Yes, I look after you. Eat now, pretty one. We travel far."

She gave him refreshment: fish, mangos, and flat bread, chased down with a cold tomato-based drink he could have done without. She led him out of the cliff dwelling to join the hunters and the shift changers. Lucas didn't mind being the center of attention, but the whole 'Juwaan' thing still baffled him.

The small expedition continued toward the coast and stopped at a breath taking view of the pounding waves and foam three hundred feet below. Lucas could feel the cool rising vapor generated by the low rhythmic thuds against the jagged rocks. To Lucas' amazement this was exactly where they were headed, descending first a log ladder to an overhang rock landing, then down a rail-less case of switchback stairs chiseled into the side of the cliff.

They helped each other off the last step to a sheltered beach where they boarded two shallow-hulled wooden sailboats.

Lucas interrupted everyone by reminding them, "We may want to rethink our safety in sailing through these waters after what I encountered on one of your beaches."

Peleg responded, "A Juwaan should not fear. We will be sailing through the rocks where the Leviathan does not like to hunt. Open sea and beach is his hunting ground. Only for a short distance will we be open to attacks."

"Why bother?" he had to ask.

Holding the keel Peleg responded pointing beyond the breakers, "We are taking you to the desert of the dark winds to hunt, too far to walk."

From the back and forth motion, rattling and knocking around in the boat, Lucas lost his equilibrium to the point of heaving his last meal over the side. Reaching the calm waters away from the coastal barrier rocks, he now could see that a few miles ahead lay tan sand dunes piled five hundred to a thousand feet high all along the shores of calm breaking turquoise waters. There was dirty white beach, then desert -- with almost no sign of vegetation except for the drifts on the beach of old kelp washed ashore.

Lucas noticed that the small vessels had now picked up speed, with wind and current fully at their back, traveling directly perpendicular to their landing spot. Also, most of the party of eighteen were holding their long spears ready when four crustaceans dove overboard transforming their appearance to seals. *A decoy? Please, no!*

The boats hit the beach, sliding up the wet sand, and everyone jumped out. Grabbing the sides of the light vessels they pulled them quickly up a shallow creek about three hundred yards and buried the anchors in sand. The creek meandered through the wind streaked sand dunes into the haze.

Wayla smiled at Lucas and pinched his bicep to follow her back toward the ocean. She pointed toward the surf down the beach in one spot where a large wave started to crest, moving rapidly inland. The four seals came gliding out of the surf at high speed and morphed into dogs -- who ran even faster. And just in time, thought Lucas, as the deathly beach greeter pursued them like a lunging orca, the massive forward-sliding jaws snapping with gallons of slimy froth spewing in all directions.

It was a torrid, humbling sight for Lucas who asked Wayla, "Why is such a voracious creature allowed to exist here?" but no answer, for the deception had worked, making the Leviathan an unhappy predator. It let out a foghorn scream as it slid back into the sea, leaving hundreds of small fish flopping on the beach. Wayla took off running to the trench the monstrosity had left behind, Lucas followed in hot pursuit, catching up with her, and nervously helped gather sacks full of crab, fish, and eel. In the ensuing hours, Lucas stood back and watched helplessly as his hunting party cleaned, smoked and salted the seafood. Afterward the archaic peoples reboarded the boats and poled up the weaving creek to its end in the dunes. A mile inland, they ate, packed what they would personally carry, relaxed, then began the track deeper into the wasteland on foot.

Peleg kept pace next to Lucas, desiring to share the details of this mission, "You are going to help us hunt the Vranti. This foe from the past has unfortunately returned to the ruins of our ancient home to make assaults on

Sharu. It preys on humanoids for sustenance and needs little water to survive. My people are depending on you."

Chapter 37

Faith, once sprouted in good soil, will grow when faced with evil.

"What is a Vranti? How do we find it?" asked Lucas.

Peleg answered as they continued to trod through the sand, "It will find us. The Vranti loves arid places. It can cloak itself, hide in your shadows, make you lose your hunger and take your own life. The collective entity will try to isolate you to cut yourself or hurt others. The Vranti is an infestation of worms eating you from the inside. This one was bold enough to kill an elder. Shem sent warning to Ouriano."

Wayla caught up alongside Lucas from the other side determined to edit her husband's words, "Peleg, tell Juwaan the truth. Do not talk to the Vranti... it lies. Do not fear it, for it feeds on fear. Close your inside ears, for Vranti sows seeds of deceit. What Juwaan thinks it may be doing, you are wrong, for it has wisdom from its clan to call on. You Juwaan, must make for us a trail to the Vranti."

Peleg added, "You must pray we regain our lost home, our given place to worship to the one who sits above the angels."

Lucas asked, "That's a high request of someone like me. You have caught one of these before? The empty stone chair you placed me in? The seat of the last one killed by this Vranti?"

Caught between the two, Wayla and Peleg looked at each other inquisitively and spoke in a dialect unknown to him but sounded like an argument. Wayla finally completed their negotiated sentiment, "By word of our fathers and mothers, Juwaans come from long ago and far place to this desert to fight Vranti and keep from harvesting my people. Vranti can be slain, driven away, never captured like dog or pig. Even in capture, it is danger! Destruction only means another Vranti comes to repay. When last Juwaan came, she first mighty in the way of Siyon. Then something not right."

Peleg and Wayla paused and looked up. There was Siyon in all its splendor. Peleg looked back at Lucas, "I did not want to tell you, but Wayla insists you must know. This last Juwaan still lives in the desert of the dark winds held captive by the Vranti. You must set her free, if possible without exterminating her."

Lucas immediately wanted clarification, "The Vranti holds this Juwaan captive? Is she tied up, in a cell, a fortress or something?"

Peleg spoke, "No, it is a captivity without external restraints. She roams freely but under the Vranti's influence. The Vranti lurks inside her. She is very dangerous. Only another Juwaan can free her."

The hike was wearing on Lucas' legs. "Slow down please, why the hurry? Let's go through this scenario. Juwaans have these incredible powers and resources according to you? However, this Vranti pest made her some type of slave? If she were a Juwaan, how could she have become prey?"

Wayla waved off Peleg from speaking and answered, "She is like you, a new born in ways of Siyon, potential great, yes? The vision beyond her eyes not clear. Fear captured her in net. Let not this snare take you."

Posing questions to what he regarded as their myth, "Maybe she was not a Juwaan after all? What is her name? I take it she was human?"

Wayla walked closer to Lucas and held his hand saying, "We made mistake thinking that Ouriano had sent her. You know her maybe. We called her Anquanga, which means little fury. This Juwaan was of the earth."

I asked, "Why would you think I know her?"

Peleg answered, "She came to us looking for one called Dr. Lucas Tanner. All human Juwaans breed only from the Earth as once did my people. We answered, 'We have never heard of such a Juwaan. He has never been here.' The Anquanga told us she was separated in travel from her partner. We believed her. Shem had taught us that the last two Juwaans would come as a pair. He thought she was telling the truth."

Showing no expression, Lucas, mulled over her identity, *Victoria? How could she have arrived here before me, the technology we were working on?*

Lucas answered them, "I don't know anyone by that title, Anquanga? Did Ouriano bring her here?"

Wayla continued, "No, she came by one like Ouriano but more flesh and eyes of serpent. The winged one insisted woman you know, be taken to desert of dark winds, where we wait for word from Siyon. We named her Anquanga, because she became destroyer in the wasteland. Six warriors die by accident, but no accident."

Peleg added, "Her intellect combined with the Vranti made her a stealthy hunter."

Then Wayla again, "Fattened with friendship, we led to slaughter. She carried Vranti inside her."

Lucas rubbed his thigh, "So this why your people gave me the thigh check and great welcome?"

Peleg quickly added, "The Vranti has the power to drain away all hope. It makes the eyes dark, sunken; and makes the courageous cower in fear. They steal the sleep from the one they inhabit. To win in the struggle a Juwaan must have eyes which are not distracted, or they will begin to sink in."

"Why of all places is this Vranti thing allowed to exist here? Isn't this the home of the angels, the good guys in white, like Ouriano?"

Peleg responded, "Shem has taught us, 'things are not complete yet. Evil must have an opportunity to hunt so it can be drawn out of its dark den. The war is still on. Some of the angelic race have blood on their hands.'"

Peleg put his hand on Lucus' shoulder and said, "You are a Juwaan but not ready for Siyon. You must learn faith, to see with the eyes of your heart. Faith, once sprouted in good soil, will grow when faced with evil. Unbelief, once sprouted in fear, will try to choke out the good. This Vranti will not leave until it faces you. May the one who sits in Siyon give you courage. We are a simple race. We are depending on you for retribution to honor those we lost."

"I hate to go here, but how will I know if I have sufficient faith? Please tell me."

Wayla put her hand on his other shoulder, "No one come to Blue Moon or Sharu by accident. This time if we see Vranti filling the cup of your heart, we kill you. We judge by your fear. You will know when it is close to you, by the flies."

Peleg added, "She is right, this is the nature of the Vranti. After it took hold of the woman and our warriors died, the Vranti came and talked to us saying, 'When her friend comes searching for her, bring him to me or in time all of you will perish in dishonor.' Then the flies began to swarm. They became unbearable. We ran."

Chapter 38

Why do the innocent suffer? Some of the loneliest lives have the greatest consequences.

Victoria waited in mixed anticipation as her mother was brought in by Colonel Smith and Ru. Three thugs in suits were carrying her luggage a few feet behind. "Be an actress," were the words she remembered from her mother when life was rough.

Her heart sank at the line up of her four foot ten mother standing next to him. The more she looked at Colonel Smith the worse she felt. There was her mother, exuding hope and innocent trust, and she had brought her here with the help of these 'nice people' but inside feared she was leading her mom into a death trap.

From silent pain Dr. Pruett screamed, *Next to my mother stands the slime of the universe and if I believe Maria the Goth, a half demonic half human lecherous Nephilim megalomaniac!*

"Mom, I missed you so much. Wow, they brought you here, to where I work, and Blitz too! What did they tell you about your apartment?" she fumbled to be convincing.

Despite that, her mother said, "I brought some presents for you. Look how much Blitz misses seeing you." Blitz jumped out of her arms and ran to Victoria, his cute little nub tail going back and forth. Her mother then handed her a gift sack.

"Mom, homemade chocolate chips? Bible? Sudoku book? Knit blanket? Popcorn? You shouldn't have."

"I love my daughter," as she looked up at Cuzak. "I am very proud of her, she has always been a hard worker. Doesn't always take care of herself, very little time for men."

"Give me a hug mom." As Victoria placed her head next to her mother's, her mom whispered, "They took my cell phone. I don't trust these people."

At that moment regrets hit Victoria. She never gave her mother the credit due for trying to play the dual role of mom and dad in her life. She had always been much stronger than she realized, and now it was sinking in. *God, help me get her out of here.* Her mom had managed a private bookstore for years. Little Vic had no choice but to be an academic at heart.

Mr. Smith interrupted the nostalgia, "Ms. Pruett, we are so proud of your daughter too. She has almost no peer in the scientific world. What she is working on is of such growing importance to our government, her closest relatives must live under special protection. We know this may not be as comfortable as you like, but your daughter feels that with her mother living safely in close proximity, she will be able to finish this critical project much sooner. Do you have any questions?"

"I would like my phone back Mr. Smith."

"You will be able to use the call center twice a week. Our compound's design renders cell phones useless. Also, again for security, for the next several weeks we will not be able to allow excursions from the research facility. But I assure all your needs will be met, and the payoff for this sacrifice will be more than you could possibly imagine. Please bear with our protocol for a brief time."

Ms. Pruett cut him off, "My phone has all the numbers I would want to call in the memory." Looking back at

Victoria, "But honey, if this sets you up for life, I can handle staying cloistered inside for a short time. Is Dr. Tanner here too?"

"No mom. But I understand he will be joining us."

Cuzak added, "In few days. In the meantime, your quarters will be adjacent to each other, we are going to install a door between your apartments. Now if there are no more questions, the quicker Dr. Pruett and I get back to our project the sooner we all will get out of this place. Ms. Pruett, please excuse us. Your daughter is of vital national interest."

She looked toward her daughter, "Don't worry honey, I'll unpack and get Blitz used to the place."

Victoria started to hand Blitz back to her mother when he jumped and ran for Colonel Smith, alias 'Cuzak' and began nipping and tugging at the bottom of his right pant leg. The Colonel cracked a smile and reached down to pick up Blitz. To everyone's astonishment Blitz bit his forefinger and would not let go. The Colonel, holding the small dog in his hands, raised him to his eyes and stared at him. In a few seconds Blitz's jaws let go, he started to whine and began dripping urine. The Colonel put him down and he scampered back to Ms. Pruett, pawing her knee.

He remarked with a smirk, "Pets are so comforting at times like this."

The elder Pruett remarked, "Do you have a dog Colonel Smith?"

He ignored her by directing his conversation at her daughter, "Let's go and retrieve Dr. Tanner to help us finish this project. Good day Ms. Pruett, Maria, or you may call her Ru, will make you feel at home."

Colonel Smith and Dr. Pruett left the reception area and headed to the lab. He led her into a room inside the blast door area. In the center was a large oblong black marble table with a pile of old linguistic reference books at the center.

"Dr. Pruett, as you can see I am fulfilling my promise to you. Your mother is here and Dr. Tanner will be shortly."

"My mother has nothing to do with my present life, or private choices of how I live or what I do. Why did you have to bring her and her little dog into this?"

"Dr. Pruett, be more direct, you mean to say, 'why do the innocent suffer?' Some of the loneliest lives have the greatest consequences. You think your life is so different than others? You can isolate yourself at will from the rest of the universe? It doesn't work that way, never has. Besides your mother has the early onset of dementia of an Alzheimer's type. Deal with it. We are doing you a favor."

Victoria conceded another victory to Smith, "How do you plan to find him?"

"You are going to help me."

"But I don't know his location."

"You have gifts which have never been opened. Your love for him crosses even dimensions, time and place. You cannot hide your affection. I am sending someone to find him and bring him back. You may bristle at this next experience. I assure you everything will be fine. Remember these ancient beings are wounded and have suffered for a long time."

"Are you going to allow one to possess me?" Victoria was having a hard time feeling any sympathy for the entity she had witnessed.

"Absolutely not! You must remain a virgin. I doubt anyone could possess you, however it must touch and search you."

His remark brought less reassurance, "What is this one's name?"

"Does it matter, Dr. Pruett?"

With this remark Victoria suddenly lost it, raising her voice, "What is its name? Look, you've meddled in my life with things beyond my comprehension. I am forced to trust you. At least tell me this dark spirit thing's name!"

"Alright, it goes by Vranti. It means 'Hunter.' Eons ago it had a noble purpose of transmigrating through the universe discovering anomalies which endangered this bubble of creation. Its job was to fix them and restore order for the local deity. It has seen the surface of the most distant stars, traveled the fabric of space and was present when your DNA was molded."

Victoria asked sarcastically, "Yeah, but where has it been recently?"

"It has had to operate underground in shadows since the rebellion. In your history the Vranti has worked through image bearers until Beltshzan's vision became crippled. This Vranti is looking for a new home, tired of waiting and residing in fleshpots like the other fallen warriors. You may call it 'possession,' but understand, this is not the first choice of its kind. In this world their power is extremely muzzled while they watch the fleshpots try to self-actualize their cosmic, sheltered lives. How would you like living in the ocean the rest of your life surrounded by squid? Your biped mobility is completely inefficient for an aquatic life."

Victoria's stomach started to churn as she felt another presence in the room. Only one of the high backed office chairs was swiveled away from the table. Something was in that chair. The hair follicles on her neck stood up while mucus flowed into her throat and mouth to prepare for the inevitable backup of digestive juices. Chills spread through her muscles and she began to pray out loud the only thing she could recall, 'The Lord's Prayer,' "Our Father who art in heaven, hollowed be thy name, thy kingdom come, thy will be done..."

But another voice drowned out her prayer, reciting the remainder with her. When the prayer finished, the chair spun around slowly. Sitting cross-legged was something totally unexpected---a youthful man of Indian heritage, short manicured hair with longer than average side burns. He wore matching white, loose cotton shirt and pants, with heavy dark framed designer glasses and Birkenstocks. She would have taken him for an entrepreneur on vacation or a modern guru. He smelled of a light, expensive men's cologne, and spoke like a high analytic.

Chapter 39

The local entity does not want to lose face with his peers and his sacred angels right now. Eventually he won't care.

The man in white smiled, slightly tilted his head and leaned forward with his forearms resting flat on the table and said in a calm British New Delhi accent, "Eve, I want to personally thank you for the technological breakthrough of the millennium. I have been looking forward to meeting you for a long time. It will be a pleasure getting to know you."

For Victoria, he continued to speak like a creep who doesn't know when to quit hitting on a woman, "For those who desire, the experience can be a hodgepodge of mutual gratification. Did Cuzak communicate how I have worked with the greatest minds and egos of the ages? He finds the specimens. I harvest and deliver."

When this silicon-valley-anointed-one finished evaluating her and received no response, he looked over at Cuzak surprised, "What, he didn't tell you more about me?"

Victoria remained silent as the young man continued his verbiage, then he turned back to her. "That's a shame, but you should be flattered. I am not the only one in the room who would like to know you. Your suitors are many Victoria, as you have discovered a powerful tool, a portable back door we have been waiting for. In the last four thousand years we have groomed and cradled an enlightenment civilization for your kind. We knew this day would finally come. Instead of fighting the local deity we decided to guide the human posterity of Stardust to leap now from its pinnacle of development."

Cuzak had his arms folded, unimpressed as the Vranti rambled on, "Regrettably, for the most part your kind has tended to take the technological innovations and apply them to eliminating their own species. It is a brutish reflection on the local deity. We must act now before this world reaches its postmodern tipping point."

Dr. Pruett answered hesitantly, "I am not sure I am following."

"Please permit me a final point. I am glad you are secure in yourself to help us. This technology in the wrong hands could lead to unprecedented devastation and accelerate the ending of this screenplay."

She had to interject, "This is what the local deity wants?"

Vranti went on, "The prayer you began and we finished, is a testimony to the convoluted dialectic the 'one' led his little dazzled disciples into, who by the way eventually turned on him. Poor Judas, he was the most honest of them. Didn't 'the one' tell Judas, 'go and do what you must do,' tipping him over the edge? The whole plot was scripted. Who believes pain and suffering can bring about good? Those who do are crackpots."

Cuzak unfolded his arms and leisurely sat up from his casual slump, repositioned his cuff-links and asked, "Are we ready to move on now, or is there anything else?"

"I am coming full circle now. Let us review your prayer, 'and lead us not into temptation, but deliver us from evil?' Does it sound like he was questioning the motive of the local deity? Could it be he was using humans as the foil for his own stage set in his last act, the judgment? No doubt, the local deity wants to wash his hands of this chaos he has instituted and pin it on the image bearers and the rest of his double-bind puppets like Beltshzan."

Victoria did not like his all-knowing attitude at first, but did find him persuading in his persistence. The longer he talked the less menacing he seemed.

"Dr. Pruett, you may feel like a victim in this compound, but I assure you, if you had remained where you were, you would have one day been mopped up and reformatted for another of the local entity's cosmic experiments. Do you want to continue at best toward a *damned if you do, and damned if you don't future*? Go back through history, why does it continue to cycle through with such violence and pestilence?"

Victoria's gut reflex leveled out and began sympathizing with what he said. She took him as a rather charming intellect with a surprising common sense. She always had doubts of her religious experience and education as a slanted conspiracy of her mother's to keep her chaste.

So she replied, "It's like you inferred, the screenplay's writer has already written the outcome and is ensuring it will happen."

The Vranti continued, dragging his arms off the table and sinking back into the leather chair like a content man who had made his point. He adjusted his glasses, "The screen writer fought his own publication until recently because he knew it leaked his real intent. The notions of creation out of chaos, the flood, Babel, Israel's history of victim-hood, the day of the Lord, apocalypse, heaven and hell -- all have a biased slant, do they not?"

Doing her best to follow and now caught up in his crooked argument, she interjected, "Yes, it's like walking into a casino. We may win for a while, enjoy ourselves but eventually the house is going to eat our lunch because it's rigged. If you try to count cards, you will get tossed out. Which leads me to ask, are we trying to count the cards or build our own casino? Why does the local entity permit this?"

He sat silently for a few seconds as he looked up and then over to Cuzak as if fishing for an answer. Cuzak broke out with a grin and spoke to him, "You painted yourself into this corner."

Continuing to stare back at Cuzak he answered, "The local entity does not want to lose face with his peers and his sacred angels right now. Eventually, he won't care."

Remaining silent for a second, Victoria replied, "Peers? God, or what you call the local entity, has peers? So we are in a bubble after all? You have touched the edge?"

He reached out and clutched Dr. Pruett's right hand. She found both of his hands were surprisingly warm. "Yes, but you, Eve, have the power to walk us out of his bankrupt story and beyond the edge. You and your partner Dr. Tanner know the technology. Shall we begin?"

Chapter 40

We don't just need help, we need someone to take us in by the hand.

It seemed strange to her that several flies in this quarantined lab area would even be present to make touch and go landings on her arm and neck. Cuzak and Vranti acted as if they didn't notice anything until she pulled her right hand out from under his and snatched one of the flies in mid-flight, mortally wounding it. Dr. Pruett then turned her hand over and let the green shimmering insect drop on the table, dead.

The young man could not disguise the sudden flood of anger brooding inside. He stared at the fly as if it were a murdered loved one calling for vengeance. Yet, in a few seconds the fly trembled, regained its healthy form then vaulted itself in the air to rejoin the growing swarm. As Dr. Pruett was distracted by the herd of flies skirting her skin and hair follicles, Vranti's hands re-embraced hers on the table. The nagging stimulation caused her to instinctively attempt pulling her hands up to swat the swarm of now over twenty flies, which were buzzing her head, landing on her lashes, ears, nose, and lips.

Victoria tried to stand but the lean man in white held her hands bolted to the table. The Vranti became a frozen manikin, face expressionless, head bowed oblivious to her struggle to pull free. All the while the flies multiplied like a locust plague over her entire body; all sizes-- horseflies to gnats, black, grey, red, green, silver, stinging and entering her available body orifices.

Anger fueled Dr. Victoria Pruett's will to fight back, as she forced herself upright, screaming, "You're both liars!" Yet as she did, insects made use of the opportunity to stream into her mouth and lungs triggering a gag reflex. Next, her body jerked out of control with a convulsive reaction from inhaling, choking and gagging at the same time. The more she coughed the deeper the flies went into her lungs. Some were swallowed incidentally. The pain in her sinuses and chest felt like burning acid. Blood dripped from her mouth, collecting in pools between her arms on the table. "Ahhhhhhh!" she moaned while her bronchi were being reamed out by the larvae injecting bugs. She fought -- crunching, spitting and spewing the insects to no relief. Through her tear soaked eyes she saw Cuzak watch on without doing a thing.

"Bast........ards!" she yelled before her knees gave way allowing her to hit her chin on the table. The would be invader still did not release her hands, leaving her to hang off the side of the table by her chin and arm pits. By now all of her exposed skin and head were covered with the insects. She escaped further trauma by passing out, and visiting another time and place.

'I've been here before,' said the dream-state Victoria. She woke in her small hometown Christian church, age five, sitting contently next to her mother, before shutting out the faith at sixteen. Her dear Mr. Smiley was coming down from the choir loft to the steps in front of the communion table. He also served as her preschool Sunday School teacher -- white hair, yellow teeth, khaki pants, loafers, long-sleeved dress shirt, bow tie. This was the children's moment in the order of worship. All the young children were told their own sacred story before leaving the sanctuary.

Along with her friends Victoria crawled out of the pews to come forward and cuddle around Mr. Smiley on the center steps before the communion table as he shared his faith story. He pulled out a large sewing needle and a stuffed camel. "Jesus said, 'it is easier for a camel to pass through the eye of a needle than for a rich person to enter the kingdom of heaven.' Children, I am going to hold up this sewing needle while I pass around a few of these stuffed yellow camels. Who thinks they can get this camel through this little hole at the top of this needle?"

Victoria raised her hand and he directed his question to her, "So Victoria, you feel like you can thread this camel through the eye of this sewing needle? I'll hold the needle for you, go ahead." At that moment it dawned on her what she had volunteered to do was ridiculous and everyone in the church was watching and giggling. But for fun, she tried. It was no big surprise when she couldn't force it through. She handed the camel back to the teacher.

Mr. Smiley went on, "Young people, Jesus was asked by his disciples, 'if it is this hard to enter the kingdom of heaven, who then can be saved?' Jesus answered his own question, 'It is impossible for people, but for God all things are possible.' Now I want to ask all of you, if it is really this hard to get into heaven, then who do you think will make it?"

For a five year old Victoria thought this was a good question, but she wasn't going to be put on the spot again, so someone else answered, "a policemen," another "the President of the United States."

Mr. Smiley's come back was, "Maybe, but as a human accomplishment, no one can get into heaven. We don't just need help, we need someone to take us in by the hand. Who would be that nice?"

Victoria so much wanted to hear the answer, but she was sucked back into her present predicament by the voice of the Vranti. "You are so lonely. Yet you cannot say how you feel towards your friend Lucas. You love him, do you not?"

Victoria sensed the Vranti's presence seeking to seep deep into the sulci of her brain. He was trying to provoke an emotional response, "You have talked to him and miss him dearly. How did you do this? And he feels the same way toward you, excellent!" At his prompt she exploded with a longing and passion toward Lucas which had been pent up for a long time. She heard Vranti, "Yes, keep it up Eve. You know this is how you feel. It has been ages since I have visited Sharu. Let's go and retrieve our friend. I just need you to hold on for a moment to locate the relative time." Finally the possessed young man released her hands, allowing her to land hard on the floor, bruising her tail bone. She rolled on her left side and began to heave and spew out clouds of flies the same way they had entered. When she had finished the expulsion, Cuzak lifted her up into a chair. She felt him wiping her face, eyes, mouth, and neck with a warm, moist washcloth and then a soft towel.

Victoria heard Cuzak ask Vranti. "Well?"

Vranti answered, "We have located him. But you may have another problem."

Cuzak spoke through his intercom, "Please come and take Dr. Pruett."

++

Blue Moon Chronicles Book III, 12.2

Date: At training of last Juwaan,
 Third generation G-Class star formation,
 Fourth generation Angelus,
 Beginning of mass exit to Sanctuary

Subject: Learning from the past

Given our current situation, what can we learn from the past?--To never give up? Grasping the subspace channel of understanding and inner power may be life or death to the last Juwaan. This faith is what Ouriano says we must awake in Lucas and even the hybrid Ru if they are to have a fighting chance. I agree, but given her pedigree from Cuzak it would be more than a miracle to rid her of the reek of death.

Moreover, recognizing the true light has become increasingly difficult for us who have lived so many generations. The secret enemy may easily be "me," as we are all tempted to look in the mirror and declare ourselves, "God," and awake that hideous dormant contagion. Some call me wise, but I hesitate to acknowledge this, because of my own questions, like: "why does the Self-Sustaining One permit everything to be put in jeopardy by working with such frail beings?" and, "why is the Angel of Light so selective in her appearing?" I have no answer.

This is frustrating. This most ominous threat to the development of humans seems to have caught many who should know better, off guard. How can this be? Therefore we must prepare to counter the powers of the Sanctuary no matter how little help we are given. I suppose what we have is enough.

Maybe this is what we are to learn from the past.

 Shem, from the Blue Moon, the caverns of Sharu

++

Chapter 41

There are winds of light who are unhappy within the ranks.

By faith, Cuzak had trusted that Yazad had harbored him through the ages to reap the day at hand. Yazad's carrot? He would provide a home for Cuzak to openly propagate his species, build a civilization to call their own. For what other sustaining purpose existed? To Cuzak, Yazad did not think of his kind as unbridled half-breeds; rather the unforeseen evolution of the species. And now, finally, with the evolution of humankind's technology, Cuzak's race was going to overcome the scourge of the local entity.

"I know all about it," he told the Vranti, "conspiracies have perpetrators at both ends. Ru, my Maria, has helped Dr. Pruett communicate with Dr. Tanner. Anywhere Ouriano is involved one must suspect a subplot like this. Did you know Maria was almost killed by the doctor and then retaliated by shooting her in the leg as a cover? She, however, then healed Dr. Pruett internally but left the external wound. I sense Maria's powers growing. She is, after all, my daughter."

Vranti leaned his chair back a few degrees and adjusted his glasses. A fly landed on his nose, then crawled up his nostril, disappearing. He didn't flinch as he put his fingertips together and flexed his double jointed phalanges in and out as he spoke, "Before you become too proud, Cuzak, what has your daughter to gain in helping Dr. Pruett? I thought amnesty was dead. Maybe she has discovered the ill fate of all your little children of the world."

Cuzak replied, "Really, some say your collective is near extinction. Imagine that? What do you know? What have you given birth to besides chaos? Don't worry, she is going to help you retrieve Dr. Tanner. We'll help her commit an unpardonable sin. And amnesty is dead -- it died long ago when most of my kind was slaughtered."

Cuzak unlocked the secured meeting room door. "Come in Maria. You remember Vranti?"

"Do I want to?"

"Like it or not you are going to accompany him on a jump."

She quickly deferred, "Jump, to where? What are you talking about?"

Her father looked at her in silence. She finally gave in, "How would I survive a jump?"

Cuzak gently held her chin and kissed her forehead, "I know all about your powers. When you were a teenager I enhanced your potential abilities by waking up your dormant genes, allowing them to replace your more human traits. The motorcycle accident? In the middle of the night you left the orphanage on the back of the young man's motor bike? You were fourteen. He died. You required skin grafts. You probably thought I knew nothing of it."

"My lab grew your skin and introduced the genetic changes through your fibroblasts. By now you could survive the jump on your own. I am sure you have already experimented. You are my daughter, in her father's likeness, but unfortunately, damned by the local entity. I suspect Ouriano has gained your confidence? Would you totally trust one who hunted down most of our kind? Ask him how he received his scar?"

Vranti added to this, "Your father is telling you the truth. Ouriano does the dirty work. You won't discover the Angel of Light sullying her hands directly."

Turning her head towards Vranti without moving, Ru shot off, "He only does the dirty work because of the likes of your symbiotic, parasitic kind. You're worse than the vilest worm. You are not even in his league. You were nothing when you were infected and still are nothing. At least he is loyal to something which brings good."

Despite his disagreement with her, Cuzak evaluated with pride her stance to the Vranti, *Yazad is going to like her. The demons must be kept in line. They have no honor.*

Vranti stood up, the muscles on his temples twitching, "Cuzak, I won't be needing her help!"

Ru stepped in front of Vranti and grabbed his wrists, her magnificent wings extended, casting fluttering shadows across the room. The veins in her biceps and forearms swelled. She stared into this demonically infested man's eyes as her predatory pupils changed from round, soft openings to snake-like vertical slits.

Cuzak saw himself in her, as she demonstrated her developing strength and demanded, "Tell me Vranti, who do you serve?" The Vranti began to panic and squirm trying to throw her off, but the power of her wings allowed her to keep him pinned. Vranti's flies began to swarm Ru as they had Dr. Pruett. She condescended to him with every word, "Your cheap medium's tricks will not work on me. Why don't you go back to telling fortunes with gypsies?"

She picked him up by his shirt. He began to convulse, legs shaking wildly. The flies exited in hordes from the young man's body, even through the bottom of his pant legs, leaving the assistant lab manager limp. Pitying the now vacated, exploited bystander, she carefully laid him back in the chair and placed his glasses in his shirt pocket.

The flies then regathered, swarming over the table in the shape of a dark, hooded head, and spoke slowly in a low hum, "Your daughter will be your undoing, Cuzak."

He responded forcefully, "She will accompany you. You shall bring back Lucas Tanner to this lab. I trust neither of you as much as I would like. Yazad waits! Do not cross him, his network is greater than you know."

Vranti spoke, "Who will give us clear passage? And what about Ouriano?"

"It has already been negotiated by Yazad," Cuzak replied, "Both Dr. Pruett and Dr. Tanner must be returned to this lab unharmed."

Vranti spoke again from the shifting form of insects, "What was traded for the protection?"

"You and your associates have neither the need nor the capacity to know all. Let me say there are winds of light who are unhappy within the ranks. They would never give allegiance to Beltshzan because of the consequences, but if opportunity arose to leave once and forever from their own homeland, protected from retribution, they would take it. They will preoccupy Ouriano, blackmail him if necessary. The winds of light fear death, too."

Chapter 42

We came into existence as we now are. They were born as infants to what they might become.

Ouriano, all alone, examined his face in the small reflecting pool behind the head of his bed. The crows' feet and weathered creases were beyond tolerance levels. This called for self-motivation through the speech he had given others a thousand times. For many by the time they stopped to notice these symptoms, it was too little, too late. The infection process had begun.

"Ouriano, you need rest. You need to forget the things which don't concern you. You are not the Existing One. You don't sustain anything or procreate anyone. You do what you're told. Let the rest go.

I know letting go is hard. Winds of light and fire have few known enemies except our pride and the infected, and that is enough. Who we are is what we do. Clearly we are not the image bearing species. Those progeny of Stardust are destined to surpass those who keep them.

Even Beltshzan realizes the humans in advanced stages are the ones empowered to bring about his demise, not us. His consortium fears not the loyal host. They fear the human harvest of the Chosen One as they transform and multiply. This is why they sow the weeds among them. Only the One who navigates the Magnificon knows what powerful form the image bearers will ascend to.

You, I dare say, have never been to the Magnificon. It is the realm that is before all that was or shall be. It is the place where the source of darkness and light are hidden. When all else ends, this is what remains. Let your worship ponder the mysteries which lie at the core of Siyon, waiting for those transformed by the Heir."

Tiring of the stale reflection in the pool, Ouriano lay down upon his bed to observe the spectrum of scattered light rays dancing out of rhythm across the dome ceiling. He critically examined the chaos above and so initiated steps towards renewal, which began with a prayer of release.

"Let all things be what they have been determined to be, and let them all be to the glory, honor and power of the Wounded One upon the throne. May I become less as the One Who Sustains becomes more. Everywhere I have been, everywhere I will go, even all things I have done, whether imperfect or perfect, let them work to the greatest good and blessing for your beloved, the first fruits of your creation. Selah."

Reflecting his countenance, the scattered lights above were now forming into patterns. He trained his thoughts on the beautiful healing river near the Magnificon entrance. "Yes!" Ouriano could feel the deep vibration of the light energy; *soothing, revitalizing, assuring.* Unfortunately, just as he was experiencing the healing recharge long overdue, a perturbing and recognizable voice spoke from the entrance to his home.

"Ouriano, Ouriano, I hope you know what you are doing?"

"This is not a good time. Please return when your call is fraternal in nature."

As Veezon entered anyway, Ouriano recalled how he had trained him well; but Veezon's ambition, never to be admitted, had long ago surpassed Ouriano's vigilant preparation. And now, uncomfortable as it was to both of them, Ouriano officially came under his command, yet unofficially operated free from his unit.

"Have you come to lecture me again on how I have grown too casual in my contacts with the dark winds and Ru?"

"I am here to remind you most of our kind need and like structure."

"Is that what I need? I know what some are saying about me, 'Ouriano has gone too far, too long, and too many times, without the required light. He brings permanent damage to himself.' You are one of my accusers."

Resenting the incursion of his rest and recovery, Ouriano remained on his back while Veezon came and stood over him. Still focusing on the ceiling he said, "Veezon, have you ever been held responsible for driving any of your legionnaires over to the infected?"

"You will be the first to know, Ouriano. Already you serve as a catalyst."

"I guess I am not surprised you are here, since you see me as a weed among your well-ordered rows. Don't lose sight that these progeny of Stardust will continue to develop into more elegant beings than ourselves. Beltshzan realizes the humans in progressive stages are being empowered to bring about his demise. His consortium must act now. He fears not the loyal host. He fears the growing human first fruits of the Chosen One as they transform and multiply. For now he has no access to those on Siyon."

"And I ensure he never will. We have the same goal in mind; the means are what make us different," retorted the stoic Veezon.

"My military friend, it is those still in early germination who concern me. The right time for us to act jointly is now. Most of the humans are like unsuspecting cattle penned up next to a slaughter house."

Veezon looked up at the ceiling and turned the blade of his tongue again, "My lights are never in disarray like these. Indeed you are long overdue on your renewal; too long perhaps? We are the warrior class, guarantors of the Magnificon, reapers of the harvest, guardians of the chosen, messengers of the sodality, watchers of the sevenfold spirits, sentinels of the Shekinah, sustainers of the throne, flames of fire, choirs of the heavens, the four winds, riders of the apocalypse. We came into existence as we now are!"

"Very good Veezon, that is my point! Agreed, but they were born as infants to what they might become. They will surpass us."

Veezon's lashing continued, "Do you hear yourself? Who are you trying to convince? You are the one sounding the horn while you purposely lower your immunity to the infection? How many have you jeopardized by your flirtation with darkness? Here you lie on the eve of being overtaken by the creeping shadow because you have failed to observe a time of healing and restoration. You have no borders. Even the great Leviathan cannot stay down forever. Haven't you heard the abandonment reports are accelerating?"

"You are in the right commander, and I too have heard, and even more, grieve over those reports. My heart is out of syncopation with the light and I don't want to be on that list. But be careful where you point your finger. It can happen to any of us. In the end, it's light which shines in the darkness, empowers and heals. That's all that matters. Without the flowing essence from the One Who Sustains, we are assured to grow dark and grotesque."

Chapter 43

*A few with faith can achieve far more than
the legions combined.*

Veezon did not hold back, "My civilian friend, since we agree on this, where is your wonder child now? And the Juwaan, are you too weak to train him yourself? You dropped him off?"

Ouriano entertaining enough of this pompous speech, sat up and stretched his wings beyond either end of the bed, then stood up to him. "Have you considered that maybe a few with faith can achieve far greater results than all the legions combined, granted grace has a messy side?"

"Messy indeed."

"I purposefully left Lucas on Sharu with Shem's colony."

"A bit dangerous, but enlightening. Lamech's bunch on Wandu would have roasted him."

"No, this is not any better. A member of the hardcore Vranti collective is coming to try and retrieve him."

"He has permission to be here?"

"Yes, but with no others. We cannot intervene. The Vranti's vanity will bring out the Juwaan's strength. Shem will help him discover what he needs."

"If he is a Juwaan? Listen to what you are saying Ouriano, by everything holy in Siyon."

"Veezon, there is no commander of the legions equal to you. Sympathy is not your weakness. I will heed your advice, but I need you to back off. We cannot approach this with traditional warfare. They will avoid confrontation, and collateral damage aside, if we attack it would be an abomination to the greater purpose. Don't you remember when you waited for the summons of the Heir, but the summons never came, even in his wounding?"

Ouriano continued, "I know where all the Nephilim in the Earth quadrant are located. No one need tell me how there is a grave danger of them crossbreeding again. Do you think I have no memory of their destruction? I abhorred the decree as if it was given to kill my own kind -- and I have done that, too. When the order came to end the Nephilim I withheld all mercy. Some of them were children. Look at the scars I carry outside and inward. I am not like you; an impersonal warrior. Cuzak left me like this because I hesitated. Then he escaped for eons with several others of his kind to find Beltshzan's fabled nemesis, Yazad."

"You are not the only one with scars," said Veezon as he crossed his arms and dipped his foot into the reflecting pond stirring the water.

"I calculated where they had escaped and began to follow. None of our kind had ever been there. Before I could enter that new realm I was told to terminate the pursuit as it was beyond our viability. After Cuzak and a few others like him escaped me, I never hesitated on a direct imperative again. That is perhaps, until now."

"I know you Ouriano, you hesitated because you judged that it was not just to extinguish an illegitimate species. But what favor did your receive in return? Tell me?"

Ouriano slowed down his words, "He used my sword against me. But that won't happen again. And now..."

Before Ouriano could continue Veezon's temper flared, "And now this mess. You are repeating yourself. Ru, I think you call her? This Ru, this Nephilim-hybrid is a potential flapping, breathing, robust breeding menace. She is not needed. Are you going to bring back the dinosaurs to earth too? Never has anyone worked with these kind successfully. Have you?

We all know you think of yourself as the brightest star, the tip of the spear, the one who needs no supervision. May I remind you some of the greatest stars turn into black holes. Ouriano, you seem to have forgotten what separates us from the others? Your primary purpose here is to help this latest Juwaan fulfill his destiny. Instead you are making it complicated, involving too many adversaries, enemies, and those we have no reason to trust. It could all backfire. Ru, your pet project, is on borrowed time."

"Veezon, if I may speak? With all respect to you. At the time I didn't recall it expressly forbidden for the infected to try such an experiment of crossbreeding when Cuzak and the others were born. It wasn't outlawed, but I agree the principle and motivation of that act of defiance was horrible.

After the infected were cast down they had nothing to lose. We didn't know what was happening. Still we followed the orders and turned our swords on the infected half-breeds. These hybrids were very powerful and made war better than our fallen brothers.

We knew there was no way we could let them live. I followed the orders to interrupt the prime directive of free will because the infected had interrupted it with their novel homo Angelicus offspring. I was not asked whether I agreed or disagreed. I saw how easily the Nephilim could have supplanted the humans and other species. The infected thought they might build a stronghold of sorts on the Earth and in turn breed until they had formed their own kingdom alliance. We made sure they had no propagation and no hope of success. But that was a one-time edict. I have not received any orders for annihilation of those who have appeared of late."

Veezon finally arrived at what he came to ask, "It is only a matter of necessity. I don't think you are up to it if ordered. What will you do when asked to kill Ru?"

Ouriano answered, "I don't think that will happen. The Existing One has been known to change his mind. The question is will anyone under your influence act on blind faith thinking they are doing a favor? They will turn as black as any Vranti if they do. Listen to me, I know it bothers you to not be in the full loop on this. You will soon. I promise. I agreed with your military assessment, that complete overthrow is the only hope they have now, though futile.

Imagine for a moment, Veezon, the fallen ones were forced to watch the image bearers up close as the seed of Eve multiplied in a way which they could never experience again. They became insanely jealous. I don't pity them – but I understand them to an extent. We are breaking no code to try and understand what used to be our brothers."

Veezon spoke again, "Why do you dance with the enemy so? Others see you do this and have followed suit. Do you suppose that you will one day become a human? Ah, this is what it is all about! Ouriano wants to become a human. We all know humans desire to become angels in their prayers all the time. But now we have an angel who is moving to please the Existing One with the hope of becoming human?"

Ouriano pointed his finger at Veezon's chest, "Do you have no love for your kind? Can I not show them some dignity? You think this is a weakness? I don't expect anything in return from them except continued treason. The Existing One loves the humans more for reasons only known in the Magnificon. I admit to you, Veezon, I have tried to understand this love for the image bearers even though most of them are completely blinded to it. Yes, you have seen through me again, I want to become like those I serve."

Veezon urged, "Give this up! You are on the verge of treason. Your hands will be called on to shed more blood in the near future of their realm. It would not be wise to get so cozy. I know you are under an oath on the details of your mission. But don't confuse this with who you are and your purpose. He is the Lord of Hosts! Do not disappoint him. You were not made for this oneness you desire.

These feelings have never gone well for our kind. It is better to keep your distance like the 'guardian angel' they speculate about, who one day must stand aside, so death can come. Ouriano, what you seek is honorable, but remain within your bounds. Do this and you will receive eternal reward for your service."

"Veezon, you are my friend. What is my life if it always remains in the strictest of bounds? Such requires no faith. The Existing One would rather his flames demonstrate faith than blind obedience. I have been left in places with no communication and barely enough light to sustain me and have had to make hard decisions, which I've had to live with, good and bad. Have you?"

Ouriano reached feebly for the bed behind him and sat down. Before he reclined to begin again, Veezon made one last attempt to compromise before leaving, "Ru is going to have to pull the others out in the open. Don't be surprised when the order to kill her comes."

Chapter 44

*Forced communion reveals the weakness of evil; it
never achieves the intimacy of unselfish love.*

Surveying the lab through her office window, Victoria
tried to process the short-term hell she had been through
in light of today's test drive with the Vranti through the
portal. She wrote a note to herself and put it in her lab
coat, "Forced communion reveals the weakness of evil; it
never achieves the intimacy of unselfish love." Based on
her recent body and mind search during that experience,
she didn't want to know what the full blown possession
would be like. The thought of another personal space
violation by the Vranti prompted her to pray, "God, if
you are real don't let them inhabit me. If I lose myself,
then what have I to give you? Please kill this thing."

By retaining her mother for insurance, she guessed
Cuzak's real purpose of the test jump was to recover
Lucas. Vranti was going to pass through the trans-
dimensional corridor via a new human for fodder along
with her and Ru. The fodder had 'Jim' tattooed on his left
hand knuckles and a syringe on his right forearm.
Assembling with the others for jump preparations,
Victoria inquired, "How is the Vranti going to return?"
Ru did not answer but bit her lip as she looked at 'Jim.'

As they mounted the platform with power supply cables
in place, a cloud of flies came through the opened blast
door and swarmed through the orifices of the weathered,
middle-aged convict. He had a clean-shaven head with
tats above the collar line of the orange prison uniform.
Shackles and chains secured him. Just as she feared, the
Vranti entered him, triggering a severe gag reflex of
coughing and gagging; dripping large amounts of mucus
and blood.

Once in control of him, Vranti exclaimed in a male, Midwestern voice interrupted by a hacking cough, "A hardcore smoker. If they only saw what it did to their lungs. Don't they read the medical warnings on those cancer sticks?"

Victoria wore a pressure suit and assumed that Ru did not require one. However she passionately pleaded for the inmate, "My God, have a heart, you must give this man a pressure suit, regardless of the sludge inside of him!"

The Vranti in turn gave a long stare and grin through Jim to her, then ordered the lab attendants, "Go ahead and suit me, this will work even better." To Victoria's surprise they acquiesced. And then, with little more than a twinge of electrical current, they began the ascent and acceleration through the dimensional brane of space-time.

By means of her helmet's radio, she heard the Vranti speak through Jim, "We are going to the island of Sharu on the Blue Moon. We will momentarily be picked up by a dark winds ambassador transport and dropped off on the island. It is one of our favorite places to vacation and work. The little Erectus and Neanderthals are so much fun to hunt, tease and torture."

As the Vranti rambled on, Victoria replaced his voice with her memories of an enraptured view of the planet Lucas had shared from his dream; a radiant gas giant painted like a harvest moon. For several minutes they flew straight at it, propelled by Ru's magnificent unfurled wings. Victoria was amazed to see Ru as her true self, thinking how powerful and graceful Ru was.

Coming within a Jupiter's distance, all of them marveled at the Blue Moon beginning to crest over the golden orb. There was a magnetic attraction for all of them, but especially for Victoria: this live planetarium exhibit injected her with a deep sense of happiness and wonder.

"Maybe I do believe in God?" she asked out loud, just before other words leaped out of her mouth, "The heavens declare the glory of God, and the sky his handiwork." The words she recognized as favorites of her mother.

But the Vranti reached over and grabbed her arm with Jim's hand, ripping into her, "Don't be so pathetic, this local entity won't hear you. His little home-base hub has more important priorities than you."

Her resentment spoke back, "How can you be so sure?"

Ru added in, "Because our ride has arrived." She suddenly pulled them to a stop.

A rip in space opened up and a dark ship, one hundred meters long with sharp crystal-cut edges -- comparable to a stealth aircraft -- aligned over them and opened a bottom hatch. Upon entering Victoria felt a low vibration rattling her bones and organs. She didn't know if it was part of the propulsion system on the space craft or something worse. Before she could remove her helmet she threw up in her suit.

Chapter 45

She is a phenomenal specimen of a rare endangered species. She is at home with the infection, a carrier.

Ru then hauled her into a pressurized side cargo processing room with the Vranti and removed her head gear. Victoria wiped her mouth and said, "Can you feel the pulse in this ship? I think that is what is making me sick."

"Yes, it probably is."

"What in heaven's name is it, radiation?"

The Vranti stood up, and pulled off his helmet. Flies covered the entire face of the man except around his eyes, nostrils, and mouth. He said, "Ru knows what the pulse is, don't you? Tell Dr. Pruett what it is."

Ru, agitated said, "It can wait."

Vranti replied through the inmate, "What she won't tell you is that the lovely pulse is the heartbeat of Beltshzan. His pulse gives life to those who have the courage to break free from the local entity. Near his portal source we grow stronger. Would you like to try?" Vranti grinned at Victoria all the while the flies were going in and out of its mouth.

As Ru continued to stand with her back to the wall, she extended her arms to each side gripping a pair of handholds. The tips of her fingers were twitching in time with the noxious energy pulse. Ru's eyes stared vacantly across the room. Her face lost its soft edges and became more masculine. With Victoria watching, her nails extended longer and her wings turned from a smoke gray to black. Her chest and shoulders expanded with each breath.

Frightened, Victoria asked, "Ru, what is happening?"

Without a word Ru spread her wings above her head to the ceiling. The swollen vessels on their underside exposed a web of throbbing arteries and veins. The circulatory vessels were engorged, feeding the upgraded and empowered form, as they too were twitching in sync with the loud pulse on the ship.

Again Victoria pleaded, "Ru, what is happening?" but she did not respond. A new growth of veins began cropping up in Ru's face, forehead, arms, and neck. Her unblinking eyes dilated to quarter-sized, a gelatin-like membrane covered her black pupils.

Victoria attempted to peel Ru's hands off the grips but it was no use. She held her hands under Ru's chin and yelled in her face, "Don't let this evil overtake you!" But like a store window manikin, Ru did not acknowledge Victoria's attempts to rouse her.

But the Vranti still had more encouraging words to share, "You are wasting your time, Dr. Pruett. Ru is a phenomenal specimen of a rare endangered species. She is at home with the infection, a carrier. Look at her now. She would betray you in an instant for a taste of this power. Feel his pulse, feed on it. It is sensual. It is dark, and it is good. Ru cannot help herself. She is who she is."

Crying in disbelief, dizzy and nauseated, Victoria backed up to the opposing wall and slid down until she was crouching on the floor, when a side door opened. Several human forms from head to toe in tight, black attire came in and quickly stood her up, removing her pressure suit, replaced her soiled clothes and injected her arm. Then without saying a word they left. Sliding back down to the floor to sulk, another flashback came upon her, undetected by her preoccupied hosts.

She was in the hospital room with her cousin Nicky, both aged thirteen. Nicky's life had been disrupted by cystic fibrosis as long as Victoria could remember. She had watched her underdeveloped cousin take many pills and breathing treatments over the years but to no great breakthrough. She felt bad for, and protective of, her 'little' cousin Nicky. Nicky's mom made her cough and pounded her back several times a day to help her breathe.

Yet, this never deterred her cousin from having fun. In her flashback, Nicky's hospital bed was surrounded by balloons and stuffed animals. Bright sun light from the window was shining down on her as she lay there. Victoria's mother had told her, "Nicky's on the verge of dying, so we'd better go and visit her in the hospital."

Victoria expected the worse, but her little cousin Nicky surprised her. When Victoria walked into the hospital room her cousin sat up in bed beaming and greeted her, "Hi Victoria. I'm ready. I'm ready to go."

"Oh," she answered, "You're ready to go back to the house?"

"No, I am just ready to go."

"What do you mean you are ready to go?" she asked.

Nicky said, "I am ready to go home. I already talked to them and they said it was OK."

With that, she closed her eyes in peaceful contentment, then lay her head down on the pillow -- drowsing off to a sleep from which she never awoke. Victoria's mother escorted Vic away from Nicky's bed as medical personnel poured into the room.

Victoria's vision carried her to her own room, where she saw herself crying and mulling the events of the night in sleepless prayer. Nicky was the first close family member her age she had lost. She remembered part of her prayer, Life's not fair God, taking my little cousin! Yet for some reason now Victoria remembered that Nicky had peace about her she had missed.

"Nicky!" Victoria called out in desperation from her half-sleep stupor. Reawakened to her plight, she saw the humanized Vranti also mounted on the wall in a zombie like state next to Ru. Victoria spoke half dazed again, "Nicky, they are both plugged into this evil pulse. Help me, speak to somebody!"

Chapter 46

I'd say you are beginning to be overconfident, given
your short life history.

A voice came over a speaker, "We are closing on the drop zone, now entering the Blue Moon's orbit, descending toward target Sharu. Communications will be temporarily cut off."

Ru woke up and began to shake her head. Victoria asked, "Ru, what happened?" for her appearance had lost some of her sleek feminine form, replaced with more masculine bulk.

To answer, the dark angel on the wall referenced an earlier ominous conversation, "Remember when I asked you, not to hold it against me for possible future actions?"

"Yes," Victoria nodded, then asked, "Is this one of those times?"

Victoria watched as without answering, Ru's eyes dilated down to half the size of what they had been just a moment ago, and blinked a few times while releasing the grips and stepping to the floor. Ru then slowly walked over to the Vranti who also had released himself after gaining new strength. He stepped toward her pressing his chest against hers. Ru spoke first, a foot from his face with her wings open, "If you even try to enjoy yourself I will make sure you spend your last days in the abyss. I understand you have some old enemies there. No honor among demonic thugs?"

Vranti grabbed the outside of her wings and folded them down against her will and held them while he spoke, "I'd say you are beginning to be overconfident given your short life history. I thought we were going to be complementary partners. It appears Cuzak has a soft spot for your life compared to your mother's. How fortunate for you. I could tell you more, but why burst your little bubble of hope?"

"No one touches my wings, release them, now! There won't be a second warning."

Vranti was pushing his captive's body to its physical limits, straining to hold her, he said, "Here is how this will work..."

Before Vranti could finish his sentence, Ru's nails from her right hand pierced the possessed inmate's chest cavity. The man's heart tried to pump but the ripped valve chambers could mount no pressure, and so instantly deflated his physical strength and circulation to the brain. She slowly withdrew her dagger like fingers from his torso as he glimpsed down at his chest in time to see the mixture of flies and blood exiting from his wounds. Victoria stepped back against the wall in fear of Ru and sorrow for Jim.

The Vranti swarmed to form a large black winged creature, bellowing in a bass toned laugh, until distilling into its finality--hooves and hind quarters of a black stallion, mid section of a human, with three sets of wings unfolding from a ridge between the shoulder blades. A thick neck-head of a vampire bat, with folds of mange-patched skin and sparse, coarse, black hair covered everything from the shoulders up; except for the mouth and eyes, which were surrounded by wrinkles of pink, cracked skin. The Vranti's fingers and arms were gangly and long, composed of exoskeleton. His ears were pointed up and moved directionally like a canine. To complete this grotesque creature, his eyes bulged blood-red and his scent reeked of gangrenous flesh.

Steam rose from his breath, as he pronounced with arrogance, "Behold my power Nephilim, you second rate Lilith!" It wrapped Ru's torso with its left hand and lifted her off the floor as she tried to struggle free. The Vranti opened its jaws, unhinging them like a python, as it pulled Ru towards its open foul mouth, lined with two rows of drool-covered needle fangs and triangular incisors. The back tissue of his throat rolled with an infestation of maggots.

Ru responded, "Go ahead Vranti! This will be the worst case of indigestion you've ever experienced. Who would want to share a home with you? And what have I to live for now, that you have pulled me into this unpardonable river of transgression with your kind?"

"My little Lilith, how difficult it was for you to kill. What powerful rage! If you do what comes natural, how can that be a sin? Look how you fed off the darkness. Feel the power, daughter of Cuzak, you have only scratched the surface. Believe me, I make a better partner than an enemy, do you not think? Be warned, I would treat you no different than Ouriano did your kind. I was an eyewitness to the atrocities he committed against your race. Did you know he keeps Nephilim trophies in his lair?"

Chapter 47

I wouldn't be surprised if he didn't secretly have the infection. Everyone is being used by someone.

Struggling in his grasp, Ru ground out, "What Ouriano said was, he was reserving a place to mount your head. I don't believe you. You are a liar by nature. He would never work with your kind."

"I have already been to the abyss. How do you think I bargained out? I have an excellent memory for innocent atrocities," said the Vranti, "I wouldn't be surprised if he didn't secretly have the infection. Everyone is being used by someone."

The ship suddenly began to shake, interrupting their confrontation. Victoria leaned back against the wall to balance herself when all sense of motion stopped. Vranti released Ru, who stumbled until she could prop against the side of the ship. Unhurt but outmatched, she vocalized her first sign of submission to his domination, "I don't trust you, Vranti, but stay out of my way, do no harm to these people of Sharu and I will deliver the power of immortality to you."

The Vranti countered her offer. "Immortality? We want a guaranteed escape! And so will you."

Putting down in the midst of a tropical jungle, the three of them disembarked for Sharu. The craft immediately disappeared, piercing the sky against the backdrop of the golden giant, taking with it the aggravating pulse.

Leaning toward her, Victoria whispered to Ru, "Are you going to save me from this beast?"

But instead of answering in the affirmative Ru asked the Vranti, "Where shall we do this?"

Vranti, taking a moment to get his bearings responded, before launching himself in the air, "The power is beyond description is it not? Grab her, follow me."

With those orders Ru opened her wings and became airborne, plucking Victoria off the ground. The wind rushed through their hair as they soared horizontally over the canopy of the prehistoric jungle dotted by turquoise lagoons, and a matching brilliant sea in the distance. Spectacular was an understatement for this first time panorama to Victoria.

Yet tragically it was offset by her feelings of betrayal against this bird of prey she had wanted to count as a friend. As they flew above the horizon of trees and sea, there loomed as a sign of hope the golden planet Lucas had mentioned, taking up most of the sky -- so surreal and peaceful. So why is this chaos permitted here? she questioned herself.

Yet in the next split second her scientific mind engaged, *Gravitationally this can't be. With no anchoring central star, and orbiting this close to a gas giant planet, this moon should be void of any higher life forms, constantly rocked by earthquakes, volcanoes, and tsunamis at best. Yet here we are, a flying trio of three distinct species on an ancient, undiscovered world.*

Just as Victoria was taking all this in, a shadow passed over them. She looked up to see a large, No it couldn't be... Pterosaur? It skipped her and Ru and dove down on the Vranti. It snatched Vranti by surprise but unfortunately the prehistoric bird sealed its own doom. Vranti disbanded into a cloud of insects incorporating the Pterosaur's head and beak, until disoriented. It then rolled over and spun crashing to the bottom of the jungle valley below wiping out a grove of trees.

Frightened, Victoria asked, "Ru, what is this place?"

"May Siyon help you," Ru said. A few minutes later the Vranti, now reformed, joined them in flight.

They found an opening in the jungle on the edge of some hot mud pits and landed. Victoria's survival radar told her she was on the menu. The Vranti walked over to her as the volume of flies buzzing round her increased through the hot mud and sulfur vapors.

Ru approached him, however, and gently caressed his wing for a few seconds reminding him, "We have to bring them both back unharmed." She then stroked his torso with one hand while running one of her long nails gently along his wing ridge, then said, "I like power. Show me more."

Ru's distraction didn't work. His superior strength tore his wing out of her grasp as he snorted, turned his head and resumed his line of sight on Victoria. Meanwhile, he told Ru, "We will set the trap for he has yet to arrive. The natives will be no problem. They eat, mate, hunt and are satisfied. Shem and his kind however have ancient wisdom not to be underestimated. You will escort me into their presence. Do not fight them. Inform them you are a friend of Ouriano filling in for him. Go to them in peace and introduce me as a Juwaan. Show them your wings if they ask. Then leave until notified."

Victoria watched his body disband and fall apart into a million flies as they further swarmed her head. Panic-stricken, she took two steps to run but Ru cut her off and held her stiff to the ground with one hand on the back of her neck.

"Ru, no!" she cried as her last words were followed by the standard gagging, choking and spewing of blood; Victoria's fear of full violation coming true. Ru, lifting her now inert form from the ground, propped Dr. Pruett's limp scarecrow body erect until the Vranti filled her and hijacked all of her motor skills -- leaving her to become a third party observer, along for the ride. When the Vranti determined, he allowed Victoria to see the external world through her borrowed eyes, but all other senses were cut off. Worse, she had to endure the constant garbled echoes of his collective thought process. This time he took up residency, and so they began to move.

For the next three months, time for Victoria was difficult to measure. The Vranti did not give her body any sleep as she either floated or tread mucky, cold water between four close scum-coated walls. From what could be observed by Victoria, Ru and the alias Vranti in her body wondered in to a welcoming Sharu, winning over the Neanderthals and their elders. She watched the people time forgot embrace the foreign visitors as a great sign of confirmation from a past epoch she did not understand.

Those of Sharu in return blessed them with a long festival of food, hunts, and religious ceremonies. They sat in their high back stone chairs, ate, discussed, hugged, danced, laughed and pointed towards Siyon. Ru sealed the friendship with the tribal people who obviously considered her a comrade of Ouriano, giving free glides over the coastline.

Victoria became convinced, however, that whatever Ru and the Vranti were planning, it would bring harm to these people for the sake of retrieving Lucas and something more diabolical. On occasion she attempted to open a form of communion with the outside even the Vranti could not choke; prayers from her dark cesspool cell, but each time emerged a counter-force of constricting water snakes. They only retreated from the dark waters when she ceased her attempts at this arcane communication. She grew weaker to where even retrieval of good memories were blocked along with the flow of the odd visions she had been receiving.

Chapter 48

This desert is devastating to those who depend alone on their eyes to see or their ears to hear.

Peleg, Wayla, Lucas and the small crew followed the winding dry creek bed deeper through the dunes into the increasingly hostile desert. The reference points of the tall, red rocks of Sharu to their north and the eastern sea behind them were no longer visible.

Lucas vocalized his frustration at this uncertainty, "This entire trip is beyond my internal compass. Who's gonna believe this? And now I face the prospect of rescuing Victoria from an enemy I am not sure exists? She must have used our technology to come and look for me but the time shift was off slightly. Do you really expect me to slay my friend?"

Wayla and Peleg heard the question but gave no answer.

In urging them to speak Lucas asked them, "So what does Shem say about the desert of the dark winds?"

Peleg answered, "Shem has a voice and we have a voice. The desert of the dark winds is place of shifting sands and changing lights. It was once our home until the purging of the infected began. Beltshzan fled here from the inner world, setting up his ring of fire and driving out or killing our people. He forced our ancestors to worship him but most refused at the cost of their lives. The land began to die--the trees wilted, the animals for hunting disappeared, farms were overtaken by encroaching sand, remaining grass lands burned. They aimed their spears and arrows at Siyon from here but their bows and shafts were broken by the loyalists, then exiled.

Most of my people's history and home was lost. Still, this land has memories. We believe this place exists for the Juwaans to face themselves and one day help us restore our home. For now this desert is devastating to those who depend alone on their eyes to see or their ears to hear. The deeper one treks into the desert the more obscure is Siyon. The continual dust storms can block the view, and worse, they can form the black cloud of unknowing."

Wayla then spoke, "Peleg, we go no further! This boundary is ruins of ring. You, Juwaan must enter alone. Inside old ring Shem says, 'heart of Beltshzan still beats.' He offers power, pleasure if heart is one with him. You will be tempted so great. Do not trust your feelings, even for woman!"

"I believe you. Is there anything else, Wayla?"

"You must be hunter."

Peleg spoke, "We entered the ring with your friend, the Anquanga. We presumed she was a Juwaan and were sabotaged. The Vranti gave her power to see in the dark."

"What will be my weapons?" Lucas asked.

Peleg spoke, "Take this ebony spear, this cloak, and your wisdom."

Wayla, to a surprised Peleg, called one of the other men over, who handed her a medium leather sack with a drawstring at the top. She exchanged it for Lucas' spear leaving him and her partner baffled. "Wayla happy to give this to Juwaan. You open."

Lucas opened the bag and pulled out a rough piece of glass about eleven inches long and seven wide. He recognized it as melted sand formed from an atomic blast, smooth and shiny on one side, about two inches thick. He tilted it towards his face and reviewed his reflection despite the tarnished surface. Lucas asked the pair, "What possible help is this going to be, to shave?"

Wayla said, "This to see through black cloud when Siyon is gone. This stone will show light of Siyon when you no longer see."

"Did Shem give this to you?" Lucas inquired.

Wayla answered tepidly, "Alone, the winged woman with predator eyes said, 'Give this to second Juwaan, a man who comes soon. Tell no one.'"

"How can I trust a gift from the winged woman after she led your people into bloodshed?" Lucas asked, while Peleg shook his head in disbelief.

Wayla continued, "She said, 'Tell him Ouriano gave it to her, but bring back.' Peleg knows our weapons are only warm coal against raging fire. Go now, we wait for you at these ruins. Avenge us!"

Lucas still unsure asked, "How will I find her and the Vranti?"

Peleg answered, "As we told you, the Vranti will find you. The only aid we might give you is if you can wound it first. Otherwise we would be like mice in a snake hole."

Lucas hugged them, then ventured through the stone rubble underneath a broken high arched gate. To either side in opposite directions were the four to six foot remains of the old thirty-foot walls. The winds, dust and sand were negotiable at first, but grew in velocity the further he walked. Below his feet the sand was soft, but the crust six inches beneath popped like thin ice with each step announcing his movements. The sky welcomed him with darkening haze the further he trudged. Half a day later and staggering in complete disorientation, Lucas ended up back at the gate where he had begun.

From his experience of hiking at youth camps roving the Rockies, Lucas understood walking in circles was a sure sign of being lost. Human nature led lost people in the wilderness to travel in circles. He knew hiking safety rule number one, "When absolutely lost the best thing to do is sit still until the authorities come to rescue you. If one doesn't heed this advice it can lead to panic attacks and death due to exposure and depression." Researchers had well documented the hallucinogenic state people achieved just after a few days of wilderness disorientation.

He confessed aloud, "This is exactly what I feared, I am back where I started." In a last resort, he pulled out Wayla's gift from the winged woman. "A little magic right now would be appreciated. Hello up there, Ouriano, anybody? Surely this isn't how it ends?"

Removing the gift from its pouch with no idea how to use it, Lucas experimented by tilting the polished surface in all directions. To his astonishment, aimed at a particular angle, the talisman sent a piercing beam of bluish white light through the hovering waste in the air. *No more walking in circles today! Confront the enemy! Now lead me to Victoria. He wrapped the cloak around his head and mouth against the swirling dust, and walked on.*

Chapter 49

*I am a terrible agnostic. My desperation led me to
believe I had nowhere else to turn.*

His ears sensed the pressure change of a heavy mass,
though quiet as an owl in flight, pass only a few feet over
him. Peering through the gaps in the makeshift air filter
wrapped around his head, something zipped across
Lucas' path before he could acquire any recognition. In
an autonomous response to an unseen presence, his
adrenals squeezed hard, elevating his blood pressure and
heartbeat.

This time a flickering shadow teased his awareness, but it
was very hard to judge through the blowing grime. Eyes
moving back and forth, he fixated on a dim illumination
to his right. It reminded him of walking through a
snowstorm toward the dull lights of a car stuck in a ditch.
He slid the mirror back in the pouch and slowly
approached.

Lucas released a whispered, forlorn prayer, "Please, if I
am supposed to be here show me something. This is the
time to help me out. I didn't ask to be a Juwaan. Eight to
five for a large non-profit or monitoring an array of
telescopes in an exotic place is real appealing. Deal?"

Encroaching within thirty yards, his target was still dim,
smothered by the dense, scratchy fog of dust, but within
ten steps the light source magnified a hundred fold. Still,
through the gritty dusk his imagination struggled to
stitch together the pieces of what stood before him, *A
white piece of marble, a Pegasus statue?*

He figured it out. From his darkened vantage point, he
was squinting at the back of a large pair of luminescent
white wings with two gold human feet at the bottom.

Mesmerized by the incredible beauty, he slowly unwound the cloak from his head for better scrutiny. But his stealth did not go undetected. This being's aura turned toward him with the bright radiance of the light he had experienced in prayer with Shem and the elders. In this helpless moment he became the deer in the headlights. Terror broached his psyche at first, but then hope returned when he heard the familiar voice.

The vibrato was similar to the penetrating voice he had heard before in Sharu, but more smooth, yet still conducting a power to draw out the truth from anyone it addressed. "Fear not, Juwaan, for this you were born. I come in peace. You may not believe in me, yet I have followed your creation from the Magnificon to the day you were planted in your mother's womb. This is all that matters: that I plucked you from my imagination."

Lucas tried to respond, but his tongue became disconnected as his inmost being ascertained his inferiority, causing him to fall to his knees and hands.

"You are right to worship me, but your heart lacks wisdom. You have no understanding of your own history, do you? You have no memory of your world's past tragedy, or thought of the long-coming intervention?"

The best Lucas could do was give a darting glance at the source of the voice, for the light was too intense to distinguish facial features. The human silhouette extended her hands towards him through the glowing haze and then separated them left and right as if holding a globe. Her radiance dimmed while a three dimensional hologram appeared between her hands, still blocking her countenance. An early teenage boy appeared, examining slides through a microscope. Lucas recognized his bedroom wall posters -- shots from the Hubble telescope and Einstein with his tongue hanging out. Ginny, his first girlfriend was sitting at his bedroom desk helping tutor him in math, of which he had feigned ignorance for her attention. More animated episodes of his life and those of previous family generations progressed as the being of light spoke.

"If you have no history then you are self-made. Your god has been your delusion of self-discovery. Even the dog who follows the crumb trail to the wedding banquet does not assume the leftovers were of its own invention. You think, therefore you are? You determined your own birth? You have determined your death as well? What are you proposing to do in this desert of the dark winds?"

Lucas, with every hair on his body contracting to the life energy before him, had nothing to say. It was all he could do to bask in the electrifying, holy silence. He did notice the wind had stopped and a clear bubble of clean air surrounded them. The angel now separated her hands vertically, enlarging his life hologram. This time he recognized himself in her hands as an old man walking through a graveyard delivering flowers. He placed the mixed bouquet on an unmarked grave. Lucas finally summoned the courage to ask, "Are all these things predetermined?"

The grand entity of light answered, "All rivers have a headwaters and an end. They carve many channels along the way to the sea. The more difficult the way, the more beauty they create. Your river has deep channels yet to carve if you so choose."

The hologram continued to evolve, red smoke now filtering out of it. There he was, in church, just before the initial jump in the lab with Victoria. He had walked in to this old downtown church out of desperation. The 1950's vintage sanctuary probably had not been full in decades, but it brought back memories. A lone church secretary in an adjacent office guarded the slow decaying museum.

He gained her permission and sat in the second from the last pew, took a breath of the musky air and let his eyes ease over the high vaulted ceiling to the large lit gold cross over the communion table. He watched himself attempt to pull information from the God he didn't believe in to help interpret the reoccurring vision.

He defended himself, "I am a terrible agnostic. My desperation led me to believe I had nowhere else to turn. I knew when the preacher questioned me in the back, someone was listening."

And then he watched her display his vision of the golden planet with the blue cresting turquoise moon. The Angel of Light held them gently between her hands without touching them.

Lucas blurted without thinking, "Will you show me my future?"

The desert angel responded with a poem,

"I will sing a song which imparts wisdom,
I will utter hidden things from of old.
Your prayers rise up like fragrant incense,
Ever before my throne.
Blessed having never seen,
Before you were born I knew you,
I will not ignore my own."

When the poem pronouncement ended she asked, "Let me have your mirror."

Still on his knees, Lucas untied the pouch and removed the rough mirror. "Here" thrusting it forward with one hand.

"Stand!"

He stood and handed her the mirror. The angel put her hand on the surface, whereby she heated it to a molten, burning orange glass. Then cooling it with her breath, she beheld the new tempered surface, and declared, "It is good." At these last words, an immense concentrated burst of light blazed from her face into it. The laser like beam reflected up, burning a hole through the thick dust clouds, stretching through the canopy of the Blue Moon toward the large golden planet.

Lucas jumped at the sound of the thunderclap from point-blank range. The crust beneath his feet shook from the concussion, knocking him to the ground, while the outbound shock waves announced his whereabouts to anything inhabiting the ring of energy disturbances.

This Angel of Light spoke again, "Take my light which makes all things new." Lucas, rolled over and raised up on one knee with his head bowed in awe, hands reaching out before him. She then placed the altered talisman back into his hands, still warm to the touch. The rough edges had transformed to blue glimmering crystals and the flat exterior now resembled a liquid silver glass. Lucas ran his fingertips back and forth across the surface, intrigued by its absolute polished perfection and the calming sensation it gave him.

Chapter 50

Divine intervention is not without its own pain

The mysterious creature said, "Look into this mirror and you will find your life."

With two hands Lucas lifted the mirror to shoulder level expecting to see his reflection, instead an image of the angel's countenance began to fade into view. Alas, he almost could see the detail of her facial features when a sudden blinding light and blistering wind blasted out from the mirror, rocking back his head.

Moaning out loud in agony, he tried to reposition the mirror and rip his fingers from the object, but to no avail. The gift remained frozen in his hands with the searing light beam locked on to his eye sockets. With his hair flaring back from the wind blast, the muscles around Lucas' eyes, cheeks, and temples cramped and contorted to block the light. His eyelids flipped back. Surges of electrical stimulus jarred his optical nerve pathways.

He knew in a few seconds nothing would be left of him by this hot white laser. At the peak of this searing pain and blindness, he heard the Angel proclaim with voice of a ten thousand watt amplified speaker, "I pronounce before Siyon and your enemies, you are Juwaan!"

And then it was over. The beam stopped. He tossed the mirror aside, but the seared nerve endings and flash blindness dropped him to his knees for the relative safety of groveling on all fours. Wailing out in anger Lucas screamed, "Why have you caused me to suffer like this!" Frantic, he grasped out in darkness for her foot, a leg, or an extended hand, "Help me. You can't leave me alone in this desert. Where are you? Tell me your name?"

Wiping the tears and mucus off his nose, "Of course, could I expect more? You won't explain yourself except to call me a Juwaan?" The silence was deafening, his cynicism high when his searching fingers stumbled back upon the mirror. Still warm Lucas curled around the fetish stone in a fetal position and cried out, "Angel, is this what you call help?"

Clutching the mirror under one arm, and laying in the sand, he stroked the mirror surface. To his astonishment the burning sensation in his face was receding. Against better judgment he held the mirror back up to his forehead, opened his blinded eyes and then gaped in shock when a blurry, then crystal clear vision of a man with a bad case of bloodshot eyes and white hair stared crisply back at him. But bloodshot eyes weren't the only change in his eyes -- he also observed new bluish white beams of light projecting through the center of his powder blue irises.

Lucas smiled and the man in the mirror smiled back. He began to laugh. "Ha, ha, ha... ha, ha," he roared.

Gasping from his laughter, he lowered the mirror. Oddly at peace now, he looked around him. The blowing dark haze glowed in front of him by the dispensation of photons from the light within his eyes. Lucas gave thanks as the strength of his body and mind charged back with a vengeance. He proclaimed, "I am the hunter. Please forgive me. I was too quick to judge you, Desert Angel."

Now, when he paused to look up through the layers of soot, he could see the faint glow of Siyon. Surveying around him, visibility was still dreadfully low except the immediate ground. Determined, he trudged for another two hours until he ran into a wall made of large pyramid cut sand stones.

"I'll find you Victoria!" he proclaimed out loud, then followed the base of the wall until crossing paths with an ascending eight-story staircase. At the top, Lucas surveyed a flat, rectangular platform by walking its borders, which he discovered to be roughly the size of a city block. Finding nothing on the edges he headed through the dark haze toward the center.

"*A place of worship?*" he asked himself, for in the center were similar elder chairs cut of the same rock as those in Sharu. Examining the first seat. he noticed a worn out engraving on the back support: two intersecting pinwheel galaxies. Walking over to the next chair was an engraving of a foreign solar system. On the back of the third stone chair were the two spheres the angel had shown him.

Peering in the fourth, he jumped back, collecting himself a moment before approaching the slumped body of a Neanderthal's remains, upon whom he found no apparent wounds. The blowing sand had worn part of the flesh away, exposing the cheekbone. A few flies buzzed around its skull and from the eye socket wiggled a few maggots. In the next elder chair he found another body, and then the same in the next, and the next.

Victoria would never have participated in this, would she? While he contemplated this, a cloud of flies stirred around his head like the genesis of a dirt devil. Victoria, if she is the monster they warned me about, must be near. *God, don't let it be her.*

He heard the shuffling of feet sliding on the sandy stone foundation. A stench came up. Two shifting red dots became visible from across the shrouded court. *The Vranti?*

He heard movement again, then a voice he recognized call out, "Lucas?"

"Vic?"

Out of the blackness her voice returned, "I missed the time mark and landed ahead of you. I see you have made it. We will be together again, forever. We can finish what we started, you and I."

Lucas assured himself the voice itself sounded exactly like her, yet not the strange romantic jabber. "They are changing everything back home for the better. Come to me my love. I've come all this way to find you. Where are you? Speak to me. Share with me your passion in this far-off place."

Something isn't right... think fast! surmised Lucas, dragging one of the emaciated bodies from an elder chair and replacing himself in it. He closed his eyes to conceal the light of his eyes, then pulled out the mirror and put it on his lap. Placing his hands to his side, palms up, he began to pray as Shem and elders of Sharu had.

He rehearsed the words of the Desert Angel, "You are a Juwaan!"

Meanwhile the flies continued to dock and dive, massing on his eyes, ears, nose, and mouth until they were several inches thick on his head. He swiped at them but it was a waste of effort, so with all his will power he lowered his hands back down into the prayer position.

The voice and the shuffling of feet were within ten yards. Waves of a dark, depressive force crashed like a tsunami over his emotions. The insects were now forcing themselves through all available avenues into his body.

Lucas recalled the warning of Peleg and Wayla. He wanted to bolt up and run in any direction rather than face this. But then, he heard the voice of the one he accused of forsaking him, "Open your eyes Juwaan!"

Chapter 51

A little light cannot get in the way of our destiny.
Sorry to disappoint.

The decision was easy. The instant he opened his eyes, the bleached laser beams bore down into his lap, becoming one as they reflected off the smooth liquid silver surface, arching a high, thick low-pitched pulsating beam through the shroud of darkness toward Siyon. Extraneous power streams also exited his nostrils, mouth and ear canals chasing out the infestation. Any insect caught in the light were fatally singed.

Lucas set the mirror on the ground with the vertical beam illuminating the entire circle of elder chairs and two other stone seats now visible in the center. A dragon was engraved on the slightly larger chair and a voluptuous woman was etched onto the smaller. He caught a glimpse of Victoria running to hide behind them with flies in retreat toward her.

Leaping up to pursue her Lucas shouted, "Victoria, wait." But when he ran to the back of the two seats she was gone. He turned around supposing Victoria's puppet master behind him, but heard the baffling of air from the opposite side and so spun his face in time to receive a solid blow to his forehead by a tattered flying shadow, "Auhhhh!"

Wobbling like a stunned boxer, his legs buckled. The beast in wasting no time descended upon him in another pass, snagging his ankles, flinging him across the fitted stone surface of the courtyard like a shuffleboard piece. He hit hard against one of the stone chairs, cracking two ribs.

Remaining focused, Lucas remembered, *The mirror, I need to get to it.* Rolling over three times put him in reach, however it suddenly moved out of his grasp by means of a lone, dirty bare foot and ankle scooting it across the stones.

Lucas peered up for the owner who now stood over him. Extending her hand down, he took it and she lifted him to his feet with ease. She forced a crooked smile, her eyes dark and sunken. Even so, he held her in his arms, noticing the light of his own eyes reflecting off *hers,* "Victoria, wake up!"

While he embraced her a large fly landed on her upper lip and crawled up her left nostril, to which she gave no notice. Girding up the courage, he shoved her as hard as he could and dove for the still beaming mirror. As he launched himself, the Vranti also reached for control of the sacred photon conduit.

Lucas clutched it first, rolling to avoid a wild blow from the forearm of the Vranti's wing, but then came around aiming the beam toward its gruesome head. The light instantly seared the flesh, causing it to screech in pain.

"We all get what we deserve in the end," scowled Lucas as he held the beam on the Vranti.

"Is that so?" Victoria said, lifting him off the ground by a chokehold while she stood on the woman's seat he had backed into. The hold rendered him helpless to do anything but gasp for air. All the while, the beast recovered itself, and pulled the mirror out of his limp hands.

Victoria whispered in Lucas' ear, "A valiant effort my love. A little light cannot get in the way of our destiny. Sorry to disappoint."

Then the beast threw the mirror into the stone seat of the dragon. Upon impact the mirror exploded into smaller pieces and severed the stone seat in half. The shards went in all directions like discarded flashlights, rolling across the pavilion. The Vranti now turned toward the coughing Lucas as Victoria released enough pressure to allow him to stand on his feet.

The monster spoke to him, "A brave image bearer you are, what a shame you are so low on the food chain. I always enjoyed permission to come back here and spar on this unholy ground of Beltshzan. Your diminutive genetic kinsmen here provide so little obstacle to the hunt, a pathetic group trying to secure their lost nobility. You on the other hand, may still find a future, as a son of Yazad if you desire."

No sooner had he finished saying this, Lucas heard Victoria grunt as the tip of a javelin spear pierced through her right side, just missing him. As she released him, he put his hand on the bloody spear point and turned around to see tears coming out of her eyes.

A spear also hit the Vranti in his thick, equestrian right hindquarter as he scoured the platform for the source. "What is this?" he said, "You do not hunt alone?"

Peleg and Wayla came out of nowhere with another spear and bow in hand. Vranti bellowed *out*, "You come before me with spear and bow? There is a reason you never survived the humans on Earth. Against you I have license to kill just for the sport. You should not have wandered into this desert of dark winds and dark wisdom. And if this girl dies I will come back and end your genus forever."

From out of the dark, Shem walked up from behind the broken seat and stood before the Vranti empty handed and pronounced,

"Listen to the prophecy from of old, my ancient foe.
'A son of hell you followed.
A son of hell you have become.
Against courage and light from Siyon,
Your life essence will soon be done.'"

Before he finished the last line, four of the crustaceous creatures in the form of grey wolves attacked his thoroughbred thighs, locking on to the hamstrings. At this, the Vranti raised his leather wings and took off to lay devastation to the warring party from Sharu. On the way up his jerking and kicking cast the wolves to the rock floor five stories below, smashing their exoskeletons. Then, as he reached his apex some ten stories high, he banked to begin his return dive, but was halted by a convergence of many small light beams.

The Neanderthals had been observing the entire episode and so reacted quickly gathering up all the scattered shards of the light-bearing object, bringing them to bear on the beast. Caught off guard, the Vranti became trapped by the cross beams of light which instantly began to cut through his hide. In defensive mode he broke down into a large swarm of insects, dispersing in all directions. In response the hunters of Sharu danced their light swords skyward in all directions zapping the insects as the beams crossed paths.

The scattered ashes and dissected pieces of the putrid insects rained down on the ancient temple mount. Lucas held Victoria, now gray and clammy, supporting the spear to relieve the pain and shock. He appealed to Shem, "Can you do something? She's losing a lot of blood."

He shook his head and said, "The tips of the warriors' spears are covered with an incurable poison." Shem, then pointed up in the sky where another flying creature was coming into sight, "The winged woman, Ru, she may help. She is the one who brought her here."

Everyone -- that is except one -- held back judgment as Ru glided in through the clearing sky, and touched down with wings beating in reverse. Upon landing, Lucas addressed Ru, "And to think I had a crush on you over coffee. You are an acquaintance of Ouriano? But you are no angel?"

Ru started to answer his statement of questions, but was cut off by another question from Lucas, "Tell me what in God's or the devil's name are you?"

"Yes, suffice it to say I am your friend, and Victoria needs help immediately. Let me hold her while you pull out the spear."

Lucas asked Victoria, "Do you trust her?"

She nodded "yes."

Ru kissed Victoria on the forehead then said, "Forgive me for the pain I am about to inflict."

The toxic head the spear came off with a quick snap by Ru. Next she placed one hand underneath Victoria' shoulder blade around the spear, and the other in the front. "Pull slowly now," she told Lucas who now stood behind her.

Victoria let out a long grunt, "Ugghhhh" as the spear reversed itself through her torso. Ru's folded hand followed the shaft into the front exit wound to stop the bleeding and seal the punctured lung and artery. "The wounds will heal. Removing the toxins is our concern now."

Ru laid her wounded friend on the ground and clamped her mouth over Victoria's. Pinching Victoria's nose Ru vacuumed the poisonous air out of her lungs and sinus cavities, causing sharp dimples in her face and a blue tinge to her skin. Finished, Ru stood, dazed, then bent over forward with hands on her knees and expunged from her mouth a thick clear fluid, including several bugs. Standing again Ru announced, "She will live to return to Earth with you soon."

With these words Lucas threw down the shaft of the broken spear and gathered Victoria in his arms, "I almost lost you Vic, but I have to ask, did you mean all those romantic things you said?"

"I don't remember what romantic things I said, why don't you tell me?" Lucas awkwardly tried to find the words to ask her, searching his mind and heart. Wordlessly, he just held her close, thankful to have her in his arms, alive.

As they sat quietly, Lucas' and Victoria's attention was caught by the Neanderthals: rejoicing, waving their mirrored lights, dancing and praising the Self-Sustaining One on Siyon. They sang about reclaiming their home and making the desert bloom as it had in the past. When they finished, as one they swept over to the couple, and, against his wishes, joyously lifted Lucas up on their shoulders with shouts of "Juwaan, Juwaan, Juwaan!"

The celebrants placed Lucas on his feet close to Victoria. The now discarded shards of the mirror were collected by Shem and put back into their sack. All the dark clouds and haze had receded, leaving the clearest view of Siyon most of them had ever seen. Even the cliffs of Sharu were visible to the North. Looking back toward the sea, the first rain clouds in decades were visible approaching the desert escorted by a rainbow.

Shem came over to Lucas and laid his hand on the back of his shoulder, "You are a Juwaan. Your eyes can now see, and your ears can now hear."

"I had help."

Shem nodded. "I know. But you cannot control the help you received today. Be thankful."

"I am, but why did you follow me in?" Lucas asked.

"Because, we cross the circle of fire for friends, and we needed your help too. None of us can redeem ourselves alone. Sit with us now in our ancient chairs and give praise. It is true, the people of Sharu want desperately to restore their nobility."

Lucas thought a moment. "Are there any more like this Vranti who will come back to hurt them?"

"Possibly, many creatures desire to get to Siyon, whether welcome or not. Eventually they discover another creature's nobility cannot be stolen."

Chapter 52

*Try not to hate--hope instead. Hate is easy to
manipulate because it plays on pride.*

"Prior to the Regnum Dei all humans are subject to the
degradation of aging. At best they may prolong this
process. Winds on the other hand don't theoretically
decline over time if they maintain the necessary light and
rest. There is however an exception to almost everything-
-the unspoken 'don't take it for granted clause.' Don't
ever forget it."

Ouriano, yet to fully recover, continued to lecture
himself, "How many times have I given this speech to the
young Morning Stars?"

With trepidation he stepped up to the reflecting pool to
judge the depth of the dark creases under his eyes--they
were somewhat receded but the crow's feet, "definitely
now engraved." Least proud, he traced the permanently
etched scar from Cuzak with his fingers, a personal
reminder and now inflamed.

"Be true to yourself Ouriano. Will my kind become
something greater in the future? If we can regress why
cannot we advance? I know what lies beneath the golden
canopy at the heart of Siyon. There lies the Magnificon,
the one place which can speed my full recovery if indeed
I have crossed the threshold of healing. Another deep
space excursion and I might become weak enough to join
the throngs of infected."

When Ouriano heard rumor that a member of the Vranti
collective had been annihilated on Sharu without his
direct intervention, he maintained his doubts. To
unofficially verify he went down to the Well, where Ru
was to rendezvous with him. He enjoyed the literal hole

in the wall, for one never knew who would show. This social refuge was an unspoken neutral zone of fraternization and sanctioned double spying located near the Trans Corridor deep within Yare'ach Kachol. Even ambassadors of the dark winds were welcome within bounds of good behavior. For Ouriano, he subscribed to "Keep your enemies close."

As Ouriano entered, Ru was receiving her share of stares. Her overt female sexuality was a giveaway that she was no angel of the ranks. That she came looking for Ouriano was no surprise to any patrons for it fit his persona, and given the chance many of the ranks relished a glimpse of a fabled hybrid. Ouriano walked up grasping her hands, "Ru, I am sorry I could not tell you."

"What do you mean Ouriano? Tell me what?"

"That everything you have done is according to a set plan."

"You've left me in a lurch with Cuzak; heads will roll, maybe mine," she said dejectedly. "Does your plan account for this?"

"In some ways, yes. You'll survive this; your status is 'favorable to necessary' for now. Cuzak knows he will need your protection when the Vranti does not return with you. The doctors' safe return are your ticket. Cuzak fears Yazad, but they both fear and distrust Beltshzan even more. Beltshzan's power and cunning have no equal. Cuzak will need you. He appreciates power and deception. You make him proud."

Ru jabbed, "We, or certainly I, lose either way."

"Listen carefully to me Ru. I said, 'Beltshzan's power has no equal,' I did not say he had no superior rival."

"You still hold that your 'Heir' can bury him? I hear he spends all his time somewhere off in the Magnificon? And what about me? I crossed the line by the killing the Vranti's host. That is unpardonable?"

"Ru, it's not proper to speculate about things you don't know. I thought you left the mirror in the hands of the Juwaan?" Ouriano said, lifting his left brow.

"No Ouriano, I didn't help in annihilating the Vranti. I gladly would have aided in that fight had you not warned me. I am talking about the human I killed on the ship. The Vranti begged me to resist his new energized power. The pleasurable pulse of the dark ship baited my own thirst for vengeance; that's when I killed his host. Afterward I felt ugly, dirty ... look at my hands, my face. I am still not the same."

"They are only shades of darkness. All is not lost, Ru; there is only one who can truly destroy an image bearer. You are still integral to this covert operation."

Ouriano didn't feel his comfort was working, so he decided to be straight. "You know I cannot make you any promises, but three quarters of you is human. His mercy for humans is legendary. You have saved lives."

She looked him in the eyes, dilating hers wide open and saying, "But one quarter is evil, maybe more. Cuzak altered my genetic makeup."

Ouriano shot back, "Things can change. There always has to be a first for everything. You are different! All of us are more than the base sum of our parts. Did you bring back the mirror?"

"In pieces. The Vranti played Moses with it. Threw it into Beltshzan's chair." Ru explained, then continued. "You didn't want me present because of the light. It would have injured me?"

"Did you look in the mirror?" Ouriano asked.

"That is a ridiculous question! I was deathly afraid, and besides now it is in pieces. Even after the Vranti smashed it, the shards wielded by the Neanderthals were still deadly. I was afraid to handle any part of it after hearing what the reflected Shekinah did to the Vranti."

Ru started to whisper now as others looked on, struggling to mentally untangle Ouriano's relationship with her. "Didn't you try to make your own bargain with this Vranti, and look what happened?"

"Yes, I had hoped in lieu of Vranti's cooperation for a short amnesty, renewed negotiations, and future adjudication by the image bearers. You know Ru, it is said that someday the winds will fall under the judgment of the image bearers. Hard to believe, right? I keep discovering myself too naive. My front line contact in the war continues to reveal the infection as deeper and darker than I imagined. Once the fleshly beat of Beltshzan's heart is shared, my kind never come back."

Ru responded with another question, her elbows propped behind her on the bar, "Why does the insurgency want their own world and self-governance? The fallen image bearers have forever tried this and have met repeated disaster. Even now they are making one last attempt?"

"Let me tell you the short story of it Ru. This Vranti knew too much. He wasn't always this ugly creature. He was part of a group called the 'blue streaks,' angels who traveled much further than I was privy to and supervised the creation of some parallel realms. Other blue streaks say this group took liberty to explore unassigned areas at

Beltshzan's suggestion, and traveled to such remote realms that rumors spread they had made contact with those like us we knew not, and another great self-sustaining entity."

"Ouriano, can such things be verified?"

"Only Siyon knows, but to this group of blue streaks, this was proof that the Existing One was only a local entity who was no longer worthy of exclusive loyalty. When they all took the infection, they went on to become a festering, mid-level, Earth-bound power. I genuinely hoped we would overcome our long past differences in light of their recent aversion to Beltshzan, but Cuzak's bringing this group in was a real wild card."

"You don't know how much I hate their collective. They are disgusting no matter what form they take."

"You will see worse. Try not to use hatred as motivation, hope instead. Hate is easy to manipulate because it plays on pride. The good thing is Yazad will be confused about this, as it was meant to be, wondering who ordered this Vranti's destruction? There is only a handful given authority for annihilation of another of our kind. The pressure will be on Cuzak to move even faster. This Vranti will assuredly be replaced by another from his collective -- one more powerful."

Chapter 53

What may soon be at stake will test the heart of all our loyalties beyond obedience and personal vendettas.

Just as Ouriano finished speaking, Veezon walked up at the Well and inspected Ru like she was a new conservation species for the Blue Moon. He slowly gave his review to Ouriano one word at a time, "Sassy, human, angelic, demonic, lustful, and untamed. So how has your pet behaved so far? I heard a report of a dark cloud pulling a complete canopy over Beltshzan's old desert salvage yard only to be broken up by dancing lights and a celebration by Shem's band of natives.

They plan on moving back to their old neighborhood? Did she have something to do with this? Who performed the annihilation? Our friends from the other side are asking questions. Oh, I am sorry, is this part your covert plan too? Now I hear you have two humans at Sharu, not just one. The legend of the Juwaan continues with those primates?"

Still lacking the proper recovery, Ouriano went off, "Veezon! This is not the place for this conversation. Your rudeness and jealousy are unbecoming for your rank. Talk of desiring to be human?"

Ru inserted herself into this conversation. Her body language alone egged Veezon on. Elbows still resting on the bar, she arched her back, pulled up one of her knees and said to him, "Who died and made you judge? Correct me, the opposite is true isn't it?" She unfurled her hand, blew a kiss at him, then caressed his face, while tilting her head back. He stood silent thinking of what to say. Then she slapped him so hard everyone in the room became motionless.

Veezon's wings twitched as if about to expand, but he held them in. He didn't move. Several seconds passed as he looked at her. Everyone at the Well continued their attention on the two and wondered what would happen next. Then through the clear back sea wall of the tavern came a great moan from a Leviathan species, a mating call, "Weeeeeough!" Any regular patron recognized the sound. Veezon cracked a smile, rolled his head back and began a hearty laugh. The tension in the angelic tavern released as all exploded into laughter with him.

He stepped forward, put his powerful right arm around her waist, pulled her close to himself and spoke softly in her ear. Ouriano read his lips, "I have never underestimated you. Ouriano is the last of his kind. If you betray my brother, even at the risk of becoming infected, I will track you down like an unwelcome rat. I swear this before Siyon."

Ru whispered back, "Angels of light are not supposed to swear by anything, are they?"

Veezon, never one to back down, snapped, "Check the rules--only in regard to registered species. You are off the record, unless we make you a specimen."

Before this escalated any further, Ouriano stepped forward and encompassed his arms around both of them, "Please, what may soon be at stake will test the heart of all our loyalties beyond obedience and personal vendettas. Let us leave this place."

Chapter 54

When all seems lost, don't confuse this with the end,
rather this is the beginning.

When Ru came back to Sharu with Ouriano, the celebration continued where Dr. Tanner could not run away from being honored as the 'last of the Juwaans.' The Neanderthals memorialized the empty Elder's chair by etching the meeting of Lucas with the Angel of Light and the defeat of the Vranti. Victoria, healed, fit, and now looking like herself again through Ru's initial efforts on her near-fatal injury, Lucas' tender care, and Wayla's homeopathic herbs, updated Lucas on the latest in Cuzak's lab.

In a closed meeting with Victoria, Lucas, Shem, and Ru, Ouriano told them, "Developments are happening faster than anticipated; we are now at the epicenter of things we have never experienced. All of us need to be in prayer."

Shem interrupted, "Before you go on, please follow me." Shem took them to his private alcove among the red rock high rises, decorated inside with depictions of all the past Juwaans in colorful hieroglyphics. Pointing to a narrative on the wall of a winged woman with long claws and fangs, he asked, "Why have you brought the winged woman Ru into this conversation? As a Nephilim she carries an incurable strain."

Begging to differ, Ouriano said, "Why does everyone see Ru as a menace? Is she the only one to carry the infection among us? She is three-quarter human. Mercy could be extended under the right circumstances."

Shem replied, "Yes, but we lost six good people by means of deception because she helped bring the Vranti through Victoria. Keep her out of the loop!"

"But your people killed the Vranti," Ouriano added.

Shem cut him off, "You and I know in time the collective is likely to replace this one, unless..."

Ouriano stepped in front of the wall, blocking their view. "Shem, listen, their lives were not given in vain. I assure you they now walk like Enoch. You shall see them in Siyon."

Shem pushed a startled Ouriano away from blocking the view of the hieroglyphics and said, "Wayla and Peleg's people have their own path, do not speak about what you don't know!"

Ouriano would not have backed off from any other being, but he respected Shem's wisdom and love for the people of Sharu. He responded to Shem, "In many things you know more than I, but something major is soon to begin in the realm of Adam's race. Do you remember a Yazad?"

Shem answered, "My father referred to many image bearers worshiping one named Yazad before the great flood. Yazad's presence through his devotees had to be driven from the Earth, for they sought to lift him up over the fallen throne of Beltshzan. No one knew for sure from whence this unclean spirit came. His followers had visions of Yazad as an infected and decimated archangel, who had been resurrected and restored. The plumes of his open wings resembled a rainbow, entrancing the gaze of anyone who had rejected the Self-Sustaining One. The awful flood came in those days to cleanse his followers from the Earth and stunt this new version of the infection. My father said Yazad was worshiped by many of our race as a god, therefore as a sign of dominion over this spirit, the rainbow was given after the judgment.

My father told me, the Vranti were somehow connected to this mysterious Yazad worship, and vowed a secret loyalty if Yazad would give them the chance of escape and help them one day throw off the local entity. Initially this appeared to end in failure, but I guess the reason you ask me, Ouriano, is because you suspect something new along this line?"

Ouriano nodded his head, affirming, and asked, "What is the connection with the Nephilim?"

"You mean those you allowed to escape before this happened, like Cuzak?"

Ouriano hung his head, "I take responsibility every day."

Shem explained further, "The Nephilim who escaped earlier may have found this fabled Yazad and tried to establish a new home with him. It is hard to determine what information from the Vranti is ever true. According to my ancestors, the Nephilim discovered a world of new star patterns, but they lacked the power to harness the laws of their new universe and the ability to procreate their kind. They lacked the life-giving force humans carry for reproduction. Yazad gave them safety and provision, and limited access back to Earth. They have been sent at various times to test the waters of the Existing One's wrath and defenses since the flood. Yazad supposes the Existing One has grown soft since the Heir of the Magnificon conferred amnesty to Adam's race.

Shem then paused, turned his head back and forth for a moment to look each one in the eyes, especially Ru, and continued, "I believe in this Yazad. He has gained more and more favor since then by spreading very selective false rumors, but one over all the others."

Ru listening intensely asked, "Yes, what is it?"

"That the Existing One is a local entity. That the Sustainer of All Things is weak in hearing, understanding, and administration. That the Existing One now confides too much in the image breeding bearers, and servants of fire like Ouriano, who are in need of retirement."

Ru, replied with a question, "If he is not just a local entity, then what is he?"

Shem drew a face of a large human eye in the fine sand of the floor and said, "In his eyes is reflected the entire expanse of all creation, time, and existence. If something is not found there, then it cannot be found, ever."

Ouriano jumped in, "Yes, this is true. I once was invited close to him with another Juwaan long ago. His eyes were something Adam's race can only dream about. They bring agony to many and complete healing to others. They search and know all things without a word being spoken. Even Yazad's home is without a cloak to this light of knowing."

"So where do we fit in?" Lucas asked drawing a picture of a stick figure man next to the eye, "Do I have a meeting with these eyes, because I would rather not? The mirror and the Desert Angel of Light was enough for me. If the nature of reality is personal in nature, that's too unnerving for my sanity."

Ouriano replied, "Yes and no, Lucas. You are indeed meeting them now because you are walking in his imagination. All of you will have to listen to the yearning of your soul -- let this be your compass. Lucas and Victoria, you are about to return with Ru to Earth to finish your project. Complete what Cuzak asks no matter what the consequences may seem, but be on your guard for your lives. These things must happen. The ship from the dark winds will rendezvous with a return waypoint I have set up. I must keep it simple for you. Shem, continue to guard the Neanderthals. Know that another of the Vranti collective will likely follow here."

"Remember, when all seems lost, don't confuse this with the end, rather this is the beginning."

Chapter 55

*You have ventured into deep waters, leaving your
wading pool of shallow pragmatism.*

Returning to Colonel Smith's secret lab through the
portal, they were greeted with a surprise, "Cuzak! What
is this you're spraying on us?" protested Ru. The more
she tried to struggle free the tighter the goop became.
Her wings would not open. "You're covering my mouth!"

"Okay, stop!" Cuzak shouted to his men, "Be careful with
her wings." Upon examining them, he relaxed, then said,
"Unbind them, use the solvent. One can never be too
careful of what might come back through the gateway. I
prepared this for the Vranti, knowing one or the both of
you could come back more powerful. Look at your hands,
you have touched Beltshzan's heart."

Ru opened her palms for a second, then curled her
fingers back into fists to hide the change, "I killed an
innocent man because of the power surge on the dark
ship."

Cuzak's answer was vacant of any empathy, "As my
favorite Juwaan once said, 'There is no one innocent, not
even one.' Welcome to your calling. Besides, the prisoner
was already sentenced to death. So many of them are."

"Ahh! Dr. Tanner I presume, and the always lovely Dr.
Pruett. You are the guests of honor. You have survived
your own invention. You will have to refresh me on the
places you have been. Extraordinary was it not? You
shall see so much more. This is your destiny."

Ru had warned Lucas not to confront Cuzak but he
insisted in taking a shot while pulling off the
disintegrating adhesive. "Let's get this straight, my

destiny and yours are completely separate! Colonel Smith, I presume?"

Cuzak as always remained a step ahead, "No hard feelings. Every destiny has two sides, and they don't ask for our opinions. Now, where is the Vranti? Did you maim him or leave him there? Ouriano have him euthanized? Shush ... I don't want to know right now. Our new slice of the multi-verse will be a better place with one less of those impotent terrestrial hermit crabs. The less I know, the more I can concentrate on work. We can all take the gloves off now can we not?" He stood there, continuing with the big fake grin.

"Dr. Tanner, stand up please." Cuzak walked up close to his face, "My, look at the white hair, the eyes. You've had an encounter with the light? You finished off the Vranti didn't you? Well done, counted worthy, bravo! Unless you were so gifted you would never have made this technological breakthrough. You have a family history of seeking the light of the local entity, yet you are not so sure, are you? Why don't you believe like them? Why have you not spoken to your parents in years? You have ventured into deep waters, leaving behind your wading pool of shallow pragmatism."

"Leave my family out of this. This is none of their doing."

"For the time being Dr. Tanner, we will. So think about this; 'What is reproducible? What is most efficient, what is the greatest good for all? What gives us the greatest freedom of choice? The research of Dr. Tanner and Pruett has answered these questions, has it not?

I promise in the long run, you will be pleased with the results. No longer will people ask, 'Who am I? Where did I come from?' Those are questions of people under the thumb of delusion, offering lame excuses for a second rate life of humility and servitude. When we finish this ultimate social experiment people will say, 'I have determined for myself the future. I am no one's victim.'"

Finally free, Ru stood up, spread her wings and broke off the last strands. She had never heard her father so full of himself; the megalomaniac within him wanted to boast in his apparent success. Ru reminded herself, *Speech, to Cuzak, equals manipulation. He makes sense in a strange way but always with something key left out.*

He continued, "Dr. Tanner, Eve, you are looking a little weathered for all you have been through. Being violated by a demon is intolerable by any standard. I am sorry you experienced the irony of how most of us arrived on this stage. Are you not humored by this to some extent? You must have been thrilled at Vranti's annihilation. He was destroyed, humanely, correct? They don't believe in torture up there? My colleagues please listen--there is no freedom unless you have power. When we complete this process you will have guaranteed the freedom for yourselves and billions.

By the way, you have made international news. Your entertainment value is way up. Homeland Security is now on your trail with egg on their face. Seems they were a day late in assessing how they could have allowed this technology to escape their priority list. Your penchant to keep your work proprietary made it easier for us to swoop in. Your University president made some phone calls and could never get a negative or affirmative reaction from the Homeland Security czar as to your disappearance and confiscation of your technology. As to your online backups, our friends own the servers. Sorry, you must read those privacy agreements.

It is a crazy world. Two Jihadi terrorist groups are publicly taking credit for your abduction, saying your technology will give them access to any place on the planet regardless of security. Of course, 'if they only knew.'"

Dr. Tanner spoke again peeling the last bit of goo from the back of his hand, "You are in control, so why not let us communicate something to our students and relatives? We'll tell them we are working with a private investor because of our security concerns. We can send out an anonymous press release. I mean, who is going to believe the truth anyway? We can give a plausible story and a demonstration of our work, an infomercial. Is there any public or private offers backing this venture?"

Cuzak was enthralled, animated with his hands, "You may think I am joking. It's already set up with Goldman Sacs. In the long run your work will render this economy useless, but until then greed will invigorate mass investors. Who cares if Rome is burning if you are making money hand over fist? We will short the stock on the backside too! I can agree to this.

Enough for now. Welcome back. Receive your needed rest. Eat, retire to your quarters. Dr. Pruett, greet your mother. Tomorrow we begin to change everything. Maria, come with me please."

Chapter 56

So this far we must assume we have the local entity's permission, which should not be confused with his blessing.

Cuzak put his arm around Ru, even though they both knew he was the pseudo father figure she never had. "I want to hear all about this trip. I know there have been others, but tell me about just this one." He walked Ru down to his bunkered apartment and mixed her a black Russian. "Sit down, I insist." Ru poured it down her throat and handed it back. "Another?" he asked.

"Yes," she nodded, then sunk into the white leather couch staring at the slowly revolving chrome fan blades suspended off the conduits bundled on the ceiling. He handed back her glass, refilled. She noticed to her relief the thick predatory nails were receding. The framed mirror showed some of the dark creases around her mouth were still present.

Ru blurted out, "I don't want to become like them, or like you."

"I can understand that Maria."

"No, I don't think you do. You must know better than the concocted bullshit you are threading together to win them over or sell yourself. You can't possibly believe this fable. Beltshzan would have done this ages ago if this would have worked."

Cuzak raised his voice slightly and kept gesturing with his drink bearing hand, "He didn't have a way out like we are going to create. His efforts did result in you, and don't ever forget it."

Ru took another big sip then let loose, "Can't you see the only reason the lights are left off in the kitchen is so the cockroaches will come out of hiding? The local entity is more than a local entity and you know it. Ouriano said that you were in the crowd at his betrayal helping incite them. Is this true? Are there other incidents as well?"

Cuzak spoke as never before, "What do you mean by incidents? The world is full of incidents. Darling, everything around you is the result of an incident. I was given permission. This all could be stopped, anytime. I saw his eyes when I passed by. He spoke 'Eloi, Eloi, Lama Sabachthani.' I came out of hiding because I thought the end was about to take place. The sky turned dark. I knew then, with no home to go to, he was about to succumb to Beltshzan.

But I should have not have been caught by surprise when the script radically changed. Who can take away the wrath of the local entity but the local entity himself? The image bearers never left the center of his vision. There is a connection between the two not all species share. Do you? Our goal is to take out all the surprises."

Ru wasn't prepared to answer this question. He suspected that her human side carried something else? "Are you asking me if I have a soul?"

"You are three quarter human. I may have altered your DNA but some things will always be beyond interference. I have suspected it for a long time. This is a gift from your mother and the one who's name I will not mention."

"Then, I am a candidate for amnesty?" Ru meekly asked.

"This has been my secret hope," as Cuzak continued, "But you must realize there are no written guarantees for you. No one knows these things. You can wait behind to take your chances or move forward and invent your future."

"What about you? You are half human?"

"Nothing can change this infection for me. I have to keep moving, like a shark, or I'll drown. You on the other hand, may have a choice. For millennia I've observed how the infection works on both races. I feel no pity or mercy for them as innocent bystanders. The infection helps them become more of what they want. Theirs is the dark light enticing them to become a god, though few will name it. This is the beauty of the infection--an unconscious shroud of pride that becomes the desire of their hearts.

Whatever their essence leads them to, is what they deserve! You probably never thought you would hear this from me, but I actually have respect for those image bearers who resist. They at least have nobility. Unfortunately, the noble are always fed on first by the piranha, who then in turn feed on themselves. I still can picture his eyes. They were full of nobility. Those truly of his kind never give up their nobility. The others are fodder. The bullshit is for the fodder. This is what they want to hear. I help them believe their own bullshit sooner."

Ru finished the second black Russian like the first, all at once, "Cuzak, you are crazy. Are you saying you know full well how this plays out in the end?"

Cuzak began shaking in laughter, "Ha, ha, ha, ha ..." He was pacing, then abruptly stopped and took in a deep breath before exclaiming, "No one knows how this plays out in the end. There isn't an end. You have seen a glimpse of Siyon with Ouriano? Siyon receives creatures from other dimensions, times and places we know not of.

We give signs, second guesses, innuendo, bluffs -- like all good poker gamers."

"Hindsight too," Ru interjected.

Quickly he added, "The hindsight only comes after the call. We are about to force the call on all the players. There is so much you don't know and I would like you to remain ignorant just in case."

"Just in case!" Ru ripped back. "Just in case of what? You start World War Three?"

Cuzak held up his hand for Ru to stop and replied, "'Are there other incidents?' Yes, of course. 'What if things don't go as planned?' you ask. Remember, there is no neutrality. If you are not behind the wheel, someone is taking you for a ride. We work closest with those behind capital markets and those who don't want to be taken for a ride by the superpowers."

Ru could not believe she was feeling sorry for him, "Do you want to know about my relationship with Ouriano?"

He sat down, focused on the carpet for a few moments. When he looked back up his eyes struck terror. Ru watched as they became like hers with an additional glistening mucosa and scaled eyelids. There was movement beneath his pockmarked facial skin. Cuzak began tilting and cracking his neck and for the first time she saw the glory of his wings.

They ripped through his suit jacket. The remaining scraps of fabric he pulled off with one hand and tossed them against the wall. The skin on his torso was heavy with sweat and marked by old wounds where he had been impaled, flayed, cut, stitched, burned, and shot. Now she was intimidated.

His voice became slower and more coarse, "Look closely. These are the wounds from my life of giving mercenary and vagabond help to humans for Beltshzan. However, there were always enough noble image bearers to wreck his restructure programs. We've failed so many times that the cat and mouse game became redundant.

Ru, please do as I say and possibly your nobility will remain intact. Cross me and I will tear off your wings and force you to participate in atrocities from which there is no forgiveness, ever. Trust Ouriano and no one else. My quarrel with him is personal."

She took a big swallow, "And the doctors?"

"It is obvious their nobility is growing. If Dr. Tanner is marked as a Juwaan then we indeed have the unknown factor. So thus far we must assume we have the local entity's permission, which should not be confused with his blessing. The Angel of Light's anger can flare up in an instant on anyone who mortally wounds one of hers. We will have to protect him until finished. Any more questions?"

"Yes, why not give this all up?"

"Because there is no neutrality--two sides to every destiny. The infected also thrive on hope."

Chapter 57

You are saying God could experience a walk out?

The coffee wasn't made with the finesse they were used to at Starbucks, but at least it was caffeine. "Let's go," said Lucas as he chugged the last cup and stamped the ceramic mug down on the table.

"Just another day in the diabolical lab," added Victoria sliding her seat back under their cafeteria table. They finished breakfast with her mother, surrounded by the inconspicuous, conspicuous security. "Mom don't forget the bacon for Blitz, here's what's left of mine. I'll see you this afternoon, work pace is picking up."

When Victoria hugged her, Ms. Pruett whispered, "I am praying for you honey, missed you the last week. I have more to tell you later." She was escorted out with little Blitz on a leash. As Colonel Smith entered, Blitz took a wide berth around his path.

"Good morning!" said the overly cheery Colonel.

Dr. Tanner interrupted, "How would we know with no sunlight?"

"Because it is what is in here Dr. Tanner," said the Colonel holding his heart. Lucas rolled his eyes. The Colonel blew right by the attitude. "Please have a seat. I have something to show you. Clear everyone out of the cafeteria."

In a very short space of time, Smith's entourage had ensured they were alone. The lights were darkened and a projector screen descended against the wall. A crystal clear image of an internet browser appeared. Lucas and Victoria looked at each other when they saw the

Microsoft World Wide Telescope program load. The Colonel began to speak. "As you know the two of you have leap-frogged us into the future. With a population nearing seven billion people, the Earth has its limitations. Within two million years the Earth will no longer sustain higher forms of life, like humans and mammals because of the bleaching affect of the sun on the Earth."

Victoria added, "A possible conclusion of the Faint Sun Paradox, first proposed by Carl Sagan; the sun will grow more efficient in its fusion furnace, turning up the radiation on our planet, to super global warming?"

"Yes, Dr. Pruett, and if it doesn't happen, long beyond this time frame the laws of our universe will begin to break down and bend because of the exponential expansion propelled by dark energy. One day all knowledge will be lost, rendering this life as meaningless. No one will ever know we were here, unless we take the same rule of law of the cosmos and use it to our advantage. This is precisely what you have done.

Billions of your years ago, creatures like the Vranti discovered far distant black holes in this universe. The local entity found these obscene apertures of time and space to be quite good at disposing of enemies and rivals of this galactic sphere. Please take a look as I pan out to deep space. You may see the coordinates relative to the Earth in the corner. There it is, far deep past the Gemini constellation. This quasar was the gateway in the past to Yazad's experiment. I say 'was' because as you know this modern picture is quite outdated by billions of years. This black hole has now collapsed.

To get to the point, your responsibility now is to set your gateway technology to these coordinates and get us to the universe beyond this dysfunctional hole. You'll have all technical assistance you will need from our other labs in the Ukraine, India, China, Brazil, South Africa. For if this gateway is successful, a corridor will be open to a new realm outside the local entiy's domain. This will be the land flowing with milk and honey for all of us."

"And if we refuse?" asked Lucas.

Colonel Smith smiled as he spoke, "Then your research will have been for nothing. Complete this and you can have all your proprietary and improved technology back. Thank you for the loan. You will have riches beyond measure. The media will be all over this."

Lucas started getting hot, "But we already discovered something wonderful. You orchestrated bringing us back from the Blue Moon. You know all about it!"

The Colonel answered quickly, "Yes, now get someone besides a tabloid on UFO cover-ups or an Art Bell type to take your report seriously. Maybe Ouriano will show up for an interview? And did you walk the surface of Siyon? That is a nice carrot isn't it? The wonders in this new quadrant shall render your recent trip pale beyond belief. You saw for yourself the remnants of an ancient war on the Blue Moon, the dark ship, felt the heart of evil, the animosity of your ancestral seed. They may have led you to believe they are negotiating a truce. Far from it.

This feud is about to spill over on this planet. We mean to escape all of this. Let them sort it out as they desire. They both appear to have been stumped and entrenched. All the while we will move on. You will help to get us to our new home with Yazad. Once you have tasted a real paradise then you can make a choice for yourself. Don't try and make that narrow minded choice for others. How dare you limit another of your genetic line the right to know?"

"What do you mean right to know?" Lucas asked.

Cuzak politely answered, "The version of light you encountered is old, outdated, and most importantly, not the only light. While it is true the light as we know it here is the essence of all existence in this piece of the multiverse, there is no exclusive ownership. This light is force fed to all who would like to maintain a diplomatic existence. Beltshzan tried to develop his own light as doctor Pruett tasted on one of his ships. His light has severe limitations and qualifies for less than a cheap substitute for the local entity's illumination. It is like drinking stale beer when you want vintage wine."

Trying to understand this Lucas had to clarify, "Then you are saying the infected and darkened creatures consciously remove themselves from a diet of the light of God--excuse me, your favorite, from 'the local entity.'"

Cuzak answered in the affirmative, "Yes, a symptom of the infection is voluntary abstinence of the light from the local entity, from which they can no longer directly feed. Their ugliness is a result of malnutrition."

Lucas sarcasm spilled out, "Then we should suppose this new corridor or gateway will lead to the land of Oz, a place founded on a different life sustaining wave length or luminescence? What in the world led me to believe this was more of 'good versus evil?'"

Cuzak displayed his sense of humor, "You can still be a deist, just switch your loyalties to where you would like to spend paradise! A successful gateway will allow those with the infection to be restored and bring peace here as well. This will be a constructive amnesty. Beltshzan will be so weakened by desertion he will cease to be a player anymore. 'The Sanctuary' of Yazad will be a place of no religion or aging. Immortality will be given equally to all."

Victoria interjected, "And Siyon and the Blue Moon?"

Cuzak thought deep, "Who knows of these things? This development could move the local entity into jealousy. He might suffer disaffection by a mass emigration of the image bearers and more from the angelic rank."

"You are saying God could experience a walk out?"

Ru stepped in to the briefing overhearing the last part, everyone turned to her as she said, "Or maybe we would be doing him a favor? I guess this way everyone gets what they want. Everything is always what it seems to be, right?"

Cuzak shot back, "Those like you Ru should be thankful. Yazad has been establishing this realm for millennia so that your kind may prosper and be fruitful, not a freak anachronism. Enough now, we have our tasks, we need the gateway as soon as possible. Think large."

Chapter 58

I see the killing fields of the innocents crying out for justice while we hold our ranks.

Veezon made his case again before the Royal Cherubim, "Ouriano is a hazard to our more traditional ranks. He pushes the envelope of unnecessary risk mimicking the faith of the image bearers. And now as I stand before you, guardians of the Magnificon, you order me to give reinforcement to his covert activities, regardless of my strategic assessment?"

One of the Royals responded, "Veezon, I assure you Ouriano is not improvising as he goes along. He must have your division's support. Your agitation is unwarranted."

"Support? Agitation?" he answered, "You are asking prime kingdom warriors to become nursemaids to clean up the inevitable loose ends of bad planning. Who does he answer to?"

"Trust us, he answers. The two of you are close for a reason."

"Wait, hear me one last time. Ouriano has a real, live Juwaan; an image bearer with an imagination who could prove to be as unpredictable and erratic as Joan of Arc. Creativity has always been difficult for many of us in the ranks to identify with. We see things as they are, not so much as what they can be. Their inspiration invents more work for us. Imagination was Beltshzan's first mistake."

After conferring and much discussion, a final decision was made: the Royal Cherubim asked Veezon to meet with Ouriano to convey the result at the Lake of Dreams, deep below the surface of the Blue Moon. Veezon had not visited there in a long time, too many memories. When angels cry, this is where they mourn. On this occasion, the lake was the color of dark blue sapphire and coated with a pearl sheen. As new prayers fed the head waters, lights randomly flashed beneath the calm surface. The slightest movement of the head or eyes caught different hues of light.

By meeting Ouriano here, they would experience no interruptions from wandering ambassadors from the dark winds. It seemed ludicrous to Veezon that the dark winds were ever given access to the Blue Moon, even in limited numbers. However, the entrance to this place was off limits and it would be a great sacrilege if they entered. Two large, fierce Cherubim guarded the tunneled entrance opening into the massive underground chamber containing the lake.

Veezon had ordered subordinates here many times to deal with the post-trauma of warfare, "It is a holy place where dreams and prayers from the children of those who follow the One who was, and is, and is to come, are stored as an everlasting monument to their sufferings and persecutions. Respect and hear these living prayers even if you suspect some to be needless waste. For if the least of their lives seems wasteful, then what is your existence?"

Overdue and under orders, Veezon took his own advice to remind himself to be thankful for his role and remain true to his service. Tens of thousands of stories in this lake were connected to him. These prayers were the only imagination he had. Veezon walked to the edge to look upon the still waters knowing a connection would be made, rehearsing a vivid narration of the struggles of a particular image bearer he had been involved with; a descendent of Abraham, a sick child, a dying mother, a slave laborer, the addicted, a joyful wedding, a worshipper, the imprisoned. Few of the beloved of El Roi, 'The God Who Sees,' ever witnessed his work.

Bending over to feel the waters with his hand, Veezon heard Ouriano's voice, "I didn't think you felt their sentiments anymore?"

Standing back up he replied, "Yes, occasionally I do, and I also live to see the day when this lake is drained. Why Ouriano, do we put up with such rubbish from these outlaws who antagonize the image bearers? And why we don't respond with annihilation against all of the insolent if their intent is to corrupt the kingdom of the Heir? I have close friends who have suffered Beltshzan's dark plague. Unlike you, Ouriano, I cannot bear to look at them."

"They were created exactly as you and I. They deserve recognition and respect. Maybe one day our fallen shall be redeemed like the humans?"

"Our fallen don't deserve relationship. Even now there are more who freely give up their ability to thrive on the light by lustfully tapping into the heart of Beltshzan. Then, worse, they take their shriveled selves and leech nourishment from unsuspecting image bearers, to squeak out a symbiotic existence. I rather look forward to their just desserts."

Ouriano thought a moment, then placed one hand on his shoulder and motioned with the other across the lake, "What do you see when you look across this lake, Veezon?"

"I see the killing fields of the innocents crying out for justice while we hold our ranks. I see slavery, suicide bombers, moneychangers, greedy doctors, crooked politicians, empire builders, and charlatan priests, sending many we aid to an ignoble early grave. Much stays the same throughout their generations."

Ouriano was slow to respond, "Veezon, you have remained more true than I. Your faithfulness will have its reward. Certainly you must also see the good? This Lake full of dreams and prayers will provide a shower of blessings on those you protect when they finally see all that has transpired. I agree only a few of them have had the imagination to see what movements took flight in response to their prayers. Their sight is so short while on the Earth because the Existing One ..."

Veezon, being in no mood to listen to Ouriano's rehashed speech interrupted him, "'Because the Existing One has something more primary to develop in them for their next phase.' Yes, and I suppose you will tell me next how they will be elevated to judge and reward my peers of the faithful rank?"

"Yes, Veezon, I was going to say something to that effect. But now let me invite you to be part of something which will please you. I did use the word 'please,' since you too have taken on a number of human attributes including your impatience, preoccupation with self and your immediate need for justice."

"Go on Ouriano, and add jealousy to the list. You know well how I was asked to meet you here by the Royals of the Magnificon."

Ouriano cast out the lure, "What if I told you your longing for justice would soon be fulfilled? Have you ever heard of the 'Sanctuary'?"

Chapter 59

You my friend have fought in the dark, but I have no such experience. How will we prevail if your light turns to darkness?

Veezon answered, "Of course. It is the distant homeland Beltshzan could never deliver on. He is too weak. He's peddled the idea ad nauseum for recruiting purposes, but this seems to have quieted in the last earthly millennium after he was stripped down. The only powers that could pull this off now are in the Magnificon of Siyon."

"Listen Veezon, you are about to be so far inside the circle in a moment you may decide to back out. This is completely voluntary. I am coming to you on this because you wear your questions, honor, and loyalty, forthrightly. You and I are not the antithesis of each other as you might think."

"I am flattered to fly wing with you Ouriano, however I could never agree to cooperate in an improvised plan with your pet project. Where there is one scavenger, there are bound to be more. The Nephilim are nasty birds and tend to roost together. However, you have me intrigued. Persuade me."

"Ru, as loyal as she is, doesn't know all of what I am about to explain. You are wise about her nature. The Juwaan doesn't know either unless it has come to him from within. This must remain concealed. You have to be in or out on this. There is no half way. Once you understand the implications, I am going to need you to hand pick a trusted few who can be ready to mobilize swiftly and covertly."

"I am listening. Get to the point."

"Here, let us take our hands together and place them in this lake. Soothing and painful are the prayers of the redeemed. Their faces, their plight, are before us. Look how it affects you Veezon. You have become more personal with them than you let on. You love them, which leads you to more pain because their cause goes unfinished. I hear of the disaffections from your own winds because they feel plans have stagnated. You suppose most of your service for the Self-Sustaining One has been for a defensive slog? This is far from the truth, but perceptions can be stronger than truth. Veezon, this lake shall supply the first source of waters for the River of Life which is about to roar from Siyon!"

"Ouriano, you are known for your long speeches. Let me save you words. I am in—if you received this information directly from the Angel of Light? Though, I'll probably regret trusting you."

"Yes Veezon... spoken to me in a vision."

"This is not as direct as I would hope, and for no other of our kind would I believe this, except you. What else?"

"The Vranti are very connected to this development. I am holding the remains of one of the collective for us to interrogate."

Instinctively, at the mention of their name, Veezon clasped the hilt of his sword, "Those blood thirsty beasts, the dark legion. What good is interrogation on chronically lying insects? They play themselves off as spearheading the insurgency against Beltshzan. I have always questioned why his royal guard would turn against him? Please continue."

"Veezon, do you know why Beltshzan could never deliver the Sanctuary, given as great a power as he was or is?

There is none who knows the architecture of the creation better than he except for the Son of the Magnificon. No created being has ever been given the power equal to what he held, yet his ability to carve into the fabric of space and time puffed up his mind to no end.

When Beltshzan was cast down, he had to be torn in half, for his power was too great. His creative personality was split from him and flung into the furthest black hole of the earthly realm and collapsed to create an impenetrable seal. Even the abyss was not secure to hold this part of him. The Vranti were still uninfected at the time and given the task to quarentine his creative self until the end.

They supposedly completed their work, but not long after, many of them started coming down with the infection. The Vranti knew of this location and may have shared this information with a few of the escaped Nephilim who also were aware of Beltshzan's secluded other half. This creative half of Beltshzan goes by another name, Yazad."

"My Ouriano, be careful what you say, for you are suggesting a new front for which we are not equipped! May Siyon save us from all that is unholy! So the insurgency against Beltshzan has been orchestrated by his alter ego, Yazad? Why are we now learning about this? How does he communicate, and if he is still encapsulated in a dead end section of the multi-verse, what is the emergency?"

The news to Veezon became worse as Ouriano explained more. "The less any of us knew, who being susceptible to the infection in the early days of the pandemic, the more secure the weakened Beltshzan would be. His final fate still awaits. It looks like he may have his last shot to prove himself right and honorable, as is his desire."

"Glad to see you're laughing at your last remark, what is the humans' part in this?"

"Unknowingly coached by returning Nephilim the last few centuries, the humans have developed the technology which may open a corridor to any multi-verse bubble, much like we do with our deep assignments launched from the Blue Moon on approval from Siyon. The technology was hijacked by a partnership of Nephilim, the Vranti, and darkened humans. Together they plan on opening a wide corridor to the new Sanctuary."

Veezon pulled out his sword, stared at it, picturing many battles of the past, "A ripe trap for any in the ranks or of Siyon. Do you think Beltshzan is aware of his other half reaching out to him? If Beltshzan makes it to the sanctuary for unification, then he could be successful in taking the war to a new level, one which we have little experience. Deep incursions are difficult enough, draining what light resources we take with us. For the honor of the winds of light who were annihilated at the beginning of the infection, I am thinking of a worse scenario! This must be stopped."

Looking dead into his eyes, Ouriano said, "Veezon, this is why I brought you in. You understand well what could happen and what is at stake. This mission could be our last. What will happen if we go to fight him in his complete dominion? Reunified and in his new realm, the combination could turn us. You are right alluding that Yazad may already have created his own light. If he drew us into battle in his realm we could eventually be cut off from our strength, could we not? The roles of the infected would be reversed. He would obviously restore his infected, trap and suffocate us."

Wondering what role they could serve, Veezon asked, "Our regular weapons could be useless if we are being asked to take the battle to him. Why would the Lord of Hosts allow this? Why do we not destroy the technology behind the corridor?"

Ouriano added fuel to Veezon's fire, "In speaking to the Angel of Light in my vision, she said, 'The One Who Sustains All wishes the corridor to be opened. This must happen. Beltshzan will be allowed to attain his full potential again for a time, times, and half a time. Many of the unborn and redeemed will believe the lie and enter into the Sanctuary of Yazad. The Juwaan must enter in, and you Ouriano must aid him. Choose your friends wisely, for the Lord says,

(As Ouriano began to quote, Veezon recognized and confessed it with him)

I will give warning signs both in the sky and on the
Earth – blood, fire, and columns of smoke.
The sunlight will be converted to darkness
and the moon to the color of blood,
before the day of the Lord comes –
that great and dreadful day!'"

Rattled by what Ouriano was suggesting, Veezon appealed to him, "You my friend have fought in the dark, but I have no such experience. How will we prevail if your light turns to darkness?"

But Ouriano did not give him the answer he was looking for, "The Juwaan will need us. We may have to learn to feed off the dark light for a season. Our swords could become useless in the realm of Yazad. But this will be your greatest moment Veezon. Your courage will be inscribed in the depths of the Blue Moon and on the gates of the Magnificon."

Veezon gave the only response he had left, "This trip will require great faith like that of the Juwaans. As for my name, the less known, the better."

"Well said," added Ouriano, "We must become less."

Chapter 60

We are the progeny of ancient myths,
so we attempt to write our own.

Ru arranged for Victoria and Lucas to share their evening dinner with Ms. Pruett. Inside the sealed lab, they grew close. A byproduct of sharing the home-cooked meals with Vic and her mom dredged up a longing for Lucas' own mother, father, and sister, whom he had drifted away from the last ten years. He wanted to keep better contact, but it was always at the end of a weekly list he never finished.

The big separation from his family started when Lucas came home from college one Christmas, having taken an elective course in religion. Shattering his stained glass concepts of God, he learned how the Bible was really edited through contentious councils over centuries along with some of the little dirty secrets, like the medieval crusades, pogroms against Jews and colonial missions. The class showed how half the book of Acts was an argument about circumcision and a few centuries later how Emperor Constantine forced Christianity to become the official religion of the Roman empire. He was caught off guard and disappointed that these items were left out of his church youth programs leaving him stripped of anything to believe in. *Or did it? Maybe that was all a prodigal's excuse? No, it was all rational.*

He was home on winter break, eating dinner with his parents when he forced the final showdown with his father over the subject of church. Lucas knew it bothered his parents that he slept in at the dorm on Sunday mornings after partying on Saturday night, and then later acquired a job at a Half Price Book store during the sacred Sunday time slot.

His dad didn't need to say much for Lucas to feel his disappointment. As a deacon in his little evangelical church the world was categorically black and white. There was God, the Father, Son, and the Holy Spirit, and then there was the Bible; handed down from on high to be taken as the literal manual for everything in life. Jesus walked on water, saved sinners who repented, but carried a big stick after people died. Heaven and hell were the mandatory destination for all humans, whether anyone had heard the story of the New Testament or not. Every culture, race, and people needed to get saved, for they were fallen.

While away, Lucas began to ask, "Saved from what, God?" It wasn't clear to him anymore. And furthermore his parent's views started sounding pretty bigoted.

His mother, Judith, made a wonderful meal that night. His father, Henry, extended his hands as always and asked if Lucas would say the blessing. Lucas looked at him, and said, "I can't pretend to do this religious routine anymore."

When Henry asked, "Why?" that is when he decided to lower the boom. Fifteen minutes later Lucas was still going through all his reasons when his father finally spoke up and said, "That's OK son, you don't have to continue. I don't have the knowledge to answer most of the things you have brought up. Your mother and I are glad you are becoming an educated man. I work with sheet metal and your mom keeps books. I hope you're hands don't end up looking like mine. I can see you are struggling with the faith we tried to give you. You are your own person now and have to live by your decisions and what you think is right. Your mother and I want you to know we are extremely proud of you despite what you think of our beliefs and how we tried to raise you. You are the first of our family to go full time to college. I wish

I could sit in those classes and learn with you. We know you are making the most of your opportunity."

From Lucas' view, Henry had backed up against the ropes and let his son whale away on him, then he countered with a punch that blew through all his defenses, "But I want you to know something else. Your mom and I are selling the house and moving to Peru to become missionaries. This is something we have prayed about a long time and are leaving next year."

Lucas attempted to counter. He was on his own mission and needed to give one more blow to his father's arcane faith, "Dad, how could you dare to take your puffed-up North American, evangelical, conservative, ethnocentric, capitalistic, colonial views, and think they are better than the indigenous people you are going to try and change? That is so myopic! How could you think of yourself as better than they are? Is it possible in your helping them, you are destroying their culture. What gives you the right? What are you, the second coming of the conquistadors?"

His mother was tearing up at this point, dabbing her eyes with the table napkin. Unnerved, Henry said, "Lucas, my world is not as complex as yours. All I can say is, this family wouldn't be here, nor you, without the Lord. Thirty-five years ago my anger and drinking almost destroyed our marriage at the outset. Your grandfather drank heavy and was very mean to my mother, and I was headed that way too. Your mom was precious to me and I didn't want to lose her, so I went down the street to church and got baptized and started studying the Bible with Brother Ray. Lucas, I can't answer all your questions, but I am positively sure, without the Lord I wouldn't be the man I am today, or your father."

With those final words from his dad, the argument ended. Lucas buried it, "You've stolen my thunder. The man with experience has won. I am sorry mom, dad. I won't bother you again."

His mother said the prayer over the food as she cried. His parents, Judith and Henry, learned Spanish and went on to become missionaries taking his little sister, Page, with them. Suddenly he felt he had no home, no faith, and no family. They wrote him, sent emails, but Lucas responded sporadically. Forgetting where he was for a second he blurted out, "No doubt they have me on a prayer list."

"What? Please call me Marge," Ms. Pruett reminded him for the third time, then asked, "How do you like chicken Marsala?"

He answered, "Ms. Pruett, sorry, Marge, chicken Marsala is one of my favorites. Is that fresh Italian bread I smell? When we finish this project, I will build a new house with a custom kitchen just so you can come and cook. Your meals are what keeps me going under these conditions and long hours. I miss seeing the sun."

Marge, with her pure bleach white porcelain smile, borrowed apron, and spatula in hand said, "Mr. Lucas, I understand where you are coming from. Sit down here at the table you two, everything is ready. Enjoy, because when we get out of here I plan on going out to eat every night with Blitz. Take all the money Colonel Smith promises and buy yourself a cook or get married to one. I'm getting claustrophobic in this place. Now if you don't mind, Lucas would you do the honor of praying over our meal?"

A premonition had occurred to him this situation might come up, so he decided ahead not to fight it. After what he had just been through, why be nervous over a prayer? Lucas said, "OK" and held out his hands, bowed his head and waited--five seconds, ten seconds, Victoria started squeezing his hand.

He was trying to decide how to begin when Marge spoke up, "That's OK honey, I'll pray for us if you'd like?"

"No Ms. Pruett, I intend on praying for us. Little rusty." He cleared his throat before beginning, "Lord, you preparest a table before our enemies. You give us life and you give us things to figure out, and you give us things we may never understand. I am truly sorry I underestimated you and never felt you, like my mom and dad. We give thanks for this beautiful meal, you know, ah, especially under the circumstances. Bless us somehow. I am sure this time you hear us. Sorry you had to expend so much energy on me. You have shown us a great deal. Tell us what to do next, amen."

Chapter 61

"But one must not think ill of the paradox, for the
paradox is the passion of thought..."
– Søren Kierkegaard

Victoria and Marge echoed, "Amen, amen." "Beautiful prayer Dr. Tanner," said Marge, then added, "And He will tell us what to do if we listen. How do you like it? I gave my list of ingredients to Maria who came by while you were working. She came back later with everything I needed. All the labels were torn off to disguise where we are of course. I am waiting for a review, so eat!"

Lucas took his first bite of pasta, and chicken breaded and basted in the white wine sauce, then dropped his fork on the table while holding a straight face. Marge puzzled, stared at him as he slowly gave her a thumbs up and broke out in a smile. "Magnificent!" Victoria gave thumbs up too, nodding her head, still chewing on a full bite. Marge laughed and said, "This is how you get a man Victoria. Trade the lab coat for an apron and fix yourself up a bit. Has she ever cooked for you Lucas?"

Victoria jumped on this, "Mom, please don't do this now. Our first priority is to get out of here, and you're embarrassing Lucas."

Marge turned to Lucas, "Honey, are you embarrassed; is that too old fashioned?"

"Not the least," he said as he grinned toward Victoria, "especially after what we've endured. I'd be flattered if she ever traded in the lab coat for an apron, did herself up right and invited me to a home cooked meal."

Victoria had to answer this, "Did myself up right? I do myself down on purpose to stay professional. I know how men think."

"How does this one think?" as he touched her hand again.

Ms. Pruett wasn't finished, "You're a fine man Lucas. Can I ask you another question?"

"Why not?" he said. Then she dug in.

"Victoria was raised in the Church then quit going as a late teenager. She believes in God and was baptized at age eleven. I don't think she goes to church much or reads her Bible like I think she should. So I wanted to ask you, what is your religion?"

"Mom, what you're asking is too private," chimed in Victoria.

Lucas saw his father's head on Ms. Pruett's body for a split second, as he said a silent prayer, *You have my attention, is this bad karma for attacking my father's faith?*

"Vic, your mom is asking good questions. Our work brought her into this compound, so I am obliged to answer her."

"Marge, I don't know what I believe in. Or, what I mean is, up to recently I worked harder at blocking out more than listening for anything supernatural. My parents are Christian missionaries somewhere in the rainforests of Peru and that makes them happy. They are great people.

Those ideals didn't make me happy, so I put them on the shelf for more sure things. Funny though, we are having this conversation under odd circumstances because of my faith in science. Right now I'd give anything to have my father and mother here to hug and ask their advice. I think you would like them and have much in common. Maybe you'd be open to share some insight."

Marge, put down her fork, "Sure honey, anything. I am just an old woman. I really don't even know why I am here. I don't need protection even from death at this point in my life. What is it?"

Lucas took a deep breath, "If a person has a vision, or circumstances which totally confuses the direction of their life, how do you begin to sort it out?"

"I'd find someone who has walked in your shoes."

"Ms. Pruett, that won't be easy."

"I am sure your road is unique Mr. Luke; forgive me, but we all like to think that. Where do you get your mail?"

"I am not sure I am following? We're not receiving any outside communication here."

"Honey, from God."

"Of course, on that I'd have to say my inbox is full, but not sure if there are some viruses attached."

"Mom, what Lucas is saying is…"

"Victoria, I know what email is. What you are asking is, 'how can I identify the truth in this soup I've been tossed into?'"

"Exactly."

"I don't know if I can answer that the way you might like. You younger people are smarter than me and have your own way of discovering things."

As she spoke Lucas tried not to pigeonhole Marge and label her as the proverbial 'church lady.' He noticed her thick hair looked like a wig, her makeup powder was caked in some places, and her lipstick was always fresh. When she finished speaking he asked, "Marge, some things have happened to Victoria and I beyond the work of this compound. Do to current circumstances I don't count on attending church any time soon. My track record in that area needs improving."

Ms. Pruett became animated at this point, telling her daughter, "Victoria honey, please bring the remaining white wine from the kitchen and a new glass."

Both of the doctors were caught off guard, knowing she was a teetotaler, and Vic asked, "Do you want a few more glasses for everyone?"

Ms. Pruett turned to Lucas, "Honey, just one will do, we can all share. Lucas, life with a single parent was not always easy for Victoria. When her father left we were members of a large Baptist church. It was embarrassing. Most of the people in the church were real nice. I was crying at night and trying to work enough hours to pay the bills. A handsome man at the church whose wife I was friends with started helping us. He bought groceries and paid a few bills.

He said the Lord told him to help us. One night he came by to check on us while Victoria was out with a friend. He offered to take me to the grocery store. On the way back he stopped the car in a secluded spot and forced himself upon me. I was in shock. I cried and got out of the car and walked the rest of the way home."

Victoria blurted out, "Oh my God mom, you never told me this!"

Chapter 62

"...and the thinker without the paradox is like the lover
without passion: a mediocre fellow."
--Søren Kiekregaard

"Honey, you didn't need to know. You needed your innocence. I made an appointment with the Senior Pastor, but no one did anything. I called the man's wife, and he had already lied to her that I was chasing him, so I also lost a good friend. Lucas, I am telling you this story because of my state of confusion. I was a single, broke, desperate mother who felt dirty. The church I trusted in stabbed me in the back. Or that's what it felt like at the time. That's when I realized, I had a brush with the devil and so made up my mind not to give in."

Caught up in her story Lucas asked Ms. Pruett, "I am so sorry that happened to you. What did you do then?"

"We switched to a new little community church. Victoria was really young and didn't know what was going on. They had no real youth group, but they had the friendliest people in the world and no one judged me. It was a place where I felt we mattered. We went to visit the first time and the minister was talking about the story where Jesus went to talk to this Samaritan woman who wasn't a bad woman; she couldn't help herself from depending on the wrong kind of men as she was desperate. She had lived with five or six different fellas doing the best she knew how.

The preacher said that this woman tried to be nice to Jesus and ask him if he wanted some well water. He said, 'no, but if you want, I'll give you a drink where you will never be thirsty again.' He told the story in a funny way, that the Samaritan woman was finally getting wise to her own relationships. She got suspicious and asked Jesus where his bucket was. He told her that he didn't need one because he was offering her some of his own special living water from another well. Anyway, I so related to that story after what I had been through. It verified somebody close still believed in me. Victoria and I took our first communion with them that Sunday and stayed. Am I boring you with all of this?"

"No ma'am, you've captured my stomach and my mind. Please, what else?"

"I trembled holding the bread in my hand that day. Right before my turn came to dip the bread in the cup and partake, a thought occurred to me, 'Lord help me forgive the men who had hurt me.'" Ms. Pruett ended her story, "I hope that helps you. I am not sure I made much sense."

Lucas added, "No, no, you made perfect sense. You connected some things for me."

"You've grown up now, both of you. I have a proposal. The Bible says 'Where two or three are gathered in my name, there I am in your midst.' You may feel funny, but we can do the communion here together if it will help."

Lucas looked at Victoria who had tears in her eyes and said, "Mom I love you. That's a wonderful idea. I am so glad you are here. I know you have prayed for me every day. Lucas, will you participate?"

"Your mother is a sage. It is no accident she is here with us. You are saying, now, at this table?"

Miss Pruett answered with a smile, displaying her bright perfect teeth, "Yes honey, under these circumstances – unless they suddenly give us a chaplain. Shall we invite the Colonel or Maria? He could use it."

"Mom, I don't know if they can do that. We'll invite them next time. Go ahead."

"Here, each of you take a piece of this bread and hold it. Just a small piece. Don't eat it yet. I've never done this outside of church. Victoria will you pray over this bread and wine. Oh, pour it in this glass first."

"Is silent OK mom?"

"Go ahead."

When Victoria finished the moment of silence, they all took turns dipping the bread in the cup. Lucas held his up and looked at it closely. Ms. Pruett and Victoria were already chewing their makeshift communion, but for him this act was now more fearful than facing the Vranti. He thought, *How else can I account for what is happening? My parents, my life, and now a little old lady, they've all joined forces to turn me.*

He then took the bread and carefully placed it on his tongue and closed his mouth. As he chewed and began to swallow, he could tell something was happening, something was igniting in him; and odd as it seemed, it wasn't the Blue Moon experiences. This was something deeper, an inner door of knowing opened. The mother and daughter sat back in their kitchen chairs looking at him with wonder as if he was a wine critic ready to give a verdict.

"Victoria, we are so far behind... oh, ohhhhh, I can't believe I missed this!" he shouted and pounded his fist down on the table causing the communion glass to tip. Ms. Pruett snatched the glass, saving it from falling, but splashed herself.

Lucas made a vow out loud, "No longer!"

Victoria, bewildered by his behavior said, "What, Lucas, you think we will land the coordinates Cuzak is looking for?"

"No, no, no," he answered. "Do you realize the gateway by which we accessed Ouriano and Siyon, the Blue Moon, has been with us all along. It's here," pointing to his forehead.

"You nailed it Ms. Pruett, communion. We all have this chance to pray, explore this divine realm. The children's stories my mother taught me were about crossing these boundaries. We just happened to come up with an artificial way of opening a door."

At this he leaned over and grabbed Ms. Pruett's cheeks and kissed her on the lips. She rocked back in her chair stunned, then laughed and said, "I'm not sure what I did, but I'm thrilled you're so happy, Mr. Lucas."

Pausing for a couple of seconds, he said, "I am happy, happier than I have been in a very long time."

Chapter 63

...you have no chance of redemption if you don't exist.
There is no resurrection for angels.

The pressure bubble of his high speed pressed a trough through the breakers as Veezon cruised low over the surface of the waters, wings stretched, saltwater misting his legs, vapor trails curling from the tips of his wings. His intent: a rendezvous with Ouriano for the interrogation of the remainder of Vranti, held in a cave complex accessed through a Sharuan cliff overlooking the sea.

The Vranti had been mutilated to where he had lost his ability to fly and organize his being into much of a threat. He was now a grounded, ugly, hostile, darkened power, but on the other hand, there was little left to threaten or motivate him with to help. This was a stripped-down demon, no way out, no chance to recover. If the two angels could take away his existence, he might accept this as preferable for what awaited all his kind.

Ouriano watched Veezon's approach, the sea breeze blowing his long hair. His mind began reciting his training speeches again, "Annihilation is a prospect most angels ignore except for the fallen. The infected spend most of their time thinking about this since their doom was assured long ago. This declared judgment, as opposed to what many image bearers think, is not annihilation, which is disintegration of their entire being. Rather, this certain doom is complete separation from their creator, while left to fend for themselves in some unknown sector of the creation.

All the aspects of the miracle of blessing without the Existing One is rendered void--lost is joy, the prospect of co-creation, the delight in beauty and perfection, the experience of sacrificial love, and the ability to become one with another being. The infected try to suppress these thoughts by avoiding the local entity's name and creating false hopes. Many of them secretly pine for their dissolution as a valid escape from eternal suffering."

But now, Ouriano knew they had a new problem which would mean a change in the training manual. Yazad and Beltshzan believed they had solved this dilemma, by creating a third option if not more. Ouriano guessed, *One way or another, we are going to find out. This Vranti has no dignity left.*

The last time information was leveraged out of an infected, Ouriano was at the center the controversy. His team had captured and flown one of the instigators of the Ukrainian starvation massacre of Stalin toward the staging area of the Magnificon. They kept him shrouded then slowly exposed his form one section at a time to the Shekinah light. For an initial moment the exposed leathery flesh experienced a restoration to its original form and luster, but then like a smoldering stick overloaded with oxygen, the restored member flash burned.

This questionable torture continued until receiving the information Ouriano and his team wanted to hear. The creature then pleaded for them to finish what they started, but they refused. By then the Royal Cherubim discovered this violation and completed the task in their fury. Ouriano and his group were charged with temporary intent of desecration of Siyon and unwarranted cruelty, and were examined to see if they themselves were infected. Ouriano replayed all this as he watched Veezon's continued approach.

To his horror, one of his longtime fellow collaborators had been contaminated by the infection, then removed from the rank ceremoniously by Michael, asked to confess his pride, and cast down to Earth. Ouriano, as well became suspect, and put on temporary leave of his duties while he was investigated. Michael visited him and said a strange thing had happened, "You Ouriano, were weighed by the Magnificon council and found clean of the infection and intentional desecration, even though you violated the non-torture clause. The council said you were *somehow buffered* from the infection by your odd faith. But I think they confused you with being human. Don't count on this abnormal trait for any sentinel to deliver you again. And expect to be reassigned."

"And Veezon, what about him?" Ouriano asked.

Michael answered, "His motivations were pure. As a subordinate he was following your orders. The other was not so fortunate; he crossed over through self-directed vengeance. But in my opinion, Ouriano, you helped him." Even with this history in mind, Veezon and Ouriano once again risked another round of questionable interrogation methods.

Ouriano began working out the justification of what they were about to do, *But if we were already being recruited for possibly a one-way trip to the Sanctuary, would it matter? Once inside the Sanctuary might we be forced to decide between annihilation or an unholy adoption at the hands of a reunified Lucifer? Could we of the non-image bearers, claim David's promise, 'that you will not let your holy one see decay?'*

I know what some of my compatriots would say, 'Ouriano, you have no chance of redemption if you don't exist. There is no resurrection for angels.' Do I really want to become human and won't admit it? Where did my fantasy of trading my elevated position for a mortal walk of faith derive? From my obsessive, compulsive, contemplation? Break out of this Ouriano!

Ouriano continued to watch Veezon's descent. He was close. *And to think, all the redeemed image bearers would one day become something greater. How many of the earthbound feet believed his words, 'you shall be called children of God?'* Veezon accelerated, then swooped up ten stories to the entrance of the secured cave compound.

Landing he spoke, "I thought this Vranti had been decimated? I have grave memories of the last time we tried something like this. I will not go to the same extreme unless we have word from the Magnificon council."

Ouriano tried to relieve his fears, "We will take a different approach, I assure you. Like you, I was surprised when I received word from Shem. His Neanderthals had gone back to the ancient worship center in the desert and noticed most of Vranti's remains were missing. They began hunting for him and found a pile of rotting flies and insects attempting to assimilate back together. They became suspicious, sacked them up, and notified me. We continued to let him assemble his toasted pieces under heavy guard. He can now talk."

They walked close to a hundred yards through a narrow corridor into the red sandstone cliffs, then down a flight of stairs through an entrance opening up to a Roman-coliseum-sized-cavern, encrusted with clear crystals that refracted the blue light from the turquoise pool of seawater at the bottom. To the water's edge, they glided down to where piles of bones and shells dotted the crushed crystal beach. Dangling from the ceiling hundreds of feet above were tree roots, just shy of the salt water. The sack containing the Vranti was hanging from one of the roots over the beach.

Veezon unsheathed his sword and was about to say something when a bullfrog-like voice came from within the bushel-sized sack. As the voice spoke, the bulges in the sack shifted, "I am afraid you have caught me when I offer no match to you. I am less than half the adversary I once was, and no one from the collective comes for me. Do you dare to look? My powers are gone and I am naked. I know what you have come for."

Chapter 64

How does it feel to be a drone? Oh, you can't answer that can you?

"Cut him down," Ouriano requested. Veezon took his sword and sliced the sack in half. Two bundles of steaming phlegm coated green matter plopped down onto the crystal sand beach. Veezon sighed in repulsion at the goo dripping off his sword. The piles slowly slid together and formed into a Komodo-like dragon. The resulting giant lizard sat up and faced the two inquisitors with its long scaled tail swinging back and forth like a pendulum.

It began to speak, sporadically testing the air with its long split tongue, effecting a pause each time, "And so now...what shall we do? ... The jester ... has been tricked!"

Ouriano appealed to their ancient bond, "Vranti, you have seen the matrix of creation and were privileged to explore where only recently some of us have ventured. Why did you turn, were we not once brothers?"

The bedeviled creature sat there idly flicking out it's tongue and slowly waving its tail. Veezon surprised Ouriano in holding back his own voice. Then Vranti spoke, tilting his head slightly to the right, his speech repeatedly interrupted by the protruding of his long forked tongue, "You are wasting your time ... in patronizing me. The plans and contin ... gencies ... are in place. This is a winner ... take all. You have nothing ... to offer me. I know well ... your lore of bloodshed and torture ... your anger ... your want to be human.

You Ouriano ... are like one of us. It is I ... who have an offer for you. Take me to Cuzak ... so I may be transported to ... the Sanctuary. You may come, too ... my friend, and become ... what you desire ... a human ... a father ... without the tag of his image!"

"Why do you speak of such things with certainty?" Ouriano asked, keeping his focus on him, "With your kind nothing is as it seems."

"Yes Ouriano ... you speak the truth ... as you know it. In the Sanctuary ... all things ... will be restored. My collective ... will have new light from Yazad."

Stepping forward Ouriano said, "And Beltshzan, does he have a say in this?"

He walked toward him slowly, the Vranti's tongue lapping his ankle. Veezon drew his sword. Vranti then let out a cackling laugh echoing through the cavern, backed off and said, "You already know ... this. Why do you ask...? The Cherubim guards ... are a dead give away!"

Veezon moved toward him and asked, "And the rest of the infected, where do their loyalties lie, Yazad or Beltshzan?"

"Who is this ... ? I am insulted ... to be addressed by ... such a low flyer ... a drone. How does ... it feel to be ... a drone? Oh ... you can't answer that ... can you? Look, you are showing emotion ... don't break ... the pixie of light would be upset."

With this biting remark, Veezon swung the flat of his sword against the Vranti's neck, flinging him into a pile of bones, "How dare you blaspheme the sovereign, the Lord's sentinel?"

The Vranti slowly righted himself and swaggered back to them with the motion of a crocodile, elongated head and in countermotion to the thick tale, then spoke to Ouriano, "I refuse ... to address the drone."

"Alright then, I am not saying we have something to offer you yet, but we might if you help us. If a corridor was opened, how many would break from Beltshzan to give allegiance to Yazad?"

"Hmmmm? The percentages ... means nothing ... but like all new social orders ... they need a purging ... your man said, 'many are called, few are chosen.'"

Ouriano continued to dig, "Then we are correct in thinking Beltshzan will punish those who act disloyal and initially flee to Yazad? And your collective, they are working with the Nephilim to restore these two perceived adversaries as the unified Lucifer?"

The Vranti sensed this was the time to make a deal, "Release me ... restore my wings ... you need someone ... like me ... on the inside. Only understand ... many things ... are in motion ... myself cut off from ... the collective ... it assures vengeance ... even now."

Veezon put the point of his sword to the Vranti's neck, "I believe this part – that his collective will descend like a dark cloud on your Juwaan and your pet half-breed in retribution."

Ouriano turned his back to them both saying, "Then he's helped all he can. We must go to Siyon. Leave him."

As they turned and flew back up to the platform entrance they heard the Vranti declare, "I have more."

But Ouriano had enough. Veezon gave him his last words,

"Oh Vranti, what you might have been,
A drone of the Most High was beneath you,
How many times you have been spared,
May your local entities save you.
Call on their names to the distant heavens,
See what love redeems you!"

With this. Ouriano and Veezon gazed one final time at the reptilian Vranti as he lay near the water's edge. He replied back, "Yes, and ... to you ... as well, '*See ... what love ... redeems you,*'" then began to wade into the hidden lagoon and swim. He may have rightly assumed there was an escape out to sea. As he started to dive, many medium-to-small sea creatures crossed paths with him fleeing to the surface, leaping for the crystal beach.

Just then, the colossal Leviathan of Sharu exploded without warning up through the underground sea passage full of rage, sucking the Vranti's form past its massive incisors and into its multiple rows of grinding teeth. The leviathan victor then beached itself on the underground lagoon's shore and celebrated, releasing its horrid death scream.

The long time friends in arms walked out to the cliff landing. Veezon spoke with a straight face, "If only the dinosaurs had been left to mix with the image bearers a while longer. Did you arrange for this ending?"

Unfurling his wings into the buffeting sea breeze, Ouriano answered, "This is the time of the image bearers, and ours as well. Siyon awaits us. By the time we arrive, the council of the Magnificon will know of this. You must show them you have the faith they suspect."

Chapter 65

I don't share your luxury. I believe in karma. I make karma happen. I rain down karma on my enemies.

Cuzak walked into the lab ingratiating himself, "Before you retire for the evening Dr. Tanner, I want you to know I am eternally grateful for the progress you have been making. Every step you and Dr. Pruett make with this technology is being followed by mirror labs around the world. You will get your credit and pay off. I have arranged a press release and interview soon. Until then I hope you are still finding your accommodations manageable? I hear Ms. Pruett is a great cook."

"She is a blessing in so many ways," said Lucas.

"Good, please tell her I admire her strength, and give Blitz a pat on the head for me," Cuzak said as he went back through the door.

Out of hearing range, he mimicked Cuzak's smirk and speech, "Very well, please give your orc-ish hordes my best regards, I hope they all get cooked." Lucas even mocked himself for his own cooperation with the enemy, putting more words in the mouth of the Colonel, "Based on your core identity, Dr. Tanner, or lack thereof, collaboration out of silent despair makes evil that much more palatable if not justifiable; unless you have something stronger on the inside you haven't shown us?"

For the past two weeks, Colonel Smith had coordinated everything needed to expand the dimension-piercing technology to accommodate hundreds of travelers at a time. While Lucas and Victoria were working fourteen hour days, they kept a level of professional excitement which brushed aside remorse for the obvious diabolical application of their creation.

They wanted the technology to reach its potential, as it was their baby. Since Ouriano had encouraged them to complete this work, they postulated, despite their feelings of guilt, that it had a greater purpose. Still, they prayed for forgiveness ahead of time.

As they went back to the apartment, Lucas confided in Victoria, "I regret that my faith is coming out now because of a survival instinct."

"What are you talking about?"

"The best faith has its roots in innocence, and then necessity as a distant second choice."

"I don't know Lucas, maybe God took you serious as a kid, even if you didn't, later on. Maybe you didn't kill off your faith as much as you give yourself credit for. Maybe it wasn't yours to kill off."

Coming around the corner toward their dorm, they saw Ru leaning against Ms. Pruett's door with one hand at the top of the frame and her head bowed over against the door. Closer, they saw she had tears dripping on the tile floor. Panicked, Victoria asked, "What is it Ru?"

Ru said nothing, but lifted her head and stepped back from the door, leaning on the opposite wall. Lucas grabbed the knob and pulled open the door with Victoria right behind. They made it to the living room and were halted by shock. There was Ms. Pruett, hanging from the small kitchen chandelier by a rope of wound sheets. The small kitchen table was kicked over next to her dangling legs. Her face was blue. A couple of flies were buzzing around her head.

Running to her, Lucas tried to lift her out of the noose but needed an extra hand, "Ru, help us!" Ru's hands ripped the corded sheet in half from beneath Ms. Pruett's chin. Catching her, he laid her in the living room on the love seat. Her wig was crooked and dentures half out. He felt her pulse, but she was gone. He gently straightened her wig, tidying her appearance as best he could, knowing she always wanted to look her best. He had not known her long, but Ms. Pruett had opened doors for him, and he would miss her. There was nothing more he could do. He could hear Victoria moaning in sobs behind him, so he turned and put his arms around her, lending her his strength while she collected herself to adjust to the shock. Dazedly, she looked at her mother, then scanned the room, when her attention seemed caught on something. He glanced around, trying to focus on what she saw.

She was pointing at the floor, to the body of Blitz. He had a pool of blood under his head, leaking from his mouth and nose. Victoria broke out in fresh sobs. Not only had she lost her mother, but Ms. Pruett's little pet, too. Lucas tried to comfort her, "Looks like he was trying to protect her. The little fella put up some kind of a fight. Look at the dozens of dead insects on the floor around him. We can guess who was here."

Lucas recognized the lingering room's scent from the desert of the dark winds when he had confronted the Vranti. "This is payback. This is retribution for the Neanderthals' slice and dice."

While Victoria continued to weep, Lucas guided her to Ms. Pruett's body, and pulled up a chair near the love seat. She was embracing her dead mother when Cuzak entered abruptly through the front door, initially dismissing everyone as he sized up the crime scene. Ru walked up to him, whereupon he whispered something to her while she nodded her head up and down. Turning around, for the first time they saw the Colonel without his positive pretense. His head was tilted down as he addressed them, "This is intolerable. We will not forget who did this. Ms. Pruett was a great woman. I am also sorry her dog was lost."

Unable to control his emotion, Lucas stepped over Blitz to within six inches of Cuzak's face. "We've kept up our side of the agreement. Why did you let this happen? I've heard about your rubbish theory that these poor demons have no choice. I've experienced differently. Looks like they've chosen to kill this time for the sport of it."

Cuzak answered, stone cold, "I was not counting on you killing or maiming one of them either during your visit to the Blue Moon. We all are to blame for this unfortunate event." Looking at Victoria over his shoulder he said, "Your mother was a true believer wasn't she? She'll be fine. All things in time." Switching his attention back to Lucas, he asked, "Do you believe in karma Dr. Tanner?"

"What kind of a question is that?" He spun back.

"Do you believe in karma?" he asked again.

He closed in until he pressed his chest against the Colonel's and then grabbed hold of his suit jacket. He quickly noticed this hybrid was not a movable object, more like a commercial fridge. "No," he answered with startled uncertainty, "I believe in a greater power than karma."

"You keep that belief Dr. Tanner. I honor that in you. I don't share your luxury. I believe in karma. I make karma happen. I rain down karma on my enemies. Being the tip of vengeance is an ugly business, a destiny. Don't let yourself think about it too much. The Vranti crossed my line. Now Dr. Tanner, please back away."

"Wait a minute," Lucas said, "You are not walking away from this so easy. You took our lives away from us, and you bear the responsibility of her death."

Lucas heard Ru's voice behind him as an emergency signal, "Please back away Dr. Tanner." At the same time she hooked his upper arms guiding him back a step, and with sarcasm in her voice said, "The Colonel has been reminded of this before." With this statement Cuzak's eyes dilated at Ru.

Cuzak straightened out his suit jacket and spoke again, "'Precious in the sight of the Lord is the death of his saints.' If you are intent on being a believer's believer, you should educate yourself. Drop the sorrow and learn quickly from this. I don't give advice for the local entity but he does show an affinity for you. I am sorry, you'll find your own reason for this. We will store her and the dog in our morgue until your release. Then you can bury her. Take the next forty-eight hours off to grieve so you can concentrate when you come back."

Cuzak then exited the room, knocking aside the help at the door who had arrived to clear the bodies. A second later every one heard a deep grunt and the vibration of a heavy sledge puncturing a hole in the hallway wall, followed by chunks of falling concrete hitting the tile floor.

Chapter 66

"For the creature was subjected to frustration, not by its own decision, but by the will of the one who subjected it," – Romans 8:20

Ru turned around and shouted at those who had come for the bodies, "Out! Haven't any of you lost your mother or were you all born in a test tube?!" She pulled the door shut and leaned against it, thinking about the lonely indignity of her own mother's death. She gathered herself in silence for a minute then walked over to Victoria to comfort her, "You were blessed to have such a wonderful mother by your side. I looked forward to checking on her everyday while you worked in the lab. She was an extraordinary human being. I delivered her groceries at noon today and left around 12:40. Like always, she held my hands and said a prayer before I left:

'Dear God, we don't like it here, but if this is your will, we will put up with it for a while, just like your twenty-third Psalm says, *And you prepare for us a table in the presence of our enemies...* Thank you, Lord for wood and water. Watch over Ru, Blitz, my family; change the heart of Colonel Smith. Amen.'

Your mother has to be the first person in history to pray for the Colonel. Victoria if I should meet my own mother one day, I hope she would be like Ms. Pruett."

"Ouriano can help you meet your mother, right?" Victoria interjected trying to smile.

Ru paused a few seconds, "There are a few places that Ouriano's help doesn't work for me." Changing the subject she added, "I know how cold Cuzak can be. He did tell me he was sealing the complex off and guaranteed the culprits would be found. He thinks they are still here."

Victoria wiped her eyes, "Thank you Ru for being a good friend to her. Mom grew fond of you and talked about how you were much nicer than your first impression suggested. The other day I told her, 'Ru is a real angel in disguise.' Mom agreed but said something which shocked me, 'Ru is not the first angel I have met.'"

Ru broke down and wept. Ashamed of her weakness, of her emotion and tears, she faced away from Victoria. "I don't want you to see me like this."

"Please Ru, don't blame yourself," Victoria reached toward her, but stopped short of touching her, realizing at the last moment that Ru would not want any more displays of sentiment. Victoria turned away from Ru and went over to the chair beside her mother.

Next to the love seat where Ms. Pruett lay, Lucas sank to his knees and gathered her cold hands in his, attempting to be indifferent to Ru's emotion. Without warning a new vision triggered, one where he stood over himself as a young boy and his mother reading together. Both were seated on the old green living room couch. Her left arm wrapped around his shoulder as his head lay under her chin. The four-year-old Lucas helped hold a thin children's book with his left hand as he turned the pages with the other. He could smell his mother's make up and Lilly of the Valley perfume as he pretended to read with her through a child's version of the Ten Commandments, "Read with me Lucas, say the words with mommy... 'You will have no other gods before me... You will not lie ... Honor your mother and father that it may go well with you all the days of your life' ..."

His mother closed the book and then began writing in her prayer diary. The boy asked her, "What are you writing mommy?"

"A prayer for you! You are one of a kind."

"Tell me what you are writing," he begged.

"I'll tell you," hugging him closer, "Keep your Angel of Light as guard over my Lucas, may his life glorify you greater than his father or I could." Almost as soon as the vision began, it ended. Lucas snapped his head back up. He gently released Ms. Pruett's hand and abruptly stood.

Victoria asked, "What?" as he got up and went toward the back bedroom, "What are you looking for?"

"Your mom was way more aware than we gave her credit for. I told you she reminded me of my parents. I want to know what else she was thinking and experiencing."

On the same wavelength, Victoria shouted amidst her tears, "Yes! I know what you are looking for, it's under her mattress! She wrote her entire life in it. Most of her recordings were prayers. I peeked inside once as a teenager, but it was a lot of religious stuff so I quit. Victoria chuckled as she cried with her last observation, "She thought no thief would ever think of lifting up her mattress."

Lucas shouted from the bedroom, "I found it," then reappeared and resumed his place next to Victoria. "There are many things I wanted to ask Ms. Pruett. I know it won't be the same, but this is gold Victoria, your mom can still speak to us." Victoria nodded her head yes, but the tears continued to seep into the fresh tissues handed to her by Ru.

"Do you mind if we read her journal tomorrow Lucas? I am not up to that right now."

"Of course, but I'm not going to leave you alone for one second. Nothing against you, Ru," he said, "but we need some time alone."

Victoria wondered about his last remark and buffered it, "What do you think Ru, are you alright with that?"

Ru answered, "Let me leave you alone for a while with Ms. Pruett and Blitz. I'll bring the men back, and we can clean up her place up then, while you go next door. We'll leave all her personal things in the apartment. No hurry."

Ru clutched her hands together, and stared down at the carpet, "A mother's desperate prayer for her children does not go unnoticed. Have you never heard, 'And your seed will bruise the serpent's head?' Maybe we have been called to continue where our parents left off?" With that last sentiment Ru walked out the front door, locked it and silently waved her help waiting in the hall to come with her.

When he couldn't hear their steps anymore Lucas asked, "Whose parent is she referring to?" but Victoria wasn't listening anymore as she wept harder. For the next six hours there were no more words spoken between them as they tried to make sense of two more innocent victims caught in the cross fire of a war they didn't want to acknowledge. Without knowing it, they both fell asleep praying the same basic prayer, *God make your voice clear among the confusion!*

Chapter 67

*My God I trust in you, please do not let me be
humiliated by my enemies.*

Six hours later, a tad rested, but almost as frustrated,
Victoria and Lucas heard the rap on the metal front door
just before it opened.

"Dr. Tanner, Dr. Pruett, we really need to take Ms. Pruett
and Blitz now."

Dr. Pruett replied, sitting across from her mother, still
rummaging through many memories, "I know Ru, please
come in alone for a few minutes."

Lucas stood up as Ru entered in, "We were just talking
about who can we trust to make sense out of all this? In
the desert of the dark winds the Angel of Light spoke to
me. Her words are stuck in my head,

'I will sing a song which imparts wisdom,
I will utter hidden things from of old.
Your prayers rise up like fragrant incense,
Ever before my throne.
Blessed having never seen,
Before you were born I knew you,
I will not ignore my own.'"

Victoria asked, "You've brought this up before. What did
this Angel of Light mean?"

"I think she meant there are many clues left for us to
discover, connections to be made guiding us toward our
destiny, but so far we haven't been tuned in."

"A spiritual hibernation?" Victoria added.

"Yes, and the clues are still here," said Lucas as he reasoned, "Planted in the past as waypoints for the future. How about if I read some of your mother's journal aloud now?"

Ru spoke up gingerly, "Lucas, Victoria, I have a suggestion. We need to let my men come in and take Ms. Pruett and Blitz, and clean this apartment up, now. Why don't we carry this conversation on next door in your apartment?" Ru motioned for the men to come in, three in lab coats, three in suit and ties.

Lucas replied, "Looks like we don't have a choice."

Before they move them, "Do one of you want to pray over her, I am not there yet. Trying," said Ru.

Lucas, shook his head. "The only thing I feel like praying for right now is vengeance against her killer and a close second to Cuzak. But for her honor I will."

Ru extended her hands to each of them. Lucas, however only took Victoria's leaving Ru's other hand awkwardly dangling alone next to his, then he prayed, "Lord of Ms. Pruett, she was one of your best. She was like a mother to me. Little did we suspect how important she was to you. Help Victoria with this heavy loss. Please unite them again one day. In the meantime, help me bring justice to this killer once and for all. We all know who did it."

The moment the prayer ended Ru barked out orders, "Be gentle with Ms. Pruett and Blitz or you'll be in a body bag! Please, doctors, follow me next door."

The three of them walked out of the apartment. Victoria stopped at the door to look back at the men zipping up Ms. Pruett in the body bag, then continued. Most of her tears were used up for now.

Ru felt uncomfortable as she led them to their adjacent apartments next door, given the harsh prayer by Lucas, but Ru had a breakfast of eggs, pancakes, sausage, with coffee and orange juice waiting for them at the table. "I figured you might be hungry. Do you want me to leave again?"

"No Ru, I want you to hear this too. Lucas can you read some from mom's journal while we sit down and eat?" Lucas took a minute to answer as he was in the middle of devouring his pancake, then flushed it down with orange juice.

"I have marked a few things you might be interested in."

"January 23rd, 2012,
All this moving? My little Vic isn't telling me everything. She needs my help. Dr. Johnson told me I only have eighteen months to two years to live before I go into congestive heart failure. If that is the case I'll just go along with the move Victoria's friends are suggesting. I don't want to tell her about my condition. She worked too hard to be weighed down by me. I hope she remembers you. Watch over her tonight.

Words for today are Ps 25:1-2,
'O Lord, I bring myself before you in prayer
My God, I trust in you
Please do not let me be humiliated by my enemies
Do not let them triumphantly rejoice over me!'

I don't like moving, and I don't trust these men who say they are with the government. I'll go along with it, since I can't get ahold of Victoria right now. You want me to do this? I guess I'd be moving to assisted living soon anyway, so take me somewhere exciting!"

"Umm, your mom enjoyed leading on with her simple little old lady act didn't she?" Lucas tacked on.

"And she was anything but," said Ru.

"Thank you for the meal Ru," added Victoria.

Chapter 68

The beginning of the end is near. All things will be made new. The rage of evil has lifted its head against the one enthroned.

"She was an iron lady, find something a little earlier in the diary," said Victoria. Please sit down with us Ru. Are you sure you are not hungry?"

"No, I'd rather remain standing in case someone walks in, but I do want to hear what she wrote."

Flipping back, Lucas peeled a page over and read,

> *"June 7th, 2011,*
> *Blitz never gets tired of chasing his ball or the neighbor's cat. If it wasn't for Blitz I'd really be lonely. The roses were bursting with fragrance this morning in the bright sun. Would love to bottle this smell. I am so proud of my girl. I read the press release of her and Lucas' awards for their experiments. I don't understand what they are doing, but others are excited about it. Maybe she will find a man. I am tired already this morning. Woke up at 3 a.m., watched weather and infomercials for half hour, then prayed, never went back to sleep.*
>
> *Finally got up at five, let Blitz out and, made coffee and read the paper. I think you kept me up last night to make sure I prayed for Victoria and Lucas. Bless and protect them. Should I move near her? Most my friends are now gone.*

"She continues," said Lucas.

> *"My words for the day are Psalms 77:1-2:*

'I cried out to the Lord for help
I cried out to God to listen to me
When I was in trouble, I looked to the Lord
During the night I lifted up my hands in prayer
But I refused to be comforted.'

Alright God, how did you time this passage? Who do you think you are? I know you're listening and I'm frightened. There is a good reason why you had me praying again last night, I'm sure. These sleep interruptions keep happening more regular. Please, lead me today down your paths. I feel like things are about to change. I can't help it, Victoria's my life."

Victoria sobbing, said, "My mom should never have been caught up in this."

Ru stepped closer to the table, "On the contrary, there was no better person to be caught up in this than her. Listen to what she wrote. She was exactly the kind of person Yazad, Beltshzan, the Vranti, can never account for. Her faith will be your strength. Your mother had a secret source we had better all tap. Please read another."

"Okay, some are very short. Here is a more lengthy one."

"June 20th 2011,
I spoke with Victoria last night. She never shares a morsel of significance, so of course I have to talk about Wheel of Fortune with her like an old biddy. She won't talk about anything personal. I am afraid she thinks she is going to disappoint me. I wish we could live just one day over again from the past; maybe go back when she was nine and make it a Sunday, with pancakes, church, lunch, movie, walk in the park. I am not going to tell her what the doctors have said.

For the life of me Lord, why does my sleep keep getting interrupted? Last night I thought I was hallucinating; I woke up with a green, dark cloud in my room. Blitz was barking like mad, perched on my stomach. I tried to yell out but my body was frozen. I couldn't sit up or do anything but open my eyes. Something was holding me down. This was the most oppressive feeling I've ever encountered. I don't think it was my imagination. I called the pastor this morning. She told me the experience could be my heart meds, emotional strain, or even spiritual warfare. She gave me some verses to read. I like this one.

2 Corinthians 12:7-9,
'Therefore a thorn in the flesh was given to me so that I might not become arrogant because of the great things I had seen, a messenger of Satan to trouble me. I asked the Lord three times if he would take this away from me. But he told me, My grace is sufficient for you, for my power is made perfect in your weakness. So then, I will most gladly boast about my weaknesses, so that the power of the anointed one may dwell in me.'

I can accept this, but don't let me die alone. I still remember the camping trip right after the divorce when Victoria and I went to the Appalachians. I heard a noise outside the cabin and through the blinds saw what looked like radiant beams of light from behind a large pine. I went to investigate and that's when I saw her. I've yet to tell anyone, but it is about time Victoria knew.

'Your fervent prayers go
where you will one day be,
for now you must keep your faith
for it is the Lord alone who sees....Marge, guard your child, you have but this life to give.'

I asked the Angel, 'What do you mean?'

She answered,
'The beginning of the end is near.
All things will be made new.
The rage of evil has lifted its head against the one enthroned.
The rebellious will raise a false hope of eternal life,
but His Holy One scoffs at their schemes,
and His Anointed laughs at their complex plots.
Have they not failed once, only to stumble into their own snare?'

I never saw this angel again. Do I dare tell Victoria, lest something bad happen or she accuses me of dementia?"

Lucas laid down Ms. Pruett's private diary on the kitchen table.

Victoria's grief for her mother mingled with disappointment and sharp frustration welled up in her eyes again as she addressed the diary, "Mom why didn't you tell me?"

Lucas spoke up, "That's easy to answer. If it wasn't for what we've seen, neither of us would have believed her. The question is what's next?"

Ru added, "We all are dealing with the *'what's next.'*"

Victoria dabbed her eyes dry, took a swig of coffee from the mug, placed it back down on the table and boldly stated, "The prophecy of my mother's angel is the 'what's next.' We're going to help evil stumble into its own snare, God help us all!"

Chapter 69

*If they insist on discovering alone where imagination
ends and creation begins, they are utterly lost.*

Golden dust clouds of Siyon's outer layers rushed by as
Veezon and Ouriano blindly dove toward their meeting
with destiny, escorted by flashes of static charges ignited
by the friction of their high velocity. Once through this
outer band, they leveled off, soaring like eagles, taking in
the panorama of the clear atmosphere resplendent with
rainbows arching between giant, churning white pillars
of glowing clouds hundreds of miles in height and
breadth, and then they renewed their dive.

Every time Ouriano had this experience the same words
echoed in his mind, "This is the birth place of worlds, of
time, and light, itself. There is an old saying, 'Siyon is
where creation goes forth from the imagination of God.'"

They continued to pass golden asteroid cities dotted with
fresh water lakes, mountains, green forests, and terraced
vineyards. Sky-sailing vessels embarked, ferrying the
citizens between countless civilizations. Here,
celebrations were frequent and new arrivals constant,
with generations uniting in joy and healing as answers
emerged. Below him Ouriano knew beauty and pleasure
are perfected as the joint heirs of Siyon move toward
beholding the Heir of the Magnificon face to face. All
scars, pain and suffering of other worlds are removed in
Siyon except for those which belong to one.

With that said, however, Veezon and Ouriano feared the
plot of Yazad and Beltshzan. Veezon himself speculated,
"Could this place be drawn into battle? This would be the
ultimate jewel of their rebellion and pride. Most of the
inhabitants of the flotilla of cities we pass have already
suffered through this once and for all, have they not?"

Half way to the Magnificon, Veezon marveled at the two members of the Royal Cherubim warriors who had joined their formation as they rocketed down... *Each one as powerful as a legion, a different sort from the ranks, called to guardianship of the Most Holy. My rank were ordered to refrain from mixing with them, as they were given to little conversation and where present, projected the imminent presence of the sevenfold spirits. Least in resemblance to humans, the sight alone of a Royal Cherubim warrior is known to cause humans immediate apoplexy and dread. Lucifer is of this kind and the most brilliant of them all.*

Ouriano, leading the formation in the dive, recounted words he had mentored others with regarding this place, "Image bearers and angels alike misunderstand Siyon, whose layers are without end. The deepest I have ascended is to the edge of the Magnificon to the council of the elders. Beyond this is a place where even the rarest of host have ventured for it does not belong to them. As much as the Self-Existing One has revealed, everything is far from being made known.

Over the eons I have watched the image bearers of Earth fly with their consciences near this holy place in search of what lies before and after the gate. Their speculation gives them both pleasure and pain. Many have gazed near the great aperture with the briefest flash of pure reason. Even greater fools have flown nearer, carried by worship and faith. They are so burdened, but do not be fooled by them. If they insist on discovering alone where the imagination ends and creation begins, they are utterly lost.

Yet, a word of caution you Morning Stars, much of this realm is yet to be charted, and will never be by our kind unless a change is made. I have been accused and ridiculed for exhibiting several human traits, speculation, one of them. However if a creature is to truly wonder in amazement, then ecstatic worship followed by hopeful speculation is the natural route. My opinion is that through the gates of the Magnificon is the other side of the great singularity so many image bearers are seeking. To go there one must pass under the great throne, past the Angel of Light, through the One Who Sustains All, and the Shekinah gate. A sifting and final transformation has to take place to pass through this entrance. Some of us on rare occasion have spoken of this and attempted to guess what lies beyond. I can tell you, Michael, Gabriel, and the greatest of Juwaans, have yet to explore this realm.

What we do know is that the vastness and the grandeur beyond the gates of the Magnificon are so overwhelming, if one were to go uninvited and unprepared their very core nature would surely evanesce into nothing. Worship and wonder on Siyon are the guiding principles. Beyond the gates of the Magnificon is the adventurers' and voyagers' dream.

I have been asked, may this be the heaven so many image bearers hope for in their earthly death, and the consummation with God at the great feast to come? Wouldn't those alone be destiny enough? I have been close and looked beyond by accident. I have few words to describe. There is a river which flows toward the great throne and under which continues through, supplied by the prayers of the image bearers.

There is a large beam of light flowing through the throne, originating from the Magnificon, the source of all illumination of Siyon. The light is so intense only the Angel of Light can stand in the beam dispersing it as she wishes, casting out new galaxies or illuminating hearts in realms of darkness yet to be visited by her. To this place every host like you should aspire to come and worship, absorbing the light that moves us to vibrate the

Magnificon gates with energy 100,000 times that of any earthly spectacle."

Ouriano continued in his private thoughts, *If I could talk to my former students now, I would remind them, 'The host and the redeemed love to sing, but they are not scheduled for that today. Today the council is meeting. They are convening about Veezon and me. They are gathering because something is about to take place which has never happened before. Pray with the image bearers you protect, and above all have faith!'*

Chapter 70

*If they must sacrifice themselves, let them do in dying
what they could not do in life.*

Approaching the Magnificon council, whose location
continually moves through the Siyon atmosphere, the
Royal Cherubim secured the two visiting winds'
weapons, then escorted them inside the spherical
labyrinth. From the outside one could not see through
the outer shining gray skin into the small moon
structure. Inside however, everything was translucent,
the outline of the corridors, platforms, columns, seats,
were visible when needed, or when you moved, but the
entire view to the outside atmosphere of Siyon -- except
for the other beings present -- was uninterrupted.

As Veezon and Ouriano entered the central council
platform they found the members rising from their knees
where they had been in lengthy prayer. Veezon and
Ouriano previously had only viewed the entire council in
worship from a distance. Their appearance was a mash of
angelic and animal; wings, beaks, eyes, claws, mixed
faces and breeds, older than the Blue Moon, holding
knowledge of another history before the time of man and
angels. *Why this heightened security?* they wondered.

Ouriano speculated correctly that the four creatures and
twenty-four elders could see what lay beyond the
paradox of creation into the singularity. Veezon too
sensed their power, not from their size, but from their
being and character. To their right, a quarter-moon
away, they saw a great beam of light from the singularity,
and heard the beating wings of thousands upon
thousands preparing for worship. Here they were close to
where all paths end, and trails birthed.

The creature with the head and wings of an eagle and the body of a lion began to speak, "My name is Gamaliel, let him who was, and is, and is yet to come, bear witness and give wisdom to our meeting with Ouriano and Veezon, two honorable host of the Most High. May courage, faith, hope, and the blessings of the sevenfold spirit be with you."

"And also with you," Veezon and Ouriano responded in unison.

Gamaliel became intense, "Do both of you know what this is about?"

Veezon's and Ouriano's responses overlapped, "Yes ... Most certainly. I'd ... Well, no ... We'd like to know more."

"You are here for two reasons. Let me explain the first. A hook has been put in the nose of Yazad and Beltshzan to bring them together. Their deceit and murderous ways against the woman's seed will come to an end. Yazad and Beltshzan will strive against them with unprecedented cruelty and deceive many. Those who have eyes to see will see, and those who have ears to hear will listen about the great and coming Day of the Lord. Unfortunately many will not heed. A lie is coming so vile even some of our Sabaoth, I am afraid, will succumb. Both of you are already engaged in this encounter."

Ouriano answered, "Yes we have confirmed this ourselves. And the second reason?" He wondered if this related to the confiscating of their swords.

One of the elders who carried a human form spoke up, "Your weapons were secured because things have changed."

Recognizing him, Ouriano blurted, "Shem, that is you? I had no idea you were an elder of this council?"

"As you say, but let Gamaliel finish."

"Veezon, Ouriano, you are as outstanding a representative of the rank as there are. For this reason we are going to ask both of you to do something completely foreign."

"Gamaliel, may I speak?" Shem said as he stood and continued, "Both of you are here because you are more than model representatives of your kind. You have demonstrated extreme faith and love in your service. Now I know that you especially, Ouriano, have received ridicule for acting human. And you, Veezon, have done all you can to mask your faith so your legion and peers would not make the same observation of you. So with that being said, we want to ask something of you. This council is not going to insist obedience to what we propose. It is strictly voluntary. We truly are asking."

Gamaliel spoke again, "Ouriano, put bluntly, we want to grant your desire to become human. This has never been requested of an angel."

"I don't know how to respond," replied Ouriano as he glanced around at the council, which included a few elders who were still perplexed at the unknown variables of this faith initiative. The Angel of Light had asked Gamaliel and the elders for a bold new plan of action, that was anything but routine.

"Don't speak just yet, you haven't heard all the details," said Gamaliel as he paced inside the seated circle of solemn faces, "There is more than reward here. We need you to infiltrate Yazad's sanctuary as a human, a son of Adam. This is possibly a one-way-trip, and your most sacrificial mission ever. Please reflect a moment."

Ouriano was stunned, unable to grasp either the concept and the mission. "My esteemed Gamaliel, elders and ancient ones, as you say, to become a displaced image bearer in a foreign world is more than a small detail to consider. You are proposing that my chance to experience life as a human would be on a covert mission? Who would go with me?"

"We shall address this in time," said Gamaliel as he walked over and stood face to face with Veezon, "Now brave one, I must also ask you about a sacrifice."

Before he could speak, Veezon cut to the chase and said, "I can do almost anything except this. I have no right nor do I wish to leave my brothers in arms at such a key time."

The elders began to stir in their seats as if this was unexpected. Again Shem spoke up, slowly stretching his long gray beard with his fingers, "Veezon, we will not force you to transform against your will, but please listen. We don't need you to become a human. Quite the opposite, we need you to do the unthinkable."

Veezon was now even more disoriented, looking down at the translucent turquoise and sapphire floor they stood on, then elevated his gaze to the distant beam and spoke, "I can only think of one alternative. You want to fake my annihilation?"

Gamaliel at this point held his back to him. Even Ouriano had no idea what was next as Veezon looked to him for an answer. Calculating his words, Gamaliel then turned around and spoke, "For the glory of the One who soars beyond the Magnificon and has asked none of us to sacrifice greater than what has been done, this is what we ask." There was a pause and dead silence in among the council, "We ask that you would become infected!"

At this heavy suggestion, both mighty winds raised their wings in reaction, alarming the Cherubim guard into lightening speed to surround them, as if these elders needed protection. Gamaliel motioned the Cherubim back to their stations.

Without hesitation Ouriano spoke up on behalf of Veezon, "With all praise to our Creator, the One who rides the clouds and surrounds Himself with winds of fire and the wisdom of the council of the Magnificon, why would this be asked of Veezon? Should we next ask Beltshzan to join this council?" The council members looked at each startled and murmuring, then he continued, "As a human I would have a chance at redemption, but if my friend should accept this infection there is no recovery for him. Everything about this suggestion is repulsive!"

Shem spoke again, "Siyon needs hosts with faith who can tolerate the cover and suffering of the infection. Veezon's faith has already made him different than the others. We need you inside the dark sanctuary as one of them. We admit, you will be vulnerable, tempted, and could fall completely toward the darkness. This is the possibility you would have to accept."

Veezon finally inquired for himself, "Has this been done before? I have never witnessed this. None has ever returned. My own home on the Blue Moon reminds me of a time past, when we were once one, when there was more happiness. And now you ask me to carry this deceitful infection within? Is this my final destiny?"

Chapter 71

"He who knew no sin, became sin for us,"
– Saul of Tarsus

Another elder stood up. He had eyes on three sides of his head, a face resembling an ox, a bear, a leopard, and began to hover as he spoke. His voice was low toned and loud, "Many of your kind will be annihilated, unmentionable abominations await the image bearers in the sanctuary of Yazad. This has been revealed to us from beyond the Magnificon gate. We have prayed for another outcome in dispensing with Lucifer. We have no others who can fulfill this role."

Gamaliel took center stage again, "What then is your answer Ouriano?"

"This is not what I expected. How will it take place?"... There was silence. "Yes!" he finally said with an enthusiasm of an eternal, one-of-a-kind purpose.

"And Veezon, what say you?" asked Gamaliel.

Looking toward the center of the Magnificon, he answered, "I saw the One who was slain before the foundation of the world. He was full flesh, divine, infected and transformed. I have always wondered what it would be like to live by faith. So be it!"

Gamaliel embraced them both then asked them to sit down, "We cannot tell you the details of how this transformation will take place or exactly when. There is only One who knows this. I can tell you it will be within one generation of the humans you are helping on Earth. Continue your duties to the best of your understanding."

Shem added, "Live as fully by faith as you can. Remember your place."

As Shem spoke, suddenly the entire floor they were seated on lit up with an intense, pure white light coming from the center of the Magnificon. In Ouriano's near blindness he saw the elders and creatures bow on their faces, so that Veezon and he followed suit. He whispered to Veezon, "It has to be none other than the Angel of Light landing among us."

Ouriano felt footsteps of thunder and a hand of sentient touch on his bowed shoulder, as did Veezon. "Stand up, humble winds, my flames of fire, for never has such a sacrifice been asked of your kind."

The Cherubim Guard were soaking in this light, glowing in radiance, covering their eyes with one set of wings, reflecting the energy and sensing the purity of this one who flew beyond the Magnificon and with one breath could ignite or extinguish the stars.

"You are willing to give of yourselves with abandon. You are willing to sacrifice your well-earned position, friendship, freedom and security of home. Where did these emotions and thoughts of self-sacrifice and love come from? You will leave this city of God, this Holy place where the Most High dwells? You will leave your home, the seedbed of these universes for an unknown place, a rogue country? Who would do such a thing?"

Veezon answered, "Yes, your light knows all things. We are honored to offer this form of worship to Who was, and is, and is yet to come."

The two felt the Angel of Light continue to rummage through their being, "Yes, we can know all things, but we don't wish to restrain all things, do we? Chosen stars must burn to the end that new ones may be born. You are willing to meet this fate with no future promise? You are willing to be cast down and cut off from what you have known, enduring pain, isolation, and shame? You have wondered what it was to be human and infected. Still you will never know unless..."

Interrupting the Angel of Light, Ouriano said what burst from his heart, "Oh One who rides the clouds of Earth and dances on the nebulae of the most distant realms, who calls things which were not as though they were, and can hide yourself in the smallest of celestial planes, revealing yourself to the humble and those who shout your name across the horizons of Siyon, did we not also watch helplessly as you were slain by those bearing the infection and abandoned for death? Yet your faith sustained you. Yet the Holy One did not let you see decay. We know of no such future promises for our service and deserve none. We are joyful to be here and believe there to be many others like us."

The Angel of Light spoke again, a mixture of comfort and raw power, "If you say to this mountain be removed, then without angelic aide, it shall be tossed into the heart of the sea. Ask what you seek now or forever wrestle with unspoken prayer."

Ouriano took the invitation to be bold, "The hybrid, Ru..."

Veezon interrupted him. "Oh Angel of Light, Ouriano knows little of the indignity of what he is about to ask."

"And what indignity would be beneath me, Simon Veezon? To bring to light that which was destined for abomination? Would you suggest I abandon a faithful one of my legion in time of greatest peril? Can you weigh the thoughts and intentions of another's heart if your own should become darkened?"

At this point Veezon did something Ouriano had never seen. He broke down on his knees and wept, crying out, "Angel of Light and of the Holy armies, I despise those who have shared the cup of Lucifer's arrogance, and so I loathe myself. How long have you known of my fall, my own infection? I only suspected it until now, but your presence has begun to sear my veins."

The Angel walked a few steps from them turning away and lifted up her hands. Her light went dim as she turned back toward them. But what they now saw was the appearance of the Wounded Innocence of Siyon, the Heir of the Magnificon! The Innocence walked up to Veezon, took his right hand and lifted him to his feet, turning his forearm up. Indeed, all present confirmed, there was the early bruised spots of the infection and darkening of the veins.

The forearms of the Wounded Innocence were then offered up in a reciprocal fashion as he asked Veezon, "What do you see?"

"I see the One without blemish who took on the infection but wears the scars forever. I see the One who drank the cup of arrogance for the image bearers."

The Innocence answered, "Then despise not yourself, this scourge must come but it is only as strong as your lack of faith. The throngs of fire followed the second Morning Star and so heaped abomination upon themselves. They became buried in the pride of their shame following the way of the Vranti. They desecrated themselves acting as if they had the power to call things that are not as though they were, and so attempted to breed as cattle without the ability to know, heaping greater darkness over their heads.

Have you heard one disparaged spirit call out for me? When I walked the shores of Galilee or strode the graves of lepers, healing prostitutes, beggars and tax collectors, did you ever hear a cry for mercy other than to escape the abyss? Do they fear the Wounded Innocence more than Yazad or Beltshzan?"

Veezon shook his head, "No" and continued to weep as the Innocence spoke more powerful words.

"No, they smell meekness as a sign of weakness. They race like sharks to the wounded prey. They writhe in darkness and hope for a different light. They blindly think they shall escape the sky in which they were born to fly and the sea that contains them.

My eyes see all and my ears are attentive to all who call on my name. If it is difficult for the wayward image bearers who have never seen me to call on my name, then it is sevenfold more difficult for the darkened winds who were raised in the caverns of the Blue Moon and who stood in the shadow of the Magnificon. Yet all things are possible, for evil and for good.

My Veezon, you will not fail. You are wounded, but you are not one of them for you have fallen on your knees. I am with you to the end of the age. You are right in acknowledging the difference in kind. But are not both the humans and winds incriminated in my slaying and benefited in my triumphs? The humans share my conscience and light and shall rise higher than the winds. The winds have shared my council and power and will one day kneel to listen for the still small voice."

The Innocence turned to Ouriano. "My long time friend Ouriano, you asked about the mixed breed Ru? Where does this compassion come from? You know Ru's nature. She could turn in a heartbeat as she is sifted by evil. She exists because of your failure to exterminate all of her ancestor's kind."

Ouriano felt the Heir was testing him so he answered, "Yes, and you are known as one of great compassion who threatened to end the image bearers, yet relented from complete erasure because of the prayers of few."

"You answer with wisdom Ouriano, and so you ask, 'Might Ru find amnesty?' Is this from who she is, or for who she is not yet?"

"My Lord, I am unfit to give an answer, but for what she shall become with your light. Her hope does not lie in the sanctuary of Yazad, but beyond the Magnificon gates, to that which you are rightful Heir."

"Then she is wise too, despite the darkness inherited in her veins. The amnesty she seeks is not a hidden secret, but it requires for her relinquishing of old family loyalties. Ru has put her life in great peril for the humans but has taken innocent life. Since you indulged her amnesty, then it will be granted. Know this however; the costs to you will be great. It will embrace all you have never before given."

As the Wounded One turned away into a blinding light, Ouriano confessed His own earthly words, "Let this eternal cup not depart from me."

The elders and living creatures stepped close in to surround them. All their wings, hands, talons, claws, were placed onto them as they knelt. The Cherubim guard left their posts and came in close extending their three sets of wings over all of them. Shem spoke these words,

"This moment we have witnessed a new turning of the heavens. Who may know the mind of the Heir, and the understanding of the Angel who ignites the stars? The time of the dreaded seals has come. Woe to those through who they come. May the Timeless One deliver the kingdoms of man and the heavens to the Son of the Magnificon. May these winds before us and their faith endure and deliver those whom they love."

With this prayer by Shem the elder, Veezon and Ouriano were released to return to their work. Before departing they flew to the rim of the Magnificon where a gathering was taking place after all. They worshiped as if this was their last breath of light, wondering how and when they might see this place again?

Chapter 72

We have never subscribed to conspiracy theories.
This one found us.

"Lucas, sounds like Ru is at the door, would you invite her in please? My feet are killing me. I left a message with lab security asking if she would stop by."

Allowing the door to open outward into the hall only four inches, peeking over the side with one eye he asked, "Has the locksmith changed the locks yet? We certainly don't want you to feel endangered." Lucas stepped back and let go of the door waving his arm with a magician's gesture saying, "Please step right in to our palatial receiving room." Ru furled her forehead at him like he had gone mad.

"Ru, thank you for coming by tonight, or I presume it's night. Please come in and sit down. Are you at liberty yet to tell us where we are? Physically?"

"Why, are you thinking of mounting an escape?"

Lucas, continuing his perturbed behavior, said sarcastically, "Come on Ru, does it really matter at this point? Like your knocking before you enter? We've never subscribed to conspiracy theories. This one found us."

She calmly answered, "Cuzak is going to free you soon. When this is done, the way it will be spun is that the two of you will be given figurehead titles on the board of a new technology company with legitimate patent rights for lesser attributive applications. He knows no one will believe you if you come off with an occult story. And, by the way, you are in France. Just off the coast of the North Sea. We are near one of the largest nuclear plant facilities in the world to mask our small reactor's signature. If you left now you could try and swim the English Channel, but if you wait things out you will be set for life."

"Remain here any longer? Ru, you have the ability to help us escape now if you wanted?" interjected Lucas.

Ru nodded, "Yes, I suppose I could," as she walked through the small apartment, checking all the walls as if looking for something, "But then I would be getting ahead of plan."

Victoria asked, "Ru, please come sit down," as Ru lifted up the living room chair cushion as if searching for another booby trap, "Yes, of course. You can sit here on the couch instead."

"No thanks, this is fine. We all need some humor here don't we?" Ru asked as she gave a mock sinister smirk and tried to smile at Lucas who pretended he wasn't looking. She sat down, crossed her legs and put her hands together on her lap, and asked, "Victoria, are you going to make it? I know you deeply miss your mom, and so do I."

"You know Ru, sometimes I feel she is with me more now than when she was physically alive." There was a pause in the conversation. Victoria interrupted the silence, "Have you spoken to Ouriano of late?"

"No, matter of fact I went looking for him, and some of his associates said he was unavailable. They advised me to keep my distance from him because, quote, 'I was the drone killer.'"

"Who would speak to you like that?"

"They were members of the legion who sometimes give Ouriano support. A past subordinate, Veezon, is the commander. Ouriano later served under him before assigned to more covert work. They don't trust me. I sense something odd is going on. It could be the infection."

Lucas sat down with keen interest though floating in a cloud of impatient attitude. He put his hand on Victoria's knee as had become normal for him when they were alone. Ru curiously stared at his hand on her bare knee, then regained her attention on their faces. Lucas pulled back his hand as if caught in the cookie jar, but with a sarcastic glance at Ru. Victoria couldn't help to wonder if Ru felt any romantic inclinations toward Lucas and what that would look like.

Lucas pounced, "I can understand the lack of trust and cold shoulder. You are friends of Ouriano, who some of that kind consider as a renegade and you as an odd gem of DNA. You fell through the cracks and no one knows what to do with you."

Ru continued to try and force a relaxed expression, "OK, what do you mean by odd?" she said slowly as she tried to guess what was egging him on to bait her, then continued, "I accept the lack of trust, but I have a strong sense about something else."

Lucas didn't wait, "Oh, what could that be?"

Ru said, "I sense that their lack of trust has little to do with my dark inception. Their lack of trust is a cover for something else."

"Hold on, you are losing me," he said, "You suspect that members of this legion may have turned away from their created loyalties? You know they make similar accusations about you, that you have made Ouriano drop his defenses?"

"Please you two, hear me! I am telling you that the hosts with clear hearts have no fear. I sensed fear from some of Veezon's troops. Lies and fear are the modus operandi of the infection. Lucas, you seem to have a similar attitude, especially tonight. Do you sense lies and fear from me?"

Lucas finally looked at her, "No, but the potential..."

Interceding, Victoria said, "We've all had a bad day. Let me bring up why we wanted you to come by. Lucas and I saw something yesterday that gave us the chills. As you know we have moved into the testing stages where we have worked out the details for correct coordinates and power for the dimensional door. It is all about the fine-tuning now. Cuzak's team of other scientists and support people are running tests while every day we are temporarily quarantined from watching the test subjects or materials in transport. But despite this, we saw something yesterday, a result from one of the lab employee's sloppiness which made us sick to our stomachs. There was an empty box labeled "Do not drop, extremely fragile," left out on the floor. I picked it up to move when I saw an invoice tucked inside."

Chapter 73

She has gone at great lengths to go against the tide of the creature she should have been.

Lucas put his arm around Victoria for support as she continued, "The invoice mentioned thirty frozen embryos."

"What type?"

"I didn't have time to examine it and the wording was in an oriental script. It may have been Korean. The statement had a stamp on it like an embryo. I tried to act as if I hadn't seen anything. One of the security crew grabbed it out of my hand. I am guessing they were human embryos?"

Ru widened her eyes, frozen in place for fraction of an instant, then took a quiet breath and spoke, "I will check into this. Maybe it was just an empty box."

"And maybe this is the plan, to multiply more of your kind somewhere?" Lucas added in an acidic remark. Ru's eyes fell towards the floor. He then tried to recover from what he said, "Look Ru, they would not be like you. These must be human or stock animal needed to germinate a civilization. No, that is not what I mean either! Look Ru, I'm sorry."

She replied gripping the armrests of her chair, "I would feel offended by your remarks, Dr. Tanner, except we know your suspicions are legitimate. If Cuzak is trafficking in human embryos to forward to the Sanctuary I am going to confront him. I want to know who the partners are working with him. There has to be rogue nation-states involved."
Ru stood up, "I have to leave now."

"Wait!" Victoria said. "There is one more thing to this which frightens us even more."

But Ru didn't stop or look back. With that last comment, she walked out and locked the door again from the outside. The two sat there perplexed. "Lucas, you crushed her feelings! She has gone at great lengths to go against the tide of the creature she should have been. She saved my life. Ru was dear to my mother. Ouriano has put his trust in her. She has to be absolutely careful."

"I haven't forgotten to be thankful for what she has done, but she should be battle-hardened. Why should she get so emotional? And what about ones like her we have not met?"

"She could say the same thing about humans. She obviously had feelings for you. Were you not attracted to her?"

"Vic, how could you ask that?"

"Lucas, I have given you numerous clues through the years about how I felt about you. Your eyes kept trolling anyway. What is to stop you now?"

Lucas pulled Victoria up off the sofa and touched his forehead against hers, "This experience has confirmed who I want to be with. I am already in love with an angel. It's you Victoria." Then cupping her face in his hands, he turned his head slightly and kissed her so as to leave no doubt. She felt as if their souls exchanged.

Gently he eased back, and facing her, he continued nose to nose, "You are the most exotic creature I know. You needn't ever doubt me, or our future together. But we have yet to discover what that future will be – we are trapped here! And Ru is right, if we were to escape today who is going to believe us? If I could contact my own parents right now deep in the jungle, as fundamental believers as they are, even they wouldn't believe this story. We need to escape, and we need to escape now without telling Ru. I have a plan. She can help us without knowing the details." Saying this, he put his arms around her waist as she placed her hands under his back shirt tail and t-shirt.

"But Ouriano told us to stay with this project?"

"We have stayed with it long enough. They are going to make the break through with what they have jacked out of us already. We are becoming less valuable. The time is now. They are at the stage in development, if we escape now, they would have to reallocate too many resources to track us."

"But Cuzak said he was still trying to find the culprit of my mother's murder. Do you think that is nothing more than posturing?"

"He held your mother captive to keep you motivated. Now he is manipulating you with your loyalty to her dead body? OK, say the man, or the whatever he is, has some core loyalties or pride. With what he is trying to pull off, one demon is not going to sidetrack him. There isn't anything about Colonel Smith I would ever hope to trust. Just the opposite. Your mom is dead because of him. He might be mad because it happened on his watch. Nothing more than control. Let him get the revenge. And if he doesn't, I will," said Lucas, working himself into a vindictive lather.

"I am not looking for revenge for my mom. How about truce for the rest of the evening?"

He looked at her, and forced himself to take a breath and calm down. "You're right Vic. I don't know why I am so agitated. We didn't build this world, and we certainly don't hold the responsibility for ending it. Two Ramen noodle specials coming up. Add a little tuna, broccoli, garlic. We are in business."

She mock grimaced. "I'll pass on that treat, thanks. I'll make dinner. You, unwind. Here, open this bottle of wine, pour us both a glass. Keep going through my mom's notes. They are on the table. You said it before, 'we need to pray.' Find something else good."

"Agreed," said Lucas as he walked back into the bedroom, then began to yell, "Victoria, come back here now!"

On the bed was a sword like that of Ouriano's, sunk into the covers, and beside it a purple cloth sack with a thin black cord pull-tie. Victoria put her hand on the silver-colored hilt as Lucas watched. The rest of the sword looked like a dull, burnished pewter with symbols engraved on its flat edge. The sword was warm to the touch, and the grip felt malleable.

"Be careful Vic! Why don't you let me handle it."

"I can't move the sword. Feels like it weighs a ton. Why would he leave it here?"

Lucas pulled off his blue oxford shirt for the freedom of his white tank top. "Let me give it a try." A new energy filled Lucas' face as he gripped the double-edged sword with his right hand, lifting it over his head. The weight of the sword became as nothing, while light glowed from his eyes. Feigning jousts, he was mesmerized by how well the sword responded. The hilt shaped to his hand, while the blade hummed and glowed a bluish white, with a hint of gleaming diamonds at the center. The light crept toward the hilt, into his hand and then flowed into his right forearm, at first illuminating his red blood cells, but turning his arm blue up to the elbow.

"Open the sack on the bed," he ordered Victoria, "I think I know what it is." She untied the knot and pulled out the restored mirror Lucas had been given by the Angel of Light on the Blue Moon. There were no shattered pieces. Her fingers glided over the smooth surface. Victoria heard Lucas in the background saying, "Don't stare ..." as she looked at her reflection. And then, in a 1,000-watt flash of light, she was blinded. A few minutes later Lucas helped her off the floor, saying, "I wanted to warn you about that."

Chapter 74

Woe to those through whom evil comes, for they have become just another tool.

From the back room they heard the front door being pried open, and ran to the dining area in time to see three strangers coming through the now bent door wearing long black trench coats, hats, gloves and boots. Clothing fell to the floor as one of the strangers' forms collapsed and was replaced by that of a large Rottweiler, snarling and baring his gnashing teeth.

The second took off her hat, removed her glasses and gloves and threw back her long blond hair. To Lucas she looked more like a model than a killer. The third person, a man, pulled a Glock from his long coat, spun a silencer into the end and pointed it at them.

The woman then brandished a large paring knife from under her coat, and poking herself with the tip through the center of her other hand, squeezed blood out onto the floor while the dog licked the drops. She spoke to them with a German accent, "This ride is over."

While the couch hid the sword held alongside his thigh from view of the three, Lucas asked, "What do you want?"

"What do we want?" the woman mimicked, "No, the question is who wants to go first? You can do this the easy way like Ms. Pruett and her little beast, or we can make it entertaining."

Victoria blasted, "*You* killed my mother? What kind of a sadistic bitch are you?!"

"I think you already know that, doctor. We left something in your head." With that suggestive remark, the deranged woman lifted her bloody open hand as a claw toward Victoria, projecting her power. Victoria's brain began to throb with horrible pain as the woman backed her down into a chair, yet Victoria managed to keep hold of the mirror, resting it in her lap.

Victoria prayed, "For the sake of my mother, I'll be damned if I let this happen again."

Lucas yelled, "Leave her alone! Is your blood thirst always against the defenseless?"

The man with the gun then spoke likewise with a Germanic accent, "Have a seat next to her doctor Tanner." He tossed a sack of spun steel cable, ready fit with a noose, on the kitchen table, "Put the noose around her neck, and loop the cable over the ceiling hook."

Lucas understood him, but he didn't move; not out of fear, but out of a confidence that the vengeance he was about to unleash was justified in all realms. Fear fled as the light of his eyes moved like white laser beams tracking multiple targets, dashing between all three of the Vranti.

Startled by Lucas' change, the adversarial woman, dropped her claw-hand away from Victoria and said, "We've underestimated him. He has the light and eyes of a Juwaan after all. Take him down first."

The Rottweiler rotated its head as he examined Lucas, its muzzle twitching, revealing its menacing canines again, still licking the blood off its teeth from the drippings on the floor.

The gunman answered back, "But Cuzak said, *'He shows no aptitude for a Juwaan,'* Look, his arm is radiating blue light from Yare'ach Kachol. What do you have in your hand? No ... ... It's a set up!"

For Lucas, everything around him shifted to slow motion. His eyes magnified the trigger finger of the gunman as it began to squeeze. In the next millisecond he glanced to see the dog sag in a slight crouch and then skimmed his eyes to spot the slo-mo action of the woman's recoil of the knife into a throwing motion.

The gunman fired a bullet toward his heart. Surprised by his power of observation, Lucas saw the bullet spinning as it streaked toward him, a thin trail of disrupted air tracing its path. Matching its timing the dog sprung in the air, traversing the furniture in one bound, with jaws wide open.

It all felt surreal to Lucas. Without a plan, he whipped up his right hand smashing the projectile with the flat of Ouriano's sword, spraying the small bits into the opposite concrete wall. Lunging forward with his right leg, he then double-backhanded the razor edge of the sword into the chest of the leaping beast, filleting it in half, all the way through the hindquarters. As the pieces hit the wall to his right, they burst into a yellow mush against the cinder block construction.

Without looking his ears estimated the trajectory of the whirling knife headed towards Victoria. He continued his spin all the way around from his right on his follow-through, until he arrived back into position to intercept the knife with the flat of his blade and fling it back at its rightful owner.

To Victoria, this all happened faster than she could keep up with, but the pain in her head ceased as she watched the blond woman try to dislodge the knife now split through her Adam's apple. Her breath leaked out of her throat as she gasped a few seconds, then fell backwards, dead.

And, as her remaining partner watched her fall, he turned his head back to squeeze yet another shot off, but it was too late. He looked down only to discover his gun hand and arm did not exist below the elbow, and then in the blink of an eye, no attached legs either, as he tumbled to the floor in a heap of parts.

To Victoria's horror the insects immediately dissipated out of the bodies, and began to form in a cloud around Lucas, spinning around him in a whirlwind. He yelled at her, "The mirror!" She flipped the smooth silver surface off her lap toward the swarm, bathing them in the lethal bright light. At once, the spinning swarm began to smoke from the beam, and peeled off to escape through the mangled front door.

Lucas hurried over to embrace Victoria, gleaming sword still in his right hand, and said, "Are you alright?"

Wiping her tears, Victoria said, "I will be in a minute. But I want you to know *I hate bugs. I mean I really, really hate bugs.*"

"Damn parasitic infestation. Part of it is still alive." Pinching his blue arm, Lucas remarked, "Let's however be thankful Ouriano's sword arrived in time. I don't feel good about what I just did to these two real people, but they're the ones who helped kill your mother."

Rubbing her temples to make sure the pain was gone, Victoria said, "I know what that's like, they had no control over their bodies. But you had no choice either. Ouriano knew this was going to happen. He left you his sword, but where is he?"

"I don't know, but before we think about it too much, we've got to leave. This sword is our ticket out of here. Let's go!"

Chapter 75

Be careful what you want to know and accomplish.
Along the way, you still will have to exist.

Inside the lab's transport room was a security office that used tandem controls to open the blast doors to the recessed sealed compartments. Only Cuzak could open them on his own. Ru presumed he preserved at least a few more vacuum dried creatures in storage for testing. She wanted to see what else might be there. Her snooping wouldn't be considered as atypical as her emotions towards Lucas were. As she approached the security post, there sat a guard who she did not recognize dressed in a standard issue corporate blue security uniform, embroidered with the Sanctech name on the arm patch. She did however know Cuzak had hired a new contractor for staffing the growing security needs. Ru noticed that the guard had her top two shirt buttons undone. On any day when Ru was thinking clearly, that should have been a clue.

This new guard was at a desk painting a bright beach orange polish on her fingernails and cracking her gum when Ru interrupted her obviously busy day. "I need in the storage area now. Here, run my clearance card."

"I am sorry Ms. Zvonimira, but you have not presented the clearance necessary to jointly open this storage section of the facility. Can I scan your retina?"

"See this profile?" displaying her concealed weapon, "You are looking at my clearance. Let's open the unit!"

"I am sorry babe, but you are not on the approved list."

"Babe?' We'll deal with this insubordination in a minute, but first, you're going to tell me who took me off the list."

"That is classified."

"Like hell it is classified! Maybe for someone else."

"Would you like to place a complaint for review with Sanctech?"

"A review with Sanctech? If they hired you they must be running a bumbling lush squad."

"They liked my assets, you know, my qualifications. I was recruited in Las Vegas. They said it would be like living on a submarine. Come back home in six months, $100,000 tax-free cash. Keep my pie hole shut."

"What do you know so far?"

"Remember? I am from the town where the motto is 'What happens in Vegas...'"

Ru interrupted, "I know, stays in Vegas."

"Well, I don't really know anything anyway. Science is not my main interest."

"What was your former occupation?"

"I was a dancer."

"And in six months what will you be doing?"

"I'll go back and relax. Then start working again."

"Dancing? Your badge says, 'Darlene Howard?'"

"Yes." She put her eyes back down to focus on painting her nails.

"Darlene, look up! In six months you won't be leaving. In one year you won't be leaving or after this shift for that matter, unless you open that door."

I've lost my objectivity, after all, Lucas had thrown some low blows. Why was I thinking there was something between us? I'm agitated, anger is rising, and so are my wings. My nails are extending like grizzly claws and my eyes have dilated. I don't want to waste this display on this idiot or a security camera. No possible way Cuzak would have approved her. I need to regain my composure.

Darlene flashed her gaze at Ru's crude nails, then at her wings, moving up to her eyes. She then focused back down and resumed work again on her own nails. "Unbelievable," Ru said.

"Those real?" Darlene asked with her squeaky twang.

Unholstering her Taser, Ru answered, "Yeah, those real?"

"No, bought 'em," she looked down toward the top of her cleavage, smiling for a moment, then continued to work on her nails.

"Stand up slowly Ms. Howard. Quit the act."

She stood up, smiling. Holding a bottle of polish in one hand and modeling the nails on the other. "Ms. Zvonimira, what do you think? Those claws look so unbecoming on you. I could do miracles for those."

Ru fired the Taser, aiming above the right breast. But, Ms. Howard was quicker than the prong and caught it between her thumb and first finger. Ru pulled the trigger and heard the pulses. There was no apparent affect as the guard examined the prong, then nonchalantly let it go, where it began recoiling at Ru's feet. The bogus bumbling guard smiled and said in a hearty masculine voice, "Ru let's be discreet."

"Ouriano?" Ru whispered her internal yell.

Darlene raised one eyebrow and tilted her head. "My mistake, your credentials are verified. Let's begin the unlocking sequence. My manicure is finished."

"Thank you, 'Miss Howard.' I will need your assistance inside. Dancer?"

She tossed the used Taser aside as they walked through the control area of the high security storage that included the temperature, humidity, and air pressure controls. Another security person walked up. This one was legit. He recognized Ru but asked them to sign for the storage area they were to enter, then became suspicious of Darlene. Darlene put her hand on his shoulder, blew in his face and he went down.

Chapter 76

Your redemption is at the gate of your conscience. You have been granted the power of a choice.

"Did you kill him?"

"No, just scrambled his conscience for about twenty-four hours."

"Why are you here, Ouriano? And like this? One of the Vranti is loose in this facility. Cuzak is sure to be alerted."

"I had to talk to you immediately and tell you some good news."

"Tell me quick, I am looking for something important."

"Ru, you won't find anything good locked up here. Sure you want to do this?"

"Keep walking and talking, Darlene."

"Your amnesty," Ru stopped when he said this, "I heard it myself, you don't have to be fatalistic. Your true loyalties will demonstrate what you are becoming. I was there, invited to the edge of the Magnificon. Your name was spoken and esteemed. Your redemption is at the gate of your conscience. You have been granted the power of a choice."

Ru picked up the pace towards the first blast door saying, "Remember, I've never been to Siyon. My flesh would sear. I am trying to do a little of your justice work right now."

"Ru, be careful. Justice also includes humility over reckless abandon. And I need to tell you something else. Before you go in, please, listen to me?" As he spoke, Ouriano transformed into his given form and stepped into her path with wings extended, "I may be leaving you. The details are known only by the Wounded Heir. I was told from the Magnificon council, that at some unknown time I will become human, an image bearer!"

Ru grabbed both of his wrists and held them tight, her nails almost piercing as she spoke, "Your becoming human and leaving me is a package deal? Why human? Why do you have to leave? You practically are my father."

"Ru, this has never been done! And I said, 'I may be leaving you.'"

"I have been alone all my life Ouriano. If you leave, how are you going to help me? Am I supposed to be glad for you? I will cave in to the forces of Yazad and Beltshzan, probably for breeding purposes. Who knows where Cuzak stands?"

Letting go of his wrists, she lifted up the edge of his bulky right wing with her arm and walked under it to the security control pad she was looking for. He put his hands on her shoulders as she punched in the sequential code, and gently reminded her, "You are not alone, to the contrary, ever. Your greatest powers are yet to be discovered."

She turned around, relishing the goodness in his weathered face as she heard the airlocks hiss, locks and gears unhitch, and the storage area door begin to track up behind her. "Do you have to take a fall to start your new life?" she asked. Ouriano had been concentrating on her, looking into her eyes while they had talked. When the door ceased its upward motion and the accompanying mechanical sounds, he glanced over her shoulder through the opening at what lay behind her. That long, deep look before his attention was distracted is how she wished Lucas had looked at her.

Ouriano answered, "Sacrifice and transformation are the norm for humans. I don't know how mine will begin."

"Why can't you remain as you are?" she asked. Ouriano didn't respond to her question, as what lay behind her drew his concentration away.

Then he said, "I warned you."

Turning around, Ru saw that this storage vault contained over thirty human sized caskets resting on hospital gurneys. The caskets varied; monolithic stone, ornate and simple crafted wood, modern metal alloy. This was a clean room for their care, vacuum-sealed, dust free.

They walked over to the closest casket: the lid was dark maroon wood with four thick cracked leather straps securing it to the main body of the casket with metal rivets. She unbound these, said a silent prayer. Ouriano stood to the side and watched her remove the lid. A dread came over her.

"Except for the long hair and slimmer build, she no doubt is related to me. The facial features are too similar." Ouriano reached inside and gently lifted then rolled the body on its side. The spindles of the top of the main wing structure were evident as Ru ran her hand over the corpse's shoulder blades.

"Roll her back," Ru barked as her face displayed the disappointing confusion of the morbid discovery.

Ru walked hastily to the nearest stone coffin, leveraged her thickening nails in the seam of the sarcophagus until she could get her hand under it. She slid it down, letting it drop with a low thud the last two feet. This body was an older male, dark skinned, bearded, missing his left arm, and dressed in a highly decorated military uniform, but again the traits of Cuzak's DNA were apparent.

"Isn't this enough torture?" Ouriano asked.

Her anger was kindling, "These are my kin. My brothers and sisters. Did you know or mortally wound any of them?"

"Yes, I knew them, but no, Ru, I did not kill them; that happened long before. These are second generation."

She moved faster, smashing the casket lids when they would not cooperate. In a modern alloy coffin rested a handsome, in human years, twenty-five year old male. He was naked. His heart had been cut out and wings torn out of his back. "Who would do this? What do you know, Death Angel?"

Ouriano's head drooped as he answered her, "Sometimes a king views his offspring as a threat to his throne."

"You cannot lie, Ouriano! Was this someone you helped to turn against him? Have you spoken with Cuzak since your face-to-face encounter eons ago?"

"This speculative interrogation serves no purpose Ru. Let's leave."

"Please answer! Are all of these dead because you tried to get them to help you and crossed Cuzak?"

The blast door had come down without notice until they heard the lock and felt the vacuum air pressure change. And then he appeared as she had never seen him; barefoot, slacks almost bursting at the leg seams, bare-chested, muscle striations and veins of a body builder, his large gray wings poised in fighting position. He walked toward them through a row of caskets, both arms extended, his fingernails dragging across their tops, first etching the lids of a stone and metal coffin, then ripping through the sides of two wooden caskets. She had underestimated his raw power.

Chapter 77

*"Though he slay me, yet will I trust in him: but I will
maintain mine own ways before him." – Job 13:15*

The embryo box incident incited Dr. Tanner and Dr.
Pruett to turn to Ru for help as Cuzak had planned. He
admired those of consistency and loyalty for they were
easier to bait. "Anger throws everyone off in their
perception of reality, because it feels good. Admit it!"
Cuzak spoke as he slowly walked toward them among the
spraying splinters and pieces of stone.

"A child's goal is to see how far they can push their
parents. Permission for a little turns into presumption
for much. I so desired Ru to keep innocent of the past
history and conflict of our kind, Ouriano. By letting her
run with you I gave you my trust that she might have a
chance to stay clear.

But now she has gone along with you and opened up the
past. These progenitors of yours, Ru, were sloppy and
needed tidying up. May their God, their local entity, help
them. If he is so great then he can sort out the details.
There is nothing in this game left except the feeling of
being alive, and I feel alive at this moment for a welcome
bloodletting! My raw nature has waited too long to be
exposed to a worthy opponent. Harnessing my true self
day after day is a despicable discipline.

My old friend, Ouriano. You always seem to drift near
where death is in the air. Do you miss being the Angel of
Death? Other angels obey like emotionless robots, but
you always were different, taking the law of the entity
into your own hands. How did you escape the infection?
There are things of this universe about which it is better
to have never known. Where are your legions of support?

Did you think coming into this domain you would not need them?"

Ouriano's answer to Cuzak was filled with arrogance, "I came not to slay anyone, today."

Ru pleaded, "Why don't you work with Ouriano? Your goals are nearly the same, are they not?"

Cuzak countered, "Move out of the way Ru, your hero has an appointment." Cuzak's rage awakened all of his senses as his second set of organs kicked in. "Tell her Ouriano. Tell her the story of each of these lying here. You know them. You sought to befriend them out of your guilt. What happened to my children? Tell her. Even monsters love their children. Tell her about neutrality in this war. Neutrality is a myth isn't it?"

Ouriano did not wait to answer, "He is right Ru. Cuzak's progeny, though ill conceived, were all incredible life forms. I wanted to protect them, lead them from being used for evil and becoming objects of wrath. Most like you could go either direction. There is no rule book on your kind. Whenever I became involved with them, they somehow became targets of Beltshzan. He would find a way to slay them. Some hid, disguised themselves by cutting off their own wings. Some sought to live a quiet private life."

"That was impossible wasn't it Ouriano? So here you stand. Their blood cries out for justice because you tried to make them into something they were not. My babies, Loyden, Joda, Wendamere, Phizil..."

"By the name of the One who holds all things, they were but chance accidents of your seed, Cuzak. They were all off the record, and forsaken by you. None of them were a child of love, were they? And now you collect their shells to perpetuate your hatred. Or is there more to this?

Where now do you judge our truce? The plan is working and now you are adding a gothic sideshow to it. Does Ru know this?"

"Dear lost angel, all truces are compromises fueled by weaknesses. We both have a common enemy who can never be trusted, but at least you have a homeland. I have none!"

Ru turned to Ouriano and asked, "The two of you are *working together*?"

Cuzak answered quickly, "We were until now. No one knows this. I wanted to keep you out of this quagmire my daughter."

Cuzak could sense Ouriano become the prey; isolated, vulnerable, confused, questioning his own motives, exposed, so he pressed him more. "I will complete the project. This was the deal. What is between you and I is separate and personal. Like you insisted, 'this project is larger than both of us.' To dispose of you would only add credence before Yazad, Beltshzan and the Vranti and give protection to Ru. Then, maybe there will be a chance that my children shall live! Have you offered them a resurrection lately? Any sign of their souls floating around Siyon?"

Ouriano responded, "You know it doesn't work like that."

"If Doctors Tanner and Pruett are disposed of as we speak, then my loyalty will be unquestioned despite my plans. Several of the Vranti collective are on their way now to lead them to a deep depression like their mother. The mother's prayers were getting annoying to them. I could have intervened, but I had to be here! How will you counsel me on this?"

"You've underestimated this Juwaan. The wind in your sail could be sucked out any time with no notice. I caution you to think about who you fear."

"Spare me the thought, Ouriano, you would like to tell me 'He is the God in whom we live and move and have our being?' And I caution you. I will not see Ru end up like these, killed by my enemy. She is all I have. 'I'll conceived,' you say? No, each of my children were conceived in calculated passion. What do you know of passion strong enough to conceive? You cannot conceive, you are pathetic. Your interference only led to my need to procreate another, and another. You killed these and forced the untimely deaths of their mothers."

"Cuzak, this is absolutely untrue! You are now twisting your tongue like a wild vine, like your father."

"You came to terminate Ru today didn't you Ouriano? I admit, she is a liability for both of us. But when we complete this project I will be able to breed a thousand just like her! And your little Juwaan, 'his power displayed in weakness?' They all suffer and die while things continue on as they always have. This is a time for those with power to use it. Without a little help from his friends like you, Lucas stands no chance. By the way, they are getting a one way ticket today to an abyss set up by Yazad. What a pity."

Cuzak realized Ouriano was hesitating. An angel of his strength could have turned this sealed room into a food processor by now. "Why don't you show your rage Ouriano? Or suffer righteous indignation? Show me the difference?" Cuzak opened up his wings and readied his strength.

"Why do you want to force violence Cuzak? Why? You must stand down."

Chapter 78

You have faith in your God and you have trust in others who were beyond redemption. One of these beliefs is your weakness.

With Ouriano's magnificent wings displayed and defensively affronting Cuzak, he unwittingly obstructed Ru from his view. And while Ouriano focused on Cuzak, Ru found herself drawn by an unseen force to open an undisturbed casket, one longer than the others. Inside she found a unique weapon; a spear sent by Yazad, an attractive talisman with the capacity to inflict the wound of annihilation. She gripped this dark instrument with both hands, carefully lifting it in silence. The mid shaft was wrapped with the flagrum of an ancient Roman scourge. A barbed dagger of a Blue Moon alloy was attached at the tip.

She was exhilarated at the power it gave off to her, a deep pulse, like that on the craft of the dark winds. Her mind said 'no', but this dark power blocked out any reticence. With the spear aimed at Ouriano's back, Ru proceeded to walk like a cat of prey toward him, her eyes blind to everything but her quarry, her senses and will attuned to nothing but the dark power. The loyalty of blood called her to obey against her better nature. Her finger nails grew longer, her arms and hands stronger.

"I cannot stand down. This plan would be extinguished," said Cuzak.

Ouriano rubbed his forehead and said, "I can assure you Ru's fate will not be like the others."

"This time, my Angel of Death, you are absolutely right." Finishing these words Cuzak, feigned a charge toward Ouriano, causing him to step back into the waiting spear of dark light. Ru followed with a thrust then pulled him back, lifting him high enough that his feet were unable to give support. With the base of the nearly petrified wood spear against her foot, she struggled to hold him immobile. His wings fluttered trying to fly off or break the spear, but the ancient lance had pierced his heart. The dark light was quickly poisoning this remarkable being of light. Moreover, she had broken his trust.

He tried to bend his head and neck back to look at Ru. He reached back and touched her face and felt her hair with his right finger tips, but she looked down continuing to work the spear, using her wings as counterbalance and power.

Stepping up to Ouriano's left side, Cuzak asked, "Where is your fight? You have fallen too easy. You have faith in your God and you have trust in others who were beyond redemption. One of these beliefs is your weakness. Which is it? Someone warned you and you paid no attention. You could have been part of a new future for all of us. But now you will disappear into a great nothing."

Ouriano attempted to speak. To Cuzak's surprise the expression of the slightest joy and peace rested on him. He was ancient, weathered, and yet there on display in front of both of them was a glimpse of youthful renewal. Cuzak commented, "There is nothing so disgraceful as when the naive are dumped into the aquarium, slowly squeezed and suffocated by the waiting serpent. You should have no joy; no one is waiting for you."

Ouriano grasped the spear with both hands and started to pull himself toward the tip. A mix of white and black liquid poured out of his wound. Cuzak stepped quickly behind him and hacked off his wings while he struggled. They fell, one gliding over into an open casket. Cuzak then helped grasp the spear with Ru and mocked, "Look up at him. He helped others!"

Ouriano then said something with his final gasps of life disturbing to Cuzak, "Ru has amnesty."

For this, Cuzak shook the spear harder but Ouriano continued to pull himself upward, trying to break off the spear's tip. Disgusted, Cuzak slammed him to his feet onto the floor, and thrust the spear forward so that the flagrum rested inside his torso. And with all of his power Cuzak spun the spear's shaft, releasing what would be like internal blender blades of the cursed scourging device.

Cuzak then rammed Ouriano into the thick reinforced steel wall and suspended him like a skewered piece of beef. He was turning dark now, shriveling as the dark light countered his inmost being. Pieces of Ouriano began to fall away like a bad case of leprosy, his hair, an arm, his head, torso, until, there was nothing left intact but the ancient spear and the straps of the flagrum leather drooping off the sides.

Ru's dark adrenalin started to subside, leaving her stunned at the realization of what she was now complicit in. By contrast her father gloated over the pieces of his fallen adversary. After a few silent minutes he addressed her, "My daughter, you have done splendidly. The converse to good isn't always evil, once the reference points have been changed," to which a shocked Ru gave no immediate response.

Regardless, Cuzak stood in silence, absorbing his victory. *At long last, I have defeated my enemy, my tormentor! From the beginning, he has obstructed my path... No more!* His mind went back, back to the battles, back to the defeat dealt by Ouriano to him, to his children... and the weight of eons slipped from his shoulders. He savored it. He relished it. He took the minutes to let his triumph be felt to his very bones. Finally, turning away from the fading remains of Ouriano, Cuzak's eyes began to roam frantically around the room, under the coffins, along the ceiling, and base of the walls. *Something is not right.*

Ru, meanwhile, grappled with her distress, her mind racing. Ouriano had, for so long, been like a father to her... and she had killed him! He had assured her amnesty... and she had killed him! What had she done? Would she have amnesty now? She grieved for her friend, her mentor, and herself – for her chance of redemption. Her mind struggled with the weight of it all. How could she survive this? She closed her eyes, and dug deep into her inner soul, her inner strength. *The way I've always survived – by my wits, by my strength, by my determination to live. I can't undo what I have done; Ouriano would tell me that if he were here. All I can do is go forward. And now, maybe I have Cuzak for my father, at last.* Still reeling, Ru steeled herself and forced her focus on Cuzak, and asked, "What are you looking for?"

"Ouriano's sword, I have the wings. Now where is his sword?"

Ru forced herself to clear her mind even more, and concentrated. *Oh, Ouriano!* She braced back from the memories, and pinpointed only on the sword. "I don't think he had it. He was in disguise when he met me."

"This is not good, we must find either the Vranti or the doctors immediately. Let's get these blast doors open now."

Fully in tune now to deal with Cuzak and the present, Ru grabbed on to calm. "Please, slow down," said Ru as she went over and pried the ancient lance out of the wall, then placed it in the hands of her father, "You told me these walls were built to contain beings like us. There's also a thirty minute delay from an internal security code entry to open these doors. What can happen in half an hour?"

"The world, Ru, the world!" said Cuzak as he pounded the blunt end of the murder weapon on the floor, changing his demeanor back to anger. "If this is a trick of yours, so help me, I will use this on you. This happened too easy. Ouriano is more formidable than this."

Ru instantly felt her inner guilt and torment rise, and grasped the top of the spear and tipped the point down to her heart, pressing against it with increasing force as Cuzak still held on and said, "Have I not done what you wanted? Is entrapping a friend what you call, *easy?* You could end me as well right now and add me to your collection. Go ahead."

Cuzak paused at the call of his bluff, released the tension on the lance letting it fall to the floor, bouncing--clanking twice, then put his arms around her and spoke gently like the parent she had longed for, "Let me start over with you Maria, you make me so proud. Do you think I would take the life of my own flesh and blood? You are my daughter, and today I have become your father. You have risen above all my former offspring."

Ru did not know how to react. Tears welled up in her eyes and dripped on his shoulder as they embraced, "Father, I killed my friend."

He spoke again, "You helped kill who you thought was your friend. Remember we now are the determiners of fate. And we will determine that this was good. Agreed?"

She squeezed his torso and kissed his shoulder as he held her, but answered him only after releasing her torment and the last of her grief through her simple, silent prayer to Ouriano and his God, *Please forgive me.* Then taking a step back and holding Cuzak's burly hands she said, "Agreed."

Cuzak responded, "Good, I promise to be the father you need... but we must secure the sword of Ouriano. This is a detail which cannot be underestimated. It must not pass through into the Sanctuary, especially in the hands of someone who knows its power."

++

Blue Moon Chronicles Book III, 12.3

Date: At annihilation of Ouriano
Third generation G-class star formation,
Fourth generation Angelus,
Beginning of mass exit to Sanctuary

Subject: Death giving birth to the new

"Fair" is not a word I like to use, for "fair" means we can take every potential into account including what we deserve. I leave that for another much greater than I to determine. As of now there is so much unaccounted for with this development, and Ouriano never mentioned that word. What he desired was to guarantee and experience for himself the transformation of those he once served. Our hearts are all torn over this, but we are glad and full of thanks he faced evil while maintaining his nobility.

I hope to meet him again soon, but will he recognize us from his past as a new Child of Stardust? I have no doubt that he was granted the gift of his desire, and I now suspect what form he takes. For somewhere in the Earth near him is his sword, forged in the fires of the Magnificon, under the safeguard of a wise Juwaan and a strong mother. May the sword and the child be reunited. We desperately need those who can fight in the dark!

Godspeed to all of them, They are going to need it.

Shem, from the Blue Moon, the caverns of Sharu

++

Preview:
The Rising

Sequel to The Exit, Blue Moon Chronicles

A SCIENCE FICTION FANTASY

TODD BODDY

The Rising is the next exciting narrative of the debut trilogy, Blue Moon Chronicles, that explores a compelling end-times conspiracy combining a heavy dose of twisted theologies with cosmological and technical wonder.

Broken Club Publishing LLC, McKinney Texas

The Rising

At the top of the towering tree, Pico had Daniel's attention, and so he also curled upside down around the branch watching the low valley clouds roll in.

"But Pico, I don't know any other sloths who speak. Why are you talking to me?"

"Quiet Daniel, learn from me, and remain completely still. Your enemies are looking for you."

"But I have no enemies. My grandfather tells me the one who never sleeps nor slumbers, watches over me, and my grandmother says I can be anything I want."

"True Pequeno, you have the canopy of many prayers, you are the core of the heir's eye, but there are those who fear what you can become. They fear the warrior in you who might cut them down from within, and for good reason."

"Pico, I don't understand."

"Like the men who illegally hunt in this forest. You have seen them?"

"Yes, and I hide, like you taught me. They hunt the deer, the armadillo, the macaw, the gold, Senior anteater, they harvest the orchids and the trees."

"Danielito, a time is coming when hiding is not enough. These hunters want you. They may be here now. Be silent." The sloth arched his head toward the ground. Two forest rangers, dark green ball caps, matching trousers and shirt walked around the trunk of the tree. At the base they noticed the boy's footprints and a four foot sharpened stick with two dead toads on the end. They both looked up.

One of them motioned to the other to begin climbing. As Daniel remained motionless, he glimpsed one of them through the foliage climbing directly vertical with ease. The ranger stuck to the trunk, went under and around branches like a giant praying mantis. Daniel froze in wonder, even I can't do that!

Daniel heard Pico's voice in his head, "Daniel, you have to jump when I tell you. Just do it, you'll be ok." If it were not for the dread he sensed crawling up the tree like a leopard coming to finish its prey, he would not have believed. "On Three ... Uno, Dos, Tres!"

He let go and began to free fall some fifteen feet from the trunk. He passed the ranger going down who put his arm out toward him but missed. Looking up he saw that Pico a second later had let go and was now in a free fall. But Pico didn't remain as Pico. The talking sloth transformed into a young man with wings.

For information, sales, or presales, contact:
Broken Club Publishing LLC,
4100 W. Eldorado Pkwy, Suite 100 #130,
McKinney Texas 75070
BCP@ToddBoddy.net 214-736-9470
WWW.Facebook.COM/BlueMoonChronicles
WWW.ToddBoddy.COM
WWW.BLUEMOONCHRONICLES.COM

About The Author

"If you play golf, you are my friend," is an invitation to building bridges with people about something you love.

Todd is a graduate of the University of Texas at Austin and Dallas Seminary. He is an ordained minister in the Christian Church, Disciples of Christ.

He offices and writes on his North Texas "ranchette" with his wife Loretta, two dogs, varieties of native plants and animals, including their children and grandchildren, who come and go.

Todd is known to frequent many coffee shops and golf courses in the Princeton and McKinney Texas area.